Penguin Books
Henry and Cato

Iris Murdoch was born in Dublin in 1919 and educated
at Badminton School, Bristol, and at Oxford, where she
later was a tutor in philosophy. In 1953 she published a
brilliant study of Jean-Paul Sartre, and in 1954 her first
novel, *Under the Net*, appeared to critical acclaim. The
many novels that followed confirmed her growing
reputation as the wittiest and most intelligent writer at
work in England. Miss Murdoch lives near Oxford with
her husband, the novelist and critic John Bayley.
Among her recent books are *The Black Prince*, *The
Sacred and Profane Love Machine* and *A Word Child*.

Iris Murdoch

Henry and Cato

Penguin Books

Penguin Books Ltd,
Harmondsworth, Middlesex, England
Penguin Books, 625 Madison Avenue,
New York, New York 10022, U.S.A.
Penguin Books Australia Ltd,
Ringwood, Victoria, Australia
Penguin Books Canada Ltd,
2801 John Street, Markham, Ontario, Canada L3R 1B4
Penguin Books (N.Z.) Ltd,
182–190 Wairau Road, Auckland 10, New Zealand

First published in Great Britain by Chatto and Windus 1976
First published in the United States of America by The Viking Press 1977
Published in Penguin Books 1977

Library of Congress Cataloging in Publication Data
Murdoch, Iris.
　Henry and Cato.
　I. Title.
PZ4·M974He4　　[PR6063.U7]　　823'.9'14　77–8044
ISBN 0 14 00·4569 4

Made and printed in Great Britain by
Richard Clay (The Chaucer Press) Ltd,
Bungay, Suffolk
Set in Linotype Times

To Stephen Gardiner

Part One

Rites of Passage

Cato Forbes had already crossed Hungerford railway bridge, three times, once from north to south, then from south to north, and again from north to south. He was now walking very slowly back towards the middle of the bridge. He was breathing deeply, conscious of a seemingly noisy counterpoint of breath and heart-beat. He felt nervously impelled to hold his in-drawn breath too long and then to gasp. The revolver in its case, heavy and awkward inside his mackintosh pocket, banged irregularly against his thigh at each step.

It was after midnight. The last tardy concert-goers from the Royal Festival Hall had passed over and gone home. Yet even now he was maddeningly not alone upon the bridge. The mist, which he had welcomed, baffled him. Damp and grey and gauzy and slightly in motion it arose from the Thames and surrounded him, seeming transparent and yet concealing the lights of the embankment on either side and deadening the footsteps of figures who, persistently appearing, would suddenly materialize close to him and go by with a suspicious gait. Or were these all shrouded apparitions of the same man, some plain-clothes police officer perhaps, whose task it was to patrol the bridge?

The air of the April night was faintly warm, carrying fresh smells, the scent of the sea, or perhaps just the old vegetable aroma of the river, lightened a little by far-off presences of springtime trees and flowers. Although it had scarcely rained that day everything was wet. The asphalt beneath Cato's feet was sticky and the thick cast-iron railings were covered with a cold sweat of running water. Cato's fingers had become damp and chilled as he walked the narrow footpath beside the railway line, steadying the gun with one hand and trailing the other hand along the bars. His face, blazing with anxiety, felt wet too, and he mopped it awkwardly with the sleeve of his mackintosh.

Behind the grille which separated the railway from the foot-path a train leaving Charing Cross station rattled slowly by, the lighted carriages jerkily illuminating the mist. Cato turned his head away.

Oh how stupid I am, he said to himself, using words which he had used ever so often since he was a child. At that moment it seemed to him that his life had consisted of one blunder after another, and now aged thirty-one he was well on into the stupidest of all. The train had gone by. A tall figure appeared and passed, looking at him intently. There was a curious taut silence within which the faint hum of the sparse embankment traffic was contained. A distant foghorn boomed sadly, then boomed again, the very voice of the night. Cato knew that he could not simply give up and go home; he had made a cage of purposes and was caught in it. Fear, feeling now almost famili-arly like sexual excitement, was at last becoming a compulsion to act.

Without even troubling to notice whether anyone was near he knelt down close to the centre of the bridge, his knees adher-ing to the cold muddy ground. He began to pull the revolver case out of his mackintosh pocket but one corner of it caught in the lining, and he knelt there tugging at it and ripping the cloth. When he had got the thing out he hesitated again, won-dering if he should remove the gun from the case. Why had he not decided this earlier? Would the case float, he stupidly won-dered? He peered down but the water below him was invisible. His cheek touched the wet cold ironwork. He thrust the un-opened case out through the bars into the dark misty air and released it. It vanished instantly silently from his fingers into the mist as if it had been gently plucked away. There was no sound of a splash. Cato rose. He touched his pocket, hardly believing that the heavy object was no longer there. He took a few steps, then looked round behind him. It did go into the river, didn't it, he thought. It can't have gone anywhere else.

He began to walk back towards the north bank. There were two chill plates where his knees had rested upon the ground. Someone, approaching him with soft gluey steps, loomed up and passed. Cato coughed, then coughed again, as if to reassure both himself and the other person. He breathed slowly and deeply, blowing his breath out vigorously into the mist. He could now see the lights of the roadway. Deliberately slowing his pace he went down the steps onto the embankment. Charing Cross underground station was closed. Of course he must not take a taxi. He began to walk up Northumberland Avenue, lighting a cigarette as he went. He felt better. The acute fear had gone and now seemed to him to have been irrational. The sexual excitement, diffused and vague, remained as a comfort, as if he had taken some warming calming drug. Oh how stupid I am, he said to himself again; but now he smiled cunningly, secretively, as he said it.

At about the hour when Cato Forbes was walking up and down in the mist on Hungerford Bridge, Henry Marshalson was awakening from a brief nap upon an eastbound jumbo jet high above the Atlantic. Leaving New York in daylight, his plane had soon risen into a sort of radiant rosy-blue stratospheric gloom. Now it was almost dark.

Awakening Henry had instantly become conscious of something new and wonderful about the world. Some unexpected marvel had entered his life. What was it? Oh yes, his brother Sandy was dead. Leaning back in his seat again and stretching, luxurious Henry flexed his toes with joy.

When the great news reached him Henry had been in St. Louis, sitting in O'Connor's bar eating a hamburger. He had opened a copy of the London *Evening Standard* which a jet-propelled visitor had left in the lounge of his small hotel and which he had idly picked up. Private Henry shunned university acquaintances in St. Louis, preferring modest hotel life, while trotting to and fro from the picture galleries and the zoo. Munching, he opened the paper and scanned the news of strikes, trade deficits, Labour Party feuds, rows about education, rows about new roads, rows about new airports. No interesting murders. Everything seemed much as usual in his native land which he had left nine years ago intending never to return. Then he gasped, rigid with shock, blushed scarlet and became white. Covered over with surges of dots the small news item danced wildly before his eyes. *The well-known racing driver Alexander Marshalson ... killed in a car accident ...*

Crumpling the paper against his chest Henry staggered up. The air seemed suddenly to have become rarefied and unbreathable. He rushed out and ran all the way to his hotel, panting with anguish. It was in the paper, but it didn't have to be true. Oh God, if it should now prove false! He made a telephone call to England. Of course he did not ring his mother; he rang Merriman, the family solicitor. It was true. They had been desperately trying to find out where he was. The funeral had just taken place. Henry put the receiver down and fell back on his bed, salivating with relief. Inheriting the property was nothing. What mattered was that bloody Sandy was no more.

Alienated Henry, now thirty-two years old, had spent his nine years of exile in America, after obtaining a second-class degree in modern history at Cambridge, England. He had spent three years at Stanford messing with a doctorate, and had then obtained an insecure teaching post at a small liberal arts college at Sperriton, Illinois. Henry's academic career had not been glorious. At Stanford he had begun, cautiously at first, to pass himself off as an art historian, an idea which would have amazed his tutors at Cambridge, England. At unexacting self-indulgent little Sperriton, where no one knew much and he could do as he pleased, he taught "fifty great historical pictures." Later he taught "fifty great pictures." His courses were popular and Henry's ramblings did the kids some good, he thought. Would he have stayed on at Sperriton if it had not been for Russell and Bella Fischer? He was not sure; and in any case there had been no rush to offer Henry jobs. Sperriton was a very long way from anywhere out in the flat cornlands where miles and miles away against the sky one could perhaps see a silo. Through the corn here and there ran the freeways, along which Henry and Russ and Bella would sometimes tear about. Once they went as far as Mexico.

The local metropolis was weird majestic St. Louis beside the journeying Mississippi. T. S. Eliot's city. Henry, who detested New York, loved St. Louis. Sperriton was tiny and lonely. St.

Louis was vast and lonely, and lost Henry delighted in its besieged loneliness. He loved its derelict splendours, the huge ornate neglected mansions of a vanished bourgeoisie, the useless skyscraper-tall steel arch through which the citizenry surveyed the view of shabby warehouses and marshalling yards on the Illinois shore. The empty palaces beside the immense eternal river: what an impressive image of the demise of capitalism. (Henry hated capitalism. He hated socialism too.) Russell and Bella went to concerts. Henry cared for none of these things; he just wandered about seeking an identity. Eventually he got onto the trail of Max Beckmann whom a fate even stranger than Henry's had exiled to St. Louis in his later years. Henry had been told by the head of his department that he must write a book, any book. He decided to write about Beckmann. Henry's book would not soon appear. Russ and Bella laughed at it.

In fact after Henry had been teaching fifty great pictures for a while he began to hate art. Or perhaps what he hated was just the old pompous cluttered-up European tradition. It was mass production before the factories. There was too much stuff in the world. Man invented time, God invented space, Beckmann said. Henry wanted to get back to space. So oddly enough did Max, although he so anxiously crammed his canvases with those tormented images. The only peaceful thing in Max's art was Max himself. How Henry envied that vast self-confidence, that happy and commanding egoism. How wonderful to be able to look at oneself in a mirror and become something so permanent and significant and monumental: a revolutionary leader, an epic hero, a sailor, a *roué*, a clown, a king. The fish-embracing women were another matter. But that great calm round face was a light in Henry's life. Two-wived Beckmann treading underground paths of masculine mysticism which linked Signorelli to Grünewald, Rembrandt to Cézanne. One day Henry would chart it all, only, given over to love and envy, he kept putting off starting.

Henry often thought of himself as a failed artist. Why failed, for heaven's sake, Bella asked him, you haven't tried! He and Bella took painting lessons but Henry soon gave up with a yelp of rage. Bella cheerfully went on painting badly. Henry grandly said that he preferred the *tabula rasa* of the white canvas. Perhaps indeed America had been his *tabula rasa*, where at first he had expected all sorts of events and adventures. There was a heroic life somewhere to which he felt that he belonged. He pictured himself like Max in a frightful harlequin world of extreme situations and inquisitions taking place somehow in night clubs or circuses. Of course Max had had his real horrors: the Nazis, and the nineteen-fourteen war with a pencil and no paint. There was certainly an America elsewhere where things happened, but the hard stuff never seemed to come Henry's way, and he could not but observe a lack of intensity in his life. He inhabited spacious easy routines of quietness and calm. His America was a soft drink. He had expected a great love, never having had one in England; but the competent hygienic campus girls, his pupils, who regarded him as comic and very old, filled him with alarm and dismay. At Stanford he had had several inconclusive miserable affairs. At Sperriton he had met Russ and Bella. When at last he went to bed with Bella, Russell knew all about it and they both discussed it with their analyst. Bella wanted Henry to go into analysis but he never would. Contempt for analysis was one of the little English flags which he sometimes flew.

Henry had meditated a lot upon what he thought of as "the great American coldness," and upon why he went on feeling such a foreigner in his adopted land. Both figuratively and literally there was a certain lack of smell. (Henry's clothes and person smelt. Bella said she liked it. Russell was odourless.) Henry had long ago adjusted himself to his modest talents and settled down, he sometimes suspected too soon, to a sense of his limitations. He took the pattern of his life and character for granted. *They* (Russ, Bella, The Americans) seemed to have no way of taking things for granted, but assumed a regime of perpetual change wherein they unceasingly asked: am I developing, am I succeeding, am I fulfilled, am I good? This made unpredictability a right and the constant exercise of will a duty. Psychoanalysis, which might ideally produce a humble self-awareness, seemed to Henry in this heroic scene to promote a restless nervous desire for change and improvement. He looked on with awe, like an idle slave watching some battle of Titans. What he could never decide was whether this grand refusal to be defined was something good, perhaps a kind of innocence, or whether it was something bad. As he would not regard himself as good he decided that the opposite must be in some way admirable, and he made that wonderful instability into an object of admiration, although he knew that he could never share it. Having had the orderly frustrated childhood of an English middle-class child he could not, in early middle age, still think that all things were possible. He gave himself no credit. He thought of himself as a demonic man, but failed. A failed demon, that would be something spiteful; only even his spite was contained by his deep sense of his limits.

In fact refugee Henry had quite remarkably settled down. In America there was nowhere to hide, so he stopped hiding. He settled down with the transcendentally nice Fischers, finding what he had never expected to find again, a *home* in their Jewishness, in the bosom of their vast intelligent American innocence. Carefully and slowly they unwound him, they unpacked him like china. His affair with Bella, now over and done with, had not ruffled any feathers except his own. It had, exactly as they had predicted, brought him closer to both of them. He had concluded, and had told them this, that he would now be quite happy to spend the rest of his life with them, studying America in their two persons. Of course (they were childless) they had adopted Henry, they had become his "parents." They even suggested that he should live with them, only Henry clung to his tiny wooden house and his tiny independence, even though he spent more time with the Fischers than he did at home. And through them he made his other friends, and through them he partook of America. Both of them taught at the college, Russell as a philosopher and Bella as a sociologist. Spiritually they desired to perfect themselves, but academically had more realistic ambitions. There was a persistently discussed dream of getting to "the coast," that is to California. Russell was once short-listed for a job at Santa Barbara. Of course they could not go until they all three had jobs. Unfortunately none of them was any good.

It had been extraordinarily painful to leave them, though naturally he was returning very soon. "Cheer up, kid, it'll be

15

over by Christmas," said Russell to leave-taking Henry. "By Christmas!" shouted Bella. "Why, he'll be back here in a fortnight, he can't live without us!" Henry's chance of sudden English adventures was discussed. "If he falls for anybody it'll be some sort of ravaged tart," said Bella. "Like you, honey," said Henry feebly. It was agreed to be unlikely. Timid Henry shuddered from indiscriminate or hasty sex. One of the things which Bella had done for him was to make him feel that he had somehow been through "all that" and come out spotless. What after all did he know about women? What big plump loud-voiced dark-eyed Bella had taught him; he was her pupil, her creation, probably her property.

Henry took off his watch and altered it to London time. Halfway there. He felt, as a very vague stirring in his bones, America begin to fall away. Not thinking of England or his mother he poured himself a quick martini from the hip flask which Bella had thoughtfully provided. Presumably he was a rich man now. Of course he had not been exactly a poor man in the States except in the sense that he had somehow conditioned himself for poverty. His father, a rigid primogeniturist, had left everything to Sandy, the elder son; everything that is except a sum of money, not fabulous though not contemptible, which escaping Henry had left behind him untouched in a bank in London. Occasionally, when economizing with Russ and Bella, he thought of bringing the money over and spending it rapidly on riotous living, only somehow he had never found out how to live riotously. He could not discover in himself any talent for buying anything expensive: girls, fun, *objets d'art*. He did not want them if bought. Even the cornucopia of the American supermarket somehow turned his stomach. He never told the Fischers about the money. Naturally he had told Bella about Sandy at a faculty party the very first time he met her, and she had soon developed her classical theory about his childhood. Only of course it was not like that, it was not like that at all, and the truth was untellable.

Henry's father Burke Marshalson, who died when Henry was a boy, ought to have been Sir Burke Marshalson, or perhaps Lord Marshalson, only unfortunately there were no titles in the family. There had always been a legend, based on nothing

16

whatever, of "grandness," which Henry loathed with every cell of his being. Burke Marshalson spent his life tinkering with the property, which relentless governments were reducing. His wife Gerda, left a young widow, preserved the legend and did her best with the money. In this fictitious importance Sandy, the elder of the two children, had early clothed himself, or been clothed by the attentions of relatives and servants. When still a boy Sandy had inherited Laxlinden Hall, the park and farm-lands, and the still substantial fortune needed to "keep them up" for transmission in due course to his son. Henry, soon made aware that Sandy owned everything down to the very earth that tolerated Henry stood upon, used to pray daily for his brother's death. Sandy always appeared to be the clever one, though he only studied engineering and even gave that up. He had identity, while all Henry's qualifications failed to endow him with any credible being. Sandy patronized Henry and laughed at him and called him "Trundletail," or "Trundle" for short. He never even noticed Henry's hatred. To Henry in America he sent Christmas cards, even birthday cards. No one had intended to be unkind to Henry and perhaps nobody had been unkind to him. He had just been born a bit unreal and second rate. "The little one is a puny child," he had heard his mother saying in a context where Sandy was being praised, and quick Henry learnt a new word.

And now handsome six-foot Sandy was dead, and he had never married and never produced the longed-for heir. Inferior Henry was the heir. And now Henry was coming back to it all, back to ancient claustrophobic wicked cluttered Europe and quaint dotty little England and beautiful terrible Laxlinden and the northern light over the meadows. And his mother whom he had not seen since she visited New York five years ago in the company of that sponging creep Lucius Lamb. (Of course tactless Henry had to ask if she had paid his fare.) Hope-fully, creep Lamb would have had time to die or get lost in the interim. What would it all be like? Was something going to happen in his life at last? Would he be called upon to make great choices, world-altering decisions? Would he be able to? Free will and causality are entirely compatible, Russell told him once. Henry did not understand. Or would it prove as insubstantial as a dream from which he would soon wake up safe at home in his little white house at Sperriton, with the telephone bell ringing and up-early Bella bright upon the line? Were there *people* waiting for him over there in England? Was there anyone there that he really wanted to see? Well, he would quite like to see Cato Forbes, he wondered over his next martini what had become of him. The plane shuddered on. Emotionally exhausted and now drunk Henry went to sleep again.

At about the hour when Cato Forbes was walking to and fro on Hungerford Bridge and Henry Marshalson was awakening from his first sleep on the jumbo jet high above the Atlantic, Gerda Marshalson and Lucius Lamb were in conference in the library at Laxlinden Hall.

"He won't change anything," said Lucius.

"I don't know," said Gerda.

She was walking up and down. Lucius was reclining upon the sofa near to the recently installed television set.

The library was a long room with three tall windows, now closely velveted with curtains. One wall was covered with a late-seventeenth-century Flemish tapestry, representing Athena seizing Achilles by the hair, the goddess and the hero being decoratively enveloped in green Amazonian vegetation. Agamemnon and his companions were not visible, but nearby Troy was represented, against a mysteriously radiant grey-blue sky, by three creamy pinnacles rising above immense leaves on the top right-hand corner. The other walls were covered by shelves containing ancestral Marshalson books, most of which had been rebound in a uniform tawny-golden leather binding: mainly history and biography and sets of standard literary classics. No book had been touched, except by Rhoda's duster, since Henry went away. The shelves stopped short of the ceiling leaving space for perched busts of Roman emperors. Nobody dusted them, but fortunately they were black in any case.

Two shaded lamps, made out of huge vases, illuminated one end of the room, and beneath the tall chimney-piece, carved by a pupil of Grinling Gibbons, a log fire was brightly burning, stirred lately to life by a strong poke from Gerda's small slippered foot. A blue cut-glass bowl beside one of the lamps contained a very large number of white daffodils whose delicate smell blended airily with the warmth of the fire.

Lucius was feeling very tired and wanted to go to bed. His back was hurting and his new false teeth, which he dared not remove in Gerda's presence, were unbearably cluttering up his mouth. A kind of itching ache was crawling about his body, making it impossible for him to find comfort in any position. Pains curled in crannies, merely dozing. How he hated growing old. Even whisky was no good now. He wanted to scratch and yawn but could not do either. He saw Gerda's face hazily. He never wore his glasses in public. She had been talking for hours.

Gerda was wearing one of the long loose robes, too elegant to be called dressing-gowns, which she now often put on in the evenings. Lucius was not sure whether this new style represented a kind of informal intimacy or simply a compromise with comfort. Gerda never spoke about her health and in general preferred her own rigid conception of style to common ease. Tonight's robe was of light wool, chequered blue and green, buttoning high to the neck and sweeping the carpet. Had Gerda, underneath it, undressed? Gerda's straight dark brown hair was looped back from her face and held at the nape of her neck with a large tortoise-shell slide. When loose it just covered her shoulders. Did she dye her hair, Lucius wondered. He lived surrounded by mysteries. Gerda, especially in this light, could still look uncannily young. Of course she was faded and her features were less fine. She had a pale rather wide face and a nose which seemed to have become larger with age, the nostrils more powerfully salient. The eyes were a dark brown and glowed—like Sandy's, like Henry's. She was neither short nor tall, perceptibly plumper. But she still had the authority of a woman who had been a beauty. Watching her stride and turn, tossing her long blue and green skirt, he thought, she's a woman every second, bless her. Her old-fashioned coquetry was so natural it had become a grace.

Lucius was sixty-six years old. It was many years now since he had become the slave of glowing-eyed Gerda. When he first

19

met her she was already married to tall red-headed Burke and carrying a lusty red-headed baby in her arms. Lucius had fallen in love, not intending to make of this his life's work. How had it happened? His fruitless passion had become a family joke. Gerda patronized him. ("At least English intellectuals are gentlemen," said Gerda.) Nobody feared Lucius. Burke, who felt, for no good reason that Lucius could perceive, superior to everyone, patted Lucius on the back and told him to make himself at home at Laxlinden Hall. Little did Burke or Lucius dream how thoroughly this would come about.

Lucius had been, making almost a profession of it, a beautiful young man. He had had long flowing light brown hair at a time when this was unusual, a defiant sign of some remarkable oddity. Lucius, very conscious of this, felt that his oddity was simply genius. How he despised Burke, despised even his younger college friend John Forbes through whom he had met Burke. Everybody in London adored Lucius then; it was only at Laxlinden that he was a failure. He belonged to a stylish literary milieu and had published poems before he was twenty. A number of quite well-known men were in love with him. He was the child of elderly parents. They were poor folk, but they had sent him to a good school. They lived to see his book of poems and also the novel which followed it. He had a younger sister but she was uneducated and they had nothing in common. Spurred by an idealism which was one with his self-confident ambition he early joined the Communist Party. He soldiered, bravely and decently enough he thought in retrospect, through the years of disillusionment. Perhaps joining the Party had been his mistake? He had made some mistake. Perhaps he should simply have sat still and worked it all out *a priori* as other people did. It seemed obvious enough afterwards. What a lot of his young strength he had wasted on fruitless controversies, now rendered dim and tiny by the relentless, and to Lucius always surprising, onward movement of history.

He had lived in this strange way with Gerda for several years now. Of course much longer ago, after Burke died, he had proposed to her. Or had he? He could not now remember the exact form of words. She turned away. He went back to London. He worked as a journalist, then for a publisher, saving

20

up for his freedom. The first novel was a success, the second one was not, he never wrote a third. Instead he wrote literary love letters to Gerda. He gave up poetry and started to write a big book about Marxism. He visited Gerda regularly and told her that she was the only woman he had ever loved, which was not quite true. He talked to her impressively about his book. One day she suggested that he should come and stay at the Hall until he had finished it. It was still unfinished. So Gerda had turned out in this strange way to be his fate after all. Was he glad? Was she glad? He had never been to bed with her. But she seemed to need him, she seemed to expect him to stay on. Perhaps, as the years go by, any woman will value a slavish faithfulness. For a while she expected him to teach her things. They were to have discussions. Once he gave her a book list, and nothing more came of that. Their relations remained intimate yet formal.

And he was really rather beautiful even now, he thought, as he often consoled himself by looking into the mirror. His flowing hair was a greyish white, and with his twinkling blue eyes and scarcely wrinkled face he looked like a sort of mad sage, and passed for vastly wise as he played the eccentric and made younger people laugh. It was a pity about the false teeth, but if he smiled carefully they were not conspicuous. He had lived on talk and curiosity and drink and the misfortunes of his friends. Only now life was more solitary and he could hardly believe that he had achieved so little and was sixty-six.

"Will he stay?" said Gerda.

"I shouldn't think so."

"You're not thinking."

"How do I know what he'll do?"

"Will he stay in England, will he stay here?"

"I shouldn't think he'll stay here, it's so damned dull. I mean—"

"Will he want to make changes?"

"No, why should he? He'll find out from Merriman what's in the kitty and skip off back to America."

"I wish we hadn't sold the Oak Meadow."

"Well, Sandy wanted that boat in a hurry—"

"Bellamy says John Forbes is going to build on it."

"I don't suppose Henry will even remember the Oak Meadow."

"Will he live in London?"

"Darling, he's a stranger to us, we can't know what he'll do, he probably doesn't know himself."

"He's not a stranger to me, he's my son."

Lucius, sucking his teeth, said nothing.

"Why don't you say something? I wish you wouldn't fidget so."

"Yes, of course he's your son. We must be very kind to him."

"Why do you say that?"

"Oh, I don't know, I mean, coming back here, so long away—"

"You meant something special by it."

"No, I didn't."

"Are you implying that I've been unkind to him?"

"No!"

"Or unjust to him?"

"No! Gerda, don't always imagine I mean something."

"Why not?"

"I mean you keep thinking he'll arrive with a plan. He won't. We'll have to make the plan. Well, you will. Henry was never able to make a decision in his life. He'll arrive a shy awkward gentle muddle-headed young man as he always was."

"He's not such a young man. And he wasn't very gentle to you in New York."

"He was jealous."

"Oh don't talk such rubbish. I should have gone to Sperriton. I see that now. I ought to have seen how he lived."

"He didn't want you to."

"You persuaded me not to go."

"I didn't! I never persuaded you of anything!"

"He didn't want me to come. I wonder if he was living with a woman. Perhaps he'll announce that he's married."

"Perhaps he will."

"You're not being very helpful. You'd better go to bed."

"I am a bit tired."

"You're looking cross-eyed. It's the whisky. Must you have another? You know what it costs now."

"I wasn't going to have another."

"I don't know how I shall live through this next week till he comes."

"You'll live. Only do stop speculating, no wonder I'm cross-eyed."

"Which bedroom should we put him in?"

"His own, of course."

"It's so small."

"If he doesn't like it he can move. After all he owns the place now!"

"I think I'll put him in the cherry blossom room. The radiator still works in there. And Queen Anne's not heated. Oh Rhoda, thank you, dear—"

Bird-headed Rhoda, the maid. had come in soft-footed and without knocking, as she had used to do when she carried in the oil lamps, in the days before electricity came to the Hall. She moved across the room in her ambiguous uniform and reached high up with her gloved hands to check the windows, her nightly task, to see if they were securely fastened. Company or no company, she came always at the same hour and never knocked.

"Rhoda, I think we'll put Mr. Henry in the cherry blossom room."

Rhoda replied.

"He isn't coming for a week, you know."

"Well, make it up in the cherry blossom room, and make sure the radiator's working. Good night, Rhoda."

The door closed.

"What did she say?" said Lucius.

Rhoda, who had an impediment in her speech, was comprehensible only to Gerda.

"She says she's already made up Henry's bed in his old room."

Lucius had taken the opportunity to rise. "I think I'll be off to bed now, darling, I'm flaked."

"I wonder if I ought to—"

"Oh do stop wondering. It doesn't matter, the details don't matter. Henry will only want one thing when he arrives here."

"What?"

"Your love."

There was a silence. Gerda, on Rhoda's entrance, had stopped pacing and now stood at the chimney-piece, one hand touching the warm burnished wood of the superstructure. A sudden flicker revealed her face and Lucius saw tears.

"Oh darling—"

"How can you be so cruel."

"I don't understand."

"Go to bed."

"Gerda, don't be angry with me, you know I won't sleep if you've been angry with me. I never sleep if—"

"I'm not angry. Just go away. It's late.'

"Forgive me, darling Gerda, don't stay up and—I know what you—do go to bed now, dear—"

"Yes, yes. Good night."

"Don't cry."

"Good night."

Lucius went upstairs slowly, as he had used to do holding his candle in the old days, in Burke's time, when he had been a guest at the Hall. Well, was he not still a guest at the Hall? A little breathless after the climb he went on over creaking boards to his bedroom. This large room, which was also his study, occupied a corner on the second floor, on the drawing-room side of the house, with a view one way towards the lake, and the other towards the grove of beeches which were always called "the big trees." The room was rather bare as Lucius, who had lived in tiny rooms most of his life, liked to emphasize its barnlike size. He liked to feel himself loose, lost somehow in the room, wandering. The cushions on the big divan bed were a recent concession to Gerda's desire to prettify. Sometimes Rhoda put flowers in the room. Tonight upon the carved oak chest of drawers was a brown jar full of bluebells. The window, which he now closed, had let in the cold earth-smelling April air. The radiator was not working, only with so much else amiss Lucius had not liked to mention it. His bed had been neatly undone and turned down by Rhoda, as it had been every night for years, but there was no hot water bottle. Hot water bottles were not issued after the end of March.

Lucius sat down on the bed. He would have liked some Bach

now, only it was too late. Why had that particular remark made Gerda cry? He would never understand her. His awful mistake, never to have forced her into bed. Did it matter now? He knew that her unspeakable terrible grief at Sandy's death was still there, hidden from him now as at first it could not be. He had thought at first that she would die of grief, die of shock, die screaming in a frenzy of bereavement such as he had never witnessed or imagined. He shuddered at the memory. But with the fearsome strength that was in her she had collected herself and retired into an almost equally terrible concealment. Avoiding him, she walked the empty rooms of the house every day, he heard her slow rather heavy tread. She sometimes wept, but would dismiss him if she could not control herself at once. She lived in private with her own horror. She was a remarkable woman.

When he was young, romantic Lucius had thought of himself as a solitary. Real loneliness was different. No, he and Gerda were not a bit like man and wife, he could not partake of her woe and she knew nothing of his soul. Their talk did not contain the affectionate nonsensical rubble which pads out the conversation of true couples. The formality, which had seemed at first like a kind of old-fashioned grace, an affectionate respect which she extended, an expression even of the admiration which she had once felt for him, now seemed cold, sometimes almost desperate, a barrier. Yet there they very much were. Of course she needed him, she needed him as an admirer, perhaps the last one, someone who valued her in the old way. She needed him, unless the horror should now place her beyond such needs. He was the prisoner of a woman's vanity. If it were not for her he might have become a great man.

Lucius thrust one foot under the bed and winkled out the suitcase which contained the secret whisky bottle to which he occasionally resorted. He filled the glass on the bedside table. It was quite easy to remove the bottles from the cellar, only getting rid of them later was something of a problem. Did Odysseus get drunk on Calypso's island? When would his travels begin again, did he want them to begin, was it not too late for travelling? He took out his teeth and laid them on the table and felt his face subside gratefully into the face of an old man.

He drank the whisky. His teeth grinned at him. Could art still console? Mozart had left him long ago but Bach was still around. He only cared for endless music now, formless all form, motionless all motion, innocent of drama and history and romance. Gerda, who hated music, would only allow him to play it very softly. He had stopped writing his book, but he had started writing poetry again. He still wrote newspaper reviews for pocket money, only now editors were less interested. Surely there was still power somewhere, that significant power which he had once felt inside the Communist Party. One by one the philosophies had failed him. Is that all? he had felt as he mastered them. He was a creative person, a writer, an artist still, with fewer brain cells but with much more wisdom. Of course he was restless, of course he twitched with frustrated energy. He would become old and wild and lustful, but not yet.

Lucius's back was still hurting and he had a pain in his chest. He finished the whisky and undressed and got into bed and turned out the light. The usual awful melancholy followed. He could hear an owl hooting in the big trees. He wished he was not always young again in his dreams, it made waking up so sad. Henry had been very unkind to him in New York. He had had a way of life with Sandy. Lucius had been grateful for Sandy's total lack of interest in Lucius's life, in the justification of Lucius's life, in the question of why Lucius was there at all. Had this blandness been assumed? Lucius thought not. Big red-haired Philistine Sandy simply did not care. Gerda saw Sandy as some sort of hero, but really Sandy was just a big calm relaxed man, unlike dark manic Henry. Lucius had never seen Sandy as either an obstacle or a critic. Semi-educated Sandy only cared, and amateurishly at that, about machines. Gerda ran the Hall, it was her house. Of course Sandy's death had been a terrible shock, but Lucius did not feel bereaved. He could not think about Sandy now, Sandy was over. He thought about the future and it was a vibrating darkness. He felt fear. He fell asleep and dreamed that he was twenty-five again and everybody loved him.

An hour later Gerda was still sitting beside the library fire in a small armchair pulled up so close that her little velvet slippers were right among the ashes. The fire had died down, there were no flames now, only a parade of red sparks upon a blackened log. The log subsided with a sigh and the sparks vanished.

Gerda had thought: if he had really cared about me he would have seen to it that I went to bed instead of leaving me here. He would have waited like a dog. He thinks only of himself. But this was just a mechanical thought, the kind of thought that came every day. She had forgotten about Lucius, forgotten about their conversation, which although it reflected some of her deep concerns had been merely a way of prolonging his presence, of using it up. She would not appeal to him, and she so feared to be alone.

The house had changed. It had lived with Burke's life and with Sandy's life, and before Burke and before Sandy it had cast its ray upon Gerda's childhood. Living nearby, she had loved the house before she had loved her husband; and when she came to it from her humbler home as a bride of nineteen it had seemed a symbol of eternity. The house had been her education and her profession, and the men, Burke's widowed father, Burke, Sandy, had made it her shrine. But now, quite suddenly and unexpectedly, she and the house were strangers. No one really cared about Sandy's death, even the house did not care. It had its own purposes and its own future. Gerda had looked at her letters of condolence and seen a heap of bones. She had been an only child, so had Burke. Burke's relations in the north were only concerned about their chances of a legacy. Her own relations in London, whom she never saw, had envied her grand marriage and were pleased at her misfortune. Her neighbours, Mrs. Fontenay at the Grange, the curate Mr. Westgate, the architect Giles Gosling, even the Forbeses, were not sincere. The only person who was really sad was the old rector, now retired, and he was thinking of his own death and not of Sandy's. Gerda had set herself apart and was now an exile in her own home. Her wandering feet roused echoes which she had never heard before.

But it was not even of this that she was thinking as she went up the dim staircase and darkened the long landing behind her. Nor would she think at all of changeling Henry. The thought of Henry was like a door which instantly snapped open showing her beyond the hospital bed with Sandy lying there as she had last seen him, as she had insisted upon seeing him. And she wondered now how she could go on existing through the successive moments of her life.

At about the hour when Cato Forbes was walking to and fro on Hungerford Bridge and Henry Marshalson was awakening from his first sleep on the jumbo jet high above the Atlantic and Gerda Marshalson and Lucius Lamb were in conference in the library of Laxlinden Hall, John Forbes was sitting beside the big stove in his slate-flagged kitchen, re-reading a letter which he had received from his daughter Colette. The letter ran as follows.

Dearest Dad,
   I think I must give up the college, I can save the fees for the term if I leave now, I just asked the office. I kept trying to tell you but you wouldn't listen and when we argue you always muddle me and I don't say what I think, please please forgive me. It is quite clear to me now, I have thought it over sincerely and I just don't feel that my studies are relevant to anything worth-while. I talked to Mr. Tindall and he agreed, I think he heaved a sigh of relief! I feel I have been deceiving myself and deceiving you and passing myself off as something I am not. Please understand me, Dad, I've always wanted so much to please you, perhaps too much! I forced myself against my nature, and that can't be right, can it. I feel very unhappy about it all. I feel I am a failure, but it is better to stop now and not waste your money any more. I think I never told you how unhappy I was all last year, I am not up to it. It has needed some nerve to be honest with myself and come through to this truth, though I know you will be hurt. At home when you say you must *try* I say yes I will try, but I've felt so wretched about it. You must think I'm spineless, but please please don't be angry. I have faced up to it and now I know myself, like you were always quoting about Socrates. I want so much to come home. Please don't try to telephone me, they can't get me anyway, the hostel phone is out of order, and please don't send a telegram or write, there won't be time,

just try to understand and don't think it's a tragedy, it's not the end of the world! I'll find my way in life but it must be *my* way. I have tried your way, truly I have. There are all kinds of growing up and getting educated which are not academic kinds. One has got to feel free to become oneself. I can learn things, but not in this way. I feel what I am doing now just lacks relevance, for me anyhow. You know I'm not just a "silly girl" like the ones you despise. Please see I have to do my thing—and I don't mean that in a silly way either. Make things easy for me. I could only explain this in a letter. I do rather dread coming home. I'm so terribly sorry I cost so much money for nothing, I want not to cost any more. I'll get a job soon, only don't be angry. I'll pack my stuff and it can be picked up later. I'll be home in a few days, I'll let you know when. Dear Daddy, much much love to you from your loving

C.

John Forbes threw the letter onto the kitchen table which was covered with dirty plates and beer bottles. Earlier in the evening George Bellamy, the Laxlinden gardener whose services John coveted, had come over to watch colour television and to bring the latest Hall news. John disliked everybody at the Hall, and since he had bought the Oak Meadow there had been a positive, though quite irrational, sense of feud. Gerda made such a muddle over the sale, and wrote afterwards implying that he had pressed her into it. Of course he had felt sorry for Gerda when Sandy died and had written her a carefully composed letter. He had never forgotten the cold letter which Gerda wrote when Ruth died. But then poor Gerda always envied Ruth her beauty and her talents. About his old friend Lucius Lamb, John often thought sadly. And now George Bellamy had brought news of the arrival, expected in a week or so, of the slug Henry. John Forbes disliked and disapproved of them all, but he was always interested in Bellamy's bits of news.

Colette's letter was a bolt from the blue, though he now told himself that of course the girl had obviously tried to prepare him for it, only he had refused to listen. He could not bear to think that a child of his was not an intellectual. He had pushed her and encouraged her and taught her himself and pulled strings and tried and failed to get her into a decent university (of course she was a bad examinee) and had had to accept that training college as a second best, not good enough for his

29

daughter but still the best available and good of its kind. He had regularly interviewed her tutor, Mr. Tindall, had explained exactly what courses he thought would suit Colette, and had even suggested certain changes in the college syllabus, to toughen it up a little. He had talked for hours with Colette herself about what she ought to do, what subjects she ought to choose, what she ought to concentrate upon, he had done the best he could to help her in the vacations. He had actually found the books for her and put them into her hands!

Perhaps he had used the wrong tactics, he thought now. Women are so odd. He abhorred bullying, and had often thought and said that the domination of men over women is the source of many of the world's evils. He had always fought for women's liberation, he had fought, to his best knowledge, for Colette's liberation! But there was a kind of invincible stupidity in the other sex which simply asked for bullying. After all it had taken them practically the whole of recorded history to invent a simple idea like the brassière. Yes, he had bullied his clever darling wife, now so long dead, and he had bullied his daughter. Perhaps he had been thoroughly unwise and it was indeed just a matter of tactics. He recalled how much he had valued studying when he was Colette's age. Colette was perfectly capable of enjoying her work and getting a college degree of some kind; then as a graduate student she was sure to do very much better. She was a late developer and a bit of a slow-coach. The trouble was her teachers never saw that, in her slow way, she was really thinking.

And now this half-baked half-witted letter. Somebody must have been getting at her. He would telephone Tindall tomorrow. Tindall was pretty flabby actually. John had resisted the impulse to send an angry telegram. Let her come home. He would argue rationally with her and send her back. He would explain to her everything that she would miss in life if she threw away her chances now. He could not let her give up her precious education and become a typist or a flower-arranging ninny or posturing mannequin like Gerda Marshalson. The young have got no backbone, he thought. They are not like we were. They can't face anything *difficult*. They haven't been taught the important difference between getting things right and getting things wrong. They just want to be themselves, but education is the process of extending and changing so as to understand what is alien. No wonder the lazy puling left-wing youth were drifting into pointless anarchism; always moaning, when there was so much good to do and so much to learn and to be cheerful about. Of course the trouble starts at school. And they are all so absolutely soaked in self-pity. I would never have told my father that I was unhappy at college!

It's a shame that I never got into Parliament, thought John. He had been an unsuccessful Labour candidate. Now he had been for many years a university lecturer. Still, we must go on and on trying to improve things, he thought. Anyone anywhere can do that and there is plenty that I can do. He had learnt his own limitations by the same dogged method that he used in the study of history. He came of a Quaker family. He had intended to spend his precious sabbatical leave, which was now just beginning, in writing a history of Quakerism; from a sociological, not a religious, point of view of course. John Forbes had no truck with superstition. As a small child he had soon realized that although his father still went to Meeting he did not believe in God. His father called himself an "agnostic," but that was just a matter of generation. He and his sturdy truthful bright-eyed father had early understood each other. "There is no God, John, not like they think," his father had told him. His father had taught him never to lie and that the world was godless almost in one breath. Now that the time had come however for John to write his history, he found that he no longer wanted to. There were far too many books already by men who were middling clever like himself. What after all justified a man's life? Certainly not a book. He would read and think and prepare new sets of lectures. He knew that he was a talented teacher. One must keep hope and sense in one's life and go on striving. John Forbes had never found these things too difficult. He could still do plenty of good in the world. Only now this valuable time was going to be interrupted by his daughter's vagaries.

John recalled his paternal grandparents, whom he had known well as a child, he recalled his splendid parents, his noble socially energetic father, his pure high-minded mother, his clever angelic wife who had died so senselessly of cancer. How could it turn out that the children of such a lineage were made of such rotten stuff? Cato had gone to the bad, and now Colette, indulged with every possibility of happiness and improvement, was whining about "relevance" and finding her little simple tasks "too hard"! What had he done to deserve such children? Ruth had named the girl, he had named the boy. What a sad eclipse of all their bright hopes.

Cato Forbes, hidden underneath a black umbrella, was walking along Ladbroke Grove with long strides. He passed under
the railway bridge and continued for some distance, then turned
down a side street. It had been raining all day. Now it was
late evening and dark. Cato usually went back after dark. He
spent the day wandering about or sitting in library reading-
rooms or churches or public houses. He had a decision to make
but he could not make it; and the time which passed fruitlessly
in this way made the decision more urgent but made the making
of it more difficult. Last night he had been sleepless. Tonight
he had an appointment.

Ladbroke Grove is a long and very strange street. At the
south end of it there are grand houses, some of the smartest
houses in town. At the north end, and especially beyond the
railway bridge, the street becomes seedy and poor, there are
areas of slum property, a considerable coloured population, a
mass of decrepit houses let out in single rooms. A small terrace
house in this melancholy labyrinth off the Grove was Cato
Forbes's destination. The house itself had been condemned
and some of its neighbours had already been pulled down, so
that the street ended in a wasteland of strewn rubble where the
citizens had already started to deposit their rubbish. The area
had, particularly in warm weather, an obscure characteristic
smell mingled of dust and spicy cooking and rats and urine and
deep black dirt. A Sikh friend once told Cato that it smelt like
India.

The surviving row of houses backed onto a narrow alley,
separated from it by a small back yard and a brick wall. Beyond the alley were other houses, also condemned. Cato swung
into the alleyway, putting down his umbrella for which there
was now no room. His mackintosh brushed walls thick with

33

growths of vegetable filth. He fell over a dustbin. The doorways into the yards, which had once had doors, gaped darkly. Some of the houses were still inhabited. Stepping carefully in the mud, he passed through a hole into a cluttered back yard and up to the back door of a house. He quietly and accurately fitted his key into the keyhole, pressed the door open and moved noiselessly inside. He closed the door and locked it after him.

Before turning on the light he checked with experienced hands that the thick black curtain which covered the window, and which had evidently been hanging there since the blitz, was pulled well across and tucked in at the sides. Then he turned the switch and a feeble naked light bulb, darkened with grease, revealed the kitchen, just as he had left it in the morning twilight, his enamel mug half full of cold tea, a ragged piece of bread, and butter in a paper packet. He took off his mackintosh and propped his streaming umbrella in a corner, whence a rivulet proceeded across the floor making pools in the cracked tiles and disturbing a gathering of the semi-transparent beetles who were now shameless inhabitants of the kitchen.

The dim light showed, immediately outside the door, the steep stairs which Cato now mounted to the room above where he once more checked the window which had been partially boarded up and more recently covered by a blanket hung from two nails. All being well he turned on the light, which here was slightly brighter. He ran down again to switch off the kitchen light, then came up more slowly. The little room was dingy and shabby but not totally comfortless. There was a chest of drawers with the drawers standing open and empty, a divan bed with a dirty flimsy green coverlet drawn up over disorderly bed-clothes, and a small metal crucifix nailed to the wall above. The speckled linoleum was worn into holes, but there was a cheap newish brown rug. A washstand with a brightly tiled back and a grey marble top was strewn with Cato's shaving tackle. On the floor was his suitcase, packed, unpacked, packed, now once more disgorging its contents conspicuous among which was a bottle of whisky. The dusty wainscot was decorated here and there by eccentric forms of flattened soup tins which a previous tenant had nailed over the mouse holes. There were two upright chairs and a number of overflowing ash trays. The

34

room smelt of damp and tobacco and the lavatory next door. Cato switched on a one-bar electric fire which stood in the corner, the element emitted a shower of sparks, then settled to a dull glow. He sat down on the divan and lit a cigarette. He was trying to give up smoking again, though really now it scarcely mattered.

After the first few heavenly puffs the cigarette began to lose its charm. He leaned forward covering his face with one hand and letting the hand holding the cigarette drop down until his knuckles touched the floor. He sat there waiting, trembling a little with a kind of excitement which was a kind of misery; and the despair which had surrounded him like a cloud all day, and from which he had sometimes literally run, hoping to leave it behind like a swarm of flies, settled quietly upon him. The surface of his body crawled and twitched all over, his mouth twitched, his teeth clicked noiselessly together, his breathing was like that of a deep sleeper, his eyes, wide with apprehension, moved slightly as if surveying the room, though he saw nothing. He waited.

Cato was a tall man, broad-shouldered and now a little stout, with a big head, thick pouting lips and plump cheeks, large brown eyes, and thick straight brown hair which, since he had become a priest, he hacked jaggedly short. Because of his plump cheeks and rather rubbery nose he had been called Fat Face Forbes at school, or sometimes just Funny Face Forbes or Old Pudgie. It was now three years since he had been ordained. Much of that time had been given over to theology. The *élite* order to which Cato belonged worshipped God also with the intellect. The "Mission," now failed and defunct, had been his first attempt at full-time pastoral work.

There was a faint click downstairs, the sound of a Yale key cautiously inserted in a lock. Cato sprang up. A door opened and closed. Cato moved across the room. A boy of about seventeen was coming quietly up the stairs.

"Father—"

"Hello."

"You were expecting me?"

"Yes."

Cato went back to sit upon the bed, his legs giving way. The

35

boy pulled up a chair and sat near, smiling compulsively. This was Joseph Beckett, known to his friends and enemies as Beautiful Joe. He was very thin and at first sight looked odd rather than beautiful. He wore hexagonal rimless glasses which slightly enlarged his light hazel eyes. His blond hair was very straight and fine, quite long, cut in a neat bob with a side parting and always recently and carefully combed. He had a short straight nose and a long thin mouth with sensitive humorous lips. His cheeks were smooth and rosy, and with his bright attentive slightly quizzing air he looked like a young American scholar or perhaps a very clever schoolgirl.

"You're all wet," said Cato.

The boy had no coat and his jeans and shirt clung in wrinkles to his body. His hair, darkened now by rain, clung to his head like a cap.

"Been wet all day. Soon dry. Got a towel?"

"Here."

"Got a drink?"

"Have you taken anything?" (this meant drugs).

"No, course not, that's all over with."

Cato sat watching as the boy first carefully dried his glasses and set them on his knee, then dried his face and neck and rubbed his hair vigorously, resumed his glasses and, with a steel comb, combed his hair down in a neat lacquered curve, all the time keeping his bright quizzical gaze fixed upon Cato.

"Got a drink?"

"Later." What the hell, thought Cato, I need a drink myself. He reached for the neck of the whisky bottle and fetched two tumblers from the washstand. "Here." He stubbed out his cigarette in a mound of ash and lit another one. Joe did not smoke.

Joe was smoothing his damp hair down with his fingers, patting out the sleek curves across his cheeks, still watching the priest with an air of affectionate amusement.

"Father—"

"Yes."

"I haven't told anyone."

"Told anyone what?"

36

"That you're still here. No one knows but me. That's what you wanted, isn't it?"

"It doesn't matter now," said Cato. That seemed to be the theme song of the present moment. He added, "I'm going away. You'd better give me back the door key."

Joe gave him the key. "That's sort of sad, Father, you trusted me, it was a sort of symbol, wasn't it, Father?"

"I still trust you. This isn't my house."

"Where will you be then, where will I see you?"

"I don't know."

"Are you going to Rome?"

"No. What makes you think I'm going to Rome?"

"Every priest goes there. I'd like to see Rome. I'd like to see His Holiness. When will you be Pope, Father?"

"Not for a while yet!"

"Where will I see you?"

"I don't know. I'll—I'll write to you."

'I haven't an address. I'll come to you. You want me to, don't you?"

Joe was smiling and swinging his hair about, transforming the lank locks into a golden fuzz by teasing them between his fingers. He twitched his shoulders, then drew his damp shirt out of his jeans and unbuttoned it a little so as to pull it free of his back.

Cato was not looking at him. Cato had imagined that after the ordeal of Easter everything would become simpler and certain moves at least would just have to be made. But it seemed that there was still nothing compulsory in his life and the horror of choice which by now should have passed from him was still there, the awful superimposition of quite different problems producing more and more glimpses and vistas, more and more superfluous possibilities, the longer he gazed.

If only, thought Cato, instinctively forming his thought as a prayer, everything were not happening to me all at once. Is this an accident, can it be? One thing at a time, oh Lord, and I can manage. I cannot deal with such different things at the same moment. Yet are they different things? They were beginning to seem inextricably connected. But that was impossible. What was the connection, what could it be? He had to solve the problems separately, he had to, and he had to solve one after the other. Perhaps *the* problem was how to separate them.

The period of Cato's conversion now seemed inconceivably remote, a prehistory, a mythical time of creation out of chaos which did not cease to be, even now in his life, a centre of authority and power. He had been invaded by Christ. That he had been "armed" by a strictly rationalist atheist upbringing was nothing. Such arms were exceedingly ambiguous. A reaction was "to be expected" some people said. But Cato had his own deep resistance against sudden emotional religion. He had, as it were, quite early inoculated himself against falling in love with that mystical beauty: the ritual, the intellectual delight, the drama, the power. As a budding historian he had gone into it all and probed in himself the weakness that made him vulnerable to what was after all, in the end, a vast vulgarity. Christ himself of course was untouchably pure and had never put a foot wrong, though this was true also of Socrates. No vulgarity there, no vanity, not a shadow of trickery or falsehood, but what this showed was how vastly perfectible human beings were after all. This Jesus was an old friend, a great saint whom he had often discussed with his father, as between them they had dissected Christianity, sorting out good from bad, truth from illusion. Christ was a great saint, a good man. But the superstition, the symbolism, the hoax: Cato had perfectly understood, had studied it all with sympathy, had seen exactly why it happened and why it appealed to him and why it could never really attract him or even, profoundly, interest him. As a historian he was more interested in Islam.

Then suddenly, with no warning and with a sense of immense barriers dissolving in the mind, he had tripped and stumbled into reality. Suddenly, with faculties which he had not been aware of, he experienced God. All that he had "known" before now seemed a shadow-land through which he had passed into the real world, into a form of being which indeed he did not "know" because he lived it and was one with it. He entered quite quietly into a sort of white joy, as if he had not only emerged from the cave, but was looking at the Sun and finding that it was easy to look at, and that all was white and pure and not dazzling, not extreme, but gentle and complete, and that everything was there, kept safe and pulsating silently inside the circle of the Sun.

And what was so strange too was that this new grasp of being came to him quite clearly identified as an experience of the Trinity. The Trinity was the Sun, so white and complete and when you looked straight at it so thrillingly alive and gentle. Of course Cato knew all about this strange doctrine, he had many times discussed it spiritedly and jocularly. Now it was present to him not as an idea but as reality, as the whole of reality, with an invasion of spirit which seemed totally alien to his "personality" as he had known it before, but which became the very selfness of his self. This selfness partook of the Oneness of Christ with Father and with Spirit. *How* the Trinity was One, and how this Oneness was the law of all being, the law of nature, the electrical universal expression of love, he now *saw* with the opened eyes of the soul, and *resting* as he had never rested before he let this indubitable vision gather him into its silent power.

In retrospect Cato found it difficult to connect these revelations with the ordinary history of times and places. He was doing some postgraduate work, writing a thesis on some aspects of eighteenth-century Russian history, at the provincial university where he had been a student, and looking out for a job. He had been at home that summer, staying amicably with his father, playing tennis with Colette. He had been tepidly in love and had had two tepid love affairs, now fortunately over. He was perfectly happy and unanxious and unafraid. Why then this visitation? Perhaps this animal happiness had led him to lay down the weapons of sharp egoism which protect the soul against God? Or perhaps it was itself a first automatic gleam reflected from the joy to come. His "conversion" did not arise out of spiritual anguish, misery, extremity, or any pressing need for transcendent consolation. He had been alone a great deal, walking in the summer heat, sitting beside rivers and watching dragon-flies, swimming naked in lonely flower-girt pools. He had been happy with the happiness of youth and innocence and intellectual self-satisfaction and infinite possibility. He was healthy, active, robust, successful in mind and body. And then—he had found, breathless with wonder and almost a spectator of himself, that this earthly joy was being steadily and entirely and quite independently of his will transformed into a heavenly joy.

Cato never, at that time or later, dignified these happenings with any grand name, such as "mystical experiences." What he had learnt was that all was mystical. He did not need any spectacular "vision" of Christ. He was with Christ, he was Christ. He was invaded, taken over, and it all happened so quietly and with such a sense of perfect reality. Cato said nothing to his father, nothing to Colette. He waited to be told, and he was told. It was not a headlong rush into a new life of self-sacrifice and strenuous devotion. It was like a river, like a growing plant. The will did nothing, there was no will. That nothing less than the gift of his entire being would be adequate to this reality was from the first clear, he was already given, indeed possessed. What exactly he had to do emerged more slowly. He must become a priest, his whole life must be a showing of what he now *knew*. And he did not even think that it would be easy, he did not even feel himself in any danger of being deluded, since with his new cleansed vision he also saw, still existing, still there as part of the world, his old self, unchanged and perhaps (and this was one of the most remarkable teachings of all) unchangeable.

After a while he visited a Roman priest (the idea of entering the Protestant Communion somehow never seriously occurred to him), not at Laxlinden, where there was no Catholic community, but in a nearby village. The priest turned out to be very unwilling to have anything to do with Cato and his new certainties. He told him to go away for six months and see what he felt like then. Cato could not wait six months. By now he was back at his university continuing his studies. Here he remembered a Catholic lecturer, Brendan Craddock, a man a few years older than himself, whom he had known slightly in his student days and who was now a priest in a religious house in the city, and went to him. Craddock treated him with the same cool suspicious detachment and passed him to Father Sidney Bell, who later became his godfather. About a year afterwards he entered the order of which Father Craddock and Father Bell were members, and a few years after that he was ordained.

Of course the glow of those early experiences faded a little with the years, as he perfectly expected them to do, although that joy was renewed for him at intervals as he penetrated into the complex simplicity of the mass and began to make his home inside the everyday life of the Church. He thought that he would faint with happiness when he celebrated his first mass, and he did indeed nearly faint. His new mentors taught him to fear exaltation, but as he lived and grew in Christ he quite sufficiently felt in every day of his life that magnetic bond that joined him to the ground of being. He lived close to, and very often inside, a perfect happiness. Yet ordinary pains and anxieties did not disappear; and the gravest of these was the extreme anger and bitterness of his father. His father met his announcements with absolute incredulity. He thought that his son almost literally had gone mad, and could scarcely have been more stunned and amazed if Cato had declared that Peter the Great was risen from the grave and was now his constant companion. For a short time John Forbes behaved with the energy of desperation, behaved as he might have done if he had seen his child drowning before his eyes. He begged, he threatened, he went and stormed at Father Craddock and Father Bell and practically accused them of sorcery, he talked wildly of going to law, he even (in a frenzy, although he despised psychiatrists) besought Cato to admit himself to be mentally ill and enter a hospital. Cato went quietly and steadily on with his plans, never arguing, constantly begging his father's pardon for the pain he had to cause him. At last John Forbes gave up and retired into a bitter contemptuous coldness which had lasted ever since. Cato wrote to his father and visited him at slightly increasing intervals. The letters received no reply, the visits passed off politely, with no discussion of anything of importance. His sister Colette was upset by the family quarrel but she loved her brother dearly and though she considered his beliefs absurd she never for a second regarded them as a barrier between them.

Cato, for a time absorbed in the busy rhythmical life of the Church and serenely obedient to his superiors, continued to work as a scholar, dividing his time between theology and Byzantine history. He lived in a community house, first in

Manchester, then in London, and did his share, first as an ordinand, then as a priest, in counselling students, talking to (as he then thought) all kinds of people, addressing meetings, dispensing comfort and instruction to believers and unbelievers alike. He sometimes, with wry self-observation, felt himself in danger of becoming a "popular figure." *Charisma Forbes the swinging priest* he once saw written beside a ludicrous drawing on a lavatory wall. Cato was not afraid. A cool sense of the tough old Adam in him had never left him. He knew how much he loved a certain kind of power, the power of the authoritative teacher, the power of the wise confessor. To be able to release a man from the burden of sin in the confessional filled him with an almost too exultant pleasure; and the precious jewel of the priesthood, the mass itself, was to him sometimes almost a temptation. He was too happy.

He had of course his irrelevant desires. He found it ridiculously hard to give up smoking, which he felt himself bound to do. He would have liked to travel, particularly to go to Rome, but this in their wisdom his superiors still denied him; and he took this as an admonition, an attempt perhaps to "cool it," to lower the temperature of his still too devotional Christianity by prescribing the most humdrum possible routine. He went at the prescribed intervals into retreat, preferring the more austere traditional practices which some of his fellow priests regarded as so emotive and old-fashioned. There was a sort of painful awkwardness about this discipline which seemed itself to figure the counter-natural demand of perfection. He had, on the other hand, always felt perfectly at home in his body, there was an athletic suppleness which was always a part of his worship, and his youthful strength moved naturally into adoration. Ever since those first "showings" he had felt that God and he occupied the same space, and he found nothing difficult or quaint in imagining, even in detail, when required to do so, Our Lord, His Mother, the moment by moment reality of the Passion and the historical eventfulness of the Incarnation. Hell he could not imagine; it was for him an intellectual idea. Damnation if it existed was God's affair.

When he meditated upon his own sins he often thought about his father and about the grim and high necessity which had led him to become a bane of suffering to one whom he so much loved; and he lodged this pattern deep in God's wisdom. He revered every austerity that was required of him and adored the strange and almost invisible tenderness that lurked inside it. At the same time he was without illusion about his ability to change. Perhaps sometimes, if he looked away from the world, if he looked only at God, there might be a little change, an atom of it. In a way *that* did not concern him. Only God concerned him, only God was his business, only God *interested* him, and man and his doings simply by extension. He did not find it difficult to listen patiently to dull confused people, to resist physical tiredness and boredom, to do without, when it was necessary, the intellectual joys which were also a communion with God. The vow of chastity and the practice of that virtue never caused him trouble. He had no major temptations except the deep subtle temptation afforded by the power itself which came from his givenness to God. He had friends in the order, especially Brendan Craddock, who had been his confessor since he came to London. He had friends outside the order and outside the Church. But these friendships had never disturbed him with dramas of any degree of intensity.

At a certain time his superiors decided to give Cato a change of scene, and he, in the harmony of his mind with his priesthood, found himself wanting exactly what they were now proposing. Without yet leaving the shelter of the community house where he had lived hitherto, Cato took up a visiting role in a poor east-end district of London upon the confines of Limehouse and Poplar. "You'll be shocked, you know," Brendan had told him. "Nothing can shock me," said Cato. But he had been shocked. He had been frightened, frightened of his penitents, frightened of the dumb failure of his authority, and of a world where news of Christ had never come and, as it often seemed, could never come. "I was in prison and you visited me" had lost its charm. Cato could sometimes discern no light at all in those whom he devoutly attempted to love. He saw for the first time the wilfulness of vice as a part of everyday life, and the way in which despair and vice were one. Just beyond the confines of ordinariness there were places where love could not enter; it was as if the concept broke. Cato knew perfectly well that the power of God could pass through the broken concept, and that this was the lesson which it most behooved him to learn. He measured now how cloistered he had been by his father's clean idealism. Perhaps it was this very breaking point that he had been seeking when he fled away into Christ. He prayed ceaselessly and hoped to find some blinded understanding in his prayer as he brought it with him into scenes where he knew himself to be powerless, detested, or even (worst of all) a figure of fun! Yet in the midst of it there were families, especially Irish families, who took him absolutely for granted. "Ah, here's Father come. Sit down now, Father, will you have some tea?"

In the course of those adventures he made only one friend, a local secular priest called Father Milsom, an old man who had lived for many years in the east end, and who regarded Cato as an innocent child. Cato was glad of this new paternity, and soon told Father Milsom all about his own father and the quarrel and his hopes in Christ that it would end one day. Father Milsom was not very optimistic, but even his realism was to Cato like a kind of hope. Sometimes in the late evenings he met Brendan and told his "day." Brendan had worked in the slums of Manchester and Cato found it impossible to astonish him. He talked to his friend and confessor about his discoveries and his fears. "All the same, one has such great power in the confessional." "*You* have no power." "Confession becomes a kind of collusion." "Of course it does. Just try to leave one little unassimilable grain of truth behind." "They confess, and carry on, in fact they confess *to* carry on!" "Who can say what draws them to confession. God's grace is everywhere." "Christ is with these people, he is in these people, in the most violent, most criminal ones, but sometimes it's impossible to see Him there." "Just see Him, look at Him. He will give you the light." "You said I'd be shocked. The misery doesn't shock, it's the vice that shocks. I thought I'd seen it all already in myself, but I hadn't. And do you know—Father Bell used to say that wickedness was dull, but it isn't, it's rather exciting." "It seems exciting. The place where one can see it as it is is above our level."

Just as Cato was beginning to feel less awkward in his duties a new idea was mooted. The order had acquired the lease of a house in Paddington, and a priest whom Cato knew slightly, an enthusiast called Gerald Dealman, wanted to set up a little community of priests to live there with the people and share their lives, perhaps even work with them. Cato was delighted when Gerald asked him if he would like to join in. That had been a year ago; and the "Mission," as the local people called it, had come into being. In the original plan there were to have been three resident priests and a visiting Sacred Heart nun. The third priest, an eccentric called Reggie Poole, was present during the initial period of house-renovation and settling in, but afterwards mysteriously disappeared and was later said to have been sent to Japan. The Sacred Heart changed their mind about sending a nun, perhaps as a result of something which they had heard about Reggie. Gerald and Cato ran the Mission very haphazardly, each with his own kind of zeal. Cato in fact found it rather hard to get on at such close quarters with his brother in Christ, who was far from efficient and never stopped talking. However, after the Mission had existed for some time and was certainly a going concern, Gerald too disappeared from the strength after a punch-up with a penitent, an incident obscure in origin which landed Gerald in hospital with a broken jaw. After this it became clear that the enterprise must be either rescued or abandoned. The local authority conveniently decided about this time that it wanted to pull down the whole street, so the project was able to end without any awful stigma of failure.

The Mission had indeed, for all that it existed in a state of unparalleled muddle, not been entirely unsuccessful. "They'll love us!" Gerald had shouted. Cato had thought it more likely that they would be ignored or mocked. But, whether because Gerald and Reggie were so picturesque or because Cato was more experienced, the priests found themselves quite popular. There was a great difference between visiting a poor area and going home to a clean book-lined room, and living in a poor area night and day. It was now impossible to escape from people. The Mission became a centre not only for Catholics but for all sorts of people who were in trouble, wanting spiritual or temporal advice, or a chance to sponge on somebody or steal something. The simple worldly possessions of the Mission. saucepans, crockery, cutlery, linen, blankets, transistor sets, even books, began to disappear during the first two months. In the early days, on principle, they never locked the door; later on they took to locking up simply in order to preserve a kit for survival. Cato, forced to be a one-man citizens' advice bureau, became expert on all sorts of practical matters concerning supplementary benefits, rent rebates, tenancy agreements, hire purchase, legal costs, insurance, and how to fill in tax forms. He had felt disappointed at first that so little time seemed to be spent talking seriously to people and getting to know them. He would have liked to bring the reality of Christ to those whom he saw sunk in misery or upon the slippery edges of crime. Later he was too busy and too tired to worry about such matters or to seek to make opportunities for such "serious talk." He went on hearing confessions but now did not experience the worries he had confided to Brendan. He celebrated mass every day, sometimes almost alone, at a side altar in the big local church. His time came to be spent, especially after Gerald's departure, more with atheistic social workers and less with fellow Catholics or "devotional" people.

During this year Cato had felt himself changing. He felt like a plant growing yet not able to be conscious of what the changes were which were daily taking place in its form and texture. He began to feel more independent, more individualistic, less, in his relation to the Church, like a child. He took to wearing a cassock all the time, unusual for a Roman priest, arguing to Brendan that if Reggie Poole could go about looking like a hippie, he could at least sport a black robe if he pleased. He felt independent, but, amid his many clients, solitary. "You'll miss us," Brendan had said. He did. It was the first time since he had joined the family of his order that he had been on his own. Of course there was, for a time, Gerald, but his mild alienation from his companion made him feel more alone. He thought a lot about his father and wished that that wound could be healed, he thought about his sister and wished that he could see her more often. The local parish priest, Father Thomas, provided no company, since he had from the start regarded the Mission as a wrong-headed adventure and an intrusion on his territory. The secular priest and the monkish priest are always likely to be at loggerheads, since the former regards the latter as decorative rather than useful, while the latter can hardly help feeling superior and "more dedicated." The general practitioner and the specialist are natural enemies. Father Thomas thought that Cato, Gerald, Reggie, and the other members of their order were spoilt idle over-educated prigs, always off on holidays to monasteries abroad, always blowing in and out of places where the real work was done, drinking sherry and showing off their knowledge of Latin and Greek and of the finer points of theology. While Cato tended to find Father Thomas's conversation rather dull, and resented his assumption that Cato was a frivolous amateur. Of course Cato and Father Thomas, being decent sincere men of God, recognized their prejudices as prejudices. But this did not stop them from quietly feuding.

The majority of the people who came to the Mission were uneducated, some of them illiterate. This did not surprise Cato who had already learnt how in a rich and civilized society large numbers of citizens can be not only miserably poor, but unable to read a newspaper. Of course he had not come to Paddington to keep cultivated company or enjoy luxuries of private contemplation. It was now difficult for Cato to follow any strict regular devotional routine, since in the house he could never rely on being alone even at night. But he knew that a priest must maintain his life of prayer against the unceasing clamour of the world, making his cell of solitude even in crowded streets or underground trains. Thus prayer is strengthened and deepened; and he had seen in Father Milsom the results of a lifetime which indissolubly combined trivial nagging practical activity with an absolute quietness in the presence of God. Cato hoped soberly and confidently for grace, the power when tested to live more deeply in and through the ground of his being.

When this hope seemed to be disappointed Cato was not at first alarmed. He ascribed the spiritual dullness which he felt to all sorts of natural causes—tiredness, lack of solitude, the irritations of his exposed existence or simply to the mysterious rhythms which, as he already knew, govern the spiritual life. The dullness, the blankness was a phase which would pass. It was just proving harder than he had expected to enjoy loving Christ without more frequent *tête-à-tête*. However the phase did not pass, and Cato woke up one morning with the absolute conviction that he had been mistaken and that there was no God. The conviction faded; but from that moment Cato began to treat himself carefully, almost tenderly, like someone who has discovered in himself the symptoms of a serious disease, and for whom the world in consequence is totally altered. Brendan came on a flying visit. Cato said to him, "Oh by the way, I've lost my faith." "Rubbish." "God is gone. There is no God, no Christ, nothing." "I expected this." "You expect everything." "That darkness comes to us all." "I knew you'd say that. But suppose the darkness is real, true?" "Hold on." Brendan went away, then wrote him a wonderful letter, but the darkness persisted.

It was all very well for Brendan, born into a Catholic family, educated at Downside, inhaling the faith with his first breath. Those born Catholics were a different breed. Faith had never been a problem for Cato. It had been absent. Then it had been present. He had not questioned it any more than he questioned the daylight. Now when it suddenly seemed to have been withdrawn he wondered if he had ever really had it at all. Had it all been utterly *private*, a subjective experience, something like a drug-induced hallucination? Or perhaps the real experience of faith was, for him, just beginning? His sense of living in and with Christ had been so positive that there had almost been no room for the concept of faith. Was he now, after so many years, just reaching the start? Or had he simply woken up from a happy dream? Brendan, to whom he talked at more length on a second occasion, did not brush his doubts aside, but said things which Cato had already said to himself about "the dark night of the soul." Cato would have liked to talk now to Father Milsom or to Father Bell, but Father Milsom was ill and Father Bell had gone to Canada.

Of course during this sudden and unexpected period of change Cato contrived to do his work at the Mission, so much of which made no explicit reference to Godly matters. He watched the atheistic social workers, now his colleagues. Several of them impressed him very much indeed. They had no faith.

48

They probably had no exalted feelings of love or care, no sense of companionship with a higher world; they just functioned as efficient machines, tireless tending rescuing endlessly looking-after machines. Cato in spirit bowed down to the ground before them. They were professionals. He took on no fresh penitents and only when unavoidable heard the confessions of those who had by now come to rely on him. He went on celebrating mass each day, but the mass was dead to him, seemed literally dead, as if each morning he were handling some dead creature. He stood at the altar excluded, blind, unable to give any devotional expression to the anguish which he felt.

The decision, not taken by Cato, to close the Mission, was both welcome and unwelcome to him. He was beginning to feel all the pain of being in a false position, of being an un-truthful lying teacher, a charlatan. He wanted to get away from all these people who took him for granted as a priest, and in their naïve way for a good man. On the other hand, what would happen to him now when at last he had time to think? Practical hard work, preoccupation, constant demands and lack of privacy had so far prevented him from fully facing and investigating his doubts. Suppose now when he was able to give the matter his whole consideration he were to decide, irrevocably and without appeal, that there was no God? So far muddle and procrastination had made the horror of it bear-able. Easter, just over, had been a bad dream, but he had managed to get through it in a state of double-thinking. To Brendan, who was still his confessor, he had communicated a rather subdued version of his doubts, but so far he had told nobody else, and Brendan, who now took the line of "jollying him along" and calling him a "poor old Protestant," had not yet revealed his plight. Cato was now to be officially on holiday, visiting his father. After that there would be no more interim, after that he would have to decide, or indeed, whatever hap-pened, would have decided. Would he stagger on, consenting, concealing, doubting, half-believing, feverishly reshaping the dogma so as to save his honesty? Many priests did this. Or would he, as it now seemed, destroy himself by leaving the house of Christ? Or would there be a miracle which would re-new his faith?

By the end of this period however, by the time of the closing of the Mission, the question of what Cato would or would not have otherwise done about this spiritual crisis was already becoming academic, since something else, also quite unexpected and extraordinary, had happened to him. Cato had met Beautiful Joe quite early on in his Paddington days, when even Reggie Poole had still been around. Beautiful Joe was one of a number of teenagers, all from Catholic families, all cheerfully "lapsed," who had adopted the Mission at the start, making a nuisance of themselves, ragging the priests, playing practical jokes, stealing things, and sometimes professing to have religious problems. The other boys had gradually got tired of the Mission after the first novelty had faded. Some of them in any case were "Reggie's boys" or "Gerald's boys." In the end they went away, and "Cato's boys" went away too: except for Beautiful Joe.

Cato had never for a second thought of himself as a homosexual. He had felt no strong emotions about other boys at school. At college he had been in love with girls, though without managing to do a great deal about it. The vow of chastity when it came had not dismayed him. Of course he felt attracted by the young maidens who came to him so confidently for advice and to confess their trifling sins, but of course he had no difficulty at all in keeping his hands off them. He had often reflected on how merciful it was that at least *that* was not one of his problems.

Beautiful Joe caught Cato's attention early on as a picturesque and interesting phenomenon. Joe had left school at sixteen, after doing rather well and being pressed by his teachers to continue his education. He was obviously intelligent. He came of a not very poor Catholic family in Holland Park. His father, who had died when Joe was ten, had been a hairdresser. His mother worked as a clerk at a primary school. There were books in the house. Cato had called there once, but Joe's mother had shown so much embarrassment, almost hostility, that he had not repeated his visit. Joe was the youngest of six boys. The others had all by now left home, left London, or simply vanished. Joe had in fact, as Cato later learnt, left home too. Cato did not know where Joe lived. Joe was mysterious. How Joe acquired money, which he undoubtedly did, was also a mystery since he appeared to have no employment. "He's a baby crook," Reggie had said at first sight of Joe. It took Cato some time and some reluctance to come to agree.

Cato had felt rather gratified at being Joe's favourite, since Joe was certainly the cleverest as well as the handsomest of the little gang of boys who frequented the Mission. What was more important, Joe was the only one who really seemed to want and to attend to spiritual advice. "He's having you on," Gerald said. "He is and he isn't," said Cato, feeling wiser. What was extraordinary from the start was how easy he found it to talk to Joe. Cato could talk to people of course, but he could not, the way for instance Gerald could, simply *chatter* to them about serious matters. He and Beautiful Joe chattered about the Resurrection, about the Trinity, about the Immaculate Conception, about transubstantiation, about papal infallibility, about Hitler, about Buddhism, about communism, about existentialism—in fact it later occurred to Cato that they had talked about pretty well everything except sex. Joe did not seem to be particularly interested in sex as a topic of discussion. "Sex is a bore," he once said, "I mean having sex is a bore." Joe had had plenty of girls, as he casually explained. "Would you like to get married?" Cato once asked him. "*Married?* Girls are muck, they aren't real people, they're a slave race."

Cato, who felt the utmost curiosity about Joe, soon began delicately to question him about other aspects of his life. Joe was remarkably, almost disarmingly frank. "Get a job, me?! Talk about a bank job, I might be interested." "But how do you live?" "I nick things. O.K. You don't believe in property, neither do I." "Surely you could do something better than that." "You bet I could, I'm going into protection, going to employ little kids, scare the shopkeepers silly." "You ought to go to college and learn things." "I learnt something yesterday." "What?" "How to slash a pig with a razor and be sure of leaving a scar." "Violence won't get you anything that you really want." "Won't it? Show a man a knife and he'll do anything. Isn't that pleasure?" Another time he said, "I want to get in with the Mafia. I know someone who knows a big man." Such talk was clearly designed to shock and to provoke arguments and reproofs, and Cato did not take it too seriously, though he believed that Joe probably did, in a small way, "nick things." On other days Joe was a revolutionary, talking about joining the IRA, destroying capitalism, bombing the prots, bombing the Jews. "I'm an anarchist, see. The straight world is just a racket, business, capitalism, TV, money, sex, all a racket. Look what happened to the Beatles. They just got bloody rich!"

When Cato realized how much he was enjoying these conversations and observed that, however busy he was, he always somehow had time for Joe, he became nervous. All his old fears about collusion came back to him. He made feeble efforts to get rid of Joe, to pass him on to Father Thomas. "Talk to that square? You're the only one who understands me, Father, you're the only one who can get through to me." Cato was touched. He had no evidence, unless the continued conversations were themselves evidence, that he was having any sort of influence on the boy. But surely it was better to go on talking to him and holding onto him, rather than to abandon him to the world about which he talked so glibly and whose reality round about him Cato had already come to discern. Of course Joe was not "vicious," he would be saved. He was just a young person with different principles, a young person in revolt against a society with which Cato was in his own way at odds. 'You're the only one who has ever cared for me, Father, you're the only one who can really *see* me at all." This was irresistible. If this is even half true, Cato thought, I must stick to this boy through thick and thin. But of course he had already decided that it was his duty to go on talking to Joe. They argued about property, about capitalism, about freedom, often having the same argument over and over again. Cato tried eloquence, persuasion, logic, everything except anger. He knew anger, which was what Joe wanted, would be the worst collusion of all. Surely that grain of truth could be deposited somewhere. Beautiful Joe was respectful, flatteringly devoted, yet also stubborn, curiously aloof and full of pretences of iniquity. Would he come to confession, would he come to mass? Maybe, one day. When? Maybe, maybe. Is he just amusing himself, Cato wondered.

Beautiful Joe was now always in Cato's prayers. The image

of the youth caused him exasperation, excitement, pity. Of course he loved Joe, after all nothing less than loving him would help him at all. How terribly he loved Joe only dawned upon him gradually. Visiting Brendan he said, "I think I've fallen in love with one of those boys, the one you met." "The angel with the hexagonal glasses? Don't worry, we all fall for lovely boys." Cato could not get Brendan to take his new predicament seriously. Besides, by now there was the other far more awful question: was there a God? On one hideous sleepless night, smoking cigarette after cigarette (he had started smoking again) Cato suddenly began to realize that the two things must be connected, they *must* be connected. Perhaps Beautiful Joe had been sent especially to tempt him. When had he begun to doubt God? At the time when Beautiful Joe came into his life. Was not the boy playing with him, coolly probing him, reaching into his soul and confusing all his thoughts? That curious amused cynical aloofness: how could a boy of seventeen be so detached and cool?

Of course these thoughts were mad, as he recognized when he next talked to Joe, seeing now no demon, but the confused silly vulnerable boy, the boy who depended on him and needed him, the boy whom only he could reach. "I'm off shoplifting." "Good." "I'm going to Belfast to kill those Protestant shits." "No you aren't." "Aren't I, Father?" "I wish I could see into your heart." "You can." But Cato could not. His own heart was swelling and aching. When they looked at each other Cato was the first to look away. Yet Joe was perfectly tactful, perfectly docile, there was no exhibition of emotion, they remained priest and pupil and a weird decorum reigned between them.

About the time when the Mission was officially closing Cato made a discovery in the house. He noticed in one of the bedrooms a cupboard in the wall which had been papered over so as to be almost invisible except when the bright sunlight shone into the room at a certain time. There was no handle on the cupboard door, there was only a tell-tale slit. Probing with his fingers, then with a knife, Cato, in search of some blankets, which might or might not have been stolen, prised open the cupboard door. There were no blankets, but stowed far back on one of the shelves there was a revolver in a leather case. Cato took it out and studied it. The case was clean and the gun had been newly polished. He had little doubt that it belonged to Joe. Joe had the key of the house, which Cato had given him as a gesture of confidence. The cupboard afforded a safe hiding-place, safer presumably than wherever it was that Joe lived. Cato could not decide what he should do. He hid the revolver in his bed, and when he next saw Joe he said nothing about it. He wondered if he were wronging the boy after all. Then the presence of the weapon in the house began to upset him intensely. He kept pulling back the blankets and looking at it and touching it. At last he had taken it and dropped it into the Thames from Hungerford Bridge. That was last night.

And now his cigarette was burning his fingers and he was staring at Beautiful Joe, while in his mind a gabble was going on which was like the gabble of an idiot: the automatic machinery of prayer, which fruitlessly continued without his will and without his heart. The beseeching never stopped, the crying out for mercy, the crying out for light, once such a ready source of power, was more like an obscene involuntary symptom of disease. No one receiving, Cato's mind raced. It occurred to him for a moment, since there is no God why should I not say all these things, *all* these things to Joe? This idea fled by. He put out the cigarette, thinking clearly for the first time, I cannot help this boy. Our relationship is a dangerous muddle and a nonsense. I must leave him absolutely and for good. I can do nothing for him, nothing. I must say good-bye to him tonight. This is the logical, the easiest, moment to do it. It is, oh God, now. No need to make a drama. I must save myself. I must go away somewhere and think. I must get back to some innocent place where I can *see*.

"Where shall I come to you, Father?" said Beautiful Joe, looking straight at Cato, his eyes, enlarged by his glasses, seeming like the golden staring eyes of a ginger cat.

How thin he is, thought Cato, how frail really, how defence-less. "Joe, I wish I could pull you out of that world."

"What world?"

"You know."

"Well, then take my hand and pull." Joe stretched out his hand.

Cato ignored the outstretched hand. "You've got wits, you've got sense, why don't you see?"

"Take me with you."

"Where?"

"Where you're going."

"I can't."

"I'll make money, then I'll retire like, I'll learn things and read books, I'll read all the classics."

"I wish you would!"

"But I got to make money first and prove myself, prove I can win at my own game. You don't want me just to join the rat race, do you?"

"Joe, if you get into that bad way of life you won't be able to get out again, if you take to violence you'll be caught by it, you'll just become the tool of very wicked men."

"Who said anything about violence, Father? You shouldn't take me so serious, the things I say. Anyway, you can't get away from violence, can you? Pigs use violence, don't they? The IRA had to use violence, otherwise they wouldn't get justice, you can't get justice under capitalism without violence, look at the trade unions. When you get down to the nitty gritty, everything rests on violence in the end."

"No, it doesn't, Joe, listen—"

"Capitalism's finished anyway. Why should a few people have everything and everybody else have nothing? Just look at Ladbroke Grove, there's the capitalist world for you. Fucking millionaires one end and us at the other. No wonder they need the army and the police! This society's rotten to the core, and you know it as well as I do, that's why you've dropped out of it, that's why you live here, that's why you dress like that, I can understand. You know property's unjust, it's wicked, that's why you've got nothing. You went to Oxford College but you're as poor as we are. You had an electric kettle but somebody stole it."

"You probably did."

"People are just slaves, otherwise they wouldn't put up with it, they wouldn't put up with starving misery when there's millionaires on yachts, why should they? But they're slaves. Just like the Jews. I was reading a paper about those concentration camps. Why did the Jews go, why were they like bloody sheep, why didn't they fight? And in the camps, there were lots of them, why did they let themselves be gassed, why didn't they kill the guards? I'd have made a fight of it if I'd been them."

"They weren't organized," said Cato. "And they weren't soldiers. Violence has to be learnt. They were just a lot of ordinary peaceful citizens pulled out of offices and shops. They were a lot of frightened individuals, and each individual wanted to survive and probably thought he would survive if he kept quiet. He didn't want to be the one to risk being shot or tortured."

"Lot of bloody cowards. I'd have *hated* those Nazi swine so much, I'd have killed them with my hands. All the same, old Hitler knew a thing or two, you can't help admiring him."

"It's easy afterwards to talk of resisting. But they didn't know what was happening."

"They knew their bit of it. They knew some bugger was pointing a gun at them and taking away their things."

"Exactly. People are afraid of guns."

"Yes, they are. And a funny thing, do you know, it's awfully easy to frighten anybody. Not everybody knows how easy it is, but it's dead easy."

"I expect it is. So you see."

"Dead easy. Do it even with a knife. I got a knife, a beauty. I scared a girl with it in the road, suddenly whipped it out and pointed it at her tummy, should have heard her screech. Just show them a knife and anybody will do anything, girls take their clothes off, rich shits hand over their wallets, anything—"

"If you—"

"I'm going to write a pop song called 'Fear is a Knife.'"

"Joe, if you play that game—"

"Well, it's just a game, you know me, scare a few ratbags, does no harm. I don't want to be a slave though. Just look at the people you see, ordinary people anywhere, they're done for by thirty, they might as well be dead, got stupid pigs' faces, can't think of anything but telly and football, that's materialism for you. I'm not going to be like that, I'm not a materialist. I know I'm somebody, I want to be different, I want to be big.

You got to be an expert. So people get frightened, O.K. And who's on top? The frighteners. No good just nicking things, that's protest but it's kids' stuff. The top people don't bother with nicking, they just frighten the little guys. That's what the Mafia do, they frighten all the other villains, that's a laugh, that's what protection rackets are all about. And Hitler and Stalin that's what they did too, that's what made them big. I'd like to be big somehow, I'd like to be famous, I don't want to be a victim of the system like all the rest. If I got a little job like in a garage mending rotten little cars for pennies a week, what'd I be? Nobody and nothing. I know I've got something in me. I just got to find myself, I got to find my way, *my* way. That's what freedom's all about. Most people are just scared, they're scared of freedom, they're sheep, they *want* to become morons, watching the telly with their mouths hanging open, I'm not going to be like that."

"All right, don't be, use your mind, you've got one! Do you think I want you to be a moron? And I'm not suggesting you should work in a garage. Get some education, that's the way to freedom, that's the way out—"

"I haven't time, Father. I'm feeling so frustrated. I wish I was a boxer, that's the way to get great. I want to live my life now, I want real things, money, fun. And I'll get them, you'll see, I'll surprise you—"

"You'll surprise yourself. You'll probably be hung."

"Not now I won't, get ten years, out in six! I'd like to kill a man, I'd like to do one sometime, just one to see what it's like. Don't worry, Father, I'm only joking! But I won't be a sheep, I'd rather die."

"Joe, I found a revolver, was it yours?"

Beautiful Joe, his dry hair now frizzed out and brushed by his thin hands into a blond mane, became very still, his mouth a hard thin line. After a moment he returned his hands to his knee and cross them with deliberation.

"In that cupboard."

"Yes."

"Did you take it?"

"I threw it into the river last night."

Joe was silent, breathing hard almost panting. He creaked

his chair backwards with a harsh movement. He was suddenly flushed. "You shouldn't. It was mine. It was my thing. *Mine*."

"You have no business with a revolver. That's one thing I can do for you, take it away."

"It's mine, it's beautiful—you don't understand—I cared so much—I'll never forgive you, never, never, never."

"Joe, you know perfectly well—"

"I hate you for this, just for this, and I'll have to—you don't understand what that meant to me, my gun—Christ, I was a fool to leave it here—"

"Oh, don't be *childish*!" said Cato. "You look as if you were ten years old."

Joe closed his eyes, then opened them and picked up his drink which had been standing untouched upon the floor. He smiled, drank, then laughed a little staccato laugh. "It wasn't a real one anyway, it was an imitation."

"Don't lie."

"Well, it's gone. Did you really throw it in the river? I'd like to have seen that. Well, Father, so you're going. Where do we meet then?"

"I don't know," said Cato, "I'm going away, absolutely away, and I can't—"

"Oh, yes you can. I must see you, I must talk to you. You're the only one I can talk to, you don't know what a star you are in my life, you're the only thing that's not bloody rotten and awful around here, you're the only *person* I know—"

"Joe—"

"If you leave me, I'm really done for, I'll go berserk—"

"All right, I'll—"

"You saw me, saw something in me, you knew I was worth something—"

"All right, all right. I'll see you—next Tuesday—this time—here."

Henry Marshalson was standing so still in the evening twilight, standing there beside the iron gate of the park, that someone coming along the little road might have mistaken him for a post, or else not seen him at all as his slim figure blended in the dusk with the dark background of the ivy-covered wall.

He had deliberately arrived several days early, not informing his mother of his coming. Leaving his luggage at a London hotel he had just packed a small bag and set off after lunch for the railway station. When he asked for a ticket to Laxlinden Hall he was met with incomprehension. The station had evidently ceased to exist. He took a ticket to the next station down the line and thence proceeded by bus to Laxlinden village. He wore his trilby hat, long preserved for the amusement of Russ and Bella, pulled down over his brow. He saw nobody he knew. He walked the two miles from the village just as it was beginning to get dark.

The hedges had been cut down and the road had been widened. Otherwise everything looked much the same. He could not easily have pictured the road, but at each turn he knew exactly what he would see next: the tithe-barn, as bulky as a cathedral, the row of elms on the low green skyline, the glimpse of the canal and a fishing heron, the *Horse and Groom* set back, with two labourers' cottages beside it (the cottages had been turned into a smart little house), the ford, no, the ford was gone and a horrible concrete bridge had taken its place, the pretty view of the Forbeses' house, Pennwood, across the Oak Meadow, the meadow itself, now sown with clover, and the huge oak tree mistily budding, which gave it its name, then at last the ironstone wall of the park with the dark conifers behind it. A host of elder saplings had grown up along the ravaged roadside and beneath them thick clumps of primroses were pallidly in flower. There was also, here and there, the faint purple stain of violets. Henry marched along and as he marched he watched himself. He felt calm, or rather cold, utterly cold. The evening was very still and windless, carrying a damp fragrance. It had rained earlier, and the road surface on which he was walking was wet and a little sticky. A few cars passed him, some with their lights on. The dim road unwound before him as if in a waking dream he were compelling it to do so. He was thinking these dusky yet glowing meadow slopes and these lonely quiet trees.

It was when he actually got to the wall of the park and to the iron gate that the thing which he had been anticipating launched itself upon him. Standing beside the gate he carefully put his suitcase on the ground and stood quite still taking very long breaths. Then suddenly he fell against the gate, clutching at the wet bars with his hands. His hat fell off. He drooped against the gate, hanging there as if he were pinned to it, his legs swaying and giving way, and the metal made cold wet lines upon his pendant body. His eyes were closed. His cheek was crushed against one of the bars, the rain water was upon his lips. He held onto the gate in a fierce spasm of emotion, as if that old gate were the first thing upon that dream journey which had remembered his name and uttered it. After a minute, as he seemed to be slipping to his knees, he steadied himself, opened his eyes, retrieved and donned his hat, and brushed down his suit and his unbuttoned mackintosh. He picked up his suitcase and pushed the gate. It clanked back a little way, then checked. He looked more closely and saw that it was chained and padlocked. He pulled vainly at the padlock, then stepped back.

He could see now that the drive beyond the gate was slightly overgrown with weeds, and a line of young nettles and docks were growing just beyond the bars. They must have changed the entrance. Now they probably used the short drive from the other road, not troubling to keep up the long drive, letting it fall into disuse. Henry hesitated, began to walk off, then came back. This was his way. Like a ghost, he felt he must walk his own path. He swung his light suitcase and sent it flying over the top to land among the nettles. He debated whether it would be easier to climb the gate or the wall and decided on the gate. The first bit was easy, just a matter of hauling himself up onto the transverse bar which ran across level with his chest. The next bit seemed impossible until he found some crumbling footholds in the wall at the side, and, holding onto some ivy, managed to swing one leg over the spikes at the top, then lower his dabbing foot gingerly until he could reach the bar. His hat had fallen off again, fortunately inside onto the drive. His body recorded for him that he was no longer twenty.

Henry resumed his damp and slightly muddy hat, picked up his suitcase and began to walk as quietly as he could along the drive, his trouser legs gently swished by the weeds which were growing in the gravel. The motionless evening air was softly exuding a faint almost tangible darkness which seemed to reveal, to body forth, rather than to conceal the masses of shrubs and trees on either side. The grass had been roughly mown, not shorn, and gleamed wet and faintly grey. Some distance away a blackbird was singing a long complicated passionate song. There was a very quiet persuasive sound of dripping. Henry breathed in the cool rainy earthy smell. He had not smelt this particular smell for nine years. It was the smell of England. He had forgotten it all. He had forgotten the unnerving uncanny atmosphere of the English spring. How it smelt, how it dripped.

The drive curved and the trees receded. A blackness upon the left, like a huge wall, was a yew hedge where there had once been statues, only they seemed to have gone. A patch of radiant sky opened ahead, dark through a saturation of powdery blueness as if the night were suspended, not yet precipitated, in tiny invisible particles. One large light yellow star was blazing, and round about it, as Henry looked, searching, were other stars, tiny pinpoints hardly able to pierce through the radiance of the twilight blue. Blinking, he looked away across the widening expanse of grass. There were scattered patches of glowing paleness here and there at which he looked for a moment puzzled, then knew of course the daffodils, all of them white, since his father would only tolerate white daffodils. The blackbird had fallen silent. The stars were brighter. The drive curved again and he was within sight of the house. Henry stopped.

The Hall was L-shaped, the foot of the L being a remnant of a brick-built Queen Anne house onto which about seventeen forty a longer slightly lower stone house had been added at right angles. This long façade now faced towards Henry, several lighted windows making pale milky rectangles in its uncertain form. Against the dark blue sky the darker outline of the shallow roof seemed to creep a little. Beyond the house, invisible, the land sloped to the lake. There was more light. A bright half-moon was now making its presence felt from behind the grove of conifers, shining over Henry's shoulder, silverpointing the slates and making pendant shadows beneath the far-projecting eves. The mown grass ahead, shaven here to a level carpet, was grey, heavy with moisture.

Something moved, just ahead of him, and Henry's gaze sharpened. A small darkness moved among bushes, detached itself, then began to travel noiselessly across the lawn. It stopped again, and Henry made out the outline of a fox. The darkness which was the fox seemed to be looking at the darkness which was Henry. Then, without haste, it moved away and in a few moments disappeared into the longer grass which fringed the birch woodland beyond. Henry looked back at the house. Then he sat down abruptly on the grass. Some huge violent emotional *thought* had come to him: the thought, he realized, that this was the first time in his life, since his early childhood, that he had ever seen the Hall without apprehending "Sandy's." He could not recall much from the time before his father's death. What he remembered, with his first vivid memories of himself playing upon the terrace, was Sandy saying, "This is my house, I could turn you out if I wanted to." "You couldn't." "I could." *"You couldn't!"*

Henry got up after a while, feeling damp. He had somehow or other failed to sit on his raincoat. He vainly tried to brush the wetness off his trousers. Then he picked up his bag and began to walk with careful foxlike silence across the lawn, leaving a wavering track of watery footprints behind him in the moonlight. He had now parted company with the drive which turned away to the left, passing round the house to the front door on the other side, and branching to reach the stable block and join the other driveway to the Dimmerstone road. Henry had intended to arrive unexpectedly, but he had not really intended to arrive at night. Coming like this, he felt himself both menacing and menaced. But most of all now he felt, foxlike Henry, as he approached the house, a piercing tender agonizing emotion which was like a desire to worship, to kneel down and kiss the earth. But what would he have been worshipping? He also, as he set his foot upon the first of the three steps that led up to the near side of the terrace, felt sick, a positive urge to vomit which he had to pause and quell. The second step was cracked, a corner missing, where a patch of thyme grew. His foot felt the crack and the softness of the thyme. He stopped again on the terrace, summoning up reserves of coldness. He could weep now, but must not. He would be cold, hard, if possible even sardonic, utterly masked. The alternative was a blubbering mess. Henry called up, and felt it come, blessing him from beyond the coldness, sheer old hatred. That was what was needful, that would stiffen him all right, thank God.

On the ground floor the lights were on in the library, where the tall Victorianized sash windows, which also served as doors, reached down to the ground. The curtains were pulled, but the light glowed goldenly through, revealing in rectangles the damp uneven ochre-coloured stones of the terrace, covered with hairy mounds of yellowish-green moss. Henry set his bag down and glided forward to the nearest window where a slit in the curtains revealed to him the scene within.

He saw first, directly opposite to him, the tapestry, the outstretched hand of the goddess buried in the hero's copious hair. Only two lamps were burning, but the interior dazzled him and he could not read how the room lay. Then his body recalled, his head moved, and he saw the big round central table with its drooping red cloth covered with newspapers and the tall Chinese screen that hid the door. For a moment it seemed as if the room was empty, then he saw his mother. Gerda was standing, almost out of his line of vision, beside the fireplace, looking down at the fire, one knee leaned against the club fender. She was wearing a long robe of blue wool, streaked in its folds with long dark shadows, and with a hood or collar which rose up half concealing her hair. The skirt fell away from the leaning knee to show a tract of brown stocking and a velvet slipper. Her hair isn't grey, was his first thought, or else she dyes it. But her face was older, older; and in that shock of seeing her he realized for the first time how much he had somehow hoped that she would still look young and beautiful. She seemed thicker, her face fatter, coarser, though not lined. Her mouth looked larger, more masculine. She looked a little like Sandy. Henry closed his eyes for a moment; then opening them saw that his mother was not alone in the room. A pair of trousered legs with boots on extended in a rigid diagonal to the floor out of the depths of the huge old sofa on the other side of the fire, the owner of the legs being otherwise invisible. A man is with her, thought Henry, with intense surprise. He drew in his breath and leaned against the wooden frame of the window. Something fell to the ground, probably a piece of plaster dislodged by his sleeve. Gerda turned round full-face, took a step, then cried out.

In equal panic Henry stepped back, fell over his suitcase, then called "Hello!" and began to tap on the window. He saw his mother's face, now shadowed, close to him, looking through the glass.

"Sorry, it's me," said Henry.

There was a sound of scrabbling as Gerda undid the catch. Then the long lower sash rose easily and soundlessly and Henry stepped through into the room.

He faced Gerda, who had receded to make space for him. Then he turned and began to pull the window down again. As he did so his mother, trying to kiss him, jolted against his shoulder. There was an awkward perfunctory embrace, and Henry finished closing the window and shot the catch which he found that his fingers could remember. He turned back and saw with annoyance that his mother's visitor was Lucius Lamb.

"Hello, Mother. Hello, Lucius. Sorry to arrive like this."

Lucius came forward, skirting the round table on the other side, and took Henry's hand. Lucius was wearing, on his now visible upper half, a royal blue corduroy jacket and a white open-necked shirt with a mauve silk scarf. He looked a good deal older, even since the meeting in New York, his flowing hair almost white, his face browner and more lined. He also seemed to have acquired, in the interim, false teeth. "Trundle, dear boy, welcome home!"

"Nice to be back," said Henry, pulling his hand away from Lucius and moving past his mother towards the fire. "Sorry to be so late, I didn't realize the trains didn't stop any more."

"But why didn't you ring up? We didn't expect you for a week."

Henry did not answer, he leaned over towards the fire, unconsciously taking up the stance his mother had held a few moments ago.

"You must eat something," said Gerda. "We dine early now, but—Haven't you any luggage?"

"Oh damn, it's out on the terrace."

"I'll go, I'll go," cried Lucius, already opening the window again. He came back with Henry's bag and brought it to him.

"Lock the window again, would you," said Gerda, who was staring at Henry with a rigid amazed face. Henry, looking at her for a moment, seemed now to see the resemblance to himself in her determination to repress emotion. "I hope you had a nice journey? Won't you take your coat off?"

Henry pulled off the coat, dropping it on the floor, whence a smiling Lucius, returning from having locked the window, hastened to pick it up and spread it on the sofa.

"Not there," said Gerda. She dropped the coat carefully over the back of a chair. "It's soaking. Was it raining in London?"

"Scarcely. Well, it was drizzling. Everything looks much the same here." There must be no pause in which something terrible could occur.

"You haven't seen much yet," said Gerda. "We've sold the Oak Meadow."

"The Oak Meadow. Oh yes."

"We sold it to John Forbes."

"Oh yes. Is Cato Forbes at home? What's happened to him?"

"He's in London," said Lucius. "You knew he'd become a priest?"

"A priest? You mean a *Roman Catholic* priest?"

"Yes, isn't it ghastly?" said Gerda. "It nearly killed his poor father."

"I can imagine that. Finished your book, Lucius?"

"Well, no—er—"

"Nice to see you. Are you staying long?"

"Lucius lives here now," said Gerda.

"No, well, not exactly, I'm just—er—your mother very kindly —I do hope you don't mind, Trundle."

"Of course he doesn't mind," said Gerda.

"Please don't call me 'Trundle,' " said Henry.

"I'm so sorry, I—"

"What time is it supposed to be here?" said Henry.

"It's about a quarter past eight. You really must eat something. Or have you had dinner?"

"Yes, thanks," said Henry, who had not.

"Rhoda can warm you up some—"

"That funny-looking girl, is she still here? I think I'll just go straight to bed, Mother, if you don't mind. I've come all the way from St. Louis, I just changed planes in Chicago, I feel pretty odd, all the time's gone crazy—"

"Your bed is made up in your old room. Wouldn't you like something hot? Ring the bell, would you, Lucius."

"No one will answer," said Lucius, "Rhoda will have gone to bed."

At that moment bird-headed Rhoda entered the room. Henry turned. Rhoda, wearing the dark disciplined dress which served her for uniform, advanced.

"Rhoda!" Henry took her hand and kissed her on the cheek, realizing the next moment that he had done something extraordinary. He heard his mother draw breath.

"Rhoda, could you turn on the electric fire in Mr. Henry's room and put a hot water bottle in his bed?"

Henry, who had thought first that one did not kiss servants, thought next that he had not kissed his mother. He suddenly wanted to laugh.

"You must eat something, Henry."

"So you keep saying, Mother. Perhaps I could have a sandwich in my room."

"Rhoda, could you make some sandwiches for Mr. Henry? What would you like, dear?"

"Anything, anything, anything."

"And hot coffee, soup—?"

"Whisky," said Henry.

"Have some here," said Lucius. "I wouldn't mind a spot myself."

"No thanks."

"Rhoda, would you take some whisky—"

"Scotch," said Henry.

"Up to Mr. Henry's room? Would you like soda, dear, or—"

"No. Anything. Good night. Sorry. I'm awfully tired. Good night."

Henry grabbed his suitcase and blundered out of the room. The hall was dark, and he suddenly felt lost, uncertain which way to go, until bird-headed Rhoda, who had left the library on his heels, sped ahead of him, turning on lights, and then vanishing. He heard her very light feet tap on the echoing floor, and then away through the swing door which led to the kitchen quarters. He glanced back as he ascended the stairs but the library door was shut.

The wide curving oak staircase led to a broad landing underneath a large oval window, and then divided into two flights to reach the first storey. Henry's remembering feet took him to the left. He walked, trying to silence resounding steps, along the bare brightly lit upper landing, passed the door which closed in the servants' stairs, and went through another door and up another short flight of stairs which led to the first floor of Queen Anne, which was on a higher level since the house was built upon a slope. As he went through the door, the temperature, already low by American standards, dropped several more degrees, the coldness being reinforced by a damp smell of mildew. A light was on upon the landing as he turned to the right towards his room. He opened the door, seeing the room already lighted up by a one-bar electric fire. He turned the light on.

The room was spruce and tidy, the curtains pulled and the bed turned down. A hump denoted the presence, already, of the desirable hot water bottle. Henry put his suitcase on the floor and quickly opened it as if it might be able to persuade him that he was in a hotel. He took out his sponge bag and clutched it. Queen Anne had always been his territory, as far as possible away from Sandy. He had listened with silent childish rage to plans for pulling it down. Fortunately these had always proved to be too expensive. Without looking, he perceived his surroundings. The massive chest of drawers with the mahogany mirror on top. The rather ugly "gentleman's wardrobe." The little writing-table with the brass rail. The red leather "club" armchair. The wallpaper, more faded, a brown lozenge pattern upon yellow. The narrow iron bed which he had insisted on keeping. The imitation Sheraton commode beside it. The dark brown well-worn woollen rug upon the dark red well-worn Turkey carpet. The rather pretty upright Victorian chair not for sitting on. The stout Windsor chair with the cushion upon it. Even the cushion was the same. Who had slept here since he left? Almost certainly no one. The room was stripped to its minimum as if in an attempt, without destroying it, to make it forget. But it remembered.

Henry went out into the corridor and into the adjoining bathroom. The bathroom smelt of damp linoleum and disuse. He turned on the hot tap but the rusty water continued to run cold. The bath was badly stained and there were dark lines upon the soap. As Bella used to say, England is great but it's so dirty. He noticed a spider, then another. The spider population of the house must run into millions. He had never seen a spider in America. He lifted the immense glowing mahogany seat and used the lavatory. The flowered porcelain bowl was the same, full of knowledge. He went back into the bedroom and took off his tie and his jacket and began to unbutton his shirt, having forgotten all about the sandwiches, when suddenly there was bird-headed Rhoda once more with a tray.

"Oh, thanks, thanks, do put it anywhere."

Rhoda put the tray on the chest of drawers, on top of a spotless white embroidered cloth which lived there, always perfect in spite of Henry's messes, changed at frequent intervals no doubt by, in the old days, the housemaid whose name Henry could not now remember.

"Thanks, Rhoda, that's marvellous, sorry to be a nuisance."

Rhoda had almost grotesquely large eyes, or perhaps it was just the shape of her head. Henry now vividly recalled his recent kiss and how her cheek had tasted of resin. He considered kissing her again, but it was already impossible. Noise-less-footed, she disappeared.

As soon as Henry saw the sandwiches he began to feel very hungry, and the odd feeling, not exactly desire but more like a special kind of fear, which Rhoda had aroused in him went away. He started to eat so voraciously that he almost choked. The bottle of Scotch had arrived with a large cut-glass tumbler and a soda syphon. Henry poured out and gulped some neat whisky, wondering if this was a mistake. No sooner was the whisky down his throat than he began to want to whimper. Legions of tears, of cries, of screams, were mustering. He wanted to lie face downward upon the floor and wail.

He adopted a device which he often used to calm himself. He looked intently into the oval of the mahogany mirror, widening his bright tearless eyes. Self-portrait. He was warily alert, thin, not tall, narrow nosed, quizzical mouthed, in his self-portrait. His copious longish very curly hair was very dark, yet shot with red. (Burke, Sandy, had been redheads.) His eyes were long and exceedingly dark brown and *glowed* under tri-angular eyebrows. His stubbly chin was neat and round and (perhaps too) small. There was a deep runnel above his lips. The small lips were finely grained with close vertical lines. Behind the head the brightly lit lozenges of the faded wallpaper hung like a shabby harlequin's dress.

Assuaged drunken Henry turned out the light, then by the glow of the electric fire pulled back the curtain and opened the window. He leaned out. There was an overwhelming smell of wet earth and plant life as the warmer air from outside rushed into the room where the electric fire had made scarcely any impression upon the archetypal coldness. Henry stretched out his hand into the windless night and thought he could feel a faint misty rain. He listened. There was a soft regular dread-fully familiar sound, the murmur of the little river descending to the lake. Clouds must have covered the moon. Leaning out, he could just see the lower façade of the main house, lightless, just outlined against the dark sky. His mother's bedroom was on the other side. He remembered with disgust the presence of Lucius. A light came on in a room just above him, on the maids' floor, and he moved back and partially closed his window and drew the curtains. He was reeling on his feet. He got his trousers off, then collapsed onto his bed and fell instantly into deep sleep, leaving the electric fire burning. When he awoke in the morning it had been turned off.

"Copper-bottomed?"
"Copper-bottomed, Mr. Henry."
"Good. That's all I wanted to know."
"Shall I show you—?"
"No, thank you, Mr. Merriman, the details can wait."

It was the next morning. After having dismissed Merriman, Henry continued to sit, quite still, at the red-velour-covered round table in the library gazing at the big tapestry of Athena and Achilles: Flemish work, probably of the late seventeenth century. Recording this, it occurred to him how much he had learnt about art in America, after having left England as a barbarian. *Seeing* the tapestry for the first time, he studied it now in the bright sunless northern light of the morning. The goddess, her long-tailed helmet thrust back over her curls, wearing a much-pleated robe with the aegis rather carelessly falling off one shoulder, was striding out of a large-foliaged shrubbery which took up most of the left side of the tapestry. A determined sandaled foot, heel down, emerged from the swinging skirt. The right hand held a tall vertical spear which divided the sky above the shrubbery, while the left, in an elaborate and implausible pattern of flowing locks and crooked fingers, grasped from behind the bright hair of the helmetless hero, who was also represented as moving away to the right, holding a sword and a foreshortened shield and wearing extremely brief glittering fish-scale armour beneath which a fancy undergarment fell in pleated flounces so as barely to cover his private parts. The long brazen-greaved muscular legs, glimpsed through the foliage, were lovingly rendered. Both figures were in profile, the goddess impassive and stern, the hero, his head not yet turning to his patroness, very large-eyed, very beautiful, very young, with parted lips, registering a mild surprise. The plain of windy Troy was suggested by a foot or two of golden sward edged by a pattern of elegant flowers; then the shrubbery began again with, beyond it, the pallid turrets of the city. The sky was a very very light radiant brownish blue. "Why hast thou come, O daughter of Zeus?"

I wish I had a goddess to grab me by the hair and tell me what to do, thought Henry. It was eleven o'clock. He had breakfasted in bed. (Gerda brought the tray this time.) He had asked to see Merriman, and his mother, who regarded the family solicitor as a servant, had summoned him to come at once. Henry's purpose in seeing Merriman was simply to discover whether the will was clear and sound. It was. Dutiful Sandy had left the estate in its entirety to his brother. So that was all right. Henry did not want to hear about the farms or about the investments, which Merriman thought were so good, or about how Merriman had advised against the sale of the Oak Meadow, or how he had with apt prudence persuaded Gerda to insure against death duties. Henry was still feeling extremely odd, a little giddy, very tired, with a sort of scraped obfuscated vulnerability to light and sound which made him think he might be better off going to bed again. A log fire was burning in the big grate, murmuring, then falling into itself softly like snow. Henry wondered if he could get as far as the sofa. He got up and then instead went to the door intending to return to his bedroom. An old familiar smell of smoky toast was still emanating from the dining-room. He saw in the hall some rather good eighteenth-century water-colours which must always have been there. He was about to peruse them when he heard voices from the open door of the drawing-room opposite.

The drawing-room, similar to the library, with three tall sash windows, faced south across the descending terraces towards the lake, and enjoyed the complete formal view of the river valley, the obelisk, the woods beyond, and on the extreme right the little green-domed Greek folly perched upon its hillock. There was a brightness now, an almost sunshine, against a darker sky, and the budding trees of the woodland were intensely green. The drawing-room was all white and yellow and rather sparsely furnished, with long mirrors and console tables in between the windows. There was a round marquetry table in the centre of the room, an enormous Chinese cabinet at one end, and a set of canary-coloured Louis Quinze chairs scattered about which were never used, the velvet having been expensively treated so as to look old. There were some nineteenth-century family silhouettes upon the walls and a French ormolu clock supported by sphinxes upon the chimney-piece, underneath a portrait of an ancestor with a dog which now looked to Henry's dazed eyes remarkably like a Stubbs. A fire was burning here too, and round it on a crumpled rug there was an encampment of easy chairs, but the room was cold and smelt unoccupied. Probably he had turned his mother and Lucius out of their accustomed haunt.

Lucius leapt up as he came in and with an ungainly awkwardness which also managed somehow to express self-satisfaction began at once to move smiling towards the door.

"Well, Trundle, slept, yes, I bet?" Lucius's enthusiastic tones betrayed an uncertainty about his own role. Was he a paternal figure, a jolly uncle, or just a slightly older contemporary? Lucius looked younger this morning, moderately bright-eyed and boyish. He tossed his white hair then drew it back from his brow with a slow long-fingered hand, twinkling and smiling.

Henry was not going to help him to solve the difficulty of tone. "O.K."

"He's got an American accent," said Gerda.

"No, no, surely not, we can't have that, can we—Though in fact—Ah well, I must get back to my book. *Tempus fugit*, eh."

"I can't remember what your book's about," said Henry. "Or rather, I think I never knew."

"Oh politics, political stuff, abstract you know, concepts. Gerda thinks it's like Penelope's web. I think it's hard work. Are you writing a book?"

"Yes," said Henry.

"Have you published any books?" said Gerda.

"No."

"What's your book on?" said Lucius.

"Max Beckmann."

"Who?"

"Max Beckmann. A painter."

"I'm afraid I've never heard of him," said Gerda.

"Oh, Max Beckmann," said Lucius. "Well I must get back to my toils. *Arrivederci.*"

Henry watched Lucius frisk out of the door, then sat down opposite his mother.

He said. "It's cold in here. In America we don't let the weather come inside the house."

"How are you feeling?"

"Terrible."

"It's the flight."

"Yes."

They looked at each other in silence which, although it expressed every awkwardness, almost the total impossibility of communication, was not exactly embarrassing. Gerda saw the dark curly-headed neat-faced youth with the small pretty mouth and round bob of a chin who seemed to her now not to have changed since he was twelve. Even the long dark suspicious glowing sulky eyes were the same, expressing resentment, self-pity. Henry saw his mother, older certainly, fatter, but still handsomely carrying that old air of a beauty's confidence, her rather large broad pale face seeming without make-up, her large fine brown eyes seeming without concealment. Her dark silky hair was loose today and made her look girlish. She was wearing a smart plain tweed dress with a pink Italian cameo brooch pinned onto the collar.

Henry felt satisfactorily hard and cold, like an athlete. No danger of blubbering today. "How long has Lucius been living here?" he said, realizing that he was speaking rather sternly and involuntarily frowning.

"Oh—two or three years—you don't mind, do you?"

Henry cleared the frown away with his fingers, and said nothing.

"You're not engaged to be married, are you?" said Gerda.

"Me, engaged? No, of course not. I'm not married either, if it comes to that."

"But you don't mind about Lucius? He's a sort of ship-wrecked person."

"Is he?" said Henry.

"One can't help feeling sorry—"

"Why should I mind?"

"Because it's your house."

Henry was silent again, as if pondering this, still giving his mother the unembarrassed slightly dazed stare.

"You are—going to stay here—aren't you?"

"Here? Do you mean here in the house or here in England?"

"Either. Both."

"I don't know," said Henry. He had noticed behind his mother on a little table a photograph of Sandy. No photograph of himself. Of course she had not had time to put it out yet. He felt a nervous compulsion to say something about Sandy. "This must have been rotten for you."

"This—?"

"This—bereavement."

Gerda was silent. She pressed her lips together and looked at Henry with a kind of desperate stoical intentness which made her look ugly. She said nothing.

"I'm sorry about it," said Henry insistently, saying what had to be said and willing his mother not to cry.

They went on staring at each other.

He got up, intending to go out of the room, but misunderstanding his movement she stretched out her hand. Henry took it briefly and squeezed it, his face wrinkled with annoyance.

"Mother, I'm going out for a walk."

"Yes, that's right," she said in a low tone.

Henry made almost a dash for the window, fumbled with the catches, pushed up the window, and stepped out onto the terrace.

A large low chubby dark grey cloud was being carried by the wind away over the house, leaving a bright blue sky behind it. The sun was shining and making the watery earth sparkle in all its recent raindrops. Henry moved along the side of the house away from the front door, trailing his hand along the big squared ironstone blocks of the wall, which were variegated with white curling patterns of crushed fossilized shells. He came to the steps and began to run down them, where the hillside descended in a series of stone terraces, until he reached the mown grass which curved more gently downward towards the lake. Up the hill to his left were the eighteenth-century stable block and the cast-iron arches and glittering glass of the huge

Edwardian greenhouse. Beyond, were the walled garden, the tennis courts, the orchard, and the Dimmerstone road. Panting Henry continued to run.

The lake, not very large, was fed by a little stream which rose in the orchard, entered the lake on what was known as "the obelisk side" of the garden, and left it again on "the folly side," where there was a small stone bridge with two arches. The obelisk, made of black granite, commemorated the Alexander Marshalson who had, early in the nineteenth century, created the lake and the folly, and, by timely speculation, much increased the family fortunes. The folly was a small empty stone building, with a green copper dome and pillared pediment, standing on a hillock and facing towards the beech grove or "big trees." Henry running, stopped on the bridge and looked towards the lake. In the vivid rainy sunlight the water was black, the wide girdle of reeds, which had so much terrified him when as a tiny child his father had attempted unsuccessfully to teach him to swim, luxuriant with new growth, green and russet. At the far end an ancient blue-nosed punt projected a little from an arch of foliage. The lake, so lately agitated by the rain, was very still now and glossy, reflecting the top of the obelisk in a sliver of enamelled blue laid, at the far side, on top of the blackness. There was a scattering of quiet coots. Henry held onto the faintly crumbling stone of the bridge, limestone here, not ironstone. Because of that muddy reedy horror he had never learnt to swim properly. Visiting California with the Fischers he had sulked upon the shore while they were being dolphins in that blue ocean.

He walked on slowly towards the edge of the wood. The trees were mainly small, birches and hazels, ash and wild cherry, and here and there a taller oak. The cherry was already in flower, a greeny whiteness spread among the still budding tree-tops. The oak was just in leaf, the ash still hard and black. Within the wood there was a haze of bluebells and, growing among them, starry masses of creamy white stitchwort. There was a smell of wet earth and pollen and the birds were singing crazily. A muddy path, fringed with nettles, wound away among the trees, bound for the further boundary of the park, for tiny Dimmerstone village and the church, and the churchyard where Henry's ancestors were buried. Where Burke was buried. Where presumably Sandy was buried. Henry had not inquired about the funeral.

He turned, receiving the shock of the appallingly pretty view of the lake, the gracious green hillside, and the house. Another chubby grey cloud had moved to cover the sun. Henry gritted his teeth. He would not think about Sandy and he could not think about his mother, though her presence was suddenly everywhere in the overcast scene. He walked back towards the bridge, blind with misery. He felt panic, terror, a kind of nebulous horror as if he were a man destined by dark forces to commit a murder for which he had no will and of which he had no understanding.

"Lucius, I do wish you wouldn't cut off little pieces of cheese and then not eat them."

"I'm sorry, my dear."

"They just get dry and go to waste."

"I'm sorry."

It was after lunch. Henry had gone off to lie down. Rhoda had cleared away and Gerda and Lucius had moved with their coffee cups into the drawing-room. It was somehow clear that the library was henceforth Henry's.

"That went quite well, didn't it," said Lucius after a moment.

"What went quite well?"

"Oh, lunch-time. Trundle talked quite a lot, didn't he."

Henry had been polite.

"You speak as if he were a guest."

"Well, he's been away so long, it is worth a comment, isn't it, if we're all so sort of relaxed together after all?"

"Relaxed?"

"Well, you know—and he asked those questions about the property. I thought that was a good sign."

"What do you mean by a good sign?"

"A sign that he'll stay. You want him to stay, don't you?"

Gerda was contemptuously silent.

"I thought Trundle might sort of reject the place and go and live in London. I jolly well would if I was him."

"Am I stopping you from living in London?"

"No, no, I just said if I was him. But I'm not him."

"Please don't chatter idiotically, I've got a headache."

"I mean, after all, young Trundle—"

"And please don't call him Trundle, he doesn't like it."

"Young Henry—"

"It's time for you to go and have your rest."

"Yes, yes, I'll be off. My dear, don't—don't—"

"Don't what?"

"Don't grieve so."

Gerda made a gesture of exasperation and Lucius got up. He touched her shoulder gently though he knew that she would wince, which she did. He moved towards the door.

"I say, Gerda, we will be able to watch television tonight, won't we? I mean, Trundle won't mind if we drift in?"

When he had gone Gerda, rigid in his presence, got up and went to the window. It was raining again. She looked at the rain rebounding from the terrace and fretting the little pools. A silver fold of rain dimmed the view of the lake and the wood. Her grief absorbed her, as if she were holding close against her breast a great basin into which her life was draining away. Had she hoped something from Henry's coming, some hitherto unconceived of kind of consolation? Scarcely, though she had somehow hoped, and still did so blankly almost because it was her duty. If she could even come to see Henry as a task, that might give a little sense to the world. But she had not anticipated how deep the instinct would go, or how violent it would be, to grieve, so that she could have wailed and cried, that Henry was alive while Sandy was dead.

*

Soon thinking about himself, Lucius went up the stairs to his big low-ceilinged room on the second floor which was above Sandy's bedroom which was above the drawing-room. No Bach night or morning, since Sandy hated music just as much as Gerda did. He sat down on his bed and took his shoes off. He clicked his teeth a little. They still felt enormous. He knew that the great grief of the house passed him by, simply missing him entirely. He felt useless and sentimental and sad. He wished that Gerda would break down so that he could console her. He had expected to console her, and this expectation had sustained him amid the shock of Sandy's death. In the end there'll be me, he thought, and she will understand everything. But she had not turned to him; and if, with a full heart, he came to her, she grimaced with irritation. Surely surely they should both, no doubt all three, be embracing each other and comforting each other and weeping. But human beings are endlessly ingenious about promoting their own misery. Even in catastrophe mysterious barriers can isolate them, barriers of fear and egoism and suspicion and sheer stupid moral incompetence. What was Henry thinking about him and Gerda? How he had resented Henry's obvious oversimplification of him when they had met in New York. Was Henry capable of mastering that much complexity, would Henry bother, would Henry ever manage to *see* Lucius at all? He must find out, simply find out, how to make friends with Henry. That was his task; as it was perhaps Gerda's to learn to love Henry as a substitute for Sandy. Ultimately, she would work on Henry and try to perfect him. But supposing Henry refused to be friends with Lucius? He suspected that Henry was *capable de tout*.

Lucius moved to his record player and put on the Goldberg Variations softly, then a little more loudly, conscious of the emptiness of the room below. He sat down at his table. It was littered with verses. What a blessing it was that he had had the sense to come back to poetry at last! A failed poet, that was what he was, it was quite the best thing to fail at. And why, indeed, should he necessarily fail? There was still time for greatness. "After long years of abstract thought, the revisionist renegade returned to poetry in his later years. The sentimentality of youth was vouchsafed to him again, irradiated now by the calm wisdom of age. Always young at heart, laying down the pen of the historian, he gave himself at last to the genius of poetry."

The thing about poetry, thought Lucius to himself, is that you can remain inside yourself all the time, the whole world is there inside, it's *safe*. All you have to do is just record your thoughts one by one, like bats emerging from a hole. Of course I'll finish my political book, I'll shorten it and cut out the history and make it into an autobiography, a sort of spiritual odyssey. Yes, I'll do that, and I'll publish a book of poems as well. He sat with glowing almost tearful eyes. He had lately discovered the haiku, and flattered himself that he had mastered the form. Instant poetry. He had written nearly a hundred about Gerda alone.

> Dully her feet call up
> Echoes that each time remember less.
> Clump, clump. The old girl.

He took up his pen.

> Oh cruel daffodils,
> Each spring commits some murder.
> Now the young master,

He began to wonder if Henry were to buy a house in London would he let Lucius come and stay in it?

He lay down on his bed. Five minutes later, relaxed and smiling, he was fast asleep.

Supposing one lacked the concept of suffering, thought Cato, sitting in his bedroom waiting for Beautiful Joe to arrive. Supposing one just suffered like an animal without thinking all the time: I'm suffering. Is it a sophisticated concept? He was not sure. Christianity hands it out even to peasants. Christ suffered, that is the whole point. But what a pointless point. It's such a selfish activity, suffering. Buddhism treats it with contempt.

Cato wondered if in order to stop himself from thinking and suffering he ought to go home to Laxlinden and dig the garden. But he could not confront his father, his father's sarcastic politeness, his father's anger with him for reasons which were already old. He would have to act a part at Laxlinden. "Going

79

on holiday" was unthinkable. He could go and stay with Brendan, who lived in meticulously spartan luxury in a small flat in central London. But Brendan would exhort him, bully him a little, comfort him, speak eloquently to him of the "dark night," subtly attempt to alter the whole pattern of his terrible dismay. And Cato would want to accept, would half accept, would perhaps yield, when he was with him, to Brendan's so magnetic persuasion. No. If he was to lose it all he wanted to lose it in his own particular individual way, just as he had found it in his own particular individual way. He was a convert and he had a convert's sense of inferiority, but also a convert's pride. He must sit alone at his own doorway until it should be finally closed against him.

The need to pray remained obsessive, profitless, like an illness, like an organ which goes on producing what the body can no longer assimilate or use. *Sweet Christ, help me.* It was so simple. It was the simplicity of prayer, its naturalness, not its awful difficulty which indeed struck him at these times. Of course prayer was the best way out of thought, but he could not move that way; and the simplicity which should most have helped him came to seem to him like an obscene childishness, a gabbling of spells. He felt so tired. The God of darkness and emptiness and dereliction peopled his mechanically praying mind with brittle images. *Recordare quod sum causa* ... He could not, any more, get through, the faith that had once taken him on into the fecund darkness was no longer there. The absence of God was not now the presence of God. And his head was full of pictures of the boy, and he could not use the method of prayer to render them harmless. Sometimes the sense of spiritual deprivation was so positive that he thought: perhaps Christ is actually leaving the planet and this is what I am experiencing.

Floods of tenderness were in him for that child. Suppose I were to stop playing a part, thought Cato, if that's what I'm doing? Suppose I were simply to put my arms around him? What does it matter whether God exists or not when there is a lost child to love? It happens, quite by accident and without any merit, that I am the bond, the connection, perhaps the saviour, for this boy at this time. Perhaps it was just for this that I was born, for this that I was converted? Perhaps even Christ is just part of a mechanism which brings me to Joe, with the kind of pure irresistible mechanicalness which makes the swallows migrate when the summer ends? Why bother about Christ when there is Joe? Why bother even about sin?

But some deep craving in him for order forbade this. It was not a matter of "disapproving" of homosexual love. Cato did not disapprove. The case before him was far too complex, far too concrete, for any such categories. He just knew that his ability to help Joe depended on a concealment, on the absolute inhibition of wild barrier-destroying tenderness. There were, here, and for him, abysses of corruption, there was depravity, the transformation of love and courage into instant travesties. Even if he could keep a pure and clear intent in such a tempest he knew that Joe could not, and it would be a final wickedness thus to try him. It would be a betrayal of a peculiar and specialized trust which existed simply because Cato had once believed in God. And even if God could not now make Cato into a priest, Joe made him into one. So there was sin after all, or something like it. The question of Joe's "loving" him scarcely arose. Joe would love power. What might yet save him was, in all ways, its erasure. Cato did not seriously contemplate embracing the boy. That was far off. The revelation of love was the revelation that must not be made. But could not the work of love go on?

I must get away, thought Cato, I must stop living here like a criminal, simply looking forward to seeing him. In this torment, how can I know what I ought to do about the priesthood? I've got to get away, but I cannot just abandon Joe, I cannot leave him to bottomless cynicism and perdition, he hasn't got anybody but me. I must create some sort of framework to hold him when I'm gone. If only I could make him learn something. But can he learn? He's lived in a dream world of his own all his school days. Who can teach him now and where is the motive that could make him try? If only I could *bribe* him to learn. He is perfectly able, he is clever, if he could only start. But that's impossible, there is no money, I have no money, and I can't ask *them* for any now.

But even as he reflected about how he could leave Joe, and

how he might somehow persuade him to go back to his studies, Cato was thinking: I shall see him, he will soon be here, I cannot leave him. I cannot leave him *ever*. It's as bad as that.

There was a soft sudden urgent knocking down below and Cato bounded to his feet. He sprang down the stairs and through the kitchen. It was early, still daylight, not yet time; but he was certain that it was Joe as he dragged the door open.

The cold evening light revealed a thin young man with a small prettyish face and a lot of curly dark hair. He was wearing a brown mackintosh with the collar turned up.

"Hello, padre!"

Cato stared at him, finding him familiar.

"Cato, don't you know me?"

"Henry!"

Cato felt pleasure, then dismay. He must somehow get rid of Henry before Beautiful Joe arrived.

"Come in! However did you find me!"

"I rang up your famous HQ and some Frenchman told me of your whereabouts. He said your phone was cut off."

"That would be de Valois. Come upstairs. I'm afraid this place is in chaos, it's just being dismantled."

"Oh, why?"

"They're going to pull the house down."

"They seem to have pulled half the neighbourhood down. I came across a place like the end of the world. I saw a hawk there."

"A hawk?"

"Yes, a kestrel."

"Symbol of the Holy Ghost."

"Your familiar."

"One does occasionally see hawks in London. Do sit down, I'm expecting a visitor, but—"

"I can't stay long anyway, I'm catching a train back. I came up to buy a car but I can't have it till Thursday."

"What did you buy?"

"A Volvo."

"They're beautiful cars."

"You got one?"

"A car? No, of course not."

"I see. No possessions. Lucky you."

Cato sat on the bed, Henry on a chair, and they looked at each other. They had been school friends, then, more vaguely, student friends, though they had gone to different universities and Cato was a little younger than Henry. They had corresponded for a short while after Henry's departure, then stopped. Detached from each other, two very private little boys, circumstances had made them allies, against fathers, against Sandy. Mutually harmless, neither had led the other. Childhood had made a strong bond. There was no great locking of temperaments or meeting of minds. They would not especially have sought each other, but were glad to meet, interested, enlivened, curious.

"I was so very sorry to hear about Sandy," said Cato. "I wrote to your mother. What an awful thing."

"Yes, *awful*," said Henry. He looked about the room. "So you're leaving here. Fancy your being a priest. What does your father think?"

"He hates it."

"Where are you going?"

"I don't know."

"What was this place? Your Frenchman called it the 'Mission.' Are you converting people?"

"Hardly! Just welfare work."

"Will you try and convert me?"

"A cynic like you?"

"So you help people. That's good. You know, I envy you in a way."

"What are you going to do? Are you going to be a country squire?"

"Don't sneer."

"I'm not. Why shouldn't you run the place, it needs running. What have you been doing all these years? I don't even know where you went after Stanford."

"I went to a nowhere in the middle west. I've been teaching mindless beautiful American kiddies about art history."

"Not married are you, Henry?"

"No. I've been living *à trois* with a married couple. Do I shock you? I suppose priests can't be shocked. You know I can't get over seeing you in that black skirt. I thought your lot wore smart suits."

"Most of them do. I'm eccentric. Written any books?"

"Books? What are they? Well, I'm writing one. On a painter called Max Beckmann. All right, you've never heard of him. It's called *Screaming or Yawning*, there's an early drawing—never mind. So you're a priest."

"You never used to like painting."

"I've changed, America has unmade me. Do you think I've got an accent?"

"An American accent? Well, faintly—"

"My mother said—Did she reply to your letter?"

"No, but Lucius did."

"Lucius. Christ. Never mind. I hate art actually, I hate all the old grand stuff, so confident, so pleased with itself, Beckmann's the end of it all, when the yawns turn into screams. I like being at the end, the scene of destruction like round the corner here. I'm the hawk watching it all. Cato, I'm so glad I found you, I haven't been able to talk to anybody. I can't tell you how horrible it is at home, it's *horrible*."

"Your mother's—grief—yes—"

"And it's all mixed up with—oh that bloody scrounger Lucius Lamb—and the whole place—it's too big—I've been feeling sick ever since I got back, *sick*."

"How long have you been back?"

"Three days, four days. She keeps watching me to see what I'll do. I think she wants me to go back to America."

"That's impossible."

"I'm obscene, I'm so alive, and I'm so un-Sandy."

"She loves you, she must need you terribly."

"Well, that's worse."

"Henry—forgive my asking—but how do you really feel—about Sandy?"

Henry was silent for a moment. Then he said, "I feel delighted, absolutely *delighted*."

"Henry, you can't—"

"No priest's stuff please."

"For your own sake and—"

"How do I know what I feel? I could say that I feel free for the first time in my life, but what the hell would that mean? Of course I'm pleased. But it's not even important. I feel I'm going to explode, there'll be some great conflagration, some great act of destruction. I've killed Sandy. Who shall I do next?"

"You need time," said Cato. "You're still suffering from shock. There must be so many practical things. And you must comfort your mother, and damn your feelings."

"O.K. damn them. But she's not easy to comfort. We can't even talk."

"But you will stay here? You could go on teaching—"

"I'd never get a teaching job here, not a hope in hell, I'm no good. I suppose I could sit in the library at Laxlinden and think. Except that I can't think."

"There's your book."

"Yes. Except that—really, it's not a book, it's a painter, it's not even a painter, it's a man, and he's dead years ago. I'm nothing."

"That's the beginning of wisdom."

"Your wisdom, not mine. I'm like the chap in Dostoyevski who said 'if there's no God, how can I be a captain?' And I'm not even a captain. But, say, do you really believe in the Resurrection and worship the Virgin Mary? It's like a visit to the past."

There was a soft sound on the stairs and the door was partially opened. It was Beautiful Joe.

Cato blushed, jumped up. "Come in, this—Come in—This is Joe Beckett, one of my—Joseph Beckett, Mr. Marshalson."

"Hello, sir," said Joe, with an air of youthful simplicity and deference.

"Hello," said Henry, smiling, appreciating.

Cato had never heard Joe call anyone "sir" before. It was presumably a joke. "Joe, could you wait downstairs? Mr. Marshalson is just going and—"

"Certainly, Father." Joe retired quietly, closing the door after him and padding away down the stairs.

"It's nice to be back where they're polite," said Henry. "The kids back home are so bloody familiar."

"He's not polite. He's going to the devil."

"That nice boy? How?"

"Crime. It's an occupation, it's a world. He's in it already."

"But he's too young—"

"Henry, you know nothing—"

"I'm fascinated. In America the good guys and the bad guys don't meet socially, at least, not at my level. But you're trying to help him, to save him from—?"

"Yes, but I can't. Goodwill is no use here, one would need money. I can't help any of them really."

"Money?" said Henry. "I can supply that."

"No, no, I didn't mean—"

"Of course you didn't, but why not? Now that it's come up it's obvious. My dear Cato, I'm so impressed by this scene, no I'm not being sarcastic, I mean this place, this frightful little room with the broken window, your poverty, your, if I may say so, perfectly filthy old cassock, what you're trying to do for these people. I want to help you. You're leaving this set-up, perhaps you'll have another one like it. Couldn't I come and work with you? Why not? Would God mind?"

Cato's eyes widened for a moment. Then he laughed.

"God wouldn't mind. But you'd hate it. It's nasty. The people are often nasty. Or else they're boring. Do you really want to go visiting old-age pensioners?"

"I've never tried. I've taught pretty boring pupils in my time. I think you do these people an injustice—"

"Yes, of course. But the work is tough and—"

"Isn't that spiritual pride? Couldn't I do what you do?"

"I don't do it."

"But you—Oh, I see, God does it."

"No, I didn't mean that. Maybe I just need a break."

"Sure—But aren't you going to have another Mission?"

"We—we can't get another house—we got this one—"

"I'll buy you a house. Cato, I'm *serious*."

"It isn't only that—I'm not sure what I—"

"Of course I don't believe in God, but it's so nice that you do! I can't tell you—oh I can't tell you—how awful—how sort of unlivable—everything is now—like a great black wall in front of me—Something's got to go smash—Oh all right, all right, you want me to go. I've got to go anyway. I'll tell you these horrors another time. Will you be home?"

"No, not—"

"Well, I'll come here again, or find out where you are. I must fly now to catch that train. Do think about what I said, and we'll make a plan."

Henry whisked out of the room and down the stairs. It had grown dark. Cato pulled the curtains and turned on the light. He had deliberately put in a weak bulb and the room was dim. Beautiful Joe had materialized noiselessly.

"Who was that chap?"

"A rich man," said Cato.

"Is he a queer?"

"No, of course not."

"He gave me quite a look. I'd like to be fancied by a rich queer. I can't stand queers though. Hitler was right to kill the queers and the gipsies. A gipsy woman just stopped me in the street selling heather. I spat in her face. Did she curse!"

"I wish you could learn kindness," said Cato.

"Gipsies look dirty. And she put her hand on my arm. I can't stand being touched."

"I wish I could teach you."

"You do." The boy sat down on the chair, Cato stood. "You do teach me. But I've had such a rotten life. People like me are a *problem*."

"You haven't had a rotten life," said Cato. "I wish you'd speak the truth, you're quite intelligent enough to be able to. You did well at school. You've got an educated mother and a decent home—"

"You mean it was clean. All you saw was the table-cloth. I was butchered. Life is a dumdum bullet. That's another pop song I'm going to write."

"Why don't you go on learning, get trained, get clever, that's the way to make money and be famous if that's what you want!"

"You're trying to con me, Father, they all do. We've had all this before. You don't understand. I'd end up in the machine shop like the rest of them."

"Well, there's nothing wrong with the machine shop, it's better than being in prison."

"Who said anything about prison? You take me so serious.

87

You're doing your thing, why can't I do my thing? I must be me even if I suffer for it. That's religion, isn't it?"

"Why not try religion, then?"

"I've had it all my life, Father, priests were beating me when I was six, I've been looking at Christ on the Cross since I could see—and it's a terrible thing to look at if you think of it, the nails and all that blood. If a gang done that they'd get ten years even if the bugger survived."

"Joe, don't pretend that you don't understand. You may be closer to Christ than I am. Anyway why speak of distances when we're all a million miles from God."

"There, you've said it, Father. A million miles. A million million. So what is a man to do? You've got to fight for yourself, like fighting is self-expression. You got to have scars like real fighters have. He had scars, didn't he? You should have heard the nuns going on, it made you sick."

"I wish at least you'd get a job, and then—"

"You got to be joking! Can you see me working for a master, honest, can you? I got to be free, it's my nature. Anyway what's the use? A lot of bloody money-grubbing bosses. The upper class are all right, it's the middle class that are hell, they're materialists. Look at Lawrence of Arabia. This society's rotten, it isn't going to last much longer. It's all right for you, you're different, you're special, you got nothing. But most people are shits. I'm telling you and I know. The lies they tell, they even tell lies to you, God if I started to say all the lies I've heard people telling you—"

Cato looked down in the dim light at the brightly self-conscious face, the eyes flickering behind the glinting hexagonal glasses. Beautiful Joe never looked wholly serious. The long dry intelligent mouth quivered at the corners with awareness and suppressed amusement. Joe had combed his straight hair carefully, probably as he came up the stairs, and it swung, silky, neat and brilliant. Touchable.

"Oh, I know," said Cato, "I know." He moved away.

"Don't be angry with me, Father, don't be sort of cold, because I go on so. You do still pray for me, don't you."

"Of course."

"I tried to pray last night. Honest I did. I knelt down and I spoke to God like he was my best friend. I said, God, why did you make me if I was to be frustrated?"

"Listen," said Cato, "if I could organize an expensive education for you, would you take it?"

There was a silence, Beautiful Joe, staring, jutting his jaw and pulling down his lower lip with one finger. "What do you mean 'expensive'? You mean sort of like Eton College?"

"No. I mean a crammer, a tutor, people to teach you specially, and you'd be financially supported while you were learning."

"You mean given money?"

"Yes, like a grant. You could have a nice room, money, teachers, but not like school, you'd be quite free. Then maybe university—"

"You know, Father," said Joe, "you're a cunning one. You're quite a villain yourself in your own way. I don't want anything like that. I just want you to love me and care for me. That's all that's needed, Father. You will, won't you? Won't you? Won't you?"

The chief reason why Hannibal succeeded in performing miracles of military organization was that he was a monster of cruelty. Henry remembered having been told that at school, and having been impressed by it, some time after he had irrevocably identified himself with the Carthaginian general. He had an instinctive identification with heroes beginning with H. Homer. Hannibal. Hobbes. Hume. Hamlet. Hitler. What a crew. Only his own name seemed empty, a sort of un-name, another cause for resentment, unredeemed by kings. And of course the letter H itself was an un-letter, a mere breath, a nothing, an identityless changeling rendered by a G in Russian. Gamlet, Gitler, Genry. H, an open receptacle, a standing emptiness, equally good or bad either way up.

Henry was standing in the ballroom. It was late afternoon after tea. Henry had not attended tea but he had smelt that special smell of toast and groaned. The room, its fine parquet floor, laid down by Henry's grandfather, dusty and unpolished, was empty of furniture except for a group of chairs at one end. Those chairs, Henry saw, were all broken, perhaps discarded, perhaps awaiting renovation : old sagging armchairs with their seats upon the floor, upright chairs lacking a leg, tilting over at crazy angles. A subject for Max in drypoint. Maimed chairs. The space. The terrible space. Henry shivered. When he was a small child his angry father had thrust him into the ballroom one afternoon and locked the door. Tearful Henry had buzzed in the empty room like a hysterical fly, that sunlighted space more terrible than any dark cupboard.

He moved to the tall northern window and looked across the terrace and the lawn towards the conifers and the edge of the birch wood. The sun was weakly shining. The daffodils were over. It had not rained for two days. Bellamy, seated upon a yellow motor-mower, was carefully and slowly proceeding along the edge of the longer grass. Only now he saw that it was not Bellamy, it was his mother, dressed in an old tweed jacket and baggy trousers. She seemed to turn her head towards him, then looked away. Yesterday, outside, he had seen his mother watching him from the drawing-room windows as he was returning from the greenhouse. He had visited the orchard, the tennis courts, the walled garden. He needed to visit everything, to tell everything the news, to reassure himself that he had tasted every memory, sprung every booby trap that the past had left for him. He had been to Dimmerstone and stood with glazed eyes beside the low wall of the churchyard. He had thought of his father there more than Sandy. Or perhaps already these two sad images were joining hands. Sandy was more suddenly present in the warm greenhouse where the smell of some aromatic herb made Henry close his eyes in sudden pain. He came running back and saw the watching figure of his mother. As he drew near she faded and vanished like a ghost. Now he, a ghost, was watching her.

Henry took a cup of coffee for breakfast and avoided teatime, but otherwise he accepted the routine of the house, the tinkling bell rung by Rhoda, the polite conversation, the amazingly meagre and parsimonious but still formal meals. Whatever would his father have thought? In the evening they watched television together in the library. Henry always went to bed early. There seemed no reason why this pattern should not go on forever. Henry sat in his bedroom and gasped at it all. Upstairs in Queen Anne everything was sober, chaste, rather cold; white towels, white lavatory paper, Pears soap. He had now explored his bedroom, opened every drawer. He had fled to America almost with what he stood up in. All his old clothes were here, carefully hung in the wardrobe, carefully folded in the drawers, smelling of moth balls. A Henry museum. A Henry mausoleum. Even his old name tapes, long ribbons of his red embroidered name, waiting to be sewn onto his shirts and socks. Henry Blair Marshalson Henry Blair Marshalson Henry Blair Marshalson. It was all significant yet impersonal, archaeological. There were no papers, no letters. Had he destroyed them? No books. Had they thought he would never return? The room was old, waiting for a Henry who would certainly never return, who did not exist any more.

Two days after his visit to Cato Henry had gone up to town again to collect his Volvo and had raced back along the motorway. It was amazingly quick and easy. When he was young getting to London had been quite an enterprise. The yellow Volvo now sat in the big garage in the stable block next to his mother's Austin and Sandy's Jensen. Sandy's Ferrari had perished with him in the accident of which Gerda had given Henry the necessary minimum account. It had been a banal pointless road accident. Henry had asked no questions. Searching about he had discovered in a loose box an old ERA, obviously lovingly refurbished by a mechanical Sandy since the days of its Brooklands debut. He had already spoken to Merriman about selling Sandy's cars. Henry was not a car fetishist. He noticed that his mother's Austin had not been out since he arrived. Did his mother usually spend all her time at home? Was she waiting to see what he would do? Become a squire? Go away?

Henry was very glad that he had been to see Cato. He had not known until he satisfied it how strong was his need to talk to a man of his own age and an Englishman. Cato gave him a sense of identity and a non-painful link with the past. Was he at thirty-two destined to achieve nothing except some as yet veiled act of destruction? The meeting with Cato had given him the glimmerings of a plan. Henry might be nothing, but his money was something, and faith was something, even if it was not his own. The idea of Cato Forbes as a priest had seemed laughable. But the black-clad man in the derelict house had been for Henry touching and impressive. That stripped life had its beauty. Holiness, that was a sense datum. And even if it was no more than picturesque, it was a sign, and was he not in the market for a sign? Christianity had made little impression upon Henry, but he and Bella had had their go, ignoring Russell's scorn, at West Coast Buddhism. Efforts at meditation did not continue for long, but Henry had gained a new conception of religion, a conception it is true which remained purely abstract since he could do nothing with it, but which now constructed a gate through which Cato Forbes could more significantly re-enter his life.

That morning Henry had received letters from Russell and Bella. Bella's letter was long. *Honey, we miss you so.... Don't go English on us ... you said so often you hated the set-up, don't buy it now.... Come home soon, won't you.* Russell's letter was brief. *Hi, kid, hope you're O.K. Write. Russ.* Henry felt incapable of answering the letters, but as he crumpled them he felt that really he missed Russ more than he missed Bella. Had he left his real self, his moral being, his only hope of salvation behind him in little plain shadowless clapboard Sperriton, baked in the *lux perpetua* of the prairies and of the great American middle west and the great American goodness? And if he did would he not one day soon have to go back to stay? Had he ever doubted that he would go back? What insane hope of what had led him to England?

He had talked to his mother but it was maimed talking. She had asked him a lot about Sperriton and he had given her clipped answers, minimizing everything, making it sound dull. Of course it was dull, beautifully dull, but not as unintelligibly dreary as Henry's portrayal of it. "Did you like your work?" "Not much." "Did you walk in the country?" "There is no country. And no one walks." Naturally these questions were not what they seemed, Gerda scarcely listened to his answers or he to her questions. What she was saying was: I need you. I want to know you. I can be patient, you'll see. And he was saying: Why do you pretend to be interested now? You never wanted to know before about what I was doing or who I was, you never even came to Sperriton. It's too late now. To which she replied: It isn't too late, it isn't, it isn't. "Did you get on well with your students?" "Not very." "Did you have good friends?" "A married couple." And sometimes it seemed to Henry that the house too was wooing him in that fruitless incompetent ultimately rather self-satisfied way, saying to him: Here I am, after all, welcome home, I'm yours. To which Henry replied: When I wanted you you were not mine, when I needed you you rejected me. Why should I cherish you now? Henry noticed that his mother had quietly removed the silver-framed picture of Sandy from the drawing-room.

Lucius continued polite, even obsequious, and Henry treated him as if he were a poor resident tutor. What indeed his role was was unclear to Henry, and he would have ignored him had Lucius, by his own fear of Henry, not constantly put himself in the young master's way in a manner which clearly annoyed Gerda. Lucius felt it incumbent on himself to pose intellectual questions about literature, about American politics, so as to set up a sort of academic masculine tête-à-tête for Henry's benefit. He would have lingered with Henry over the claret (when there was any) if Henry and Gerda had permitted it. Henry was casual. He would deal with Lucius later on. For the present, Lucius must simply look to himself in so far as he dared to parade about between the fell insenséd points of mighty opposites. Meanwhile Henry mystified him. Lucius wanted to find out what Henry was up to. But Henry was up to nothing. Henry was waiting. He was waiting, with a kind of awful anguished confidence, for something to happen.

Seeing his mother employed upon her yellow mowing-machine so far from the house Henry decided that now was the moment to do something which Gerda had, with evident pain, requested him to do, and which he had put off doing; this was to sort out the things in Sandy's room. Plainly, Gerda had been unable to enter the room. Also perhaps she felt that it would be appropriate, even salutary, for Henry, the heir, to sort out Sandy's papers. Merriman, whom Henry had seen again, had also suggested that this should be done. Henry ran out of the ballroom and up the back stairs, catching a glimpse of bird-headed Rhoda sitting in the kitchen reading a magazine. He sped along the corridor past the gallery to the door of Sandy's room which was opposite to his mother's room at the west end of the house. He looked round guiltily, then quietly turned the handle and let himself in.

For no good reason, as he now realized, Henry had expected the room to be all cleaned and tidied, turned already into a Sandy museum with everything neatly piled up or put away in moth balls. But what confronted him was a living-room, a room that had not yet been informed that its owner was no more. It was as if the occupant for whom the room lived and breathed were surely still nearby, thinly and anxiously concealed beside a cupboard, behind a shutter. The room was exactly as it had been on the morning when Sandy rose, shaved, dressed, had breakfast, got out the car, and set off for London. There was a faint smell of pipe tobacco. The curtains were rather roughly pulled back so that the room was a little dark. The big roll-top desk was open and strewn with papers. There was a newspaper unfolded on the table, two pipes, a pair of spectacles. So Sandy had taken to wearing spectacles. Several ties and a towel lay upon the floor. There was a smear of soap on the mirror above the wash basin. The bed was undone, a hot water bottle lying upon the pillow. Mechanically Henry pulled the curtains well back, then picked up the hot water bottle. He took it to the basin and unscrewed it and poured out the water. Seeing the white basin and the flowing water he had a sudden desire to be sick.

He turned towards the bookshelves and held onto them, breathing slowly and deeply, feeling sick and slightly faint. Carefully he began to read the titles of the books. *Naval Aeroplanes in the Second World War. Jane's All the World's Aircraft. Traction Engines Past and Present. The Vintage Alvis. The Railway Enthusiast's Handbook. Railway History in Pictures. The Tay Bridge Disaster.* He felt better. A Latin tag came into his head. *Delenda est Carthago.* That was something Sandy used to go around saying. It amused him for some reason. *Delenda est.* He now went over to the desk, with a little curiosity, but mainly with a desire to get it over with and then call in the tidiers, the cleaners, the refuse collectors. He pulled the big waste-paper basket near to him and began to shovel into it, after a cursory look, papers which were lying about on the desk. Receipts, advertisements, club notices, motor car stuff. A few singularly uninteresting personal letters and invitations. What, if anything, did Sandy do for sex? Henry quested quickly through the drawers and pigeon-holes. Cheque books, bank statements, insurance, income tax, the stuff Merriman wanted. Keys, bank notes. A blue velvet cuff-links box, empty. Odd chess-men. (Sandy excelled at chess. Henry never learnt.) Old photos of the Hall with family and fourteen servants. Henry's methodical hands flew about, discarding, sorting. He had nearly finished when he noticed that the long low open slot below the pigeon-holes, which he had thought to be empty, contained something, a sort of folded paper which had been pushed away to the back. Thrusting his arm in to the wrist Henry's fingers plucked at the paper, then drew it out.

It was a legal document, typed upon thick glossy slightly faded paper and tied up with a red ribbon. Henry untied the ribbon and opened the document. It was a lease. He read the first part of it, taking in that it was a lease, still with many years to run, of a flat in London. In Knightsbridge. Henry stared at the paper. The owner of the lease was Sandy. So Sandy had a flat in London. This was not very surprising. Only no one had mentioned this flat. Neither Merriman nor his mother had said anything about it. So presumably they did not know it existed. So presumably Sandy had a secret flat in London. The flat had not figured in Merriman's lists of assets. Who owned the flat now? Sandy had left everything of which he died possessed to his brother Henry Blair Marshalson. So Henry now owned the flat. And of course Henry would keep it secret too. He folded up the lease and put it in his pocket. He then also pocketed the bunch of keys. He left the room on tiptoe.

*

The garden was darkening a little towards twilight. His mother would be coming in, so Henry decided to go out. He ran noiselessly down stairs and out through the front door, noticing how the old brown paint had flaked off and how the glass panels, which used to rattle so in the wind, still did not fit properly. He leapt the steps. He ran down the long steps of the descending terraces to where at the bottom Gerda's well-kept herbaceous border ran along the ochre-coloured wall. It was a windless evening, full of the rapt awfulness of spring. The grass, intensely green, was thick and spongy underfoot, already wet with dew. The sky had clouded over but was still bright, a radiant blue-grey, turning a little yellow near the horizon. There was a slight mist over the lake and the trees on the hillside were bathed in a misty radiance as if grey luminous gauze were hanging down from their still almost bare branches. The birds were crowding the evening with thin crazy continuous noise.

Henry began to walk towards the river, intending to climb up to the folly. Terrible sadness, dread, an agonizing desire for happiness swelled in his heart. He had grown up in one of the most beautiful places in the world and he had wasted his childhood in stupid resentment and jealousy. Now when, so strangely, he had been permitted to return, it was to find himself still an alien. Could he learn this music or would it forever float by him? Was there some ritual, some ceremony of possession, for which he was never to become worthy? Had his grandfather, his father, *possessed* this place? Had Sandy possessed it? He could not doubt it. Only excluded Henry saw it untouchably through a glass, utterly lacking the key to the enchantment. He seemed to stand between crime and crime, not knowing where his fulfilment lay or whether he were not always condemned to be a small whining man. He felt empty and purposeless and young. If only he were a painter, or could even feel that there was any point in going on and on and on trying to become one.

He crossed the bridge and looked up at the folly, which was dark against the yellow sky. The birds had become quieter. He decided not to climb the hill, but walked back along the stream towards the lake to where there had been a little path, overgrown now. Perhaps it had been worn by his feet and Sandy's. He skirted round a little grove of lacquered green bamboo, touching the wet rigid stems gently with his finger-tips. A moor-hen, flirting its white tail, scurried across in front of him and took noiselessly to the still water among the reeds and swam jerkily away. The reeds were motionless, the wreckage of last year's growth still arching among the young spears. The mist had cleared a little. Henry walked with a deliberate quietness, breathing the moist air, and feeling now the wetness underfoot where the spring rains had made the lake overflow a little onto the grass. He looked out over the expanse of the water. He stopped still.

Near the middle of the lake was a blue punt, and in the blue punt was a girl with long hair. The girl was motionless, stand-ing on the slats at one end of the punt, her feet wide apart, her body braced, and both hands holding the punt pole. The punt was swinging very slowly round the pole. A few ripples came almost soundlessly to the shore. Then the girl said softly and distinctly, "Oh *damn*."

"Good evening," said Henry.

The girl let go of the pole and sat down on the end of the punt, which dipped abruptly. The punt began to move very slowly away from the pole which remained upright in the water. Recovering herself the girl lay full length at the end of the punt and just managed to grasp the pole with one hand before it passed out of reach. Still lying down she pulled the punt back towards the pole, then levering herself upon the pole stood up again. She worked the pole to and fro and then began to pull it out of the water. From the way she handled it Henry could see that she was an adept.

"I said 'Good evening.' "

"I heard you," said the girl, who was now driving the pole in again. "But this punt's sinking."

"Sinking?"

"Yes, why do you think I'm stuck here, for fun? The water's coming in and I can't move it."

Henry watched while the girl positioned the pole, then put her weight upon it. The punt, evidently waterlogged, moved slightly.

"I see your problem," said Henry.

"Well, what are you going to do about it?"

Henry considered the matter. "I don't see there is anything really that I can do. Can you swim?"

"Yes, but I'm not going to!"

"Well, I can't swim," said Henry, "or at any rate I can hardly swim, so I'm afraid I shall have to be a spectator."

The girl pulled the pole out and dropped it in again. The punt, some thirty yards from the shore, scarcely moved.

"The water's over my ankles. It'll sink under me."

"I'm sorry," said Henry, "but perhaps you should not have been in it in the first place."

"Can't you do anything, can't you get a rope?"

Henry reflected. "I don't know of any rope near here. I suppose I could plait a rope out of reeds, but it would take a long time."

"Please don't make jokes. Use your mind."

"Anyway, not being a cowboy I doubt if I could throw a rope that far. Now if we had a dog—"

"Oh *damn*. I'm soaked."

"The punt won't actually sink, you know. It'll fill with water, but it won't sink."

"Maybe not, but what about me, do I stand here all night?"

"I suggest you abandon ship."

"Can't you do *anything*?"

"Well, I suppose I could go and get a rope and—"

"Oh, hell, *hell*—"

There was a splash and a little shriek. The girl had dived from the end of the punt. The punt tipped, lurched, and moved a little away from the erect pole, settling in the water. The lake foamed and boiled about the swimmer who now with a very vigorous and splashy crawl was making for the land.

"How do I get through these bloody reeds?"

The girl's face, wet and rather red, appeared close to, her hands scrabbling at the outer fringe of the reeds, the lake water round about her bubbling and black with mud. A strong rotten smell of deep disturbed mud was released into the air.

"I can't get through, they're grabbing my legs."

"Don't be silly," said Henry, "just float yourself through, don't thrash around like that."

"Help me, can't you, I'm dying of cold."

Henry took a step forward and felt the icy grip of the water take one foot at the ankle. He gasped, feeling his leg suddenly sinking into the mud. He stretched out one hand to steady himself, trying to draw his foot back again. At the same moment his outstretched hand was grasped violently and pulled. He plunged forward, his other foot now ankle-deep in mud. Something large and wet and muddy fell against his leg and he collapsed backwards, sitting down in the water on the grassy verge of the lake. "Oh *fuck*!" said Henry.

With vigorous movements, like a seal, the girl wriggled past him and got to hands and knees, and then stood up and shook herself like a dog. Henry got up, soaked to the waist.

"Confound you!"

"Sorry," said the girl. "It was just the last bit. Are you all right?"

"No. What the hell are you doing anyway on my land and in my punt?"

The sky had darkened during the few minutes of the punt drama, becoming a slaty blue. A granular obscurity of darkness was creeping out of the trees. Henry peered at his companion. Her dress, blackened with mud, was clinging to her and her hair was streaked about over the neck and shoulders. She was leaning over to wring the water out of the skirt. Even her face seemed to be blackened, or perhaps it was just the twilight.

"Well?"

"Don't you know me?"

"No," said Henry. He stared. "Oh—no—heavens—not Colette Forbes?"

"Yes. I say, I'm *freezing*."

"But aren't you a little girl of ten?"

"No, I'm not. Oh *dear*—" Her voice wavered to a wail.

"Now, don't start crying," said Henry. "You've caused enough bloody trouble without crying. You'd better go home and change. It's only about twenty-five minutes' walk."

Colette turned abruptly away, and almost at once disappeared into the twilight among the bamboos, walking at a fast pace. Henry walked after her more slowly, and after about a minute met her coming back.

"Hello. We meet again."

Colette said nothing, but going down on her hands and knees began to search frantically about on the outskirts of the bamboo thicket.

"What on earth are you doing now?" said Henry.

"I'm looking for my SUITCASE."

"Well, don't shout. Naturally you have a suitcase and it is hidden among the bamboos—"

Colette pulled the suitcase out and set off again at a smart pace in the direction of the bridge.

Henry followed her. He began to laugh. His first laugh in England this time around.

Gerda, standing at the windows of the drawing-room and pulling off her gardening gloves, saw Henry clear the semicircular front steps at a leap and career off across the terrace and down towards the lawn. A little later she saw him walking across the grass in the direction of the bridge. She turned back into the room.

Kneeling by the fireplace, bird-headed Rhoda struck a match to light the wood fire. The paper caught with a yellow glare, illuminating Rhoda's huge eyes.

Gerda, alone, sat down in an armchair looking at the flames racing through the dry wood. She wanted to put her head in her hands and wail, but she did not.

Lucius came in switching on the light.

"Sorry, my dear, I don't know—"

"I wish you wouldn't always do that."

"I'm sorry—"

"Listen," said Gerda. "I've been thinking."

Lucius's heart sank. He knew from experience that when Gerda had been thinking she usually had something rather unpleasant to announce.

The drawing-room had a slightly more cheerful air this evening, since Gerda and Rhoda had spent the earlier part of the afternoon carrying bits of furniture and ornaments down from the gallery; a sewing chair, an embroidered stool, a card table, a pair of Dresden vases, a long Kazak runner. The gallery, which was really just a long narrow room with no particular function, was used as a furniture store. It was sometimes called "the music room," since Burke's grandfather used to have chamber music there. And Gerda and Rhoda, working silently together as they often did, had also concocted, in a big rectangular glass fish tank, a huge arrangement of chestnut buds and hazel and white narcissus. The smell of the narcissus, lifted by the kindling warmth of the fire, circled the room.

Lucius had spent most of the afternoon asleep. For some time he had concealed his afternoon naps from Gerda, who, of course, never rested during the day; but she finally found out and now never failed to say, soon after lunch, "Time for your rest!" Lucius had formerly felt guilty about this practice, only allowed himself a furtive twenty minutes' nap. Now he felt older and more relaxed, although still vulnerable to Gerda's taunt, and looked forward to pulling the curtains and closing his eyes. Unless his back was hurting very much he could soon doze off pleasantly, and now disposed in this way of considerable periods of surplus time. At night he took, in moderation, sleeping pills. Ever since childhood he had appreciated unconsciousness.

During the morning he had been very busy with his writing. That is, he had spent nearly an hour looking at his politics book to see how it could be shortened into something publishable as a sort of spiritual autobiography. Or perhaps it might be easier to abandon this work and start again from scratch, crystallizing a lifetime's experience into a hundred forceful pages? Lucius began to feel rather tired. He put on the Partita in B minor and returned to writing haiku. He was experimenting with the form now. Were rhymes admissible?

> Cruel the daffodil
> All springtimes tend to kill
> Ah well, ah well, his will!
> The young master.

"What have you been thinking, my dear?"
"I think you should go on holiday."

Lucius reflected on this with puzzlement. "But I'm always on holiday. At least, I mean—"

"You need a change. You might have finished your book long ago if you hadn't been shut up in this ivory tower. You ought to be out in the world arguing with people, really living."

This prospect did not seem to please Lucius very much. "But my dear—"

"Now, don't start—"

"I thought you wanted me to argue with people!"

"I don't want you to argue with me. I want you to go away for a while. You could go to your sister."

Lucius's sister Audrey was married to an estate agent and lived in Esher. They had not quarrelled, but hardly ever met. "Audrey's pretty busy—and the children—"

"Surely they've grown up now?"

"Not all of them, there's Timmie and Robbie—"

"Well, I don't mind where you go."

Lucius was silent. Bird-headed Rhoda came in soft-footed and pulled the curtains. When she had gone Lucius said, "Gerda, dear, you've been marvellous to me. When this began we didn't think, well, I don't know what we thought or what I thought anyway—it's been a long time and I've been so happy here and it just sort of happened and we never ever really discussed it—and I've sometimes felt—I mean I've wondered if you felt—if you wanted the arrangement to—after all there's no reason—"

Gerda was frowning. As he spoke Lucius had a sudden picture of himself living in a bed-sitter in north London on his now almost worthless savings and the old-age pension, and spending the day in the local public library. It was a terribly possible possibility.

"Do you want the arrangement to end?" said Gerda.

"No, of course not—"

"I don't want it to end. I recognize that I have an absolute obligation to you, just as I have to Rhoda and to Bellamy."

This was not a very felicitous way of putting it, but Lucius felt relieved.

"I mean, not that I regard you—"

"Quite, my dear, quite. *Mutatis mutandis.*"

"I just want to be alone for a bit with Henry."

"Ah, I *see*, yes, of course. I quite understand, I'll go away, of course—"

Lucius was glad to receive this rational explanation, though the mention of the young master also made him feel: but supposing I go, perhaps Henry just won't allow me to come back?

Gerda, still in her gardening trousers, was staring into the fire. She had not been following Lucius's sensitive changes of mood. "I think if we're alone—he'll—it'll be better—"

If we are alone he will pity me, she thought. I will make him and he will have to. The alternative, for me, is misery, madness, and I cannot go on like this, I must know my fate. I seem hard to him. Oh if only he could begin to understand me. The last few days of seeing Henry running free, of experiencing his polite alien unattached coldness, had wrought a change in Gerda. The strange shock of resentment which she had felt at first was over. Then, if Henry had wished to take her in his arms and talk to her of her loss, if he had sworn to look after her and take Sandy's place, she might have withdrawn from him in horror. Now, when no such thing was in question, she saw clearly her destitution, the desperateness of her situation, a desperateness that made her entirely oblivious of Lucius's feelings, of his pathetic pride and of his fear of being sent off to Audrey. Gerda felt now that if Henry simply, as he might, gave her back her home and went away, if he simply left her here forever and went back to America, she would run mad. Henry was all that she had got and she could not and would not lose him.

There was a sudden loud noise outside in the hall, the front door was noisily thrust open and there was a sound of raised voices. Gerda and Lucius looked at each other, then jumped up. They emerged into the hall to see Henry with an extremely bedraggled-looking girl.

"Oh Mother, here is Colette Forbes. She is soaking wet and so am I, we've been in the lake!" Henry spoke with more animation than he had yet displayed to his mother since his arrival home.

Gerda, who had not seen Colette for some years, shared Henry's initial reaction. She recalled a little girl, but now the years seemed to have brought about a young woman. In spite of Henry's childhood friendship with Cato, the Marshalsons and the Forbeses had never otherwise seen much of each other, even when Burke was alive. Gerda had never quite got on with clever Ruth Forbes. Later, there had been the quarrel about the right of way; and Gerda had somehow gained the impression that John Forbes despised her, regarded her as uneducated, a jumped-up *grande dame*. It was conceivable that, without intending to, Lucius had strengthened this impression. Lucius had met Gerda through John Forbes, and though of course John had never said anything about it, Lucius felt that John did not understand or appreciate his remarkable friendship with Gerda. He suspected that John regarded them both with derision. And, sensitively, Lucius had withdrawn. So it was that Gerda, though she had certainly seen her since, best remembered Colette as a little girl, toddling along after Henry and her brother.

"But you're both soaked," cried Gerda. "You must change at once, you must be perishing with cold—whatever happened?"

"Mrs. Marshalson, I'm so terribly sorry, I do apologize, I'm dripping mud all over the carpet—"

"Henry, you're wet through, you must go and change."

"I'm only half wet. Colette suffered total immersion. Fortunately she's got a change of clothes here. I think I will go and change if you don't mind, my teeth are chattering. Mother will look after you." Henry put Colette's suitcase down on the floor and sped away up the stairs with a maniac laugh.

"Mrs. Marshalson, I'm so sorry, it was all my fault—"

Lucius, noticing how attractively Colette's clothes were clinging to her body, said, "Here, have some brandy, shouldn't she?"

"Come upstairs," said Gerda. "You must have a hot bath. Lucius, carry her suitcase."

The procession went upstairs, Gerda exclaiming and Colette apologizing, and into Gerda's bedroom, where Lucius was dismissed. Gerda turned on a hot bath and Colette disappeared with her case into the bathroom, while Gerda sat on the bed and talked to her through the door.

"I was so stupid, I went out in the punt, and then it sank, Henry will tell you—"

"What did Henry do?"

"Oh nothing really, I mean, what could he do—"

"How did he get so wet then?"

"He was pulling me out—Oh, I feel such a fool—and I'm covering your bathroom with mud and the towels are *black*—"

During this time Henry, splashing in his hot bath, could not help smiling. Emerged, he put on warm clothes, a woollen sweater. He vigorously towelled his wet hair, then stared at himself in the glass. He was a blue acrobat high up on a trapeze, squatting huge-eyed and wary and calm in the yellow air. A minute later he was down in the drawing-room.

"My poor Trundle, here have a drink, brandy, whisky, you must be half dead, I think I'll have one myself, what a business—"

Gerda and Colette arrived. Colette's long hair, hastily dried in front of Gerda's fan heater, stood out about her head and shoulders in a vast glittering fluff, which the girl was self-consciously trying to smooth down. She was now wearing a tweed skirt with shirt and woollen pullover.

"Come near the fire, here, have this, it will warm you up—" Lucius hastened forward with a tumbler of brandy.

"No, I won't, thank you. I must go home, I really must, I was just on the way there, you see I was hitch-hiking back from college and I got a lift on the other road as far as Dimmerstone, that's why I was coming across the park, I'm terribly sorry, then it was such a lovely evening and I saw the punt—"

"Of course, of course—"

"I'm so sorry, I've been an awful nuisance to everybody—"

"Not at all—"

"I really must go, good night, and thank you all so much—"

"Where do you think you're off to?" said Henry, who had been standing back looking at her.

"I'm going home. Good-bye and thank you. Of course I know the way and it's not really dark—" Colette had got her suitcase and was making for the door.

"Stop," said Henry. "Don't compound your felony by being totally idiotic. I'll take you back in the car. Just have the decency to wait for precisely one minute, will you, while I finish my drink."

*

The headlights of the yellow Volvo rotated slowly on the gravel outside the stables, flickered on the greenhouse, the caged enclosure of the tennis court, the white-banded orchard trees, the elms of the park. It was raining slightly. As they passed over the cattle grid and turned left onto the Dimmerstone-Laxlinden road, Colette said in a tired dead voice. "I'm not going to tell my father."

"About our lake exploits? O.K."

"I feel such a perfect idiot."

"I daresay you do," said Henry, keeping his eye on the golden ironstone wall of the park. The wall was in excellent condition. Henry was not yet quite used to driving on the left.

"Is your father expecting you?"

"No. That's another stupidity."

"What are you doing?"

"What do you mean?"

"I mean are you a student, a teacher, a housewife, a ballet-dancer—"

"I'm not married. Of course."

"Of course."

"I was a student but I've chucked it."

"But why?"

Colette was silent for a moment. "It's not my way."

"Oh you've got one have you, lucky you."

"Do you think I'm wrong?"

"I've no idea. Education is so easy nowadays, they cut out all the hard bits, it's just a form of entertainment. I should have thought it would have suited you all right while you were waiting for the lanky long-haired boy who is your natural mate."

"You could drop me here."

Henry stopped the car at the corner of the lane which led to Pennwood. "You promise you won't be molested and raped before you reach home?"

"I'll be all right. Thank you very much."

"What for? Good night."

Colette got out, slammed the door, vanished.

Henry drove on a bit, then pulled the big car onto the grass beside the wall, switched off the headlights and got out. He was back at the padlocked iron gate where he had stood in the twilight days ago, months ago. He spread out his arms again upon the wet iron bars, grasping them, shaking them a little. He forgot Colette. Meditating a crime, he looked into the blackness of the drive, overhung by the conifers and the low clouds of the moonless night.

It was very dark and muddy in the lane. Holding her suitcase out awkwardly away from her legs Colette ran. She could now see a light on in the kitchen. Her homecoming fingers unlatched the wooden gate and she flew up the path to the door, knocking loudly and impetuously upon it with the speed of her flight.

Footsteps. The hall light. The door opened.

"Colette!"

John Forbes, an early bedder and an early riser, had had a busy day and was about to retire. He had driven to London to see Patricia Raven. Patricia was an old friend, originally a girlhood friend of Ruth's, then a friend of both of them. Patricia was an archaeologist, now the head of a women's college in London. She had never married. John had sometimes wondered whether she was really interested in men. He had only managed to interest her, in that sense, in himself by representing his need as purely mechanical. Now he saw her regularly at her flat. They had lunch, talked politics, then made love. At least John made love and Patricia, always disconcertingly humorous about it, let herself be made love to. It could only be possible with such an old friend. John felt a wry surprise, but of course no shame, at the relentless pestering continuance of his sexual urges. He kept this part of his life strictly secret from his children though they occasionally still saw "Aunt Pat." He never never stopped missing Ruth.

Today he had got back home for a late tea and to watch the replay of a football match on colour television with George Bellamy. Of course George had his own television, but he liked to come over to Pennwood to escape from his wife and daughter and get a free drink and a bit of masculine company. Sometimes he met John and Giles Gosling, the borough architect, in the *Horse and Groom*. Long ago, Gerda had tried to make a match between Bellamy and Rhoda. Bellamy was interested. Rhoda looked odd, but one could find that attractive, there was much to be said for a wife who couldn't talk, and Mrs. Marshalson would give them a cottage as a wedding present. Rhoda made it clear that she scorned Bellamy. Bellamy, only then aware what a concession he would have made in marrying her, chose a Laxlinden girl whom he bullied, and to whom he felt that he had stooped. He lived in a Marshalson cottage in Dimmerstone.

This evening he had come round as usual bringing news of the Hall, in which John took a malign interest. "Seen the squire?" "Young Henry? Yes. He was in Dimmerstone looking at the cottages." "I hope you told him about those roofs." "He doesn't care about roofs. He's like an American, he just gawps, and he talks all Yankee." "I suppose he thought it was rather picturesque and tumbled-down." "Tumbled-down, you can say that again! He didn't want to know. I wouldn't be surprised if he was a pansy, he looks like one."

John Forbes opened the door for his daughter and Colette went on into the kitchen and sat down at the table where the remains of John's bacon and egg supper were still set out.

"You said you'd let me know when you were coming."

"Sorry."

"I suppose you haven't eaten anything?"

"No, but don't worry. I'll just have some bread and cheese. *Don't worry*, I'll have this."

"All right, all right. You look a wreck."

"Is there any wine?"

"Won't beer do?"

"No."

"That's one thing you seem to have learnt at college. I'll open a bottle. How did you get here?"

"I thumbed a lift. Then I walked."

"I've told you a hundred times not to hitch-hike."

"Is there any jam?"

"Bread and jam and vintage claret."

"It isn't vintage."

"What a wonderful thing education is. I rang up your tutor."

"I know."

"Do you know what he said?"

"No."

"He said you were unteachable."

"He told me he thought I was wise to quit."

"I bet he did!"

"I hope you're not cross."

"Of course I'm cross! Why are you unteachable? You've got perfectly good wits. You just won't try. You young people just don't know what trying's like. It hurts."

"I don't want to be hurt. Is there anything on television?"

"You arrive back without a word and march in and want to look at television! Don't you want to talk to your father?"

"Yes. I just wondered."

"Why didn't you let me know you were coming?"

"I was in a muddle."

"Your bed's not made."

"I'll make it. How's Cato?"

"How should I know?"

"Daddy, I'm so sorry—I know how you feel about Cato—and now me—"

"You're a priceless pair. I can't understand you not *wanting* to be educated. You always were a complainer and a fretter—"

"You talk as if education were a kind of special stuff and nothing else would do, but there are hundreds of ways of discovering the world."

"It is a kind of special stuff and nothing else will do. It's precious. You're damn lucky to be capable of receiving it."

"You won't accept the fact that I'm not like you."

"You needn't be like me. You could be like your mother."

"You won't accept the fact that I'm not an intellectual, that I'm not clever. You think it's a sort of sacrilege—"

"Of course you're clever! To hear a child of mine sitting there and saying it's not clever—"

"Everyone says how wonderful it is to be young. I've never seen it. I want to enjoy being young. I don't want to spend my youth pretending to be somebody else."

"And how do you propose to enjoy being young? Stay here and arrange the flowers?"

"You always put me in a false position—"

"Do you really want to be an empty-headed kitten, a little fluffy sex object?"

"No! I hated the way people talked about sex at the college—"

"I never thought you were a timid girl—"

"I'm not! I'm—"

"You'll have to get a job, you know. And what can you do? You can't even type. All right, you're free, you're perfectly free, it's your life, I'm not going to advise you. But I'm damned if I'll support you here to be a grand country lady like Mrs. Marshalson."

Colette began to saw some cheese off a large chunk of bright yellow cheddar. The kitchen table smelt of cheese and wine. She said, "Has Henry Marshalson come back?"

"That drip. Yes. He's been swanning around pretending he owns the place."

"Well, I suppose he does own the place."

"He's not worthy to own it. He'll slink off back to America with his tail between his legs. 'Trundletail' Sandy used to call him."

"I'm going to bed," said Colette.

"The sheets are in the airing cupboard. Sorry I've been sounding off like that. I just feel so disappointed that you've left the college."

"You forced me into it."

"I didn't force you—"

"Yes, you did. And you forced Cato into the Church."

"I—what?"

"Well, you made him run away, he had to escape to somewhere, he was frightened of you! I'm frightened of you. You always ridiculed us when we were young. And you raise your voice so. You mustn't talk to people like that, even if they are your children. You don't know how strong you are, how you can hurt. Ever since I got back you've been lecturing me, and I've had such an awful day and I'm so tired—"

"Look, I'm sorry, but don't—"

"And another thing, in case it interests you. I'm still a virgin and I'm going to stay a virgin until I meet the right man, and

110

then I'm going to marry him and have six children!" Colette went out slamming the door.

John Forbes sat motionless feeling subdued and guilty. Did he really frighten his children? He could not believe it. It was a terrible thought. Oh if only Ruth were here ... All the same, Cato wanting God and Colette wanting kids! What a defeat. He opened a can of beer.

"That rich chap—"

"Henry Marshalson."

"I liked the look of him, he's a gentleman. Some gentlemen dig us villains. We give them kicks. Was he really interested in me?"

"No."

"But you said—"

"I thought I might ask him for money to help your education, but as you don't want any—"

"Well, I might too, who knows. You see, nobody cares about me except you. You don't know what that's like. You've always had people who cared. You've always had *people*. I've never had anybody. No wonder I feel frustrated. Now if that rich chap—"

"Forget it."

"You're the only *real* person I know. Do you think that rich chap would set me up—"

"No."

Cato, coming from the church back to the Mission, had seen a sign in a clothes shop window which said, in neon lights, TROUSERAMA. He felt a piercing desire to laugh and cry. There was no God and the world was damned and everyone had quietly gone mad only they were carrying on as usual. The universe was funny brittle awful momentary. Human life was the pointless wandering of insects. TROUSERAMA. That's what it was. Life was simply a trouserama.

That morning, though at first intending to do so, he had not

111

celebrated mass. He had suddenly felt the need for the mass as a nervous compulsive superstition. It was not that today especially or at last he clearly "disbelieved," but he felt that the mass was now somehow preventing him from thinking and moving. It had become a dead idol, something which he must for the present at any rate, let go of. And he said to Christ, stretching out his hands, I am sorry, forgive me, I cannot.

Instead he sat, resisting the compulsion to kneel, in the early morning in the dark church where only a cluster of distant candles gave a little light. He sat motionless and open-eyed for more than an hour as gate after gate in his mind seemed quietly to open, until there was no person there any more. He did not seek, he did not speak, he just waited. There was stillness and emptiness. Superficial thoughts moved, passing him by like quiet birds. He thought of Beautiful Joe and let the image of the boy stay there in the stillness as if exposing it to blessing. He thought about his father and his sister. He wondered if he had now celebrated his last mass and whether the deep love of God which is joy had departed forever from his life. In the stillness there was no quickening, no joy. He had tasted a rapture which it would be hard to live without. Was he now indeed called upon to surrender the precious privilege of the priesthood, the dedicated role which had seemed so essentially, so naturally, his? He was a priest, he felt, with all the atoms of his being. Unpriest him, and there would be nothing left. He was so much a priest that surely he must be able to make God to be in order to sanction his calling. But this was exactly what he must not think.

When Cato left the church he found that, although he had not been reflecting about his more mundane decisions, certain immediate matters appeared in a clearer light. Brendan had written again, asking him to come and stay at his flat. Cato decided that he would probably go to Brendan, not at once, but in a few days. Not that he expected any fresh illumination, but he wanted, before seeing his friend, to have put some more form into his existence, in particular to have taken some rational step about Beautiful Joe. He feared seeing Brendan, not of course fearing reproaches, but dreading his own deep desperate desire to be persuaded to stay in the order, in his home, with his love.

As far as the immediate future was concerned, what had become plain as he sat in the church was that he must stop hiding. For the days which remained before he went to Brendan or back to Laxlinden or wherever he did finally go he must live openly at the Mission, see and be seen, and also, and at last, talk more openly with Beautiful Joe. He felt now how unwise it was for him to have allowed this sort of negative teasing relationship to arise between himself and the boy. The relation itself was a dangerous kind of barrier. No wonder Joe made extravagant fanciful remarks with the hope of establishing a more direct bond simply by making Cato angry. He must take the risk of speaking more simply and frankly. He really had no evidence, except Joe's own wild pronouncements, that the boy was involved in anything illegal or even in danger of being so. Well, there was the revolver. Joe had said it was an imitation. For the first time it occurred to Cato, perhaps it was an imitation. It had weighed enough. But perhaps—It was then that he had seen the sign TROUSERAMA. His resolutions remained however and he felt grimly grateful to the brittle funny awful universe for having prevented him from saying mass.

As he was walking along the sun came out, and when he got back to the Mission Cato left the back door ajar and propped open one of the windows in front, to air the house and as a sign that he was in residence. The house could do with some airing. He could do with some airing himself. His clothes were filthy, his underwear unchanged, his cassock stinking. The suddenly warm spring day made him feel noisome and shaggy. As he had told Henry, his persistent wearing of the cassock was eccentric. Most of his colleagues had by now abandoned even the dog collar. Cato could not approve of this, nor of the young nuns who now ran around London dressed in short skirts and high-heeled shoes.

Noon had brought Beautiful Joe, light-footed and fresh, wearing a crisp flowery shirt, a broad velvet tie, and a tight-waisted suit of mauve linen. He danced in. "I saw the front window open—" Cato invited him to stay for a bread and cheese lunch, and sent him out to buy cigarettes and beer.

Lunch was now over. The sunlight revealed the grey news-paper stuck to the kitchen table by layers of grease, two burnt saucepans and a boiled-over mess upon the stove, a wide scat-tering of crumbs and cigarette ends upon the floor, a group of milk bottles containing various levels of coagulated sour milk, and a mass meeting of the pink transparent beetles in a far corner. Through the open door came, somehow, from distant gardens, smells of earth and green leaves. Cato stared at Beautiful Joe. He had not yet managed to break through to the new frankness which had this morning seemed so necessary and so simple. He could not find the opening, the tone. The boy's expectant quizzical eyes, half hidden by glinting reflec-tions, disturbed and confused him. Joe had removed his tie and opened his shirt. Now, with a clean steel comb, he was meticu-lously combing his hair into a neat square head-piece of blond silk and staring back at Cato with an intentness which con-trolled the possibility of wild laughter. Cato felt stirrings of desire, the need for contact.

"You know I'm not a villain, Father. Not yet."

"I hope that's true."

"You think too badly of me."

"I don't know what to think of you."

"Don't think of me. Just love me."

Cato looked into the glinting golden eyes which now seemed to him to burn with sincerity. "Joe, I must try and speak more openly to you."

"I hoped you would. You've treated me like a child, you know."

"Have I? I'm sorry. Joe, listen. I've got to leave here and go away God knows where. I may even have to leave the priest-hood, leave the church, and—"

"Why, what have you done?"

"I haven't done anything, I've just decided, that is, I may decide—"

"Oh no, *no*, you can't, you *can't* not be a priest any more, it's *impossible*, don't you see it's impossible, you *are* a priest, you can't mean it, you can't mean what's impossible, you can't stop being a priest ever, ever—" The boy spoke quietly, but with

114

vehement will, stretching out one hand palm downward on the table.

With a thrilled emotion not unlike relief, Cato said, "Well, impossible, yes, perhaps you're right—"

"What's impossible can't happen, can it—"

"No, well, I expect I'll stay, yes, of course I will—"

"You had me worried, Father, for a moment I really thought you were serious! Why if *you* went whatever would happen to *us*? There must be something holy somewhere, it's got to be there, somewhere."

Cato was appallingly touched. "Yes, yes, but the holiness—it doesn't depend just on ordinary sinful folk like me—it *is* there, Joe, and it will be there, whatever I do and whatever I think —so you mustn't—"

"I know, I know, *that's* believing in God. But I don't believe in God, I believe in you."

"Heaven help you!" said Cato.

The doorway darkened and somebody came swiftly into the kitchen, a tall girl with a ridiculously short dress and a stream of long brown hair.

Cato stared, blinked into the sunlight. "Colette!"

They rushed, laughing, exclaiming, into each other's arms. Cato's large black shoes and Colette's flimsy sandals executed a dance upon the slippery greasy floor. The summer dress, the slim shoulders, were enveloped in the old musty cassock. There was a sudden whiff of apples, of flowers, of thin freshly laundered cotton.

"Oh my dear, my dear—" The dance continued for a moment.

Joe had leapt up and was standing by the gas stove, smiling and gaping.

"Joe, this is my sister."

"Come off it, Father!"

"I am his sister!" cried Colette. They were all laughing now.

"May I introduce, Joseph Beckett, Colette Forbes."

"Hello, Joe." Colette advanced with a beaming face and extended her hand. Joe rather diffidently shook it.

"He's called Beautiful Joe."

"I can see why! I'm so glad to meet you. Oh isn't it a lovely day! Oh Cato, I'm so glad to see you. I feel so happy all of a sudden, I just knew I had to see you, and—"

"Have you had lunch?"

"Oh I had some sandwiches at the station, I see you've had yours—Cato, what a *mess*, shall I wash up? Look, can I just have that bit of bread and some cheese? But oh dear, I'm interrupting you. I'm so sorry, shall I go for a walk?"

"No, don't go for a walk," said Cato, still laughing with pleasure. "I must just talk to Joe for a moment—could you go upstairs—"

"No, it's so nice, I'll stroll about in the street, just give me a shout. Good-bye then, Joe. Don't worry, I'll take the bread with me." Colette seized a piece of bread and disappeared through the door into the yard. The gate banged.

Joe sat down again at the table. "I say, I say—!"

Cato pressed his hands to his head. Some quite alien spirit of hope and joy had flown into the room with Colette and touched him lightly, as a child touches another child in the game of "tig." "Now where was I—Look, Joe, you'd better go now. But I really must talk to you. Come back tomorrow morning and we'll—"

"Do you know something, your sister is a beautiful girl."

"Is she? Yes, I suppose she is."

"I tell you she is. And she's so—sort of different. No girl ever looked at me like that before, so sort of straight, and shaking hands like a man—All the birds I know just never stop wiggling and giggling—they're so dumb they don't know how to put their tights on—Father, do you think, would she come out with me?"

Cato stopped smiling. "My sister—come out with *you*—?"

There was a moment's silence. Beautiful Joe rose. He picked up his tie from the table, shook it fastidiously, and began to put it on. "Father, you're a bloody snob."

Cato blushed. The blood rushed hotly to his cheeks, to his brow. Beautiful Joe moved towards the open door.

"Stop," said Cato. He stepped quickly round the table and barred the way. They looked at each other.

116

"I'm sorry," said Cato, suddenly stammering. "It's—its not snobbery—you don't understand—I don't know you—"

Joe lowered his eyes. Cato moved aside and the boy stepped out into the sunshine.

"Joe—please—come tomorrow—please—"

"Oh—well—yes—" He turned and sped away, running through the yard and through the gate.

Cato sat down.

Colette came in a moment later. "That boy went by me like a—are you all right?"

"Yes, fine. Have some cheese."

"Cato, look at those beetles!"

"They live here."

"This place smells. Can I clean it? I'll go out and get some disinfectant. Can I stay here with you and help? I could be some use, couldn't I? I could clean things."

"No," said Cato. "This is no place for you."

"You sound so prim and old-fashioned. I'm quite tough, you know. Even though Daddy does think I'm a sex object."

"Did he say that?"

"Well, not exactly. But he's very upset that I've left the college."

"So you did decide to?"

"Yes. Like I wrote you. It was no good. I got home last night."

"He's not really angry though?"

"Not like he was with you. Perhaps he's getting resigned to his awful children."

"You're looking lovely,' said Cato. He took her hand for a moment across the table.

Colette's hair, dead straight and rather silky, was a many-hued light brown, a colour of brown salty trees beside the sea, and reached almost to her waist. A number of shorter locks, falling straight and flat, framed her face with an effect like leaves. She had salient cheeks like her brother, but looked thinner and finer with a straight nose and a long mobile mouth which twisted when she smiled. Her eyes were a clear light questing brown. There was a slight gap between her two front

117

teeth. Cato stared at her unmarked radiant face. She looked childishly young and healthy and chaste.

"Why can't I stay here, Cato?"

"This place is closing. They're going to pull the house down."

"Oh what a shame! I do wish I'd come here more. I was afraid to because of Daddy. I either had to lie or to make him cross. Now I don't care."

"You won't lie?"

"No, I shall make him cross. When are you going?"

"Tomorrow or—well, maybe the next day—or—I'm going to stay with Brendan Craddock."

"Give him my love, if he remembers me. Do you think I'll ever become a Carmelite nun?"

"I hope not!" said Cato. "What are you going to do?"

"I don't know." She looked at him, with her pleased childish brown eyes. "I think I shall just—wait—for the gods—to tell me—what to do—next. Not God. The gods. Daddy wouldn't understand, would he?"

"Enjoy the springtime. Don't be anxious about anything," said Cato. "It must be so beautiful down at Laxlinden now." He sighed. "Oh I tell you who turned up here the other day— Henry Marshalson. He's back from America."

"Oh really?" said Colette. "I say, can I have some of that beer? I suppose you haven't got any wine here, have you, no."

I wonder if Max ever saw that? Henry wondered to himself.

He was in the National Gallery, examining the most important acquisition made during his absence, Titian's great *Diana and Actaeon*. The immortal goddess, with curving apple cheek, her bow uplifted, bounds with graceful ruthless indifference across the foreground, while further back, in an underworld of brooding light, the doll-like figure of Actaeon falls stiffly to the onslaught of the dogs. A stream flashes. A distant mysterious horseman passes. The woods, the air, are of a russet brown so intense and frightening as to persuade one that the tragedy is taking place in total silence. Henry felt such intense pleasure as he looked at the picture, he felt so purely happy that he wanted to howl aloud with delight. Smiling, he sat down nearby.

It was certainly dangerous to tangle with goddesses. Athena was a fearful authoritarian and very austere even with her favourites. Hera was thoroughly vindictive. Artemis and Aphrodite were killers. What poor thin semi-conscious beings mortal men were after all, so easily maddened, so readily destroyed by forces whose fearful strength remained forever beyond their powers of conception. Surely these forces were real, the human mind a mere shadow, a toy. Yet if this was so, why was he smiling? At least those dolls could adumbrate, in homage, their own frailty. And the piercing joy which he felt now, and which he knew to be so momentary, was surely as real as the gods.

Henry sat quietly, his outer eyes now veiled, and saw another picture. Against an empty blue sky, an empty blue horizon, a masked helmsman takes a fisher king, his queen, his hair-haired child away to sea, while an old divinity clutches the edge of the boat and an immense wise blue fish lies looking upward. On either side of this great confident calm are scenes of torture. But Max didn't get away, thought Henry. He stayed, and the Nazis came and he couldn't get to America, his America came later. The ruthless gods looked after Max all right, undid him by two wars, made him forget all he ever knew, left him with nothing but a pencil. Years without colours taught him that fearful Gothic stare: Max and his masculine mysticism. Grünewald, Breughel, Van Gogh. Why do I love him so, wondered Henry, why do I feel I am him, when he is so unlike me and I hardly know how to judge him? Sex is everywhere in Max, well, sex is everywhere in art only usually they keep it secret. Max never bothered with secrets. Candles and catfish, lucky old Max: pure vision plus pure egoism, objective perfect happiness. The gods invented space, the fearful space that he spent his life cluttering, lest he should die, and which spreads out so enigmatic and empty and blue behind the masked helmsman and the fisher king. What a nervous crazy self-indulgent artist he was in a way, what a spawner of obese and dotty symbolism,

119

and yet how happy, even the scenes of torture radiate a mysterious joy. And all those manly self-portraits. Rembrandt-Beckmann, what it is to be a man. The hedonist, the prisoner, the acrobat, the clown. He was so wonderfully pleased with himself. Oh God, oh God, oh God if only I could paint. Henry's joy left him abruptly and he began anxiously to think about himself.

He did not look at the Titian again, but scuttled blindly from the Gallery and came out into the bright open light of Trafalgar Square. The sun was shining and the air was full of pigeons. Some golden-white clouds were slowly moving downward over Whitehall, and Big Ben, visible straight ahead, said eleven o'clock. Henry raced down the steps and hailed a taxi. He was going to investigate Sandy's secret flat. He had of course said nothing to Gerda and Lucius, and by a few casual questions had confirmed their ignorance of Sandy's London hide-out. Merriman equally knew nothing. Henry felt a small livid excitement at the thought of penetrating into Sandy's secret life, though he did not in fact expect to find anything very extraordinary there. There was a sort of lucky dip interest, a prospect as of loot. Of course Sandy was a total Philistine, so there would be no interesting *objets d'art*. Henry chiefly feared that some trivial discovery might touch his heart.

The taxi took him to a small street at the Kensington end of Knightsbridge, which had progressed rapidly and a little uncertainly from dowdiness to smartness. There were a few shops, mostly selling antiques, small terrace houses painted different colours. The taxi halted and Henry paid. Somewhat to his dismay, the street number which he had hastily copied from Sandy's lease denoted a large ugly block of flats which had been built at one end of the street, presumably in a gap created by Hitler. The main door stood open. Nervously, rather guiltily, Henry entered the hall. He felt alien, almost criminal, hoping that no one would notice him or speak to him. He stood there irresolutely. Clearly the place was a warren of small flats. How was he to find out which one was Sandy's, since he had failed to note its number? Then suddenly catching his eye with a white flash, he saw a wooden board, a row of names. FLAT 11, A. MARSHALSON. How strange, how touchingly lost and insignificant the name looked here, unowned and uncared-for in the midst of London. Henry advanced to the lift.

The flat was on the third floor. The lift door opened automatically onto a carpeted corridor, windowless and lit by electric light. Henry's heart had now begun to pound uncomfortably hard as he fumbled in his pocket for the bunch of keys. He reached number 11 and, after glancing up and down the corridor, began trying the keys with a hand which was suddenly trembling violently. The third key fitted and turned, and the door opened, scraping a little on the carpet within, and a profound silence came out to greet Henry. He sidled in and closed the door softly. He was in a tiny hall with several doors opening from it. Quickly, before panic set in, he grabbed the nearest door handle. Clearly the sitting-room. He darted about opening doors. Sitting-room, two bedrooms, kitchen, and bathroom. *Silence.* He returned to the sitting-room and looked out of the window. A view of the antique shops, some roofs, a tree or two, and more distantly the fungoid dome of Harrods. He stood still, calming himself down and looking about.

The flat was small and rather cramped. The yellowish carpet from the corridor continued underfoot. Some large dark pieces of furniture, a dominating wardrobe, a big square desk, created equally dark spaces into which nothing else could reasonably fit. A long brand new leather sofa, with the price tag still attached to one foot, stretched diagonally across the sitting-room. The rest of the furniture was shabby and looked as if it had been assembled from the maids' rooms at the Hall. There were two wobbly bamboo tables with thick green glass ash trays upon them. Some varnished bookshelves were empty except for thrillers and a book about speed boats. All the furniture seemed to lean and push and lower, and Henry found himself instinctively veering and ducking. The atmosphere, stuffy with tobacco smell and with a sweetish odour which Henry could not diagnose, was oppressive, irritating rather than sinister. There were some random prettifying touches: an embroidered footstool, a pair of soap-stone elephants, a water-colour of the Hall from a set at Laxlinden. There was also a comical-faced Chinese lion which Henry remembered from long ago. Averting his face from this little presence he hurriedly rifled the drawers of the desk finding theatre programmes, the menu of a club dinner, pamphlets about boats, nothing of interest. Most of the drawers were empty. What after all had he expected? The place was tidy. The beds were made. Henry walked about breathing deeply and inhibiting emotion. What came nearest to making him gasp was the provisional almost juvenile nature of it all. Against what had Sandy fought this losing battle? Doubtless he would never know.

Suddenly overcome Henry ran to the kitchen in search of a drink. He found a bottle of whisky in one cupboard, a glass in another. He automatically opened the refrigerator in search of ice. As he was trying to pull out the ice tray he became aware of some food in the fridge, tomatoes, cress, a jug of milk. He picked up the milk and smelt it. Fresh. Henry considered this. He extracted the ice and put it into the glass. He closed the fridge. Then he noticed a folded newspaper which was lying upon the dresser. He took up the newspaper and looked quickly at the date. Yesterday. With a shaking hand he poured the whisky over the ice and retreated to the sitting-room.

His first thought was that Sandy was not dead at all but living secretly in London. But this was insane. His next thought was that Sandy must have sold the flat. But if the flat had been sold would not the deeds have been passed on to the purchaser? A confused feeling of guilt and fright dimmed Henry's mind. This was no empty derelict flat, it was *someone's* flat. This now seemed obvious. He thought he could hear a clock ticking. He decided to leave at once. He gulped down the whisky and seized his hat. And at that moment he heard the soft tap and click of a key being inserted and turned, and heard the front door scraping across the carpet as it slowly opened.

The sitting-room door was ajar. Henry stood still, paralysed with fright, expecting something unspeakable and uncanny. He could not move or speak. The front door closed. He heard someone sigh. Then the sitting-room door was pushed open and a woman came in. When she saw Henry she gave a little cry.

For a moment neither moved. Henry was rigid, hat in hand. The woman, still with coat and hat on, stood with her hands at her throat in an attitude of terror. Henry, to drown the echo of that cry, relieved too that he was not confronted with his brother, willed himself to speak. "I am terribly sorry—I didn't want to—I am so sorry—my name is Henry Marshalson."

The woman very slowly moved, taking off her hat which she threw onto the red sofa which stretched between her and Henry. Then she dropped her handbag onto the sofa and began mechanically to comb back her hair with her fingers, her mouth slightly open, still staring at him.

"Please forgive me," said Henry. He was frightened of her fear. "I didn't mean to alarm you—you see—I'm my brother's heir—but there must be a mistake—perhaps this is your flat and—"

The woman came round the sofa and sat down upon it, one hand pressed to her heart. He could hear her breath. "Excuse me—being here—" her words were almost inaudible.

"No, please—it's for me to—but—I mean—is this your flat?"

"No—well—you see—he said—he would leave me the flat—in his will—but—"

Henry listened to this murmur, not understanding. He began again. "I'm very sorry—"

"You see—I am—I was—his friend."

This baffled Henry. He moved, dropped his hat on a chair. "I'm afraid I don't quite understand. You knew Sandy—?"

"Yes—I knew—Sandy—"

Henry understood at last. "I see—I do apologize—I'm being very slow—I quite understand—of course—you—you have been living here with my brother?"

"He said—if anything happened—I was to have the flat—but of course I didn't expect him to—and now that you—I'll move out as soon as—"

"You certainly won't!" said Henry. "You must stay here, you must have the flat, I wouldn't dream of—after all you have a right, and Sandy must have wished—really I am so sorry— I mean about your—loss, your bereavement—How long had you—been with Sandy?"

"Oh—a long time—it has been a terrible—"

"Yes. I can understand. Do please feel—that if there is anything at all that I can do for you—"

"Oh I'll manage—I'll be all right—you're very kind—"

"After all I feel—responsible—just as if—Oh please don't cry!"

Her cheeks were glowing red, wet with tears. With a little distraught gesture she drew her hair across her eyes. Henry came and sat down beside her.

"You are—so kind—Look, you are sitting on my hat."

"I'm so sorry!"

The woman, receiving her crushed hat from Henry's apologetic hand, shifted a little away from him, wriggling her coat back off her shoulders, extracted her handbag from behind her and with a quick nervous movement, turning her head away, began to dab powder onto her nose and cheeks. The cosmetic smell, the cheeks red and shiny with weeping, now coated with pale pink face-powder, all suddenly so absurd, so close, made Henry's head swim. He felt awful pity, for her, for Sandy. The little instinctive defensive gesture with the powder touched his heart. She turned to him again, and with the hasty powder, the lipsticked mouth, the pencilled eyebrows, she looked like a doll, like a clown. Sandy's girl.

In fact she could not be very young, doubtless over thirty. She was plump and not tall. A frilly blouse, not perfectly clean, was stretched over a large bosom. One button had already given way. He could see her breasts heaving quickly. Her face was round with a heavy jaw line and a big prominent chin. The sticky red mouth was full-lipped beneath a faint moustache and rather small, the nose wide, with flared nostrils and assertively *retroussé*. Her eyes were large, round, set far apart, of an obscure darkish blue, and her hair, a bright brown, was arranged in a shaggy bob. The face was tired, experienced, certainly not the face of youth. Two deep lines framed the mouth. She presented herself now to Henry with a kind of desperate boldness.

"May I know your name?"

"Stephanie."

"I mean your—"

"Stephanie Whitehouse."

"It is—Miss Whitehouse?"

"Yes, I—I was never married—only—like with Sandy, and

124

he never—you see, I'm not his sort and I never expected he'd marry me—I'm like out of the—not good enough for him—and I never thought—"

"But he lived with you for years?"

"Well—yes—we were—He kept it a secret. I expect he was ashamed of me, he must have been. But he did say I could have the flat if anything happened—"

"Of course you shall have the flat!" said Henry. "I'll make it over to you. Don't worry, please. And as for his feeling—why that's ridiculous—you mustn't feel in any way—You must let me help you."

"Oh, you are so kind—I can sort of manage, I've always had to—"

"But Sandy supported you?"

"Well, yes, he was very good about that."

"I should hope so. But what are you living on now?"

"Well, I get my National Assistance and—"

"I'll look after you," said Henry.

She closed her eyes and turned away with a little gasp. She was fumbling for her handkerchief, tears streaked the pink powder. Henry got up.

"You mustn't," she said. "It's too much. I can get a job. I would have only I haven't been too well since the abortion."

"The abortion?"

"Yes, I got pregnant, only Sandy didn't want the child so we got rid of it."

"Oh—" Henry's mind reeled. Would an illegitimate child of Sandy's have inherited the property? How perfectly extraordinary everything was which was happening to him now. Henry, noticing himself, found that he was exhilarated but had no time to ask himself why.

"What is your job?" he asked. "I mean, what was it?"

"Well, I used to—I'm an orphan, you see, and I never had proper school. I ran away when I was fourteen and came to London. I came to Piccadilly Circus, it was the only place I'd heard of in London. And then—you'll think I'm awful—I became a stripper."

"You mean a dancer?"

"Well, if you call it dancing. I used to—the men were so

awful. I was frightened all the time—you had to do—what they told you—so then I became a—"

"You became a prostitute?"

"Yes. Now you won't want to—"

"Miss Whitehouse, please. I respect you absolutely, I beg you to believe me—"

"It was an awful life."

"I'm sure it was. I regard you as a victim. But how did you meet Sandy?"

"He saw me at the strip club."

This sudden image of Sandy sitting in the darkness watching Miss Whitehouse undress touched Henry's heart with an awful thrill of truth. It was in some weird way the nicest thing that he had ever imagined about his brother. Sandy, the stranger, was there in that scene which Henry now in an instant pictured so vividly, the stuffy room, the silent staring men, the awkward vulnerable naked girl.

"I was younger and thinner when I started, I was beautiful once so they said. You see I put on weight and—"

"So Sandy—got to know you, and—"

"He saw me, then we met again later on. He saved me really, I suppose. I don't know what would have become of me if Sandy hadn't cared."

"And he loved you."

"He said I was the *femme fatale* type. I think he was pleased that I was, like, what I was—"

"Poor Sandy," said Henry, to himself. The loneliness, the deadness of the dead. He felt touched fascinated curiosity, but a kind of shame prevented him from questioning her further, even now told him that he ought to go, to reassure her and then to go.

"But of course I didn't know if he'd have gone on caring. I lost my looks, and when you aren't married to a man you have no security, and I was always scared he'd just say it was over."

Her voice, with a slight midlands accent, had a deep coaxing caressing rhythm which sounded all the time like some desperate pleading. Perhaps she had talked like that with the men who—And then there had been Sandy and of course she was not his sort and she never expected him to marry her—

"Miss Whitehouse, I must go, I feel I am an intruder here."

"Oh please don't go!" Her hand was fluttering nervously at her breast, seeking to do up the errant button.

"No, no, this is your flat, your property. And I hope that you will allow me to give you some financial assistance. After all—"

"Please don't go! I'm glad you've come. I've been so anxious, I thought I might get a letter from a lawyer. I sort of hid all my things in case anybody came. I felt I oughtn't to be here, but I had nowhere else to go. We hadn't any friends, you see. I just saw about him in the newspapers, and I've had no one to talk to. I lived here like a prisoner, really, Sandy never liked— He was that jealous, he'd ring up all the time to be sure I was here—"

Sandy full of jealousy. Full of guilt too, no doubt. Henry felt wild confused pity for both of them.

"Don't worry, Miss Whitehouse, don't worry about anything now, I don't want you to worry about anything—"

"But you will see me again, tell me what I'm to do—?" The big red-rimmed dark blue eyes looked up at him timidly, submissively, the little rhythmic coaxing voice pleaded. Henry thought, this woman must have made old Sandy feel like a rajah.

"Of course I will."

"I loved him so much."

"Please don't cry again—"

"I won't be a nuisance, I'll get a job, of course I don't mean *that* job—"

"No, of course not. But what—er—else can you do?"

"Well, nothing really, but—"

"Don't worry—and, Miss Whitehouse, don't run away, will you—I mean what I say, I'll look after you. I want you to stay here."

"Oh thank you, thank you—"

"Now I must go."

"You said something about—I hate to ask for money, but I'm down to my last—"

"Oh of course, I'm so sorry—Look, I'll give you a cheque. Here, will this keep you going?"

"Oh, that's far too much! I only meant—"

"Nonsense, here, take it. I'll—I'll ring you. Let me just note the telephone number. Now you won't go away, will you, you promise?"

"Oh I promise, yes! Thank you so much, you have given me new hope! You will come again, please?"

"Yes, I will—very soon—I'll telephone you—I'll help you in any way I can—I give you my word—I'm so glad to have met you—I mean—"

Henry scudded towards the door followed hastily by Miss Whitehouse. They stood a moment together in the little hall. Henry held out his hand, then in a flurry of awkwardness took hold of her hand and bowed a little as if to kiss it, but did not do so. His head brushed the tight front of the frilly blouse, he felt a few hairs tangle on a button. He glimpsed fingernails, cracked and covered with flaking pink enamel. Her hand was small and plump and smelt of cosmetics.

Then Henry was outside, running. He passed the lift and flew light-foot down the stairs. He ran all the way to Harrods and sprang up the steps into the men's department. He walked springily about on the thick carpet looking at himself in mirrors. A warm cauldron of emotions bubbled within him. He felt frenzied compassion, desire, triumph, wild amusement. He felt kingly self-satisfaction. As he began to calm down he bought himself four very expensive shirts.

Lucius, packing his suitcase, thought: they are all of them young, concerned with a young future. Only I am old and have an old future of illness and pain and solitude and death. Even Gerda is healthy and energetic and full of projects and full of will. And now, just when I should have thought she might have needed me, she is sending me away, and perhaps Henry will not allow me to come back. His false teeth were hurting him. He had a pain in his chest. A tear came into his eye and he mopped it off into the hairs on the back of his hand.

Audrey had grudgingly accepted his proposed visit. Audrey's husband Rex treated Lucius like an old man and clearly regarded him as an old bore. Timmie and Robbie were at home so there would be ceaseless noise. Lucius could not communicate with children. He would not be able to work, so there was no good taking his manuscript. Besides, he might lose it. His bedroom would be unheated, he would have to sit with the family and watch their choice of television. There was nowhere to go for a walk. He would have to go out to the public library and write haiku. The consolations of art at least remained to him in his old age. He was experimenting further with rhymes.

> Cruel the daffodils
> Every springtime kills
> I perish faster, faster!
> Ah. The young master.

*

Gerda, looking from the terrace to see if Henry was in view in the garden, suddenly saw Sandy's green Jensen emerge from the stables and flash away along the drive. A few minutes later the ERA, towed by a Land-Rover, emerged and bumped slowly off. Gerda recognized the Land-Rover as belonging to the garage man and car salesman in Laxlinden. Evidently Henry had decided to sell Sandy's cars. He had said nothing to her about it. Nor had he consulted her about the fate of Sandy's papers. Gerda had watched tight-lipped as Rhoda had carried out boxes of stuff to the bonfire.

Henry had become a little more communicative, a little less sulky. Returned from taking Colette home on the night when they fell in the lake, he had described with animation the scene with the punt, Colette's desperate plunge, his own unheroic role. They had all laughed. Henry had shown more gaiety and ordinary human friendliness than at any time since his return, and Gerda's heart stirred with timid hope. After his recent visit to London he had seemed to her even more cheerful. But he still remained somehow secretive and detached. He often disappeared. He had had two long sessions with Merriman, and the solicitor had left on each occasion without seeing Gerda. Henry had also gone over again to Dimmerstone, he said to

129

look at the state of the cottages. (The Marshalsons owned Dimmerstone.) Gerda wondered if he had been to the churchyard.

*

Henry who had walked over to the post office at Laxlinden to buy stamps for several very important letters, turned round to find Colette Forbes just behind him.

"Why, hello, water nymph!"

"Hello, hero!"

"None the worse for your dip in the lake?"

"Of course not!"

"May I buy you a stamp?"

"How generous. I've got one."

"May I walk back with you?"

"What about the yellow Volvo?"

"How did you know about the yellow Volvo?"

"You gave me a lift in it the other night."

"Oh yes, so I did, I'd quite forgotten."

"Anyway, you're famous in these parts. Everyone is talking about you and your doings. Didn't you know?"

"One prefers not to know such things. As a matter of fact it was such a lovely day I thought I'd walk, like the pigeon."

"What pigeon?"

"Any pigeon."

"Did you know you'd got an American accent?"

"Yes. Who was that young man we passed?"

"Giles Gosling, the architect. He's making—"

"What is he making?"

"Sorry. Daddy said he was making Sandy's tombstone. He's a stone-cutter in his spare time."

"How is your pa?"

"Cross."

"With you?"

"Yes. He thinks I'm not grateful enough for the liberation of women."

"Women aren't liberated yet, thank God."

"He thinks I should have an occupation."

"You have. Being female."

"Is being male an occupation?"

"No."

"I suppose I shall have to get a job."

"What can you do?"

"Nothing."

"Excellent girl."

"What are you going to do?"

"What do you mean, what am I going to do?"

"If being male isn't an occupation, what occupation are you going to take up?"

"Painting."

"Really? How marvellous! I didn't know you—"

"I don't. I'm doing it by proxy. I'm writing a book about a painter. You wouldn't have heard of him. Max Beckmann. He liked goddesses and prostitutes. Not schoolgirls."

"I'm not a schoolgirl!"

"Then why do you wear your hair in a plait like that? You look ten."

"You look a hundred. You've got grey hairs."

"I haven't!"

"Well, one anyway."

"So there's nothing to choose between me and Lucius Lamb."

"I like Lucius Lamb."

"Why are you so aggressive?"

"Why are you? Here's the turning to Pennwood. Will you come and see Daddy?"

"No. He despises me."

"He doesn't."

"He does. Good-bye."

"Why are you going that way? The gate's padlocked."

"I know, stupid. I'm going to climb over it."

"Then I shall come along and see you climb over it."

"Who lives in those converted cottages by the pub?"

"Giles."

"Giles?"

"Giles Gosling, the architect."

"I hear your father has bought the Oak Meadow."

"Yes. I hope you don't mind?"

"Why the hell should I mind?"

"He isn't going to build on it."

"Pity. I think everybody should build on everything."

"Here's your gate."

Henry climbed over the gate, not in haste, taking care with his trousers as he swung over the top. He descended on the other side and stood holding the bars and looking through them at Colette. The sun was shining between stripes of yellow cloud out of a pale blue sky. Blackbirds and thrushes were singing in concert. Colette was wearing a flimsy smock dress with a pattern of tiny green and blue flowers upon it. She had pulled her plait of hair forward over her shoulder and was holding the end of it in her hand.

"Good-bye, water bird."

"Good-bye, squire."

Henry began walking slowly along between the fir trees, listening to the birds singing and feeling the moist warmth of the spring sunshine and thinking about Stephanie Whitehouse.

Lucius puffed down the stairs with his suitcase and put it down in the hall and dropped his overcoat across it. He wondered whether he should take his straw hat. The weather could become hot and he got terrible headaches if he failed to shade his eyes. If he took the straw hat he would have to wear it on the journey. His cap could be packed, but not the straw hat. Or perhaps Rex could lend him a hat? But Rex's head was certainly smaller than his, after all poor Rex was bald. Sheer despair at the idea of the disagreeable journey and the annihilation of his accustomed world overwhelmed him. Coming down the stairs had made him giddy. He felt thoroughly ill and wanted to lie down. He collected his cap and his straw hat from the cloakroom and put the hat on his head and pocketed the cap. He lifted the telephone to ring for the village taxi to take him to the nearest station. There was no afternoon bus.

Gerda came out of the drawing-room. "What do you think you're doing? And why are you wearing your straw hat?"

"I am telephoning for a taxi," said Lucius in a ringing voice.

"Why? Why aren't you having your rest?"

"BECAUSE I AM GOING TO AUDREY'S!"

"Don't shout," said Gerda. "I'd forgotten it was today."

"Oh had you! You order me to go away thereby inconveniencing me and my sister very much indeed and then you haven't even enough concern and enough courtesy to remember when I'm going!"

"Have you been drinking?"

Like a wraith, light-footed Henry, entering from the front door, passed between them and flew up the stairs two at a time. His skipping footsteps could be heard receding along the landing in the direction of Queen Anne.

"Come in here," said Gerda, "I want to talk to you."

"I shall miss the bloody train."

"Come in here."

Lucius took off his straw hat and threw it on the floor and kicked it. He followed Gerda into the drawing-room and closed the door noisily.

"How dare you speak to me like that in front of my son!" Gerda, her dark hair pulled austerely back into the big tortoise-shell slide, her eyes glowing, her pale broad face thrust forward, her large nose wrinkled with anger, confronted him, practically stepping on his feet.

Lucius sidled round her. "I'm sorry, my dear, I'm sorry—"

"I will not be shouted at in my own house!"

"I'm sorry, but I thought you might at least have remembered—"

"Why should I remember?"

"I did mention it at breakfast—"

"Well, I wasn't listening. I have more important things to worry about than your time-table."

"I know, it only matters to me, everything about me only matters to me."

"Oh, stop whining."

"If I don't telephone I'll miss the train."

"Look, I've changed my mind. I don't want you to go."

"What?"

"It's just as well I caught you, otherwise you might have slunk off."

133

"You might have told me before I packed, I feel quite—"

"Look, sit down, no, put some more wood on the fire first, will you."

"Do you want me not to go today or not to go at all? It would be a great relief to me if—"

"Oh stop bothering me. Sit down."

"I'll have to telephone Audrey."

"Lucius, stop fluttering and chattering, will you. Now listen—"

"Why don't you want me to go now?"

"I want you to go and see John Forbes."

"What?"

"You have been seeing him occasionally, haven't you. I mean you are on speaking terms?"

"Well," said Lucius. They were both sitting by the fire. "I meet him now and then in the village. I haven't been to his house for ages." Gerda, who had encouraged him to neglect Forbes, now seemed to be blaming him for having done so.

Bird-headed Rhoda entered soft-footed with the tea things and laid them out with deft gloved hands upon a little frail tea-table close to Gerda's chair.

When she had gone Gerda said, "I want you to call on him."

"Just like that? Won't it look odd?"

"You can find a pretext, anything will do, take him a book or something."

"A book?"

"Don't keep repeating what I say. Here's your tea."

"Oh, Gerda, I'm so pleased not to be going away. I'm so sorry I was rude just now—"

"You go and see him tomorrow."

"But why—why do you suddenly want me to visit John Forbes?"

"I want us to be friends with the Forbeses again. I want there to be coming and going between their house and ours."

"I don't understand—" said Lucius. "Oh, good heavens, you're not match-making between Henry and Colette Forbes?"

"Yes, I am," said Gerda. "Of course it may come to nothing, but it's not a mad idea and it is *an* idea. I want Henry to stay here, I don't want him to go back to America, I don't want him

134

to marry an American. Colette is young and silly and she's not exactly what I would have chosen as a daughter-in-law, but she's a decent girl, of reasonably good family, capable of loyalty and capable of learning sense, and she's used to living in the country. I talked to her a little the other night and I got quite a good impression. At the very least I'd like to see more of her. And Henry seems to like her, in fact she's the first thing he seems to have liked since he came back to England. You remember how cheerful he was that evening after he had taken her home. And altogether he's been much more lively and talkative since then. Even if nothing develops, the girl will be young company for him and he may get into the habit of staying. I want him to feel he lives here and isn't just visiting. So all this is why you've got to go and see John Forbes."

"But supposing John Forbes won't be friends?"

"He will be. He must have thought of this. And I'm sure the girl would jump at it."

"I wonder. Perhaps she's already got some chap."

"I don't think so. Anyway you must find that out."

"Well, well," said Lucius. He added, "Of course if Henry married Colette we'd get the Oak Meadow back, and John owns all the land on the other side as far as the river."

Gerda said nothing, but frowned slightly. She was thinking how little, in a way, she wanted Henry to marry, but since it was necessary to have an heir he could certainly do worse than marry this girl whom Gerda could so easily control and mould. She had been worrying in case Henry had become a homosexual in America.

Lucius, who had been moved by Colette's young beauty on the evening of the lake incident, was thinking how sad it was to be old and to have no exciting plans any more, and was feeling bitter envy of Henry who could go up flights of stairs like a bird and for whose benefit attractive girls were being schemed for. And he did not particularly look forward to going to see John Forbes. What pretext could he possibly invent? But he felt extreme relief at not having to go to Audrey's. He surreptitiously helped himself to a second piece of cake.

*

Meanwhile upstairs harlequin Henry was looking at himself in the mirror. He was wearing a grey top hat, his own from long ago, which he had found on the floor of the wardrobe. He adjusted the hat, tilted it just that millimetre backward, enlarged his eyes, tucked his dark curly hair away, and glared luminously at himself. Although it was still daylight he had turned on a lamp. The yellow lamplight made his face look haggard but noble, aristocratic. He took off the topper and put on a black beret, also a relic. He narrowed his eyes and let the corners of his mouth droop cynically. Neurotic, dangerous, *louche*. He took off the beret and put on a bowler and smiled with secretive powerful ironic amusement.

He put the hats aside and lay down on the bed, drawing up his knees and clasping his hands behind his head. His gaze was far away. Beside him Calypso, wearing a blue necklace, crouched with plump limbs and gently caressed his body, leaning her lovely bright face towards him. But far-scheming Henry heeded her not. His grave frowning gaze betokened weighty thoughts: desperate plans, destruction and escape.

Henry saw before him now a full-lipped mouth all moist with red sticky lipstick and tears. He saw pink shiny fingernails all lined and cracking. He saw timid pleading round dark blue eyes, gentle eyes. Sandy had behaved like a cad to that girl. Yet in reflecting upon his brother in this new and unexpected role he came nearer than he had ever been since his return to feeling compassion, something which might make a man weep. Sandy was gone. Stephanie Whitehouse remained. He could not let her drift away and vanish, he must control and keep somehow safe and uncontaminated and pure, in a mingled *élan* of piety and revenge, this secret of Sandy's past. Stephanie Whitehouse was his captive, his legitimate booty from this expedition into his brother's life. Money had made her Sandy's prisoner, and would, if he wished it, make her his. He looked forward intensely to seeing her again.

Constant employment was the rule at Pennwood. John Forbes was quietly glad to see that his daughter was never idle. He wondered if this industry was spontaneous or whether Colette was trying to please him. She had cleaned the house from end to end, weeded the garden, washed and mended his clothes. In the evening she watched television or read. She left the book she was reading (purposely?) on the table. *Religion and the Rise of Capitalism.* Her cooking had improved. John could not help being pleased at the improvement in his standard of living.

Where the mind and spirit were concerned matters were a good deal less clear. John was still feeling puzzled and shaken by Colette's unusual outburst on the evening of her arrival. Was it conceivable that he had been a tyrannical father? He could not believe it. He was sure he had never ridiculed his children or made them fear him. He had always treated them as if they were adults, mature free people. He had not pampered them or regarded them as sensitive plants, but that had surely been right. They had been so robust and sensible, his open frank way with them had seemed to be absolutely right from the start. He had always told them the truth, however unpleasant, and they had never cringed. They were a strong pair and when they were young he could have sworn there was not an ounce of silliness in them. Cato's defection still remained to John a totally incomprehensible horror. It had all started with that fashionable sherry-drinking with public school boys from "old Catholic families." And now Colette. John could not conclude that he had been at fault. He certainly could not see himself as a tyrant. Colette had been very tired and nervy on that first evening. They had not reverted to the subject or indeed discussed anything serious since her return.

John, observing his daughter, saw her now as more grown up, less childish. He of course accepted her statement that she was still a virgin, as he knew that she would never lie to him. Sexual adventure had not caused the change. After a while however he decided that what he saw in her was not exactly a new maturity, but some kind of absurd burgeoning of a young girl's confidence. Perhaps it was simply that she had become more attractive and knew it. Colette was now about the age which Ruth had been when John first met her, when they were both studying modern history at Birmingham. Ruth had been stockier, less tall, her hair short and mousy, her face plumper and more like Cato's, not pretty, but with a marvellous calm sage clever humorous expression which made John delight in her at first sight. Colette's face was bonier, more like his own. John and Colette were thin types, John looking gaunter now that his pallid gingery hair was a little grey and getting thin on top. Cato would be stout later, as Ruth would have been. Colette had her mother's limpid brown eyes, but whereas Ruth's eyes had always been screwed up with thought or fun, Colette's were always, as if rather deliberately, wide open, secretively staring, and shining with a sort of power or simply a young girl's self-satisfaction.

John began indeed to conclude that his daughter's air of confident maturity as she performed her simple household tasks was no more (and of course no less) than a perfectly irrational cheerfulness at being good-looking and healthy and young. And after all, why not, he rather grudgingly admitted. As she ran or pranced about the house, long-legged on light feet, deft, half smiling, her long hair plaited now for ease of her work, he felt the power in her, as if some new strong centre of radiation had been placed near to him. It was not an intellectual power, but it was not purely sensuous either, it was a spiritual power, but spirit in a raw young almost fierce almost dangerous almost unconscious form. She is like a young knight, he thought, believing so strangely and so simply in the efficacy of innocence. She dreams perhaps of adventures, of just causes, where her purity will be transformed into courage and power. She thinks that she will be a pure influence, a saviour, that she will save some wretched man "from himself." With a touching insolence she values herself simply because she is an untouched young girl. Poor child. There she is, all ready and prepared to cause endless trouble to herself and to others. All the *training* he had put into her had issued not in the pursuit of learning but in this particular childish sort of spiritual pride. Yet in a way also he was impressed by her and pleased with his own awakened sensibility.

"Daddy, Lucius Lamb is coming up the lane. I saw him from the landing window."

"Lucius? Is he coming here? Well, I suppose he must be."

It was early evening and John had just switched on the lamp on his desk, where he was writing the first sketch of an article. A misty sky of a uniform darkening luminous grey-blue hung behind the garden, where the trees were all hazed and plumped with greenish and reddish buds. Some birds were singing carefully as if threading their songs together in garlands.

John threw down his pen with annoyance. A moment or two later there was a knock at the door and Colette ran down to open. John followed more slowly, seeing through the doorway, brightly illumined by the lamp which Colette had turned on in the porch, the smiling features of Lucius Lamb.

"Hello, Colette, my dear. Hello, John. I was taking an evening stroll and I just thought that I'd call in and see how you were."

"How kind," said John.

Colette stood looking at Lucius with her bright inquisitive wide-open eyes, her hands hanging down in the graceful immobility of youth.

There was a moment of awkwardness which John deliberately prolonged before saying, "Won't you come in?"

He went ahead to the sitting-room, noisily switching on the lights and dragging the curtains across the windows. He turned on an electric fire. He and Colette usually sat in the kitchen. Lucius, holding his cap in his hand, followed, still smiling.

Pennwood, originally called Rosebay Cottage and renamed by Ruth, who also came of Quaker stock, had been built soon after the first war. It was a solid small pretty house. The sitting-room, with its glossy cream-coloured paintwork and its bow window and low window-seat, was a simple pretty room, still unchanged from the days when it had been decorated by Ruth, soon after their marriage. The brown and yellow Leach bowls, the sky-blue pottery candlesticks with the self-same black candles stood where they had always stood upon the painted shelves which framed the fireplace. The woollen rug was Ruth's work. The photographs which she had taken of Greece and framed herself still hung upon the walls. Ruth's money had bought the little house. Her money, what remained of it, had bought the adjoining Oak Meadow, hastily sold because of the boat which Sandy never lived to purchase. An economist colleague had advised John Forbes to turn his savings into land.

John of course saw his old former friend now and then upon the road or in the village, but they had not now had an extended conversation for some considerable time. Since the breach between Pennwood and the Hall seemed to John so inevitable, almost natural, it had not occurred to him to regret the loss of Lucius, whose company he had certainly used to enjoy. Most of John's social life took place at the university, where he usually spent four nights a week during term. At Laxlinden, unless he invited friends to stay, he had little company beyond Bellamy, the schoolmaster Eccles, now away on an "exchange," and acquaintances such as the curate, and Gosling the architect whom he met in the *Horse and Groom*. Lucius never came to the pub, doubtless because Gerda forbade it. John was fond of solitude and always told his academic friends that constant human company would drive him mad. But he could have used the odd talk with Lucius, were it not for Gerda's "grandness," her old hostility to Ruth, the quarrel about the right of way, the coolness about the meadow, and the absurdity of Lucius's own position about which John felt scarcely able to refrain from sarcasm. Lucius had his own touchiness and John his own pride, and so the schism had come to seem a permanent state of affairs.

Now, however, after his first irritation at being interrupted, John felt quite pleased to see Lucius. An old friend, that too after all is a permanent state of affairs. Preliminaries, posturing, fencing, these can be dispensed with. There is an absence of those barriers which as life goes on seem increasingly to divide human beings. Friends made at twenty and retained can keep for each other something of the naïve openness of youth. Lucius in fact was older than John Forbes, already abandoning his thesis for the literary life when John appeared as a student, but they had become close friends, initially, it sometimes amazed John to remember, because John had admired Lucius's poetry.

Colette, who might have sat and talked with them, had decided to be the female ministering angel, and had brought a sherry bottle and two glasses and then retired, still smiling her private smile of self-satisfaction. The scene was cosy. Even Lucius seemed to relax a little.

"Well, Lucius, how's the big book? How I envy you having time to write."

"Oh well, the book, yes. I've decided to shorten it, make it more sort of personal."

"I'm sorry to hear that. We have enough personal books, I should think. I was looking forward to some deep analysis of Marxist concepts."

"You know John, it's awful to say it, but I think I'm through with Marxism at last. I've got the virus right out of my blood. I'm writing poetry instead."

"You can't be serious. Nothing is more important than how we stand with Marx. You've got the knowledge and you've got the time, unlike us working hacks who have to earn our living—"

"I find as I grow older it all seems less interesting. I'd rather think about myself."

"It sounds as if you're ready for a geriatric ward."

"Capitalism, the Soviets, just two methods of government, equally muddled and clumsy, only ours is better because it isn't a tyranny. Socialism is just an out-dated illusion. Ask anybody in eastern Europe."

"Lucius, for God's sake! How did you vote in the last election?"

"I didn't."

"*You didn't?* How can you make sense of things or hope to improve them—"

"I can't, I don't."

"Unless you hang onto Marx? I don't mean Stalin's Marx?"

"I know. You mean the real Marx, your Marx. Every idealist has one. It's like religion."

"You used to be a historian. But I suppose country house life—"

"Frankly, I give the whole thing up. I think Marxism is just an awful mistake."

"All right, forget about Marx if you don't like the name. What about the English tradition, what about—"

"Oh the English tradition is fine, but it's a way of life, not a pseudo-science."

"Lucius. You have become a Tory!"

"Perhaps I am just realizing my limitations at last. Talking about religion, how's Cato?"

"Don't!"

"And Colette—how pretty she's grown."

"She didn't vote either. Christ!"

"Gerda sends you her good wishes, by the way."

"Oh!"

"And Henry sends you his good wishes."

"How's that young squirt?"

"Oh he's—he's much improved—very much improved, I'd say—"

"He could do with some improvement."

"He's taking his responsibilities very seriously."

"What responsibilities? Oh, you mean being rich."

"He's been inspecting the property, he's going to renovate the cottages at Dimmerstone—"

"When is he going back to America?"

"He isn't, he's going to—"

"Lucius, you can't mean what you said about Marxism. Any rational scheme for social justice—"

"By the way, is it true that you're going to build on the Oak Meadow?"

"I haven't the money, if I had I'd build twenty houses like a shot. The housing shortage in the village—"

"So you aren't going to build?"

"The housing shortage in the village is nothing short of heartbreaking—Bellamy was telling me—"

"But to come back to Colette—"

"Housing is the chief social problem today—"

"Has she got a boyfriend?"

"How many rooms are there up at the Hall? Twenty, thirty?"

"I was just wondering if Colette had a boyfriend."

"Colette! How do I know? I'm only her father."

"Not engaged or anything?"

"They don't get engaged these days, they just get pregnant."

"By the way, Gerda sends her love to Colette and—"

"Lucius, what is all this? Does Gerda want to buy the Oak Meadow back?"

"No, no—"

"Because if she does—"

"No, she just sends her love to Colette and hopes to see her up at the Hall, and you of course—"

"Gerda must be getting softening of the brain. Lucius, why don't you come round sometimes? I must set you right about socialism, or won't Gerda let you?"

"You don't understand—"

"I hate seeing you being that bloody woman's pet, any man of spirit would have cleared out long ago."

"It just happens that we love each other!"

"Fiddlesticks! Married people love each other, they have to, they grow together. You and Gerda have been living for years in a stale old fag-end of a sentimental friendship which was only an illusion anyway even at the start."

"You can't speak about other people's lives in that way, you don't know—"

"Christ, I saw it, I *saw* you falling in love with Gerda, it was like a bad film!"

"Of course you thought you had the perfect marriage and everyone else is living in a bad dream—"

"You shut up about my marriage. You encouraged Gerda to laugh at Ruth, you said she was a blue stocking—"

"I didn't—"

"I won't let you speak about Ruth, I won't have her name in your mouth or in the mouth of that snobbish bitch you sponge upon."

"I didn't say anything about Ruth—"

"You did, you implied—"

Colette came in. She had undone her hair, which just combed flowed neatly down her back. She had changed into a billowing ankle-length dress of lilac-coloured cotton. She came in quickly, like someone bringing a message.

Lucius and John rose.

"You look like Athena on our tapestry," said Lucius.

"You mean Gerda's tapestry. Colette, for God's sake keep your skirt out of the electric fire! What have you changed for? There isn't a party."

"Gerda sends you her love and hopes—"

"Colette, I forbid you to go near those bloody people, not that you would anyway. Look, Lucius, I'm sorry, one must be rational and not quarrel, I apologize, do come here and let's talk now and then, but just don't bedevil me with her ladyship and that weed Henry, the mere thought of them makes me want to spew!"

*

Safe at home later, beside a warm log fire, Lucius had been interrogated.

"So he's not going to build on the Oak Meadow?"

"No."

"And she's not engaged or anything?"

"No, free as a bird."

"And they were friendly?"

"Oh very."

"You gave them all my good wishes and so on?"

"Oh yes."

"And they seemed pleased?"

"Yes indeed."

"Those Quakers have their heads screwed on all right. John Forbes was off the mark like a flash when he got wind of the meadow being for sale."

"Mind you, they're proud people."

"Oh I'll be tactful, I'll invite the girl to—"

"Better wait a bit, it doesn't do to be too eager—"

"Perhaps Henry could— Anyway as far as you could see they were interested, that's good, you have done well."

"Thank you," said Lucius.

Henry came in in search of brandy. His presence during dinner had precluded discussion.

"Henry dear, why don't you ask Colette Forbes over for a game of tennis?"

"I can't play tennis."

"I thought you might have learnt in America."

"I didn't." Henry went out, slamming the door.

*

John Forbes, going to bed, said to his daughter. "What the hell was all that in aid of, Lucius Lamb coming round like that?"

"I've no idea," said Colette.

"It beats me. Perhaps he's decided to escape at last. I ought to have been more sympathetic."

"I saw your kestrel again," said Henry.

"Oh, you came that way," said Cato.

"The wasteland is rather dramatic, you get all sorts of views. What are they going to build?"

"A luxury hotel."

"Well, I suppose people need hotel rooms."

"They need cheap hotel rooms."

"I wasn't sure if I'd find you still here."

"You nearly didn't. I'm going tomorrow."

"Where to?"

"To stay with a priest, Father Craddock. I'll give you the address."

Cato had been putting off seeing Brendan until he had thought out his position. Now suddenly, in what seemed to him a merciful collapse into weakness, he had decided to put off considering his position until after he had seen Brendan. Did he then want Brendan to influence him, to say, stay with God, go on loving Beautiful Joe? These ideas now constituted, for Cato, the sum total of heaven: if he could only continue inside his religion and learn from it how to keep that boy near him without somehow destroying them both. He had packed his suitcase. He had summoned Joe to say good-bye. He was not yet sure how he would say it; a short good-bye, a casual good-bye, a portentous good-bye? Cato felt that there was something hard and clear which he ought to say to Joe if he could only find the words. It seemed to him now that their conversation was always the same, always a sort of self-indulgent emotional sparring match, which in some deep subtle way was being organized by Joe. If he could only break through to some kind of real directness, to some kind of *truth* with the boy. Cato did not fail to notice that the prospect of this "break-through" also filled him with self-indulgent emotion, and he wondered how much he ought to, or wanted to, tell Brendan about it. However, he was relieved to be able to feel that nothing could be decided until later on, and also that his good-bye to Beautiful Joe was in no danger of being a final one. The thought that later in the evening he would see the boy again made him, and he did not attempt to evade the knowledge of this, physically disturbed and crazily happy.

Perhaps I should relax more, accept it all, wondered Cato; and then wondered if he were only thinking this because to-morrow he would be safe with Brendan. He also noticed that, in the great metaphysical crisis of his life, he was now thinking more about Beautiful Joe than about God. Was that too because he felt that, soon, Brendan would *tell* him about God, that Brendan was keeping his God safe for him, unhurt by dangerous thoughts? Or was it, more deeply, that in all these troubles he still inevitably, trustfully, and after all without doubt believed in God, knew Him as the ground of his being, and turned to Him for light upon the very thoughts which threatened His existence? Who am I to *think* about God, wondered Cato. Lord, I believe, help Thou mine unbelief.

Henry had arrived unexpectedly while Cato was packing. He was glad to see his friend, but he felt tired and preoccupied and unready to respond to Henry's evident programme of talking a lot about himself. Henry, he noticed, treated him with a naïve and touching trust, as a priest, that is as one who has no problems of his own and is unweariedly prepared to give his whole attention to others.

"I'm sorry this place is closing," said Henry. "I'd have liked it here. I warn you, you are soon going to have an atheistical lay helper following you around."

146

"You mean you? Don't be silly. Anyway, I don't know where I shall be. I don't even know if I'll still be a priest."

"Now, Cato, you are not to lose your faith just when I need it! I can't believe in God, but you can do it for me, that's what priests are for." Henry was clearly unwilling to discuss Cato's difficulty or even to think it existed.

"That's not a bad idea of a priest," said Cato, "but I may not be up to it."

"What happened to that boy, the pretty one with the glasses and the girlie hair?"

"Oh, going to the devil in his own way. He spotted you as a gentleman."

"Discerning child. Cato, you must help that boy. That's just the sort of work I'd like to do, rescuing delinquents."

"It's not easy. He said you were the sort of gentleman who gets thrills from villains."

"He's been reading a psychology book. Anyway I'm glad America hasn't altogether declassed me. But you're not going to leave this sort of work and enter a monastery, are you? You'll have another set-up like this one?"

"Maybe. But what about yourself? What have you been up to since you got home?"

"I'm going to tell you," said Henry. He added, "Oh, I saw Colette."

"Did you? Did you call at Pennwood?"

"No, of course not. Your father always scared the pants off me, he's got such a loud voice. I met her—in the village. She's quite grown up, isn't she."

"Yes, she's a big girl now."

"It's funny being back. All the old rituals still go on, I mean we don't exactly dress for dinner, but it's like that. It all goes on, only it's all dead, dead as a door-nail."

"I expect your mother's relying on you to make it alive again."

"I can't."

"After all it isn't long since—"

"I can't play Sandy's part."

"I wasn't thinking of your playing Sandy's part. Of course you'll do it differently—"

"Ah. So you think I'll do it?"

"Why not? You're not planning to go back to America, are you? You were talking just now about coming to help me. But perhaps you weren't serious?"

Henry did not reply to this. They were sitting in the bare upstairs room, Henry on the bed, Cato on the chair. It was evening, and Cato had just turned on the light, to reveal Henry's small alert face. Henry was clearly in some sort of state of excitement, tangling the small curls of his dark hair into little frizzy balls with nervous fingers, his bright restless eyes darting quick glances at Cato. He seemed half solemn, half inclined to giggle.

"Cato, did you see much of Sandy, while I was away, I mean?"

"No, I hardly saw him at all."

"You didn't see him in London, or—meet any of his friends —or anything?"

"I ran into him at Laxlinden in the village now and then. I asked him to dinner once in London. But look, Henry, I wasn't suggesting you should just become the country squire. You're financially independent now, you can go on writing your book on that painter chap I'd never heard of—"

"I may chuck that."

"Well, a book on something, you're an academic type—"

"Ha ha."

"Or you could do some teaching, if you want to handle delinquents, after all they're everywhere these days. That would make a lot more sense than following me about as you put it."

"I need you in the picture, Cato, I need you."

"What picture? You seem quite excited. Of course you needn't spend all your time at the Hall. Your mother can run it, I suspect that she did most of the work when Sandy was around. You could live in London, Paris, anywhere. But you may as well, even if it's only to please your mother, take an intelligent interest in the place. After all it's got to go on."

"Has it?" said Henry.

"If you want to change the ritual—What did you say?"

"I said, 'has it?' Has it got to go on?"

"Well, hasn't it?"

"I don't see why."

"What do you mean?"

"And what's more, Cato—*it's not going to.*"

"But Henry, what—?"

"I'm going to sell," said Henry.

"To sell—what—?"

"I'm going to sell the whole thing, lock stock and barrel, the Hall, the park, the cottages, the farms, the lot. *Everything.*"

Henry was staring directly at Cato now, his eyes glaring with brightness, his lips trembling with a subdued smile.

Cato hitched up his cassock and crossed his legs. "Look, Henry, you're not serious."

"Why not? What makes you think I'm not serious? Look at me. Don't I look serious?"

"You look crazy."

"It's going to happen, Cato, and it's going to happen very soon, just as quick as I can fix it. It's my property. Property can be sold. They sold the Oak Meadow to pay for an expensive toy which Sandy wanted in a hurry."

"But—why be so extreme—why be so hasty—?"

"You're surprised!"

"You want me to be surprised. Yes, I'm surprised—if you really mean it. But whatever does your mother think?"

"I haven't told her yet," said Henry. He laughed shrilly and threw himself back on the bed for a moment, then resumed his attitude, leaning forward and staring at Cato with bright expectant eyes.

Cato looked into the animated impish face. "Look, Henry, just sober up. You can't do this."

"You mean legally? Of course I can. An estate isn't an heirloom. I've gone into the whole thing with Merriman. I swore him to secrecy. I think he's going to have a nervous breakdown."

"I don't mean legally, I mean morally. It would kill your mother."

"I was waiting for you to say that. It won't you know."

"But you mean—sell everything—sell the whole place—where would your mother live?"

"Oh I've thought that all out. You know we own Dimmer-

149

stone. Well, there are two derelict cottages there which could be made into quite a nice little house, there'd even be a decent garden."

"You can't expect your mother to leave the Hall and go and live in a cottage at Dimmerstone."

"Two cottages. Why not? *Why not?*"

"Well—she'd be miserable, she'd die of shame."

"Shame? Shouldn't she feel shame to be living in a big empty house when people are homeless? Isn't what you've just said topsy-turvy?"

"I'm not saying what she ought to feel, I'm saying what she'd feel. And then there's Lucius—"

"Is there?"

"Where's he to go? Is he to live with her in the little house?"

"Look, Cato, I don't care a fuck where Lucius goes. When I've told my mother all about this I'm going to give Lucius a pretty strong hint to take himself off. He's sponged on her long enough, and she's fed up with him. He drinks, and he shouts at her, and she shouts back. I've heard them at it having screaming matches."

"People can have screaming matches and love each other."

"You're not suggesting my mother cares for that old charlatan? Don't let's talk about Lucius or I shall start getting angry. She'll be jolly relieved when I boot Lucius out."

"But what'll she live on?"

"She's got a perfectly good annuity of her own, quite enough to keep her in comfort in Dimmerstone. After all, she's old now, she's had her life. She wearing herself out trying to keep that ridiculous place going, she's always working in the house or the garden. It's about time she retired and sat still."

"That may not be the way she sees it. But, Henry, you can't— I mean, what are you going to do—just sell it all anyhow, to anybody?"

"Not quite. I thought at first I might develop the place myself and make it into a model town—"

"A model town?"

"But it would be too difficult and I don't really see myself as Maecenas, what I want is negative action. I don't want to go on and on being absorbed in the place and making decisions and having responsibilities and so on, that would just feed my sense of property. I want to get absolutely rid of it all and be free. I'm going to split it up into lots. The bit round the lake would go with the Hall, and the Hall could make some sort of institution, like a school or a training college. I'd sell the farms to the farmers who lease them and the Dimmerstone cottages to the local labourers. Then the upper park on the Laxlinden side could be a housing estate for the village. There's that young architect chap Gosling who built those council houses near the motorway, he would do a good job—"

"But wait, stop—I can see that you might want to help the village, in fact you *ought* to help the village, and sell the cottages cheap to the people who want them and so on—but why rush into selling everything? Besides, what happens next? There you are with a lot of money instead of a lot of land, what will you do with the money?"

"Give it away."

"Who to?"

"Anyone. To the Laxlinden Rural District Council, to Shelter, to Oxfam, to the National Art Collections Fund, to you, to that boy with the golden hair—"

"To me?"

"Yes, to finance your next Mission, or whatever it's called. Why not? You could use money, couldn't you?"

"Yes, but—"

"Can't you see that I just want to *get rid* of it all?"

"All right, and maybe you should get rid of plenty of it and do some good, but I don't think you ought to sell the house and—"

"Why ever not? What value are you defending here? Because bloody Marshalsons have lived at the Hall ever since—?'

"Not while your mother's alive. And somehow—yes, I am surprised—your childhood home—"

"Cato, you make me ill! My childhood home! I loathed my childhood, most people do. Do you care tuppence for Pennwood?"

"Well, not exactly—but I'd like to see Colette living there one day with her husband and children."

"Colette with—Cato, you shock me, I thought you'd applaud."

151

"You should consider your mother."

"Why?"

"Because she's your mother."

"As far as I'm concerned she just counts as one."

"That can't be true. And I think you're rushing into this in some insane frame of mind, you haven't really seen what you're doing. Why don't you wait?"

"Because I might change my mind."

"Well, there you are."

Henry was still leaning forward, his lips moist and weirdly smiling. He reached out a hand and touched the black stuff of the cassock, caressed it a moment. "Yes, but don't you see. I know I'm in the truth now. I *know*."

"It's all so irrevocable, so destructive—"

'Destructive, yes. But there are good destructions, Cato. You know, you do shock me. You are a holy priest, you possess nothing yourself, but it seems that in a deep way you've still got an old irrational reverence for property."

"Oh maybe—I don't care if I have, after all there's property and property. I just feel you're tearing things to pieces for the sake of doing so, and if you even admit you'll regret it later—"

"I said if I didn't sell now I might change my mind. That's different. Cato, I don't want to let myself become the person who will change my mind. I don't want that property to *get* me, I don't want to be corrupted by it, I don't want to give it my precious life."

"I don't see why you'd have to give it your precious life. You could be teaching art history in Edinburgh. You could even go back to America."

"No. If it continues to exist it will get me. I don't want to become like Sandy, a sort of playboy, keeping a tart in a flat and—"

"I don't imagine Sandy kept tarts in flats!"

"No, I'm just generalizing. I mean a sort of bloody useless squire with a yacht and a racing car and fussing about my plants and trees—"

"But, Henry, why should you become like that?"

"My mother's living in a sort of feudal dream world. It's all false, it's a lie, and I'm going to smash it up."

152

"I think one should go easy on smashing other people's lies. Better to concentrate on one's own. There are hundreds of things you can do with the place. Why not compromise? There's even a sort of innocence in having property, you could work on it, modify it, develop it—"

"I'm surprised to hear *you* suggesting making a god out of material possessions! No, I hate the whole bloody set-up, I hate it and I'm not going to become part of it. Didn't Jesus say sell all you have and give to the poor?"

"Yes. But listen, consider your motives."

"And he didn't say do it from the highest motives."

"No, but He thought that motives were important."

"When?"

"When the woman broke the vase of very precious ointment."

"He was just answering the skin-flints. And he didn't say to her like you're saying, wait, think it over, this stuff is valuable—"

"So you admit your motives are lousy?"

"I can't be bothered with them. Of course they're complex."

"You're taking revenge."

"Who on?"

"On your mother. On your father. On Sandy."

"There'll be a certain satisfaction," said Henry, "I don't deny it." He drew his feet up under him and stared at Cato, catlike, electric, fascinated by himself.

"Don't do it. It's a crime. As you're doing it, it's a crime."

"Maybe. But my guilt won't rub off on the money. Money's clean."

"You have a duty to your mother."

"Didn't you have a duty to your father?"

"You'll plunge her into misery."

"You underestimate her. She'll pick herself up and live to be the scourge of Dimmerstone."

"And somehow you'll wreck yourself."

"I'm saving myself. My mother and that place together could just about digest me."

"You want to destroy the past. You must wait."

"I can't wait, Cato, and I won't. I want to dump this load. Christ, you gave up the world, why can't I?"

"You aren't necessarily called to do what I'm called to do."

"That sounds like spiritual pride."

"You're filled with hate. I can feel it now, like electricity."

"Cato, I don't believe in God and you do. Perhaps that makes the difference. I don't think anything very coherent goes on in my soul. There aren't any witnesses. Of course it's full of old irrational rubbish, the sort of muck people love picking over in psychoanalysis. I don't care. The thing is to act decently and make practical plans for going on doing so. Can't you see?"

"I see what you mean," said Cato reluctantly, "but—"

There was a faint creaking sound on the landing outside and Cato, suddenly blushing, got up. "Oh hang!"

Henry rose.

Cato opened the door and Beautiful Joe sidled in, smiling.

"Oh hello," said Henry, "it's you."

"Hello, it's me."

"Well, I'll be off," said Henry. "My car's probably been arrested by now, it's on a yellow line." They stood awkwardly. "Could you let me have your new address? Try to see my point, Cato."

"Try to see mine. Don't do anything yet." Cato wrote down the address.

"I can't think why you care so much. Ah well. Good-bye, Cato. Good-bye—I've forgotten your name—"

"Joe."

"Good-bye, Joe." Henry vanished.

Cato uttered an incoherent exclamation and sat down on the bed. Joe swung the chair round and sat down on it astride, leaning his chin on the back.

"I say, does that rich guy really want to get rid of his cash?"

"So you were listening?"

"Yes, a bit. I didn't want to bust in, you know. But does he really want to give it away?"

"No," said Cato. "He'll change his mind. People who have a lot of money very rarely give it away. Some invisible hand prevents them."

Cato felt so agitated he wanted to cry out incoherently. He was angry with himself because he had been upset by Henry and had not been able to argue with him effectively or even to understand why he felt so disturbed. He was annoyed with Henry for having come. He had wanted to wait peacefully for Beautiful Joe's arrival, to think about Joe and to welcome him calmly. There was some crucially important illuminating thought about Joe which would have come to him if only he could have waited quietly instead of being interrupted and annoyed by Henry. "Oh *hell*!" said Cato.

"What's the matter, Father?"

"Nothing. I'm tired."

"He thinks the world of you, doesn't he, that chap, the gent?"

"I don't know. We're old friends."

"You're going away," said Joe. "You've packed your case."

Cato stared at the boy while Beautiful Joe's enlarged yellowish eyes blinked through the glasses, looked and looked away. He had evidently just washed his hair and, neatly combed, it stood out a little round his head like a wiry golden wig. He had tilted his chair and was swinging it upon two legs, casting a grotesque shadow upon the stained wallpaper.

Cato had a quick fantasy. He would reach out one hand, grasp the back of the chair and gently pull it. Joe, understanding, would shift the chair, jerking it forward like a wooden horse. Cato's arms would reach out around the boy's neck, the radiant golden hairs suddenly outspread upon the dark stuff of the cassock. Joe would sigh and drop his head forward onto the priest's bosom, and the chair would slip sideways to the ground. Awkwardly embraced they would fall back together onto the bed.

"What are you thinking, Father?"

"About you."

"What about me?"

"Don't get yourself into any awful trouble."

"I won't. I promise!" The glinting screwed-up eyes, bright with youth and dishonesty and laughter, returned Cato's gaze. "When are you going?"

"Tomorrow."

"Where to?"

Cato was silent.

"You will give me your address?"

Cato said after a moment, "No."

"But you gave it to him. Father, you're not—leaving me—you're not going to abandon me, are you?"

"No."

"Then, why? Are you afraid I'll come round with the gang?"

"What gang?"

"I'm just joking. But why won't you tell me?"

"I'll write to you at your mother's."

"I don't want to go to her for your letter, Father. I'd rather do without."

"Then you'll do without."

There was a tense silence, Joe rocking the chair, Cato quiet upon the bed. Cato's legs were trembling, he hoped invisibly.

Joe said, "I care for you a lot. Father, you know that. You're about the only person I do care for. But you're like so hostile to me now, you know you sort of tease me and reject me. You make me feel all anxious and frustrated. Why can't you be open and honest with me, or do you really think I'm bad? I wish you wouldn't go away. You ought to stay here with *us*, not go away to *them*. You will come back, won't you? Will you promise? Will you promise not to leave me ever?"

"Joe, I can't promise anything," said Cato. "You know I care for you. Oh God—"

Joe tilted the chair abruptly back onto the floor. "Father, it isn't good-bye, is it?"

"No, no."

"You can always write to me care of the corner shop."

There was silence. Cato's desire to touch the boy was so intense, he lifted up his right hand and looked at it with amazement. If he now took Beautiful Joe in his arms would it be a means of salvation or simply the end of any possibility of grace?

"Aren't you taking *Him* with you?" Joe, now suddenly smiling, was looking up above Cato's head at the metal crucifix which hung over the bed.

Cato realized that he had not thought about it. "Yes."

"I'll get Him down."

In a second Joe had sprung up onto the bed. Cato rose quickly and stood aside. The boy handed down the crucifix to him. For a moment, one at each end, they both held it. "Wouldn't do to forget Him, would it, Father?"

"We must never forget Him,' said Cato. "Joe, hold onto your faith, won't you. You were born to it. It's so precious. Hold onto Christ. Never mind what it means. Just hold on. Now go please. I promise I will write to you. God bless you, dear Joe."

The boy, who had leapt lightly to the floor, stood for a moment and his eyes were suddenly guileless and vulnerable, childish, ready for tears. Then he lightly touched the sleeve of the black cassock and left the room without a word.

Cato laid the crucifix down on the pillow and sat down beside it upon the bed. He buried his face in his hands. As the great sea of emotion gradually became calm he began to feel a deep refreshing happiness.

Gerda was standing in the ballroom. It was rather dark and full of people. She was wearing a long white dress and a white lace shawl and white evening gloves, and feeling expectant and excited. She could see the garden visible in a lurid green twilight outside. Sandy in evening dress was coming towards her through the throng and she felt intense joy. So he is not dead, she thought, I only dreamed that he was dead. It was just a nightmare after all. He came up to her and without speaking lightly took her two hands and, in a space cleared by the guests, they began to dance. There was no music but a kind of throbbing sound. Gerda understood that it was a Scottish dance and that she must watch Sandy's feet and copy his movements exactly. It is some sort of magic spell, she thought, and if I make any mistake something dreadful will happen. It was difficult to dance because it was becoming very damp underfoot and now they were dancing on wet stones. Sandy let go of her hands and moved away down some steps to where a motor boat was waiting. Gerda could see the steps far down under the water. Sandy stepped lightly into the boat, which ducked at his weight. Gerda tried to follow, but felt an iron bar across her breast. Sandy held up a warning hand. I must have got the dance wrong, thought Gerda with anguish. He started the motor which throbbed with some deep silent rhythm. As the boat drew away she could still see Sandy's white shirt front in the darkness. She clutched at the iron bar and screamed.

She awoke with the cry upon her lips, not sure if she had uttered it. The sense of Sandy's presence was so intense she lay still for a moment and let it overwhelm her. Then she sat up. She could see from the curtains that it was getting light. Feeling stiff and heavy she pushed back the bed-clothes and put her feet down, still clutched by the dream. Reluctant to turn on a lamp, she hobbled across to the window and pulled back a curtain to look at her watch. It was a quarter to six. She looked out at the garden, looking across the sloping lawn to the grove of the big trees. Above them a half-moon was still bright. The garden was present but colourless and utterly quiet, still wrapped in the dissolving mystery of its night life, not yet animated by the simplicity of day. Gerda, in her flimsy night-dress, shivered with cold. Then with a gasp she saw a dark motionless figure standing upon the lawn, a little to her right, and gazing up the hill towards the trees. The figure was nothing but a black smudge, but Gerda knew from its shape and its unmistakable attitude that it was Henry. Fearing to be seen, she stepped quickly away from the window and went back to sit upon her bed. Awful dread and misery rose up in her heart. She could still feel the light touch of Sandy's fingers as he tried to guide her through the complicated dance. She shuddered with fear, fear for herself, for her sanity, for her continued being. She thought of the awful desolation of old age and death which she could share with no one. Tears welled up and filled her eyes and her throat and she lay back moaning upon the bed.

*

Lucius was awake too. He had had one of his bad nights. He decided to see his doctor, though he knew that his doctor could do nothing for him and would be concerned only to get rid of him politely. His lower teeth were climbing up and he felt as if he might swallow them at any moment. He took them out, and after fumbling vainly for the bedside table, dropped them on the floor. He sat uncomfortably with his pillows all awry watching the daylight come. Then he got up and went to the window to see the first cold sunlight touching the reddish tops of the woodland. He could not stay still, but twisted and paced, entertaining his various pains. He kicked his teeth away under the bed. He put on his glasses and stared at the table where he had sat up late last night composing.

> Tell her I was young once and star-bright
> Who am now invisible ...

Only I am not invisible, thought Lucius. I can still make a perfect idiot of myself. Why on earth had he lied to Gerda about John Forbes? To save himself a moment's discomfort he had acted in direct opposition to his own interests. The longer Gerda cherished this idea about Colette the more obstinately devoted to it she would become. Why had he not truthfully and firmly warned her off it? Did Lucius want Henry to marry Colette and live happily ever after at Laxlinden? No, of course not. He wanted Henry to go back to America and leave him and Gerda in peace. His feeble inability to look after his own welfare disgusted him. He felt ashamed of his muddle-headedness, of his mean envy of Henry's youth, of his stupid stiff aching body with which nobody would sympathize, of his decayed intelligence, of his age, of his mortality. He recalled with distress and resentment his talk with John Forbes, and shuddered at the picture of himself which he had glimpsed in John's mind. I lead a worthless life, he thought, I live in unreality and untruth. If only there could be total change, regeneration, escape. If only I could run and run and get back to the people, back to where real wholesome, ordinary life is being lived. I have given myself a mean role and cannot now stop enacting it. Oh if only I could get out! But even as he thought these familiar thoughts he knew: unreality is my reality, untruth is my truth, I am too old now and I have no other way.

*

"Did you see any sign of a ring in Sandy's room?" Gerda asked.

"A ring? No." Henry, wolfing toast, had made a brief appearance at breakfast-time.

"You know the ring I mean. The Marshalson Rose."

"The thing you used to wear, with rubies and diamonds?"

"Yes. It's the Marshalson engagement ring."

"Why aren't you wearing it?"

"I gave it to Sandy. I hoped—"

"I didn't see it."

"I expect it's there somewhere. It's in a blue velvet box."

"A blue velvet box? Wait a moment." Henry vanished, returned quickly with a box in his hand. "Is this it?"

"Yes."

"It's empty. I thought it was for cuff-links. No ring."

"I expect you'll find it. It must be somewhere there."

"Why do you want it? No one's getting engaged that I know of—"

"Well—it's a valuable ring. Rhoda, dear, could you go, there's someone at the door. I expect it's Bellamy. The mower has got into the marsh again."

"No, it's Gosling the architect."

"Henry, you don't need an architect to fix up those cottages at Dimmerstone. Regan the builder will do it."

Henry was gone.

"You're very silent," said Gerda to Lucius.

"I'm in pain."

"I'm worried about that ring."

"Henry will never marry Colette Forbes."

"Why is everyone so rude to me these days? Henry's rude, you're rude. Can't you even try to be pleasant?"

"No."

"Why not?"

"I'm in pain."

*

"Colette—"

"Oh, Mrs. Marshalson—"

Gerda had driven Lucius to the doctor's surgery. Now, shopping in the village, she had met Colette.

Colette was in jeans, her tail of polychrome brown hair

160

tucked down inside her speckled blue sweater, the shorter locks blown into tangles, her cheeks shining and red in the east wind. Gerda was tucked up in furs.

"Cold, isn't it."

"These spring days are icy."

"April's worse than February."

"Colette, won't you come up and see us at the Hall? Henry would be so pleased."

"Well, I—"

"Please come. Come to tea or for a drink. What about to-morrow?"

"I'd love to, only I have to go to London. Perhaps I could ring up—"

"Yes, do. Just invite yourself. We'd all love to see you. How charming you're looking, my dear. I love your sweater."

"It's Norwegian. I love your coat. Is it mink?"

"Oh, nothing so grand. At your age you can wear anything and look lovely."

"But Mrs. Marshalson, *you're* lovely—I don't know if any-one ever told you—but you're, well, even now—someone must have told you when you were young—"

"Well, that was a long time ago. I must run now. Come and see Henry, he'll be so delighted."

When Gerda reached the car Lucius was already sitting in it.

"What did the doctor say?"

"Nothing."

"What did he give you?"

"Nothing."

Gerda drove in silence for a minute.

"Why, there's Henry." She stopped the car. "Want a lift home, Henry?"

"No thanks."

"Was that Merriman you were with? He vanished so quickly. He's very elusive these days. If you walk back you'll meet Colette Forbes. She was asking after you."

Gerda pulled the car out and drove on towards the Dimmer-stone road. Lucius, looking over his shoulder saw that Henry had not turned back towards the village, but was proceeding along the lane, stretching out his hands on either side and executing dancing steps. Gerda, glancing into the driving-mirror, could see nothing because her eyes were full of tears. When she was young there had been scores, hundreds, to laud her beauty.

"Oh, I'm so glad. I thought perhaps you wouldn't come."

"But of course I've come. I said I'd come."

"I'm so relieved."

Henry had telephoned Stephanie Whitehouse and invited himself to lunch.

For the last two days, since his talk with Cato, Henry had been in a state of unholy excitement. He felt that he had been struggling with demons, and the struggle itself, whatever exactly its outcome, had given him a kind of satisfaction. He had been shaken by Cato's opposition; so much so that he had, without changing his mind, allowed it to haze over a little, to become, in relation to his project, cloudy. He felt instinctively that after a period of comparative vagueness he could return to a greater certainty. And this instinct, this slight warding-off movement, had made it easier for him to do what he now more immediately wanted to do, think about Stephanie Whitehouse. In fact the two things hung together. Until he had somehow "settled" Stephanie he could not, would not be worthy to, proceed with any drastic plan concerning his mother.

Henry had, since his first meeting with Sandy's mistress, watched himself with interest and with a kind of glee. It was as if for a brief while he had allowed himself to be "taken over" by his brother. He could scarcely doubt that it was open to him to "keep" Stephanie Whitehouse in exactly the same way and on exactly the same terms. As he had gloatingly thought, lying on his bed soon after that extraordinary first meeting, she was his prisoner. She would not run away. She would, submissively, wait. Yet as those visions, with a remarkable speed, proliferated and developed, he attempted too to resist them.

How could he so grossly classify another human being? This girl had loved Sandy. Why should she care for Henry? Because she had once been a prostitute why should he assume that she would welcome him as a lover? They were two strangers who had just met. Why should a myth out of the past determine their dealings? Stephanie was a mystery, a secret, something to be warily studied. And even supposing, because she was his dependent, as it were his serf, she were to take him into her bed, did he want that? The idea of her certainly excited him. But was not this a weird, perhaps bad excitement, something to do with Sandy? Did Henry want a serf, especially now when he was about to defeudalize his life? What an amazing problem. He found himself smiling as he reflected upon it.

Of course Henry knew that he would have to see her again and that everything in his world was waiting for this meeting. And, Henry knew, this would be no mere business meeting, but a part of the deep drama, the very metaphysics, of his life. Simply to "pay her off" and say good-bye, which would certainly be one solution, was morally and psychologically impossible. He was responsible for Stephanie Whitehouse and he must rise to the level of this responsibility. He must go to her in simplicity and in honesty, respecting her, seeing her as secret and separate, seeing her as free. He must shake off all the seedy obviousness, the banal smirking vulgarity, which could so easily demean his view of the situation. He must purge his excitement. He must become humble.

So he had felt, and for this reason he had put off his visit; for this reason too, though he had no intention of mentioning her, he had gone to Cato, juxtaposing with his thought of her his own plan for his salvation. Now, with that plan for the moment postponed, he felt the urgency of testing himself. Yes, it was a test, a trial. And if he could with Stephanie "get it right," then he would feel in the matter of his mother that much more confident. Thus had he wrestled with himself. But when he at last lifted the telephone, and when, soon after, he made his way to Knightsbridge, entered the lift, and walked on the yellow carpet towards her door, the wildest emotions filled him and all careful thoughts and plans were obscured.

Stephanie Whitehouse looked different, younger, prettier.

Perhaps it was just that she had taken greater care with her appearance. Probably she had had her hair done. It was sleeker, wavier, curving with her head. Her slightly bouncy smallness, the wide tilted nose, the roundness of her head, her face, her eyes gave the effect of a little horse. She was, in a way which startled Henry, new, a presence. Her face was ostentatiously but carefully made-up, the pouting lips scarlet, the eyelids mauve, the line of the eyes discreetly pencilled. There was a pleasant warm smell in the flat.

Henry, without extending his hand, moved rather awkwardly past her into the sitting-room, as if he were pushing his way in.

They stood in the room, beside the red leather sofa, looking at each other. Then Henry stretched out his hand and she not even pretending a handshake, took his hand, his wrist, in both of hers. It was a grab, a clutch. Henry's fingers gripped her cuff. Then, both breathing deeply, they stood apart. Henry said "What a lovely warm sunny day, isn't it."

"Yes, it's like spring at last."

They looked at each other with wild eyes.

"You didn't mind my just suddenly inviting myself?"

"No, no—But I haven't had time to cook anything or—"

"But that's lovely, a picnic—"

"Yes—a picnic—"

Today she was smarter, wearing a black linen pinafore dress with a flowery blue blouse foaming out at the neck. Henry lowered his gaze, seeing how the linen curved over her rather large bosom, seeing her breathing. He looked down at her glistening black high-heeled shoes. He was reminded of the little elegant hooves of a young donkey.

"Won't you take your coat off? Would you like a drink?"

"Thank you. Sherry. I see you have some."

"I got—You gave me so much money—"

"Please don't speak about money, Miss Whitehouse."

He dropped his coat on the floor. She picked it up and took it away into the hall. Then she poured out a glass of sherry and gave it to him. Her movements seemed to him gentle and humble, indescribably graceful. Doubtless a geisha would move like that.

"Mr. Marshalson, I'm so grateful—"

"I wish you'd call me 'Henry.'"

"Oh thank you—but then please—could you please call me 'Stephanie'?"

"Stephanie. Thank you. But you haven't given yourself a drink—won't you—sorry, I seem to be offering you your own sherry!"

"But it's your sherry."

"It isn't. Look, are you all right? I mean—has everything been all right—since I was here?"

"Oh yes, yes. I've been just waiting for you."

"I'm sorry I didn't come sooner. I've been busy down at the Hall. I suppose you never—went there with Sandy—no, well, of course not—"

"Went—?"

"To the Hall, to Laxlinden."

"No."

"It's a beautiful place. Well, you can see from the picture."

"The picture?"

"Yes, here, this water-colour. Did Sandy never tell you that that was his house?"

"He hardly ever talked about it—perhaps he knew I didn't want to hear about that other life—of course I couldn't go there—"

Henry looked into the picture. Francis Towne, seated probably upon the obelisk hill, had painted an April evening, the southern façade a light brilliant gold in the sun, the big trees in first leaf, casting their huge round shadows upon the green slope, the blue sky scattered with little radiant clouds. He turned back to Stephanie. Her eyes were full of tears.

"He was secretive. I was just a little part of his life. He didn't tell me things."

"Oh—Stephanie—I'm so sorry—"

He extended his hand again and this time she took it in a handshake grip. They looked at each other. The tears, unwiped, overflowed her eyes. One leapt onto her bosom.

"I'll just go and—see the lunch is ready. It's in the kitchen. I hope you don't mind."

With a quick embarrassment she withdrew her hand, dashed the tears away and hurried from the room. Left alone Henry

165

circumnavigated the absurd sofa and went to the window, grimacing with excited tenderness, pity, a desire to laugh, a desire to cry. Then he followed her into the kitchen. They sat down to lunch.

Stephanie's "picnic" was simple but extensive: ham, salami, a meat pie, olives, tomatoes, a potato salad, a green salad, sliced cucumber in yoghurt, cheese, celery, an apple tart. Also a chilled bottle of rather good white wine. Sandy had evidently taught her something.

Henry, usually a hungry man, found that he could eat nothing. It was simply impossible. He pretended to fiddle with ham and cucumber. He noticed that Stephanie too was only pretending to eat. Some more tears came, she tried to conceal them. He drank some wine and felt immediately drunk.

"Are your parents alive?"

"No."

"Brothers, sisters?"

"No, no one."

"And you ran away from home?"

"Yes, when I was fourteen."

"What did your father do?"

"He was a labourer. I never got on with him. He beat my mother. Please let's not talk about it."

"I'm very sorry. I do understand."

"I wish you'd tell me—Sandy never told me anything—I don't even know—"

"About me, us? My father died a long time ago when I was a small boy. My mother's still very much alive down at the Hall. There was only Sandy and me of course."

"Your mother must be so sad. Sandy did mention her sometimes. How much I should like to meet her—but of course that's impossible—"

"It's not impossible," said Henry. He put his fork down. "There's no earthly reason why you should not meet my mother." He looked into the round moist dark blue eyes. Feeling slightly giddy he looked away again.

"Oh no—"

"Look, Stephanie," said Henry. "By the way, I want to hear you call me 'Henry.'"

"I feel I—all right—Henry—"

"Good. Now look. What's past is past. I mean, I don't regard you as—I'm not trying to step into Sandy's shoes—"

"Of course not—" The tears overbrimmed again and she began to mop her face with a paper napkin, smudging the lipstick about.

"I mean—I want us to be friends, I want to know you as you, for real, I—I won't ever abandon you, Stephanie—oh my dear, please don't cry—" Henry got up and came round the table. Stephanie rose and the next moment, with all the naturalness in the world, he had taken her in his arms. Her hands gripped his sleeve. Her hot wet smudgy face was buried against his jacket, and he felt her wild captive heart pounding against his own.

Very gently he led her to the bedroom.

"I heard from Gerald Dealman," said Brendan.

"Where is he now?"

"He's running an encounter group in Glasgow."

"I wonder how long that will last. Any news of Reggie?"

"He says he's become a Buddhist, but we assume that's a joke."

"I hear Father Milsom is still ill."

"Yes, poor old man."

"Do you remember Sandy Marshalson? I brought him in to dinner once."

"That tall red-headed drunk who smashed himself up in his Ferrari, not on that night, thank heavens?"

"Yes. We were all rather sozzled that night."

"I wonder if he was drunk when he killed himself. He seemed to me a man filled with desperation."

"Poor Sandy. Well, his brother's back, I think you never met him, Henry Marshalson, he was in America."

"I remember you mentioned him. Your childhood friend. I suppose he's inherited that big place."

"Yes, but he's going to sell it and give the money away."

"Good for him. Who to?"

"He wants to give it to us."

"Us? Oh *us*. Grab it quick before he changes his mind."

"His mother won't like it."

"It'll make a change for the good old lady."

Cato was irritated because he felt that Brendan, having virtually summoned him in order to have a "serious talk," ought not to be carrying on the trivial gossip which had now lasted all through supper. Cato, continuing the gossip and bored by it, was determined not to be the first to speak seriously. Of course Brendan, who had been teaching all day, was tired. Or perhaps he thought that Cato was tired and would want to go to bed and not to have to talk late upon grave subjects. But Cato did not want to go to bed, he wanted to talk properly to Brendan, only Brendan would go on and on being flippant.

Cato had had his lunch at a pub and had arrived at Brendan's flat in the afternoon, letting himself in with the key which was always left under the mat. Alone in the flat he had given himself the luxury of a hot bath, and had then lain down in the little slit of a room which was Brendan's spare bedroom. He had at once gone to sleep and had been awakened by Brendan's arrival home. They had drunk some wine and eaten some of an excellent stew which Brendan, who was quite a good cook, had made on the previous day and heated up. Cato, now drinking whisky, was walking restlessly about the room, stopping to examine Brendan's books, then pacing again. Brendan, not drinking, had taken his shoes off and was lying flat on the sofa with his feet up on one of the arms. Sometimes his eyes closed. Hang it, thought Cato, I suppose he wants to go to bed.

Brendan lived in a small flat in Bloomsbury, circled about ceaselessly by traffic whose noise the double-glazed windows muted to a steady murmur which soon ceased to hold the attention. There was, especially now with the lamps on and the thick curtains pulled, an atmosphere of secluded quietness. Brendan came of an old Catholic family, the sort of "public school Catholics" whom Cato's father regarded with such suspicion. He had come straight from Downside to train for the priesthood and had studied at Oxford when already a priest. He lived simply, but his narrow room somehow reflected confidence and ease. The silk-fringed lamps cast a subdued golden light and the long central rug, which lay upon other rugs, was a sort of embroidery of brown and golden roses which one hesitated to step upon. An ivory Spanish crucifix, the Christ figure only, very pale and blood bespattered, hung against a black velvet curtain.

"What's Henry Marshalson doing besides selling his patrimony?"

"He's writing a book on a painter called Max Beckmann."

"Oh yes. A rather frenetic German symbolist."

"I'd never even heard of him."

Cato looked down on his reposing friend, was he really falling asleep or was he watching Cato through those rather long eyelashes? Brendan was good-looking and foppish, wearing a well-cut black suit with his dog collar, a black velvet jacket in the evening. He was tall, with glossy straight black hair and brilliant blue eyes. Cato had disapproved of him at first, taking him to be merely a charmer. As often happens it was Brendan's cleverness which taught Cato to see his virtue.

Cato thought, if he goes on chatting until I've finished my whisky I shall go to bed. It had also occurred to him, as if he had been somehow informed by Brendan's books, by the golden lamps, by the crucifix, that Brendan, whether in a sense he liked it or not, now represented authority. Cato was sure Brendan had not told anyone else in the order about Cato's doubts. But Brendan would have to decide after talking to Cato whether to tell or not, and would then do what he thought right and not what Cato wanted. Perhaps it might be better after all to wait until tomorrow.

"So you're thinking of leaving us," said Brendan, his eyes still apparently closed.

Cato felt relief. There was a change of atmosphere, a change of tempo.

"Can I have some more whisky?"

"Help yourself."

"You?"

"No, thanks."

Cato paced a bit in silence. There was no urgency now.

"I don't know—"

"Not thinking of leaving us?"

"I feel as if—I may have to—"

"Why?"

"I don't believe any more. It's pretty crucial. Of course I don't want to go. But I just don't believe."

"What don't you believe?"

"I don't believe in God the Father or God the Son."

"What about the other fellow?"

"Without them he's either non-existent or non-Christian."

Brendan laughed. His eyes were open now, but he continued in his relaxed position, his hands behind his head. "Well, let's stick to them. What's the absolutely radical central thing which you once believed and now think you don't? What's gone?"

Cato reflected. What had gone? "The person. The person has gone. There's no one there."

"Christ?"

"A holy man. A marvellous religious symbol. But not God. Not the Redeemer. Not the kingpin of history. There is no king-pin, there is no redemption."

"It isn't just the odiousness of Mother Church?"

"No."

"When did you last say mass?"

"I *can't.*"

"Well, let's leave that for the moment. I wonder how you know what you believe and what you don't believe. You were bound to have a crisis in your faith."

"I know. You saw it coming!"

"I saw it coming. We all did."

"Bloody convert."

"Bloody convert. This sort of infantile disorder—"

"Of course you think my faith was born in a drama and never recovered!"

"How well you put it. Yes, it is something to be got over. You've been living on that drama. Now it's simply exhausted. You were in love, you know."

"In love?"

"With Him."

"Oh—Him—yes, I suppose I was. He invaded my life. Everything dissolved, everything fell. Oh God, Brendan, I'm so bloody unhappy." Cato had not intended to say this. The sudden turn of the conversation confused him. He saw the face of Christ as he was accustomed to picture it. Then the face of Beautiful Joe.

"What about that boy?" said Brendan.

"You're telepathic."

"I'm just trying to see the context."

"There isn't a context."

"There must be a context. Your doubts and your speculations live in time. They're not metaphysical entities hanging in the void."

"You're not suggesting it's all caused by—"

"I'm not suggesting anything, I'm just fishing around."

"If you think my motives—"

"Oh, hang your motives—any theory you have about your motives is likely to be humbug anyway."

"I thought you weren't interested in the boy."

"I was, I am."

"Well what can I tell you. I love this child, I'm mad about him, I can't think about anything else."

"Does he know?"

"I'm not sure," said Cato. "No, I don't think so." Did he know?

"You haven't, then, grabbed him or anything?"

"Grabbed him? No of course not!"

"I was just asking. But you have high-minded emotional conversations about his future and so on?"

"Well—yes—"

"Constructive?"

"Not very. But I just can't stop seeing him. It's as if—there isn't any love ... anywhere else ..."

"I understand that."

"But, Brendan, don't get this wrong. My doubts, the way it's all—gone blank and gone dead—that was happening before. It's nothing to do with Joe."

"O.K. Let's leave the boy. You say you feel now there's no one there. Is this a sense of dereliction or an intellectual conclusion or—"

"There is an intellectual conclusion. There must be."

"Why must there be?"

"Because I'm an intellectual being. And because it's a matter of truth. If Christ be not risen then is our faith vain. I mean, it's either A or not-A."

"Of course you are an Aristotelian. Aristotle was the beginning of the end. We've had to spend all the time until now undoing the damage."

"I'm not a philosopher," said Cato impatiently. "And I'm not a Buddhist either, like Reggie Poole! I accept that Christ is the stumbling-block and I stumble."

"We all stumble."

"And please, Brendan, don't do that old thing of trying to persuade me that faith is doubt and doubt is faith and where faith ends faith begins and so on! I know all that."

"Don't be so peevish, my dear. I'm simply trying to see where you are. The priesthood is a long job. It's a marriage. One doesn't rush out instantly when things are dull and the rewards fail."

"I'm not doing that! It's a matter of truth, I tell you!"

"Truth is very complex here," said Brendan. He swung his legs off the sofa and sat up, looking at Cato with his blue eyes which showed their colour even in the dim room.

"When people start saying truth is complex they are usually starting to tell lies. The dogma—"

"There are worlds and worlds beyond the dogma."

"How far can Christianity go beyond the dogma and still remain a religion?"

"As far as the human soul extends."

"That's no answer. Anyway, for you there's no problem. You swim inside the dogma like a fish in water and have done ever since you could talk!"

"Wait a moment, and don't get cross with me. You say that Christ invaded your life."

"Yes."

"Something happened."

"Yes. Now you will say it was all emotion—"

"It seems to me that's what you're saying. Something happened. All right. But shouldn't you let it go on happening?

172

Christ isn't a sort of once-and-for-all pill that you take. He's a principle of change in human life. And a human life takes a good deal of changing. 'Not I but Christ!' Your complaints seem to be all I and no Christ."

"I'm not complaining."

"You said you were unhappy."

"We're not meeting. You're saying let Christ work and I'm saying there is no Christ."

"I think you should wait. Inhibit this state of certainty. And pray."

"I can't pray. I try to, but it's a lie, a level of myself that's a lie."

"Pray all the same. Damn it, you're a priest not a schoolgirl."

"You speak of efficacy. I speak of truth. No meeting."

"Being a priest, being a Christian, is a long long task of unselfing. You are just at the very beginning, Cato, you are now meeting the very first real difficulties. You dress these difficulties up in a certain terminology. I think you should wait a while and consider whether this is the right terminology."

Cato was silent. He sat down opposite Brendan, staring at him.

"I am not saying," Brendan went on, "that you are necessarily wrong in wanting to leave the priesthood. I am saying that you should wait. The spiritual life is a long strange business and you've got to be quiet and docile enough to go on learning. You're doing the strong-man wrestling act, you're still at the heroic stage, you want to do everything yourself. And now that you've got an inkling of what's really involved you're appalled, or the ego in you is appalled. It's like a death sentence. It is a death sentence. Not pain, not mortification, but death. That's what chills you. That's what you experience when you say there is no one there. Up till now you have seen Christ as a reflection of yourself. It has been a comfortable arrangement."

"Really—!"

"You are in a dream state. Ordinary human consciousness is a tissue of illusion. Our chief illusion is our conception of ourselves, of our importance which must not be violated, our dignity which must not be mocked. All our resentment flows from this illusion, all our desire to do violence, to avenge insults, to assert ourselves. We are all mocked, Christ was mocked, nothing can be more important than that. We are absurdities, comic characters in the drama of life, and this is true even if we die in a concentration camp, even if we die upon the Cross. But in reality there are no insults because there is nobody to be insulted. And when you say 'there is no one there' perhaps you are upon the brink of an important truth."

"I don't understand," said Cato.

"You say there is no one there but the point to be grasped is that there is no one here. You say the person is gone. But is not the removal of the person just what your own discipline as a priest has always been aiming at?"

"Well—the human person—"

"And if the human person is the image of the divine?"

"This is philosophy!"

"It's theology, my dear fellow. And you were boasting just now about being an intellectual."

"I can't think—" said Cato, covering his face with his hands.

"Don't try to for a while. I'm not saying anything very odd. Humility is what matters, humility is the key. All this connects with things you were told when you were an ordinand."

"Oh if only I could get back *there*."

"When it was all so simple. It will be simple again later."

"Truth must be simple. You're muddling me with all this talk of illusion. Of course a lot of our goals are illusory goals, illusory goods. But I am not all illusion and I have to judge as best I can with what is best in me."

"Not I but Christ."

"That begs the whole question! Some of the things I do are real—loving people for example."

"Loving people," said Brendan, "is often the most illusory thing of all."

Cato was silent again.

"We're tired," said Brendan. "Let's sleep on it. Come on. Bed."

Cato said, "Have you told *them*?"

"No."

"But you will now?"

174

"Maybe. Probably."

"Uh-huh."

"And, Cato—"

"Yes?"

They had risen and were standing by the door.

"I've got one other piece of advice for you."

"What?"

"Stop seeing that boy."

"I can't," said Cato. He gripped the edge of the door. "I can't abandon him—"

"You mean you can't surrender this pleasure. Are you doing him good? Is he doing you good?"

"I'm the only person who san save him."

"I doubt that. There is hope for him of which you do not dream, because you insist that you and only you must be the vehicle. Let someone else have a try. Give this to God. Make a hole in your world, you may see something through it."

"I can't."

"Give him up absolutely. Don't see him any more at all. You know this is good advice, you know I'm not just being—"

"Yes, I know. But I can't."

"Write to him if you like. But don't see him again. Then go into retreat. I won't say anything."

"Brendan, I can't."

"You talk about truth—but it seems to me you are being totally frivolous and self-indulgent. It's a dream, Cato, you are only saving him in a dream. In reality—"

"*Stop*," said Cato. He pushed out of the room and without saying anything more went into his bedroom and shut the door. He expected Brendan to follow him but Brendan did not and could be heard a moment later going into the bathroom, then into his own bedroom.

Cato sat for a while on his bed beside his half-unpacked suitcase. He thought, Brendan is praying for me. Can I not pray for myself? He did not kneel, but closed his eyes and in the darkness called out silently, as he had done when he was younger. And he gazed into the darkness and the darkness was not dead but terribly alive, seething and boiling with life. And in the midst of it all he saw, smiling at him, the radiant face

175

of Beautiful Joe. This is love, thought Cato, and it is not an illusion and I must be faithful to it and undergo it. And everything to do with his belief and his faith seemed to him at that moment flimsy and boiled and seethed up in this darkness which was his love for Beautiful Joe; and he felt himself confronted with an ineluctable choice between an evident truth and a fable. He opened his eyes and saw the bed, still tousled from his afternoon sleep, and his suitcase with his crucifix lying there on the top. Cato took the crucifix and laid it on the pillow, as he had done on the previous night after Joe had taken it down from the wall and handed it to him, and he recalled the feeling of joy which had come to him then. Why did I feel joy then, he wondered. Was it because of *Him*, because of some moment of divine tenderness when love was suddenly innocent? Or was it because, somehow, confidently, I knew that I would not lose Joe, that I could not lose him, that I had to stay with him and love him, and that everything, Christ Himself, was as nothing, mattered not a straw, compared with that certainty and that future? The joy of yesterday had been quiet, veiled. But now a fiercer joy, a flood, a fire, composed of fear and yet consuming fear, rose up inside him so that he gasped. There is no other path, thought Cato. And if this is what destroys me, then so be it. All is one, there are not two problems, only one. And if there is God, He is on the other side of *this*.

He quietly repacked his suitcase, leaving the crucifix lying on the pillow. Then, after having listened for a while to the silence of the house, he rose, put on his coat, and very quietly opened his door and emerged into the hall.

Brendan, in his dressing-gown, was sitting on a chair beside the front door. He looked very tired.

"I thought you might try and bolt."

"You don't imagine you can stop me?"

"You're a bloody nuisance. I've got a class on the *Timaeus* at nine o'clock tomorrow morning. Well, this morning. It's three."

"I'm sorry, go to bed then."

"Don't go, Cato. It's important that you shouldn't go. I said everything wrong. I was tired. I should have waited. Nothing I said matters, not the details I mean. Maybe I'm wrong about

176

the boy, I don't know enough, maybe everything I said was phoney. But don't go away from this. Wait, stay, rest. Forget about retreats. I won't say anything to anyone. Just stay here."

"What do you want?"

"I'm being selfish. I just want you to be here. Not somewhere else."

"You think I'm going off to some sort of perdition?"

"Nothing so dramatic. Please stay here. So that I can sleep. Because of my class on Plato. Because I'm a priest, and because you're a priest. Because of anything."

"I'm sorry," said Cato. "I'm very sorry." He opened the front door. They looked at each other. Cato said again, "I'm sorry."

He went away down the stairs and heard the door close softly behind him.

It took him forty-five minutes to walk back to the Mission.

Henry was standing on the terrace. Sunlight and shadow were moving steadily across the slope below the big trees, making it seem rather like Francis Towne's picture. Up above a sky of cold brilliant blue was striped with moving layers of *café-au-lait* clouds. The sun was now touching the light grey tower of Dimmerstone church, visible over the woodland trees. The sun was lighting up the tops of the trees and picking out each tree individually. Dimmerstone tower glowed, then was extinguished. On a clear day it was possible, from beside the obelisk, to see both Dimmerstone and the slim spire of Laxlinden church. A damp cold east wind was blowing. Henry had his overcoat on.

Henry's mind was in a gay wild turmoil. He felt as if he were seated on the sail of a windmill, rising and falling, gazing about him, strongly and rhythmically carried, conveyed. He had not intended what had so beautifully happened with Stephanie. Or had he intended it? It was hard to say. He knew that, as far as it lay in him to do so, he had come to her humbly, honestly, willing her good, determined not to take advantage of the strange relationship in which he stood to her. Had he taken advantage of it? With a kind of glee he went over and over the events of those precious hours in his mind. What had happened was extraordinary, wonderful. And really, he felt, it simply couldn't not have happened. Never had love-making been, for Henry, so inevitable and so perfect. And so silent. It occurred to Henry that all his previous mistresses had been Americans, and they had never stopped talking. Especially Bella. Going to bed had been accompanied by a ceaseless running commentary, a stream of jokes. In a way Henry had liked this, though he sometimes had an uneasy feeling that it was designed to reassure him. Before, he had always felt, even with the youngest of the bright young things, that he was the junior partner. They were all so experienced and competent and efficient. They set the pace. Bella even called him "Junior." But with Stephanie he had felt, had perfectly been made to feel, that the world surrendered to his will.

Of course Stephanie too was "experienced." Whatever had it been like for her with all those men? He thought, with a strangely satisfying pity, of her life as a victim. No wonder she did not talk. He felt, when he thought of her, which he now did nearly all the time, a warm frenzy of compassion, a desire to hold her, to protect her, to save her. When he had said to her with such sincerity, "There is no earthly reason why you should not meet my mother," he had felt the pattern of their relationship obscurely change, as if everything were being quietly lifted to a higher level. No, he had not taken advantage of her. He had been right to put off seeing her, to reflect seriously, to attempt to be worthy of what he had discerned as a prime responsibility. He had not failed the test: and this made him now stronger, more able, more free, for the next business of his life. He felt intense gratitude to Stephanie. He felt happily securely obsessed. He did not exactly feel himself, as yet, in love with her, but he conceived that he loved her in a pure way and that was new to him.

The love-making had been good. She had been, with him, curiously awkward, and that had touched his heart. Perhaps a prostitute, not used to tenderness, would be awkward? It had not occurred to him before. He wondered what it had been like with Sandy, and at first the mere idea was horrible. But, with an odd sense of duty, he kept his attention upon it, determined not to be appalled; and gradually this too was transformed for him by the power of transformation which seemed to be emanating from this woman. And Henry felt gentle, humble. He pitied her, he pitied Sandy. He felt that they, and he, we·e all of them victims together, all of them somehow shifted, separated, juxtaposed by the necessary movements of a relentless fate. And this thought comforted him much.

Not least was Henry pleased with himself for his inspired resolution in simply and without preliminaries taking the girl to bed. It was so *right*. She had trembled in his arms as he undressed her, gazing at him with such a look of submissive gratitude in her round blue eyes that Henry himself had wanted to shout out with gratitude and joy. And when he had embraced that plump warm trembling body, those large breasts, he had been carried far beyond doubts. For the first time in his life he felt, without calculation, without thought, quite simply in the right place.

Afterwards they had had tea. Completely, strangely calm, as if he had known this woman for years, Henry lingered on. They talked now, easily, about every sort of thing and their conversation often had the triviality of a converse of old friends. She talked a little about her past, but reluctantly, and Henry did not press her. She was thirty-four, two years older than Henry. She talked a bit about the strip club, and how she was supposed to dance, only nobody taught her to dance, it was just assumed that all women could dance. Henry told her, in a rather muted and selective way, about the Hall, about his childhood, about America, even, with important omissions, about Russ and Bella. He held hands with Stephanie and they talked like confident children. He left her happily, unintensely. "You'll come again soon?" "Yes, I'll telephone you, soon. Don't worry." "I'm not worrying. Thank you, God bless you."

Electric with physical vitality, rejuvenated Henry ran down the steps of the terraces, leaping the last flight onto the springy turf. He bounded away in the direction of the stables, and ran breathless onto the gravel underneath the clock. The sun was shining on the stable block, making the grey-blue slates, wet from last night's rain, glisten dazzlingly. Henry noted that some slates needed replacing, then smiled at himself. He went into the loose box where the yellow Volvo was stabled, and lifted the bonnet and leaned for some time studying the engine with pleasure and satisfaction. Russ and Bella both drove cars but without any conception of engines. Henry had been the mechanic. However could they be managing without him?

In answer to their first letters Henry, unable to utter any serious statement, had sent them each a comically worded picture postcard. To Russ he had sent a card of the Post Office Tower. To Bella he had sent a coloured card of Laxlinden Hall which he had bought in the village. He wrote on the back: *See ancestral home overleaf. Life here is, roughly hell. Missing you, honey.* Today replies had come from both. Russ had countered with a postcard of the St. Louis Arch, and the message: *Redbirds beat Braves. Wish you'd been there. When coming home?* Bella had written a long letter. *When can we come and stay? But, seriously, darling, if it's hell, or even if it isn't, come back to us soon, or you'll have us worried....* Henry was glad to hear from them, he was glad they loved him, glad that they existed, that they were *there*, establishing for him a refuge, another place. But he knew that he would not write to them properly until the next things in his life had been settled. He wondered, where shall I be this time next year? Back in Sperriton, coming home from the campus to Bella's powerful martinis, telling them his day? It seemed, in its separated way, an image of innocent happiness.

Henry closed up the yellow Volvo and shut the door of its house and strolled away in the sunshine, now walking uphill, without crossing the stream, towards the greenhouse. This had been for him, as a child, a mysterious attractive slightly sinister palace, and as he approached it now his heart beat suddenly with old undeclared memories. The greenhouse was a large Victorian cast-iron structure with a big central dome and two smaller supporting domes. Its glory had now mainly departed, the heating system was no more, the decorative tiles were cracked or missing, and much of the glass was broken at one end. Many of the plants and trees, put there by Henry's grandfather and great-grandfather, survived, however, grown into huge ragged forms, pressing against the roof, and on a sunny day perfuming the hot air with exotic smells: camellia, plumbago, bamboo, mimosa, oleander. Bellamy grew his tomatoes and early lettuces under one of the smaller domes and kept the whole place watered, but most of the greenhouse now simply ran wild. Gerda and Rhoda came in sometimes to pick flowers.

Henry entered with a sudden instinctive quietness, almost furtiveness, which must somehow have belonged to his youth. Perhaps he used to hide in here from Sandy, he could not recall. The sudden warmth and the peaty spicy smells made him gasp with memory. A particular smell among the others declared itself, animating a much earlier Henry. Azalea? No, crown imperial. He noiselessly closed the door and stood still. In front of him a vast camellia tree, glossy-leaved and covered with white flowers, rose in an arch, soaring to the roof and bowing to trail along the glass and droop its furthest branches down into a clump of big bamboo. The earth from which it rose was covered with a mauve-flowered aromatic herb whose smell now seemed to Henry dominant in the reminiscent medley. He moved forward, plucked some leaves from the herb and crumpled them beneath his nose. Then, with a little difficulty, he twisted off a camellia flower and put it in his buttonhole. The flowers were double, almost perfectly white, some with a flecking of pale pink in the centre, beneath the stamens. He walked a little, soft-footed, smelling, remembering. The sunlight was curtained on one side by a rampant passion flower which had crawled up the glass almost to the top of the central dome and was now already dotted with its wierd pale green and purple blossoms. Henry looked up, seeing the small intent faces of the flowers above him. Then, in the green shade, he looked forward, under the curving plumes of the bamboo, and stood still, rigid with surprise, seeing a girl.

The girl, oblivious of him, was leaning over intently, her head and shoulders only visible through the foliage, her long hair largely obscuring her face, looking down at something below her. Henry, in another second, from something in the attitude, the hair, the curving cheek, recognized Colette Forbes. He felt pleasure, and stole quietly forward to surprise her.

When he was a few feet away she turned her head, saw him

and smiled, but returned at once to what absorbed her. Henry saw that she was leaning over an old water tank filled with black glossy water which had been set into the midst of the plants to assist watering. Waterlilies grew at one end of it and its surface was scattered with a reddish water weed. Colette had put one hand into the water, and her hand was surrounded by a swarm of little bright goldfish with silvery bellies, who kept darting and wriggling around about her fingers, which showed a slight peaty brown underneath the surface.

"They're eating my fingers!" said Colette, giving Henry her radiant twisted grin.

Henry examined the fish. "Can you feel them biting?"

"Just a little. It tickles, it's so nice."

"There usen't to be fish in here. I wonder who put them in."

"Do you think they get enough to eat?"

"Yes, I should think so. It's become a sort of natural pool by now."

"It's so pretty. The red water weed is enchanting. And the little fish are sweet." She drew out her hand and shook the water drops off it.

"I note that you are trespassing again."

"Do you mind?"

"I'm not sure. I'll think about it."

"I saw you dancing in the lane the other day."

"Why didn't you come and dance with me?"

"I thought it might be a private dance."

Henry inspected Colette. The sun, speckling through the passion flowers, was tracing red and golden lights in her brown hair, and her face, after exposure to a few warm spring days, glowed with a creamier and more transparently youthful hue. She was wearing a summer dress underneath a rather shabby tweed coat.

"You've grown into quite a handsome strapping girl in spite of the fact that you're only ten and your mouth is much too big and your teeth don't meet in the middle."

"You don't look too bad either, in spite of being so small."

"*Small?*"

"Yes. I'm taller than you."

"You're not!"

"Your hair stands up more than mine."

"You're wearing high-heeled shoes."

"I'm not. Let's measure then. Face me, and each of us look absolutely straight ahead. You'll be looking at my mouth and I'll be looking at your eyebrows."

Henry looked straight ahead into Colette's laughing brown eyes. "This is ridiculous. You're thinner than me."

"What difference does that make?"

"It's easier for you to stand up straight. And there's more of me above the eyes than there is of you."

"That's your hair."

"It isn't, it's my brain, I have more brain cells."

"No, you haven't, you're older than me, they disappear thousands a day after you're twenty."

"Rubbish."

There was a faint sound at the other end of the greenhouse. Colette suddenly turned and melted away like an animal into the light and shade of the overarching bamboo. Henry was after her like a flash, but when he got out the door she was already some way off, bounding across the grass towards the drive. He walked after her and she waited for him on the gravel.

"What's the matter?"

"Bellamy came in. Anyway, I've got to get home, I'm late."

"Which way are you going?"

"Your way, over the gate, it's quicker."

They walked along past the stables and past the birch wood in the direction of the big yew hedge. A faint pearly mist covered the longer wetter grass and the budding birch trees emerged a brilliant green, dripping with light. A laburnum, drooping on the edge of the grove, made a streak of yellow against the blue and misty interior. The daffodils were over and the leaves were already becoming limp. Dark vigorous clumps of green betokened the early tulips, some of which were just coming into flower.

"Those tulips are all yellow. I don't like yellow tulips. They should be red and white."

"I'll make a note of it."

"I like white flowers. Your yew hedge needs clipping. The statues are quite overgrown."

"I'll make a note of that too."

"Who are they?"

"The statues? Goddesses."

"They look rather creepy peering through the greenery."

They came among the conifers and reached the gate. In a second, without halting, Colette had sprung up onto it and was lifting one long leg over the spikes at the top. The other leg swung over and she leapt to the ground on the far side. They looked at each other.

"I must get this gate unlocked."

"No, don't, it's fun to climb."

"You're younger, as you pointed out. Here's a white flower for you." Henry took the camellia from his buttonhole and held it out to her through the bars. She snatched it, flourished it, and ran away down the road. Henry turned back smiling, then began to think about Stephanie Whitehouse.

He returned along the drive, kicking at the weeds as he went. When he came into sight of the house he saw with irritation his mother advancing towards him over the lawn. In the farther distance, Lucius, wearing his straw hat, was strolling back from the direction of the big trees. Henry, hesitating, began to veer in order to avoid his mother, but it was too late.

"Henry!" Gerda was beaming. She was wearing an old mackintosh and wellingtons and carrying a flat basket on which lay a variety of clippings for one of her flower arrangements: chestnut buds, beech buds, cherry, a few of the tulips.

"Hello, Mother."

"I saw you with Colette Forbes."

"Oh."

"How did she get out?"

"Over the gate."

"I'll get Bellamy to unlock it."

"I like it locked."

"It's the quickest way to Pennwood."

"Who's going to Pennwood?"

"It's so warm isn't it, like summer. Let's sit on the seat outside the drawing-room and sun ourselves, shall we?"

Henry followed his mother up to the terrace, where they

walked round to the south side and sat down on an ancient teak seat against the wall of the house. The sun-baked iron-stone exuded warmth and the little shell-fossils glittered in the bright light. Gazing down at the lake, Henry blinked into the sun.

"I saw you looking at the yew hedge. I'm afraid it needs attention."

"I see the pleached limes have gone to hell too."

"Bellamy gets round as best he can. It's not like in your father's day. Henry—"

"Yes."

"I did just want to say—how much I like Colette Forbes."

"She's a scream."

"She's a thoroughly nice girl, it's a thoroughly nice family."

"Except that her father's a coarse bullying swine."

"Henry, no! He's an excellent sincere person. And her brother's your best friend."

"My best friend is a man called Russell Fischer."

"Well, Cato is an old friend, and old friends are important, aren't they?"

Frowning down towards the valley Henry saw in the distance straw-hatted Lucius coming into view again, strolling now in the direction of the lake. "Like him," he said.

"Like—oh, like Lucius—I'm getting so short-sighted."

"Is he your lover?"

Gerda, who had been holding the basket of cuttings on her knee, put it down abruptly on the stones. "Henry, don't use that tone to me."

"I'm sorry about the tone. I trust you don't mind the question—"

"I object to the question too."

"I think I have a right to ask it. I'll explain why—"

"My relations with Lucius are nothing to do with you."

"He lives in my house."

"Henry, you are being very rude and unkind."

"I'm sorry, Mother, I don't intend to be."

"I think you do intend to be. You've been sulky and rude ever since you came back, I simply can't imagine why, we've made you welcome—"

"It's just this 'we' that I object to, Mother. Do try and understand."

"Since you ask in this gross way, no, *of course* Lucius isn't my lover, and never has been!"

"Yes, well, I assumed that, I just wanted to be sure. Just an old friend—"

"Not even that, Lucius is a pathetic dependent, he's somebody who can't look after himself and has to be looked after, he's like a demanding child, I can't tell you what a burden and a nuisance he's been to me. My lover indeed!"

"Thank you, Mother. That was just what I wanted to know."

"As if I'd have a lover at my age!"

"I don't see why not, you're still quite a good-looking woman."

"Quite a good-looking woman! Yes, Colette was asking me the other day if anyone had ever told me I was beautiful!"

"I think that was rather forward of her."

"I assure you, I do not think of myself in any such light, nothing is more distasteful than an elderly woman who acts young and wants to be in the limelight all the time. And let me tell you that the sooner I can retire and get rid of the responsibility of running this house the better I shall be pleased."

"I'm glad to hear you say that—"

"It's time you were married, Henry. When you bring a young bride to the Hall I shall hand over all the arrangements to the two of you and retire absolutely into the background. And let me say now frankly that I think Colette Forbes would make you a very good wife."

"Oh—oh—" said Henry, shifting on the seat, still keeping his narrowed gaze fixed on the distant Lucius who was now walking slowly back in the direction of the house. "I see. I've been rather slow-witted. *That's* what it was all about. I'm afraid it never occurred to me. And looking for the Marshalson Rose—"

"Did you find it?"

"No."

"I think that Colette would be ideal, she's a good girl, she's young and charming, and healthy—"

"Oh awfully healthy. But I'm sorry to disappoint you, dear

Mother—I am already engaged to be married to somebody else."

Gerda moved away, turning towards her son. "Not—an American?"

"No, an English girl. Her name is Stephanie Whitehouse. She's a prostitute." Henry laughed wildly.

"You're not serious," said Gerda, after a pause. She was stiff, her hands thrust deep into her mackintosh pockets, her legs in their muddy boots sturdily apart. Her dark eyes glowed fiercely. Henry moved a little further away. "Don't laugh now," said Gerda.

"I'm not laughing," said Henry, glaring back. "Listen, Mother."

"Please don't joke about this."

"I'm not. This girl Stephanic Whitehouse was Sandy's mistress for years, she's a tart, he kept her in a London flat. You didn't know, did you?"

"No," said Gerda. She looked away.

"Well, naturally not. Sandy kept her dark. In fact she's rather a marvellous person. And I love her."

"But you can't—you must have only just met her—"

"Yes. But a lot has happened. One can be certain. Sandy treated her like a—"

"Like what she is," said Gerda, "according to you." She was looking away into the distance, rigid with the attempt of self-control.

"I'm sorry, Mother. I can't help bringing Sandy into it. Because of him I felt responsible. And then it all became so much more important—"

"You have been behaving like a perfect fool. There is such a thing as depravity. This woman is after your money."

"Oddly enough," said Henry, "I don't think there is such a thing as depravity. And there won't be any money."

"I don't know what you're talking about. I can't imagine that you're really serious. I think you've simply been affected —in some strange way—by this woman's connection with Sandy. You always used to copy what Sandy did. I suppose she's totally uneducated."

"Oh totally. But so are you."

Gerda pressed her lips together. She turned round to look at him again, her glowing eyes, so like his own, full of unshed tears. "I don't want to quarrel with you, Henry."

"It is sometimes impossible not to quarrel. I'm sorry."

"I don't think you're serious. If you are—it seems to me—that you are not following your heart, but following some sort of—plan of cruelty."

"You know nothing about my heart," said Henry. "You never did. You despised me and neglected me when I was a child."

"That's not true," said Gerda softly. She wiped away the tears with the back of her hand. She said, "Do you mean to say that you are going to bring that woman here?"

"There won't be any 'here.'"

"What do you mean?"

"Mother, don't scream or faint or anything. And don't think I'm joking. I'm going to sell the place."

"Henry, what are you saying?"

"Just this, Mother. I'm going to sell the Hall, the park, the cottages, and all the farmland. I do not want to be a land-owner, I do not want to be an English country squire. I do not want to be a rich man. And I do not see why, out of piety to a tradition which I regard as stupid and wrong, I should sacri-fice my life to these values, to these *things*. You've had your life here, Mother, and you've enjoyed it, at least I hope you have. I am not going to follow my grandfather and my father and Sandy. Why should I? I am a different person and I belong to a new age. Sandy belonged to the past. I don't. If you reflect you will see, see that there is nothing very extraordinary in what I say. I can't stay here and become a Sandy, even to please you. And if I go away, I'm still tied by these things, so long as they remain my property and my responsibility. To run away, to leave it to you, to leave it all to carry on as before, to keep this house, this useless land, all the money that lies behind it, as a sort of Marshalson mausoleum, would be not only frivolous but absolutely macabre. I didn't want this to happen, I didn't want to inherit the place, I didn't choose this fate, but now it's come about and I have to cope with it, I have to decide. Please don't accuse me of cruelty or of doing it out of any funny thing about Sandy or—I've never been more serious or more rational in my life. Mother, it's got to go, this way of life has got to go. When there are poor people and homeless people I can't just sit on all this property and all this money. I'm going to disperse it, I'm going to give it away. I can't live as you do. You care for trees and plants more than for people. Forgive me, I know it's a shock. But in a little while you'll see I'm right, or at least you'll understand—"

Gerda showed no signs of screaming or fainting. There were no tears now. She sat turned towards him, looking at him intently. With her wide nostrils expanded, her large face red, her shabby mackintosh collar turned up about her hair, she looked suddenly strong and brutish, like a man. "Henry," she said, "this is not going to happen."

"It is, Mother. It's all planned. I've been into it with Merriman—"

"With Merriman?"

"Yes. I'm sorry. I had to ask him to keep it a secret. The whole estate can probably be on the market in a matter of weeks. Of course I shall make arrangements for you. I am having two of the Dimmerstone cottages made into a little house, it'll be very nice and there's quite a good garden. I shall give Bellamy his cottage and sell the others. You'll be comfortable in Dimmerstone, and it'll be away from the housing estate—"

"The housing estate?"

"Yes. I'm going to give the upper parkland on the Laxlinden side to the rural district council, on condition they build a model architect-designed council estate, in fact Giles Gosling has come up with a splendid plan, all faced with local stone—"

"I don't think I want to hear about that," said Gerda.

"I don't want the place to be spoilt—"

Breathing hard, almost panting, but controlled, Gerda had turned away. She gazed down at her boots and began pushing the encrusted mud off with one finger. "And what does that girl—your—Sandy's friend—think of all this?"

"Oh, she loves it," said Henry. "She hates the rich! She's a communist!" He laughed again, crazily, curling his feet up under him upon the seat. "Oh God, I feel so relieved at having told you. Mother, don't think this has been easy—it's been a test and a challenge. Forgive me for thinking about myself here —about my integrity and my future—I couldn't compromise. I just couldn't. Please say you understand a little, you don't think it's just madness or—I don't know—revenge—or—You'll get used to it and see it's best. After all, you did things your way in your own time—and now it's my turn. Please say you're not angry."

"Revenge," said Gerda thoughtfully, still busy with her boots. Then she said, "Oh I can imagine that it hasn't been easy—"

At that moment Lucius arrived, having climbed up the terrace steps from the bottom. Ostentatiously puffing, he laid his stick on the balustrade. "What a pull! I'm not as young as I was. Good morning, Henry. I'm afraid I was late for breakfast again. Well, my dear, what a lot of lovely flowers you've picked—" Lucius became aware that something was wrong, and stopped.

"Henry is going to sell the estate," said Gerda. "The Hall. Everything."

Lucius threw back his head, and with careful deliberation undid the front of his overcoat, the buttons of his jacket, then of his shirt. He loosened the silk scarf around his neck. Then he took his hat off and ran his fingers carefully through his fine mane of white hair, tossing it back.

"Did you hear?" said Gerda.

"Yes, my dear."

"You don't seem very surprised. Perhaps he told you?"

"No, no, he didn't. But—well—in these days—one must expect changes—"

"I'm glad you understand so quickly that I really mean it," said Henry to Gerda, ignoring Lucius. "Please don't think it malice, it isn't, it's not like that at all. I've just got to survive— and of course I'll do all I can—"

"I am to live in a cottage in Dimmerstone," said Gerda to Lucius. "I don't think there are any plans for you."

"I suppose I can live with Audrey," said Lucius. "I might get some sort of little job—it's not the end of the world."

"You see, he's not as feeble and pathetic as you imagine," said Henry. "We shall all manage."

190

"Did you say I was feeble and pathetic?"

"He asked if you were my lover," said Gerda. "That was part of the reply."

"Well, I suppose I might be your lover, it isn't inconceivable—"

"What about Rhoda?" said Gerda, to Henry.

"I'll pension her off."

"No problem about Bellamy. John Forbes will snap him up, or else Mrs. Fontenay."

"I'm glad you're both being so decent—"

"When are you getting married?"

"Oh, are you marrying Colette Forbes?"

"No, I am not marrying Colette Forbes."

"He is marrying a prostitute called—What is she called?"

"Stephanie Whitehouse."

"She was Sandy's mistress. Sandy kept her in a flat in London."

"*Did* he? What surprises one gets about people. I would never have dreamt—"

"I don't know when I'm getting married. Soon."

"Fancy old Sandy—"

"I'm going to lie down," said Gerda. She got up abruptly and went into the house through one of the drawing-room windows.

Lucius said, "How long did Sandy—"

But Henry was gone. He had whirled on his heel and sped away down the steps, leaping down the first flight like a wild goat, and vanishing downward in the direction of the lower terraces.

Lucius stood for a little while leaning on the balustrade and pressing his hand against his heart. He noticed that Henry in his speed had dislodged a large cushion of furry yellow moss from between the paving stones. With his toe Lucius pushed the moss back into place and patted it down. So disaster had come, more completely than he had ever imagined. At least he had behaved in a seemly manner and had had the grace to despair at once. If Henry were to offer him a small pension would he be humble enough to accept it? There could alas be little doubt about that. But Henry would not offer it. Henry obviously thought that he was a mere burden on Gerda. Gerda herself had probably told Henry so. As separate pains he felt distress at Gerda's contemptuous words, despair at her unspeakable defeat, helpless squirming rage against Henry. So Gerda could be defeated and the world could change; and what would now become of him? Rex would never let him live at Audrey's. He stooped and picked up Gerda's basket of flowers which she had left behind. Most of all the vision of a collapsed defeated Gerda appalled him and filled him with a child's terror. He went into the drawing-room.

Gerda was sitting facing the window, bolt upright in a chair, with fixed staring eyes. For a moment Lucius thought that she had had some kind of seizure.

"Are you all right, my dear?"

"Yes, of course. Shut the window, there's a frightful draught."

"So I'm feeble and pathetic. Well, I suppose I am. Did you tell Henry I was sponging on you?"

"I can't remember. I may have done. I was annoyed at his assumption that you were my lover."

"I don't see why you should be annoyed."

"That's not important—Listen—"

"It's important to me. Perhaps it *is* time that we parted!"

"Oh stop being so *frivolous*, Lucius."

"I think it's very brave the way you've accepted it—and come to that, the way I've accepted it."

"I haven't accepted it," said Gerda.

"You think Henry's not serious?"

"Oh, he's serious. He's been influenced by that woman. But it's not going to happen. We are going to prevent it."

My dear Cato,

I am sorry you went. I'm sorry I lectured you, I got everything wrong. As for the boy, that was just a hunch. Maybe kicking over the traces and loving him is the way to save him. Who knows? I certainly don't. Why don't you bring him here? I could even put up both of you if necessary. Anyway, please come back and for God's sake don't now regard me as the Inquisitor's clerk! I had to say a word about this in higher quarters, but no one got excited, you know how they take things. Your antics are likely to be ignored for the present, so don't feel that you have to decide anything quickly or that, by running away, you have in fact decided. It's not so easy to get *out* of that net, my dear, and of course I don't mean the stupid old order or even, *sub specie temporis*, the odious old Church. Fishes move in the sea, birds in the air, and by rushing about you do not escape from the love of God. I feel inclined to say: don't even worry about the priesthood. I mean, you could give *that* up and not lose your religion. Though, on the other hand, I also feel inclined to say: for *you*, being in God is being a priest. If ever I have seen a priest I see one in you. And though it may seem almost frivolous to say so, you did make a solemn promise. Do not reject the one who made that promise, be faithful at least a little longer, wait to be taught. The spirit as experience, as vision, as joy will return. Wait. I am not belittling your "intellectual crisis." We are intellectuals, we have to undergo these crises, in fact to undergo them is an essential part of our task. We have to suffer for God in the intellect, go on and on taking the strain. Of course we can never be altogether in the truth, given the distance between man and God how could we be? Our truth is at best a shadowy reflection, yet we must never stop trying to understand. You know all this, Cato. I am not saying that you should not "wrestle," but that you should do it inside the Church, close to what you once felt so certain about. You said "Christ invaded my life." Whatever it was that happened then, *something* happened. You have not just "made a mistake." Hold on and accept change with the openness of faith and the hope of grace. Do not run, do not hide, stay beside your revelation and be faithful to it as it renews itself. For this is what will happen if you will only wait. There is a mystical life of the Church to which we must subdue ourselves even in our doubts. Do not puzzle your mind with images and ideas which you know can be only the merest glimmerings of Godhead. Stay. Sit. You cannot escape from God. And meantime let your task of priesthood hold you. Say mass even if you feel it's *really* "hocus pocus"! And come back here.

Ever, *in Christo*, yours with love,
Brendan

My dear son,

Brendan has told me of your troubles. I hope you do not mind his telling me. As you may know, I have been ill. Will you not come and see me? I was worried and saddened to hear that you had been speaking of leaving the order. Do not hasten to decide, and do not mistrust the revelation that led you to God. You saw Him then in a clarity and with a gladness that is denied to many who are holy. Abide for this time in that former assurance. Darkness comes to us all and we must attempt humbly to guard the flame of faith in our hearts when there is no light. Do not strain anxiously after any new certainty. Your will power can do nothing. Your task is love and love is your teacher, rest there and wait quietly to be shown truth. You know I am not a learned man, or a philosopher or a theologian like Brendan, who I'm sure can argue with you far better. I cannot argue, only point to Him who is our way and our truth and our life. Look *there* to Christ and see the living truth of perfect love. There all speech is silence, and there is all that matters and is needful. In charity and austerity of soul, hold to what you know to be precious and holy in your life, my dear child. I would be happy if I thought that you were with Brendan and not alone. If it is not too difficult, please come and see me. I hope you can read this shaky writing. May God bless you, dear Cato, and keep you safe within His wisdom.

Your loving friend,
J. Milsom

With these two letters in his pocket Cato was knocking on the door of a little ground-floor flat in Holland Park. It was late afternoon, a murky yellowish light, raining slightly. His cassock was wet. He had been unable to find his umbrella.

The door opened a little on a chain and a woman's voice inside said, "Yes?"

"Mrs. Beckett?"

"Yes. What do you want?"

"I'm Father Forbes. You remember, I called on you once before. I'm a friend of Joe's."

"Of who?"

"Joe. Joseph. Your son. May I come in?"

The door closed. There was a scraping sound as the chain was removed, then the door was not opened but left ajar and Cato heard the slip-slop of the woman's slippered feet receding. Taking this as an invitation to enter he followed her into a dark narrow passage, closed the door and moved towards a lighted room ahead.

Mrs. Beckett was removing from the table a half-empty flagon of red wine and a glass. There was a smell of wine in the room.

Cato said, "I'm sorry to trouble you. I hoped I'd find you back from the school."

"The school? I don't go there any more."

Having put the wine away inside a small sideboard, Mrs. Beckett turned to face Cato. She had a black eye and extensive bruising down the side of her face. Her lip was swollen. Cato had seen enough in Notting Hill to know what this betokened and to make no comment.

Although it was light outside the curtains had been pulled and the room was lit by one little green-shaded lamp. Mrs. Beckett sat down heavily at the table. Cato sat down opposite her.

"Which of them did you say it was?"

"What—oh, of your sons—Joe. You remember I called on you—"

"I don't remember. You people are all alike. One was here last week collecting money for something. They never leave you alone, it's like the secret police, you're always being pestered and spied on. I suppose they keep a list. I'm not in the church any more, that's all finished, done with."

"I don't want to pester you," said Cato. "And I won't keep you."

"You'd better not. If he finds you here he'll arrange you like he's arranged me. I suppose Joe's in trouble."

"Not yet, but he probably will be. He hasn't got a job and my guess is that he's living on petty crime—"

"That's fine, let him stick to petty crime! His brothers are all in big crime."

"I'll be brief, Mrs. Beckett."

"Dominic's in prison, Pat and Fran have emigrated, at least I suppose they have, they said they were going to and I haven't heard in years, Benedict's being kept by a tart in Birmingham, and Damian died of drugs in January."

"I'm so sorry—"

"Oh don't be sorry, I don't care, he only came here to curse me. What's this about Joe?"

"I wondered if you had any influence over him, if there would be any point in your trying to see him and—"

"No. Just no. Would you like some wine?" Mrs. Beckett tilted her chair and reached back to retrieve the flagon of red wine. Sighing heavily she got up and found two glasses.

"Not for you? Mind if I do?"

"I wondered if there was anyone in his family who could help, even get him away for a holiday—"

"It sounds as if his life's all holiday. There isn't any family. My brother doesn't want to know. The rest are lost, God knows where they are, or rather it's me that's lost. I think you'd better go now. God, I feel so tired."

Cato looked at Mrs. Beckett. Her straggling dark hair was full of slides and clips and she had put lipstick onto her swollen mouth. Her hand trembled as she held the glass. She looked at her trembling hand. She said again, "Oh God, I feel so tired." Tears filled her eyes and lapped out a little onto her cheeks.

"Mrs. Beckett, forgive me for speaking to you, but I am a priest and you are, whatever you say, a Catholic. I came to talk about Joe, but how I wish that I could help you. You must find your way back to hope and joy again. The way is open if you will only take it. The way is Christ, the hope is Christ. Take your burdens there and receive His love, hide yourself in His love and be healed. Don't despair. Whatever has happened, the world can be made new and good again. Come to church, why not, come to mass. I don't know what your troubles are and I didn't come here to question you or to pester you. But I wish so heartily and so humbly that I could help you. Come to church sometime, just sit there perhaps. The love of God is with you if you will just breathe quietly and let it fill you."

"Fuck off," said Mrs. Beckett, still staring at her glass which was now jolting in her hand. "Otherwise you'll meet him. And don't come back. If you want to be kind to me, don't come back."

"About Joe—"

"Don't bother me with Joe. I hate Joe. I hate all my children, they hate me."

196

"Go to church. Just look at our Lord, just speak to Him. Or think about Him here. He is here too, at this table, in this wine. God bless you. Forgive me."

Cato blundered out into the dark corridor and out at the front door into the street, where the lamps had just been turned on. As he came out he ran into a burly man who was just about to enter the house. The man, who smelt of drink, made a vomiting noise, then spat onto the front of Cato's cassock. The door banged.

Cato hurried away down the blue darkening street under the lamplight. It was still raining. He turned the corner. There was an Anglican church a little distance away and he hurried to it and entered. He sat down at the back in the darkness, sensing the desolate empty feeling of the bare rather damp church. How quickly and easily the patter had all come out. But now he knew no other words of consolation and if these words were false then there was no consolation. He drew out Father Milsom's letter to read it again, but it was too dark to see. He took the letter out of the envelope and held it to his face, pressing it against his mouth.

Henry was awake in the early morning. Or perhaps it was not so early, as there was a long sparkle of sun at the top of the curtains. He could not look at his watch because his arm was around Stephanie Whitchouse who was still asleep. They must have lain like this embraced all night, how touching. And how unlike anything that had ever happened to him in his life before. Last night, or as it must have been, this morning, had been their third occasion of making love, but this was their first night together. Of course he had spent nights with women before, though not so very many. But he had never done so with such a quiet unanxious untalkative sense of inevitability and rightness. He knew that this lack of fear was partly brought about by Stephanie's dependent status. She was the prisoner of his will, and in her humble little way she both exhibited and rejoiced in her captive state. Henry had often heard about women's "intuition," but he had never experienced it before. Perhaps in the case of Bella and those smart campus girls intuition had been eroded by intellect.

But his unanxious satisfaction did not consist simply in his sense of "owning" Stephanie. Sandy had spoken of her *femme fatale* charm. This seemed to Henry a coarse title for what he discerned in her. For him she was more like a mysterious silent woman encountered in a temple with whom it becomes quietly evident that by the god's will you must couch. Never had Henry felt more blessedly devoid of alternatives. He felt himself curiously reminded of a picture of Max's, in which a man is tied upside down to a beautiful lamp-bearing woman. What perfectly ridiculous images old Max could invent. The odd thing, it had earlier occurred to Henry, was that although the man has his hands bound and has perhaps been stabbed in the back, he appears to be quite comfortable in his unusual position! The woman presses one caressing hand to his thigh as she peers through the lamplit dark. Her face now reminded him very slightly of Stephanie's. And he was now aware that he had always a little identified himself with the comfortable upside-down man. So it turned out that in an upside-down way he was her captive, not she his.

Of course Stephanie was not beautiful and she was not young. How strangely and mysteriously evident was the ageing of the body. A weariness in the breasts, in the buttocks, a certain coarsening and staleness of the flesh, proclaim the years as much as lines and wrinkles can. Bella, who had always been very sensitive about her possible nineteen-year-old rivals, had talked a lot about this, only fastidious Henry had shut his ears. Now, holding Stephanie Whitehouse in his arms, he apprehended her lack of youthfulness with compassion and pleasure. He could see, looking carefully at the roots of her hair, that it was dyed. Her face, disfigured by the two harsh lines which framed her mouth and which sleep had failed to smooth, looked older now. Of course her make-up had been worn away by his kisses. A defensive seductive alertness which waking she wore as a mask was touchingly absent. She moved slightly, and one heavy soft breast nestled against him. He felt the sudden blazing warmth of her thigh against his leg. She murmured something and her face twitched. He wondered: does she think she is with Sandy now? The idea did not distress him, but on the contrary made him feel visionary, serene, full of mercy.

The scene with his mother, after which he had, without seeing her again, driven to London, had shaken him in unexpected ways. He was not of course deceived by his mother's sarcastic show of acceptance. He knew that he had struck her a terrible blow and that he must, for this, bear a heavy responsibility. He knew too that he was only at the beginning of learning what it was exactly that he was up to. He had no doubts about the rightness of his plan. That he had no doubts was the absolute prerequisite of a drastic move. He was committing a sort of murder. Matricide, in fact. But he was saved and justified by, again, the absence of alternatives. Henry felt like a man into whose hands a huge crippling weight had suddenly been put. He had to drop it, however much damage that would cause. (Max could have painted that.) He could not, morally, spiritually, psychologically become the person into which that odious ownership would make him. He had always hated possessions, always wanted to travel light and live a stripped life, and was he now to be crippled by a sentiment about an ancestral home? Giving away the money would be easy. It was, admittedly, the traditional part of the picture which threatened to hold him, and not just because it sometimes seemed monstrous to ask his mother to live in Dimmerstone. Yet after all he could coldly judge the irrationality of the bond which still tied him to Laxlinden; and could he not make a similar judgement for her? She had enjoyed the Hall; but most elderly people have to accept some diminution in their lives. His mother was old enough for such a change and certainly young enough not to be slaughtered by it. In the longer run the challenge might even do her good. She would be so determined to show her son that she was undamaged that she would perhaps discover, in her diminished scene, quite new sources of the joy of life.

Henry had felt, after the revelation had been made, relief; and he was duly grateful to his mother for her enacted stoicism.

He felt an almost affectionate admiration for her toughness. Of course it must have been a terrible shock, especially as she had quite evidently had the intelligence to discern at once that he was serious. Nor had it been easy for him to take the plunge; he had not in fact, at that moment, particularly intended to. What had precipitated his revelation had perhaps been the inconceivably irritating reference to Colette Forbes. His statement about Stephanie had then constituted the bridge passage. He would, in any case, have had to be somehow angry with Gerda in order unambiguously to bring it all out. An important stage had been passed and Henry felt himself after it a new man, even a more merciful man. He had had to "totalize" the thing to make it thinkable, to make it, for purposes of an announced decision, portable. Now that the announcement was over he could consider, more coolly and at length, the details.

When Henry had told Gerda that he was engaged to Stephanie Whitehouse he had done so very nearly as a joke. Of course it had been a cruel joke whose purpose was to shock. And Henry in saying it had not really "meant it," though equally he had not been producing a "pure fiction." Somehow the idea had come up with a certain naturalness and Henry had only twisted it into a spiteful joke by announcing Stephanie at once as a prostitute. That his mother should become sentimental about a friend of Sandy's was the last thing that Henry wanted. Stephanie had to be instantly announced as "impossible" and the impulse to torment his mother with her had seemed momentary. But when he saw Stephanie again he found that he had already been changed by his "absurd" idea. For of course it was by no means absurd. There was no reason why he should not marry Stephanie Whitehouse. He loved her. She loved him.

Am I mad? thought Henry. No. I feel more absolutely *real* than I have ever in my life. My action in being here with this woman is more absolutely mine than anything I have ever done, though also it is more involuntary, more destined. Only now I see that this is exactly why it is more mine. I am deep in my own destiny at last, I am up to the neck in it, and this is, is it not, where happiness resides. It all somehow mysteriously hangs together, selling the estate, finding Stephanie. Only in just this way, it occurred to him, *could* I get married! What a miracle, what perfect luck; and how sweet and strange that I am lying here in bed with my arms round Sandy's tart, and there isn't a grain of resentment or malice left in me at all. She has performed this miracle of reconciliation, she with her humility, her truthfulness, her deep unconscious intuitive beingness. She is all here, all woman, I can possess her totally, nothing of her will escape from me. Also, he thought, it is only by marrying her that I can have her at all. This has suddenly become clear. I cannot "keep" her as Sandy kept her, that is not a moral possibility. And if I set her "free" she will return to— No. I cannot set her free, I will not, she is mine. It comes to this: that I cannot not marry her!

Stephanie woke up. Her eyes flew wide, rounded, dark, moist with sleep. Her lips parted in a *moue* of surprise which at once became a smile. She pulled Henry's head towards her by the hair. "You're so young!"

"That's nice," said Henry. "I often feel a hundred. But not today."

"Do you like tea or coffee for your breakfast?"

"You want to serve me as soon as you are conscious. Why not stay here and enjoy the view?"

"Stay with one who loves you, look no further, dear."

"Is that a poem?"

"A song."

"I like it. Isn't this fun, Stephanie, you and me. It is fun, isn't it? I feel happy. Do you feel happy?"

"Yes." She thrust him away and smiled at him. Then her smile clouded. "I must get up." Eluding Henry's grab she slipped out and ran to the bathroom.

Henry got lazily out of bed and put on his dressing-gown. He had brought a few things with him in his flight from Laxlinden. I suppose I live here now, thought Henry. Well, I do, don't I? He strolled into the kitchen and drank some water. They had both become fairly drunk on white wine the night before.

The sun was shining into the room and making its sprightly cleanliness glisten. There was a pleasant smell of some kind of soap. Tingling with health and well-being Henry stood there, rising gently onto his toes, and looking out at the gilded dome of Harrods and the blue sky overflowing with spring sunshine.

Stephanie, in an exceedingly frilled and flowery *négligé*, came noiselessly into the room.

"Why, you silly goose, you've made up your face, you've combed your hair!"

"I must have looked awful."

"You looked lovely. We've passed that stage, you know."

"What stage?"

"Where we look critically at each other's appearance. We're just together now, like two happy good animals in a pen."

"That's nice. You say such nice things."

"Is there any orange juice?"

"Yes, here. You didn't say about tea or coffee."

"Coffee. And toast and some of that honey. Stephanie, you do like me, don't you, you do like me as me, it isn't just—I mean—"

"Yes, yes, I do. You *know* I do. I do."

"Good." He sat down at the little clean white table. "Stephanie, I do like your wrists, they're so plump, like a baby's."

"Like—yes—oh dear, it's so strange—" She paused, staring at him.

"Yes. And yet I feel I've known you for years."

"I feel that too."

"Stephanie, tell me one thing. Did Sandy ever give you a ring?"

"A ring? No. Of course not." She turned to the coffee pot, then with a sudden little whining sound began to cry.

Henry jumped up and seized her by the shoulders, then pulled her to sit on a chair beside him.

"What's the matter, dear little one, what is it?"

"I'm so happy—and I've never been—happy before ever."

"Well, that's nothing to cry about. Here, take my hankie."

"But, you see, it's all a lie—"

"It's not a lie, Stephanie, how can it be, we're here, we're us, it's real."

She mopped her eyes, then gritted her teeth for a second in a sort of snarl. "You'll go away."

"I won't."

"And I'll go away. Oh I'm so grateful to you, you've been so kind, ever since you called me 'Miss Whitehouse' in that wonderful way. But I'm so stupid and ignorant, I'm nobody, I know nothing. You don't know what I'm like. This is—it's all untrue—it's—Oh forgive me, forgive me." She seized his hand and kissed it, pressing it against her wet cheek, shiny now with tears.

Henry pulled her more closely up against him. "What was your song? 'Stay with the one who loves you, look no farther, dear.'"

"But it's just a—silly—song."

"Stephanie, let's get married, shall we? Would you like that?"

He felt her stiffen in his embrace, then say, "What? What did you say?" Her voice was harsh.

"I said, 'Let us get married.' Or if you prefer it in a more traditional form, Stephanie, will you marry me?"

She stared at him with her big tear-filled eyes and he could feel her grip tightening on the flesh of his arm until she was pinching him violently. Then she began to laugh. He saw, as he now struggled to hold her, her wet lips and the red interior of her mouth. Hysterical laughter poured from her in a seemingly involuntary stream. Her high-heeled slipper kicked his ankle and he let go of her and she fled from the room.

"Stephanie, Stephanie, stop!"

Still laughing crazily she ran, losing a slipper, into the bedroom, slamming the door in Henry's face. He dragged the door open and sprang after her, half falling on top of her where she lay upon the bed drumming her feet and shaking with the terrible mirth.

"Stephanie, be quiet, stop that dreadful noise."

They struggled for a moment then lay embraced in silence. After nearly a minute she said, murmuring into his shoulder, "Yes, yes, yes."

Henry lay with eyes closed, triumphant, appalled. He lay prostrate in a great red grotto which was like the inside of Stephanie's mouth, and he shuddered with achievement and joy and fear and the vast sense of an irrevocable destiny.

"This is the first time we've ever got drunk together, Father."

"Dear me," said Cato, "Is that what we're doing?"

They were sitting by candlelight in Cato's bedroom. The electricity had been turned off. Soon the bulldozers would be coming and the street would be demolished. The house, knowing its end was near, was strangely rickety and frail tonight, a kind of swaying cardboard house inside which Cato sat gazing at the boy. The wind was rattling the window panes and the closed doors were shifting and tapping. Cato sat on the bed and Beautiful Joe close to him upon the chair. The big jar of wine which Joe had brought was on the floor. There were two candles, one upon the chest of drawers and one upon the window ledge. The candle-flames wavered in the strong draught.

Cato had spent a crazy day. It had started with an almost sleepless night. His bed was damp, the house was suddenly very cold. He had dreamt about Mrs. Beckett. In the morning he wondered if he ought to go and see her again but decided it would be pointless. He began a letter to Brendan but tore it up. He went out intending to ring up Father Milsom but all the telephone boxes in the area had been vandalized and were out of order. He became extremely hungry and then realized that he had no money left. Hunger at last drove him reluctantly to Father Thomas's house where he borrowed a pound. Father Thomas had the advantage of being a comparative stranger. However some rumour must have circulated. Father Thomas looked at him with kind and pitying eyes, asked him to stay to lunch, suggested that he should stay the night. Cato fled. He ate some bacon and eggs in a small café, then began to feel sick. Walking back to the house the world was suddenly full of signs. ACTIVATE KUNDALINI he saw written upon a wall. And once again, TROUSERAMA. Only now the word was no longer ludicrous but sinister.

He came back and lay down on his damp bed and instantly

fell asleep. He dreamt that Father Milsom was opening a door with one hand while with the other he was gripping Cato's wrist and Cato was struggling to be free. He awoke in the twilight to find Beautiful Joe standing beside his bed, holding the wine jar and looking down at him with a strange intent unsmiling stare.

"You're like a jack-in-the-box, Father. Now we see you, now we don't."

It was late. They had drunk nearly all the flagon of wine.

"I'm sorry," said Cato. "My life is—well you must know by now—in a muddle, in a mess—I don't know what to do—"

"You're a tease, Father, that's what you are, a tease."

"I don't mean to be," said Cato. "I want to be sincere. I'd like to talk to you about everything, to tell you everything." Am I drunk, he wondered. I can't be on that amount of wine, can I?

'Well, tell me then. You know I'm your friend."

"How nice of you to say that, Joe, to say just that. Yes, we are friends, aren't we."

"That's it, Father. Now tell me something and let's have another drink on it."

"I went to see your mother yesterday."

"Ah now—why did you do that?"

"I want to help you, Joe, I feel desperate to help you. I thought she might be able to—influence you—or could tell me of somebody who could. But it was no use."

"She's just a drunken tart."

"Don't say that about your mother, Joe. Can't you pity her? She needs love so much. Can't you find any love for her in your heart? If you could it might be such a wonderful thing for you both."

"She'd scream and curse if I went near her. Don't talk of her, please. She's over and done with. She might as well be dead, the bitch."

Cato sighed. He decided there was indeed little point in pursuing the matter or in bringing Joe up to date with the situation of Dominic, Benedict, Pat, Fran, and Damian.

"I have tried," said Cato. "I have tried other ways. There aren't any."

"What are you saying, Father?"

"Sorry, I was just thinking aloud. Do you think you'll ever get married, Joe? It could do you a lot of good to get married."

"Married? Nah! The sort of birds I get near are muck. If I had a wife I'd kill her. I like men more than girls really. Girls are just for sex. And even that can be better with a chap."

Cato considered this. He felt that he was in a labyrinth in which he must very carefully and meticulously find his way. Except that everything was moving so fast that it was more like being in an aeroplane than in a labyrinth. There was a sense of physical rushing as if the ceiling were somehow sliding away over his head. With an effort he focused his eyes on the shuddering candle-flame. He knew that he ought to terminate the conversation but also knew that he would not. He thought, get things sorted out, get them into some sort of order, tell the truth. Everything would come right if he could only get to the bottom of it all.

He said, "Joe, there's something important that I have to tell you about myself."

"I know it, Father."

Cato could make nothing of this answer. He went on, "I've decided that I have got to stop being a priest."

This was evidently not what Joe had been expecting. "Oh, no! You don't mean it, Father. You can't be anything else but a priest. If you weren't a priest, you'd be nothing."

"Then I shall have to be nothing," said Cato. He had never seen it so clearly.

"No, no, Father. You're not serious. You'll never give it up, I know you won't, you can't. You're just worried about me."

"About you?" There was some logic somewhere, but where was it? Logic was a frame tilting over him, coming down upon him, about to mince him up with its sharp edges. "Joe," said Cato, "tell me the truth. Are you really a criminal?"

"I don't mean worried like that, Father."

"What other way is there to worry?" said Cato. He was trying so hard to keep his mind clear, but everything Joe said sounded wrong, as if it were the answer to some quite different question. "Joe are you a criminal? Are you involved with really bad people?"

206

"No, of course not, Father. Nobody's really bad. It's society that's bad. As for being a criminal, practically everybody's a criminal. You aren't, that's why I love you. That's why you'll go on being a priest. There's got to be some people who aren't involved."

"But do you break the law?"

"Yes a bit, but so does everybody almost. Everybody cheats, everybody steals. They'd break the law all the time if they could, help themselves, only often they don't know how or they're afraid. I just nick a thing or two, and I never nick from poor people, only from big places like, big shops, they won't miss it, they reckon on a lot of hoisting. It's not stealing really, lots of people do, respectable people too, you don't know. You live in a funny world of your own, Father. You don't know how ordinary folk go on. But I like you like that, I'm glad you exist, for us, for the others, in your funny world."

"What you call the funny world is the real world," said Cato. "It's where God is, where truth is anyway, I don't know about God any more. Joe, you're young. And you're very beautiful." Cato had not intended to say the last bit, but when it came out it quite blocked what he was going to say next, which had been something important.

The swaying candle-flames sent big shadows and a small restless light spiralling about the room. Beautiful Joe's face seemed in this rhythmical obscurity to glow rather than to be illuminated. Intermittent light fell upon his thin legs, showing the faded colour of his jeans at the knees, and upon his rather large long hands which dangled as he leaned forward or rose expressively to pat his hair or administer, as he spoke, a kind of blessing. In spite of the coldness of the room, he had taken off his jacket and neatly rolled up his shirt-sleeves. His glittering tidy hair had been recently trimmed.

"Yes," said Cato, and he stretched out his hand.

Joe took the outstretched hand in both of his with a gesture of confident calmness for which Cato felt impulsive gratitude. Joe shifted his chair a little nearer. How tactful he is, thought Cato, how charming, how just bloody intelligent.

"I care for you a lot, Father," said Joe. "I didn't think I would at first. It was just kicks, like a joke. We all thought it was funny. We used to have you on, you and the other two, more than you ever knew."

"I expect you did," said Cato. He left his captured hand limp, moving it very slightly in response to the pressure of Joe's fingers upon his palm.

"But now it's different. And you feel the same way. You mustn't let it worry you."

"Joe, I love you," said Cato.

"I know, Father, and I'm very grateful to you, it means a lot."

"But, Joe, what can we do?"

"What do you mean, Father?"

"I must help you, I must save you, you're all I've got left now, you're the only good thing I can do any more in the world. I must stop you destroying yourself, I just *know* that if you go on as you're going now you'll become a terrible person."

"You are very fanciful, Father." Joe pressed Cato's hand, released it, and reached for the wine. He filled Cato's glass, Cato put his hand on Joe's knee, feeling the bones, the warmth of the flesh.

"My dear boy, don't become a rogue, a ruthless selfish person. It doesn't have to happen. Just tell me what I can do to help you. Let me be with you and share your life. We could leave London and go and live somewhere else and work, help people maybe. You could like that, you have it in you—"

"I doubt it, Father. Your mind's running away with you altogether. What would we live on now? Would your rich friend support us, the one who wants to get rid of all his money?"

"We could work. I could teach. I could support you while you get some training. You're a clever boy, there are all sorts of things you could learn to do—"

"Would your rich friend help us?"

"Well, he might. But we must help ourselves, Joe. We could do it, the two of us, why not? I wouldn't be a burden or a nuisance to you, you could live your own life, I'd just be there helping. And once you got on the right track—"

"You're too unworldly, Father. What do you want really? Do you want us to be lovers?"

208

Joe took Cato's hand off his knee, squeezed it and dropped it. Cato sat back. He looked at the glowing face, letting his gaze wander over it. In thought and vision he outlined the bright hexagonal glasses. The hazel eyes were amused, alert, gentle. Cato felt curiously calm before the, after all, perfectly fair question.

"I don't know," he said, "I don't think so."

"Then what is this all about, Father dear?"

Suddenly the candles ducked as the door swung open, and one of the flames disappeared. Joe's chair jerked backward and Cato gave a gasp of alarm. He saw the gaping blackness of the open doorway and beside it a tall pale faintly luminous figure. It seemed for a moment as if some commanding angelic presence had come into the room. Then by the fainter light of the single candle he recognized his sister.

"Colette!"

"Hello," said Colette, who was wearing a long silver-coloured mackintosh. She turned to Joe. "Hello, Beautiful Joe."

"Hello, Beautiful." Joe was standing behind his chair with the candlelight beyond him. He lifted up the chair, then let it drop with a sound as if he were clicking his heels.

"Colette, what on earth are you doing here at this time of night?"

"It's not very late. I'm staying with Aunt Pat. I say, it's terribly cold in here. Why are you sitting in the dark? I couldn't find the light downstairs."

"They've turned the electricity off. What do you want?"

"Don't sound so cross. I was just feeling happy so I thought I'd come and see you."

"Joe, could you light the other candle again," said Cato. "Shut the door, Colette, please—It's so—" He could not find the word.

In the swaying dancing light as the boy lit one candle from the other, Cato looked at his sister and she seemed immensely tall, a heavenly being radiant with some sort of pure joy. She had said she was happy and this somehow made Cato feel sad. Was he damned then? There was a connection of thought. He focused his eyes. Colette was smiling and wriggling her shoulders inside the silver coat.

"Aunt Pat wondered if you could come and have lunch with us tomorrow."

Cato was feeling very strange. He had wanted to get up when Colette came into the room, but his legs from the knees down felt weighty and cold, as if they were encased in plaster. The upper part of his legs did not seem to be present at all. What has happened to me? he wondered. It can't be just the drink. He stretched out one hand rather slowly along the bed beside him and saw it receding into the distance like a pale armadillo.

"Your friend could come too if he'd like."

"Come where?" said Cato.

"Come to lunch with Aunt Pat tomorrow. Cato, are you all right?"

"I am afraid lunch tomorrow is completely impossible," said Cato. "But thank Aunt Pat all the same. I'm sorry, I must be a little—intoxicated, or else it's the flu. You'd better be off now, Colette. Come again when it's daylight. Everything's so extremely—difficult in the dark."

With a great effort he got the lower part of his legs up onto the bed. The mechanics of this new position meant that he was now lying flat on his back. At least he assumed that this must be the case since all he could see now was the ceiling, light green in colour, covered with black crevasses, and suddenly flickering wildly in the candlelight as the door of the room opened and closed again.

Cato heard Beautiful Joe speaking again. "You say you love me, Father, but you won't let me come near your precious sister, will you!"

"Joe," said Cato, "did you put anything in the wine?"

"Why couldn't we have gone to that lunch? I wanted to go."

"Did you put anything in the wine?"

"Well, yes, just a little bit of something—not like for a real trip—I thought it might sort of make things easier for you."

"I fell very odd," said Cato. "It's not unpleasant. Just—odd."

He heard Beautiful Joe speaking again, farther off, his voice echoing in a great hole. "I wish the bloody cunt hadn't come."

Cato closed his eyes. At once the chequer-board mincing

machine of logic came swooping down towards him, and its squares were a hundred windows and in each window he saw his father dressed as a cardinal, laughing, laughing. Bells were ringing, happy bells, wedding bells.

"Mother," said Henry, "may I introduce my fiancée, Stephanie Whitehouse. Stephanie, my mother."

"I'm *very* glad to meet you," said Gerda.

"It is so kind of you to invite me," said Stephanie.

Henry had been amazed and pleased by his mother's change of attitude, by, as he saw it, her realism. She seemed to have accepted his plan for the estate without another word of complaint. He had even had quite an amicable discussion with her about the future of Rhoda. Of course, thought Henry, now that the essential idea is accepted, I can make all sorts of humane modifications. How right I was not to present the thing apologetically or piecemeal. Now, having had the main shock, they will be grateful for any little changes I may decide to make later. They will feel I am being generous. How perfectly mad it all is, though.

Henry felt at present that he was living in a sort of myth. It was nothing to do with happiness, happiness seemed a kind of frivolity which belonged to some much lower form of consciousness. Henry felt that he was huge, like a giant, like an ancient hero, and the other people with whom he had to deal were huge too, and brilliantly coloured, under a sky as cloudless and brilliant as that of Max's Fisher King. They had emerged from the cellar, they had emerged from the cave. Gerda, Stephanie, even Lucius, were huge and significant and dignified, even bird-headed Rhoda was. Henry was the arbiter of their fates; yet he knew that he too, at this time, was far from free, he was a creature of some higher destiny, a creature of the gods. Why had he *got to* get rid of his inheritance? He did not even any more know why. He just had to transform all these objects, these things and spaces, into clean

211

easily disposable money, and then to get rid of the money and be—what—free, good? Even these names were too flimsy for what god-possessed Henry had to achieve.

Gerda's volte-face about Stephanie was another mystery of the situation. His mother, having taken the line, "I will not have that woman in the house," had lately actually suggested that she should be invited. Henry was amazed, a little disconcerted. "If you are determined to marry her, I have got to like her, haven't I?" said Gerda with a sudden access of calm reasonableness. Henry was touched. He had previously decided that there was absolutely no point in bringing Stephanie to the Hall, partly because of Gerda's opposition, but also because really, as things were to be, Stephanie and the Hall belonged to different orders of reality. This was indeed rather the essence of Stephanie, that she belonged to the world of the deprived whom Henry was going to *join*. Also, more simply, why show Stephanie a bauble which he was shortly proposing to dispose of? Not that he thought that Stephanie would be in any way shaken. He had already, though perhaps a little incoherently, explained his plans to her, and she had made no objection. She remained touchingly submissive and grateful, and Henry viewed the future with a still somewhat anxious satisfaction. In America he had lived simply. Even his apparently complex relation with Russell and Bella had become, because they were such splendid people, simple. When he had left America his deep fear had been that he would never be able to go back and that he would never elsewhere be able to live simply again. Now when he saw himself in a vision, living an ordinary existence with his wife, working for her and looking after her, he felt a pleasing glow of virtue. The great destructions led, and had to lead, back to simplicity after all.

"You and Lucius run along," said Gerda to Henry. "Stephanie and I are going to have a talk over tea."

Bird-headed Rhoda, who had set out the tea things, said something to Gerda in her incomprehensible *patois*. "Yes, Rhoda, four for dinner. Don't forget to ask Bellamy for the onions."

Henry grinned at Stephanie and waved as if saying "good luck." What a very peculiar scene. But after all, peace was better than war and reconciliation than resentment. He and Lucius followed Rhoda out of the drawing-room.

"China or Indian?"

"Er—China—please."

"Milk, sugar?"

"Yes—please."

"You had better put in your own sugar. Now do eat a sandwich, you must be tired and hungry after your journey."

The journey, by Volvo and motorway, had taken about three quarters of an hour, but Gerda behaved as if Laxlinden still had to be reached over a bad road by a carriage and horses.

Stephanie hesitantly took a damp limp sandwich, instinctively peered inside it, then blushed and raised her eyes. The two women looked at each other.

Both had taken trouble with their appearance. They were dressed very simply. Gerda was wearing a light wool dress, mousy brown in colour, with an open neck and a brilliantly blue and green silk scarf. Her dark hair was loose, combed sleekly to her shoulders. Stephanie was wearing a plain black dress with a diamanté brooch in the form of a fox terrier upon the collar. Her chestnut brown hair had been discreetly layered and a little fluffed up by an expert hairdresser. She clutched a shiny black handbag. She was wearing very little make-up.

She told Henry she was thirty-four, thought Gerda, I wonder if that was true? I wonder if she really loved Sandy, or if it was just for the money? I wonder if Sandy ... This was a mystery, an obscenity upon which she knew that, for her sanity, she must not meditate. Yet if Henry married this woman how could she not become obsessed with it? How could *he* not? Of course Gerda's realism was not as benevolent as Henry imagined. It was necessary for her to meet Henry's fiancée. But thereafter, when she had assessed the situation, there were many possible courses of action.

She smiled encouragingly at Stephanie. "Henry told us you were a communist, but now he says that was a joke."

"Oh, no, I'm not a communist. I'm not political at all, really."

"Neither am I. I don't think it suits a woman, do you?"

"No, I er—No."

There was a silence. Then Stephanie said, "I hope you don't think it's too awful—I mean, I believe Henry told you—"

"No, no, I—you must have suffered so much—we regard you as a victim." This was Henry's word and Gerda found it useful. She resolved: I will never let this woman talk to me about her past. And I will never let her talk to me about Sandy.

"Thank you!" said Stephanie. She too seemed to regard this aspect of the matter as satisfactorily closed, at any rate for the present. She helped herself to another sandwich, then coughed with embarrassment. She said, "You are very kind to me. I never thought that I would get an invitation to the—er—to the Hall."

Gerda, hastily, in case Stephanie was going to say something about Sandy, said, "It's pretty place, isn't it."

"Yes, it's as pretty as a dream."

"You know Henry is going to sell it."

Gerda had not intended to broach this matter straightaway, she spoke out of sheer nervousness.

Stephanie showed agitation. "Is he?"

"Yes. Didn't he tell you? He said he'd told you. He said you were pleased. He's going to sell everything. The Hall, everything, and give the money away. I am to live in a little cottage. Surely he told you?"

"He said something but I didn't understand. I thought he was just going to sell some fields or something, I didn't realize he was going to sell the Hall. He can't sell his ancestral home, surely that's impossible."

"Not a bit impossible. But *aren't* you pleased?"

"No. I think it's awful, *awful*, you must stop him."

"You must stop him," said Gerda. She added, "We must stop him." She thought, is this what I am scheming for, that this woman should be mistress of the Hall? Is this my best future, my one hope? It's that or Dimmerstone. Out of a perverse bitterness she said, "But honestly I don't think we *shall* persuade him. I suspect you don't know Henry very well yet. He is extremely obstinate. I doubt if you will ever live at the Hall. Henry will be a schoolteacher somewhere in Scotland or America and you will be living on his salary. He is so idealistic and romantic."

"And you will be living in the cottage. I think it's cruel."

"Well, when many people are very poor—"

"I know all about that, poverty wouldn't be any change for me. I can tell you what it's like and having no place and nothing, and it's not funny and it's not romantic and I'm tired of it, I've had enough—"

"Then you'd better not marry Henry, had you," said Gerda. "Have some chocolate cake."

"You don't want me to marry Henry."

"I want Henry to be happy," said Gerda. "He thinks that he will be happy with you. He may be right. In any case, what I think is not important. I am old."

They stared at each other.

"I'm sorry," said Stephanie. She looked down at her plate. She said suddenly, 'I'd like to see a photo of Sandy—he never gave me one—it isn't that I've—forgotten what he looked like —but I would like to see a photo of him—"

Gerda drew her feet in under her and held the arm of the chair. Then she got up and went to the Chinese cabinet. She drew a bulky envelope out of a drawer and laid it on the table. "Here you are. There are a lot of him—"

Stephanie immediately began looking at the photos avidly. "Oh thank you—yes—he was so handsome, wasn't he—much handsomer than Henry—and taller and—oh dear, oh dear—" Her eyes filled with tears, and she began awkwardly searching in her handbag for a handkerchief.

"Excuse me," said Gerda. "I have to go and see about the dinner. Put them back in the envelope when you've finished. Then I'm sure you'll find Henry somewhere outside on the terrace."

She quietly left the room and went without haste upstairs to her bedroom. She kicked off her shoes and lay down upon the bed. She did not weep but her eyes glared. Her mouth opened. She felt that her life was over and that all she wanted now was to hide the scandal and the shame of it, the shame of being old and mad with misery and having lost her son. She would hide herself in the cottage at Dimmerstone and shut the door on the world forever.

Henry skipped along the hall leaving his mother and his fiancée thus strangely in conference. In some odd way, though he was glad that it could happen peacefully, the meeting sickened him. He noticed some letters in the cage on the inside of the front door and took them out. There was one for Lucius, he guessed from Audrey, two bills for his mother, and two letters addressed to him. He put his mother's and Lucius's letters on the table, and bounded up the stairs and on into Queen Anne to his room. Stephanie was to sleep in the cherry blossom room next to his mother's bedroom. How odd, how weird. Would he visit Stephanie secretly at night, would she visit him? The sense of sacrilege excited him, the shattering of old taboos, the luridness of it all. But he felt sick too. His mother was quite noble enough to attempt to love Stephanie. Such a triumph of cosiness would not be however, Henry would see to that. He did not propose to let those two contaminate each other. He was beginning, dimly, to have a picture of the future. It did not include his mother. He determined to remove Stephanie back to London early tomorrow morning. He suddenly thought, so perhaps tonight will be my last night at the Hall, ever, ever. It was an awe-inspiring idea.

He sat down on his bed and looked at his two letters. One writing looked vaguely familiar, the other unfamiliar. He opened the familiar one first. It was from Cato and ran as follows:

My dear Henry,

I have been thinking about you and do hope to see you soon again. I expected you might turn up at the Mission. There's a lot I want to tell you of which I can only give you the barest outline in this letter. First, and I suppose most important, is that I have definitely decided to leave the priesthood and the Church. Becoming officially "laicized" can take time, but that is a mere formality. It has all been, as you can imagine, painful and humiliating. I bitterly regret having to do it, while at the same time feeling certain it is right. I feel that I have possessed something precious and beautiful which has been lost by my own fault; and yet it is the truth itself which compels this severance. I cannot quite feel that it was "all an illusion," even though I know now that it is not for me. Put it this way: there is no God, it's all a *story*. But it's a story which is full of spiritual power for those who think that they can honestly use it. I feel very unhappy about it and very lost. Being a priest has been the only thing which I have really *learnt to be*, and I find myself now quite untrained to be anything else. The order has been my family and my home. To live without Christ: I would once have thought this impossible, I would have thought that I would die.

I did not mean to pour all this out. I intended this to be a very practical letter! Well, that's the first thing. The second thing is this. You remember that boy, Joe Beckett? (The one who discerned you as a gent!) I love him dearly and have decided to go away with him to somewhere where we can work together out of London. This statement sounds as if it covers something else, but it doesn't. I don't even know if I am homosexual (I suppose I must be a bit, many priest are) or whether he is or what on earth will happen to us in the long run. It is just clear that I ought now to take him away from the world of criminality which he is getting entangled in here. This is the only decent and important act which I can perform at this present! I am the only thing in his life that represents any sort of value, and though I have no merit of my own, I can (my last task as a priest?) enact a sort of symbolic role for him, I can influence him and no one else can. So we are going. He has just, miraculously, agreed to come. And I have now I hope (again miraculously!) actually got a temporary job for the summer term, teaching history at a polytechnic in Leeds. I rang up old Fitzwilliam, you remember, our history master at school, and he put me onto someone and this job has turned up, at least by telephone. I haven't had it in writing yet. And even if this fails, I now feel more confident that I can get something or other. So I shall be able to support Joe. Now (and this is where you come in) I want the boy to get some sort of training and he says he might like to become an electrical engineer. Would you be willing to invest in him? The notion that *you* might give us some of the money you are so keen to get rid of somehow appeals to him—he regards you as a rather romantic figure!—and I have a little encouraged this idea though I know there is an element of bribery involved! I don't want Joe to feel that it'll be all grinding poverty up there in the north—and of course in the long run it won't be. I shall have a salary, he, I hope, will have a student's grant. It'll just be tough at first. And if you could help us over that first bit I'd be eternally grateful and I think honestly that money would be scarcely better spent. I wonder if you could let us have, say, five hundred pounds? I hesitate to call it a loan, as God knows when or how you'll get it back, but I would hope to start repaying some of it within a year, according to circumstances. I really would be *very* grateful, and I won't go on about that. Please send it first-class post by return to the Mission address. I'm not sure how much longer I shall be here.

Forgive me for going on so long about my own problems. Now, thirdly, about yours. I don't think you should sell the Hall. I've thought about it and of course I understand the good motives (as well as the bad ones!) which could lead you to want to do it. I just think it's a mistake. It's cruel to your mother. And I think you shouldn't be in a hurry to shuffle off this responsibility. Developing some of the land is another matter. But you shouldn't sell the place *or* give away all your money, though I certainly hope you'll give some to me! How can I put it? You're not up to it, Henry. You couldn't do it properly, and as done by you it would be ill done and have bad results. In this context you don't seem to me to understand yourself. Sorry if this sounds obscure, and not very polite! But do wait and see. And meanwhile look after your mother and Lucius, and (odd advice from a "priest") try and *enjoy yourself* a bit!

All the above needs to be explained at greater length. Please don't be offended by anything I have said. Let's meet soon. I'm in a terrible state of mind, actually.

Au revoir and love

Cato

Henry was interested moved and annoyed by this letter. What egoism! Was this what the religious life did for you? All this long spiel about his own plans, and this calm assumption that Henry would hand over the money. Of course the assumption was quite correct and Henry would send the money by return of post, but still his generosity should not be quite so coolly taken for granted. As for "going off" with that striking but rather apelike young man Henry (who could not conceive of being attracted by a male) felt that his friend must simply have taken leave of his senses. Doubtless the aberration would not last too long. And Henry could have done without the advice at the end. So Cato thought that Henry was not

218

worthy to perform a great moral act! Henry would show him. But what chiefly distressed him was that Cato would not be a priest any more. About this he felt a curiously deep sense of personal loss. Cato had somehow figured in his future plans as a sort of mysterious guide or sage, full of radiant certainties. Henry felt betrayed, let down. A struggling secularized Cato, no better than himself, would be of little use. However he looked forward to seeing him again. What would Cato think of Stephanie? Yes, he would show Cato how radically he could change his life.

Dreamily Henry put Cato's letter aside and took up the other letter. He opened it and began to read it. It was a little while before he could take in whom it was from.

Dear Henry,

You will think me mad, but I must write to you just like this out of the blue. I have to write. Since the idea came to me that I might it has been agony not to. I feel so sure, my heart is so clear and so entire, it just seems absurd not to speak out, and there is no question of any stupid "pride" or "modesty" which should make me keep quiet. I won't keep quiet!

Henry, listen, I love you. Are you surprised? I wonder. It must have been awfully obvious when we met lately, especially that time in the greenhouse with the fish. But the point is that it isn't new at all. I loved you a long time ago when I was a child, when you and Cato used to run and run and I would try to run after you when I was very small. Loving someone is just a fact. I don't mean by that that there were, and are, no reasons why I love you. I could think of thousands. But about the past, the always-has-beenness of this love, it's just there and I think I can scarcely remember a time when I didn't love you. As if I was asleep, and I just opened my eyes and there you were. Of course this was just a child's love and when you went to America though I did miss you I recovered and got to think you wouldn't ever come back. At least, I say I re-covered, I mean I wasn't pining for you, but I went on thinking about you, you are, you were my first man, apart from Daddy and Cato, and so you were my first real separated man, if you see what I mean. You were a sort of ideal figure, and when I grew up and got to know men I never thought they were as good as you, or as good as the dream you, and by now I did regard it as a dream since I thought I would never see you again. Then when I heard you were coming home after all I could think of absolutely nothing else. That

219

was why I left the college. At least I would have left anyway, but that was why I left then. I couldn't bear it, it would have been a physical torment, to be away there while you were here, though of course I thought that when I saw you it might all break and fade away. Well, it hasn't. Of course you're not the dream figure, nobody could be. (Actually you're funnier and nicer!) But somehow the you, the Henry that I always wanted, has remained there safe inside you —the you which I feel has always belonged to me, though I know this is a kind of blasphemy and you can't own somebody else like that. I doubt if you can even if you're married to them. And I was so frightened in case you'd be married or engaged or something and I was so relieved when you weren't. Well, Henry, that's the story. I know girls aren't supposed to tell, but I've got to tell—just in case you should fail to love me because you never knew how much I loved you. I want not to have to say later—I wish I'd told him. I want you to be able to *see* me, and as my love for you is so much of me (all of me, making me more than myself) then you must see that too. Not to see it would be not to see me, and not to tell you of it would be to deceive you. I haven't told anybody else, not even Daddy or Cato, they have no idea. And I want to tell you this, that I've never been to bed with anybody. I thought I'd wait, though I never dreamed that it was really you I was waiting for. I don't know, and I shake and tremble when I think about it, how you feel about me. Your mother has said more than once how much you like me—but that may have been just politeness or a mistake. Henry, I love you, and I want to marry you and live with you forever and be happy and make you happy and be entirely and absolutely yours, that's what I want. And don't think it's a silly young girl's infatuation or just because of my childhood, this is deep true love and not a fantasy. Of course I want to say, tell me at once, write to me at once, ring me up—but also, because I'm so frightened, I want to say, don't. Think it over. Consider what I say. Consider what you feel. There is plenty of time. You may feel that you don't know me enough. Please please don't drive me away because you want to spare my feelings. I would a thousand times rather suffer from being known and rejected than from being kindly set aside without being known at all. So don't be in a hurry to reply, there is no need to write any big letter, let us just meet in ordinary ways and I will not pester you with my emotions.
Forgive me.

So lovingly,
ever yours
Colette

Henry whistled. Then he lay back on his bed and found that he was laughing. He stopped laughing. This was no laughing matter. Poor little Colette. But how immensely sweet and touching it was that she loved him, and he could not help being pleased, though he felt sad too to think he would have so soon to render her unhappy.

Cato Forbes, looking around guiltily, pressed the bundle well down into the pile of old bricks and cracked cement in the rubbish tip. He had wrapped the cassock up carefully in newspaper and tied it with string but the paper had burst now and the powdery cement was whitening the black cloth. He pulled more of the rubbish over it until it was hidden. A horrible smell rose from the cassock and mingled with the rotten and limy odours of the rubbish tip. Had he been going around smelling like that? Had he smelt like that in the presence of Beautiful Joe? When he had completely buried the bulky parcel he felt wicked and relieved, as if he had been burying a dead baby. No one had seen him. He dusted off his hands against each other and began to walk back across the waste ground.

Then he saw the kestrel. The brown bird was hovering, a still portent, not very high up, right in the centre of the waste, so intent yet so aloof, its tail drawn down, its wings silently beating as in a cold immobile passion. Cato stood looking up. There was no one else around upon the desert space where already, after the rain, upon the torn and lumpy ground, spring was making grass and little plants to grow. The kestrel was perfectly still, an image of contemplation, the warm blue afternoon spread out behind it, vibrating with colour and light. Cato looked at it, aware suddenly of nothing else. Then as he looked, holding his breath, the bird swooped. It came down, with almost slow casual ease, to the ground, then rose again and flew away over Cato's head. As he turned, shading his eyes, he could see the tiny dark form in its beak, the little doomed trailing tail.

"My Lord and my God," said Cato aloud. Then he laughed and set off again walking in the direction of the Mission.

He wondered what Joe would think of him in mufti. It felt very strange to be in ordinary clothes after wearing the black gown. Cato was transformed. He was dressed in a dark grey corduroy suit, and red and white striped shirt and red silk scarf, the property (temporarily borrowed) of Gerald Dealman, which he had found under some paper in the bottom of a wardrobe during some final tidying-up operations at the Mission. Cato, in the unfamiliar garments, felt as if he were in fancy dress. He felt a kind of lurid shameless relief, more deeply a sense of guilt and shock. He was surprised to find how instantly eager he was to get rid of the old cassock and never see it again. Henry's precious cheque, now in his pocket, had arrived, but thanks to Gerald he need not immediately waste any of it on clothes.

At moments now Cato felt as if he must have gone mad. He had at last brought himself to write his formal letter of "resignation" to the head of his order. It had been extremely difficult and painful to bring himself to sit down and actually compose the letter. When it had been written he posted it quickly without re-reading. The technicalities of laicization could wait. As far as he himself was concerned he was out. The matter was settled now between himself and "God" and the formalities would merely be a matter of courtesy to his former colleagues. What made him feel that he must be crazy was this: he had given up the most precious privilege in the world and he could not determine exactly when or exactly why he had decided to do it.

It has all dissolved, all faded, he thought, trying to find some image for his loss of faith. Had it been some weak substance then, some mere reflected picture? It has gone, hasn't it? he constantly asked himself. Yes, it had gone, that seemed clear. But what had he lost? His livelihood, his friends, his mode of being, his identity. But what else, surely something else had gone, surely *the* thing had gone? But the thing is no thing, he thought, is that not the point? What is it that hurts me so, that pains me as if I had committed some awful crime or made some awful mistake? He thought, God is nothing.

God the Father, that is just a story. But Christ. How can I have lost Christ, how can *that* not be true, how can it, how can it?

And how can I not be a priest any more? That was a more manageable question, since there were so many practical problems involved in beginning to live without the priesthood. He was amazed at the ease with which he had got a job. This had not only been a good omen, it had somehow been an exercise of his new self, its will, its kind of satisfaction. It was the first ordinary good thing that had happened to him in his new life. The extraordinary good thing that had happened was of course Beautiful Joe's remarkable acquiescence in the idea of accompanying him. Whatever would it be like? And what had, so surprisingly to Cato, made up Joe's mind? Was it the idea, which had remained with the boy as something almost magical, of, perhaps indefinitely, sponging on Henry? Or was it, as Cato hoped, that Joe could now at last see how much Cato loved him? He did think that the boy had been impressed. And now: Joe who had never yet seen him without his cassock would be able to understand how absolutely free Cato had made himself so as to be bound again. He needs love, thought Cato, he wants love, every soul wants it. There is a simplicity here which human egoism is too devious to accept. Pure love can cure evil, ultimately nothing else can.

As he walked back across the wasteland which was beginning to look so like a meadow in the sunshine he felt himself full of that power. All the pain was with him, the searing sense of loss and shame, but he felt filled with the power of love, as if a scarred body could, with all its scars, be glorified. He smiled at the image which had so spontaneously arisen. Not I but Christ. Now only I. There is only I to *be* Christ, thought Cato. And as he thought of Joe, who was soon to come to him at the Mission, his heart was so rent with love that he almost staggered, and a great passionate power seemed to be flowing into him out of the steaming ground: for he was not imagining it, the ground was actually steaming a little after the rain in the hot sun. Cato stood still and let the joy of loving anticipation lick him like a flame.

He had no long-term plans. He had told Joe that he would go north tomorrow to find them somewhere to live. The term

223

did not begin for another fortnight. Joe had seemed to think it would be an adventure. Cato did not imagine that he would be able to keep Joe with him forever. He wanted to do two things, to convince the boy of his love, and to persuade him to learn a trade. Here Henry's money would certainly be of use, and Cato felt no qualms about asking for it. If necessary he would ask for more. He had faith that once Joe started to *learn* his intelligence would awaken and save him. Then, or sooner, Cato's part might be over. Meanwhile this comprised his task as a saviour and indeed his duty and Cato had ceased to have any doubts on the matter. About the details of their relationship Cato felt calmly agnostic. Love had led him in. Love would enlighten him from time to time as should be most expedient for him.

As he turned into the little truncated street, Cato saw a young man waiting just outside the Mission house. When he saw Cato he came towards him, and Cato recognized him as one of Brendan's students, a young ordinand. The youth was holding out a letter.

"From Father Craddock."

"Oh, thank you," said Cato.

He took the envelope and tore it open. Brendan had written upon a postcard:

I am sending this round by hand because I feel I should let you know at once that Father Milsom died last night. He spoke of you when he was dying.
How are you? Please come back here. Never mind about God. Just come.   B.

Cato looked up into the mild slightly inquisitive eyes of the young ordinand.

"Thank you for bringing this."

"Can I take a message back, a letter?"

"No. Nothing. Well, wait a moment." Cato took out a pencil and wrote on the inside of the torn envelope: *I am going away with that boy. Good-bye.* He paused, looking at the words. Then added *Pray for me.* He folded the envelope over and handed it back.

"Thank you, sir. I'll give it to Father Craddock."

Cato stood alone in the street looking down at his shadow on the uneven pavement. He felt a pure pang of grief about Father Milsom. Would he have gone to see him, had he still lived? No, thought Cato, not for a long time at any rate. The telephone would always have been out of order for that communication. Poor old man. Yet also, lucky old man. He had not outlived the joy of his faith. If there was a heaven, Father Milson was certainly there now. *Requiescit in pace. Lux perpetua lucet eo.* What a comforting idea. Only there was no heaven. Did I ever really believe there was? wondered Cato. He wished so much that he had written some sort of reply, some words of affection and thanks to Father Milsom's letter. He was still carrying the letter, now in the breast-pocket of the corduroy jacket. He put Brendan's card away into the same pocket, and turned down the alleyway so as to enter the house from the back. Only as his hand touched the gate did something strike him out of the recent past. Brendan's pupil had called him "sir." He thought, it's a bit like when Caesar was angry and addressed the tenth legion as *Quirites!*

The kitchen door was unlocked and Cato went in and closed it behind him. He went over to the sink and looked at himself in the mirror he used for shaving. He saw, as in a picture, his head, the striped shirt, the red scarf. It was a long time, it occurred to him, since he had looked at himself in this way. He had shaved carefully and combed his roughly cut hair. He looked much younger. There was a ridiculous almost perky air. Funny Face Forbes. Old Pudgie. He smirked at himself.

"Why it's *you*. I couldn't think who this chap was, gawping at himself in the mirror." Beautiful Joe had come in behind him.

Embarrassed, Cato turned. Joe, in a short black military-style leather jacket, looked about fourteen. His face had a youthful scrubbed look, his hair had been clipped a little shorter, damped, perhaps greased, and combed into two stiff curves behind his ears. Cato felt suddenly as if they were strangers again. It was an exciting feeling.

"Hello, Joe. I hope you like the gear."

Joe, still staring, sat down at the table in silence.

Cato began to feel uneasy. "Well, Joe—"

"Is this some sort of bloody joke?" said Joe.

"What is?"

"The get-up. You've no idea how bloody funny you look. Only I'm not laughing."

"The gear belonged to Father Dealman—"

"The gear! I'd be laughing only I'm crying! You look just about ready for Southend Pier."

"I suppose it is a bit of a shock."

"You can say that again!"

"But my dear Joe, I told you I was leaving the order, I told you—"

"I didn't believe you."

"Maybe you do now!"

"I didn't believe you would leave, I don't believe it."

"Well, have a bloody try," said Cato, sitting down at the table.

"And you've never used bad language to me before."

"If you call that bad language!"

"It is for you. But perhaps you'll go to the bad now. Failed priests always do."

"Well, maybe they do. We'll have to see in this case, won't we. Let's have a drink. I've got some wine here."

"You'll take to drink."

"Joe, just stop drivelling, will you. Can't you face the fact that I'm simply an ordinary person like yourself?"

"No, I fucking can't."

"And now we're quarrelling just like two ordinary people and isn't that rather wonderful? We're just two ordinary men at last. I want to help you, but I don't want to be some sort of false saint in your life. I simply love you. And I couldn't say it then, I had to leave to say it. Christ, can't you see?"

"Can't *you* see?" said Joe. He suddenly bit his lips into a straight line and frowned down at the table as if he were about to cry.

Cato looked at him carefully. "Joe, my dear, you've got to help me. We may have to get to know each other again, differently. All right. This hasn't been an easy change for me, and it won't easy. But if you love me—"

"I never said I loved you," said the boy, still staring at the

226

table where he was following the lines of the wood with his finger.

"You can learn to. I can do enough for both to begin with."

Joe looked up. He said, "Father, you're like a child. You don't know about the awful things."

"Joe, you're wrong, I do know about the awful things. And listen, you must stop calling me 'Father.' "

"What am I to call you then?"

"Don't you know my name?"

"No."

"Cato."

"What?"

"Cato."

"How do you spell it?"

"C A T O."

"That's a bloody funny name. Is it Italian?"

"No, it's Roman. You'll get used to it. You'll get used to—"

"No, I won't. I'm going to go on calling you 'Father.' Nothing else makes any sense between us."

"But I'm not a priest any more! I gave it up because of you—"

"That's not true."

"It's partly true, I've—"

"Partly true! Everything about you is partly true!"

"I've made myself free of everything else so that I can be with you, so that we can go away and start a new life together. We will do, Joe, won't we—I'll work and you'll train—and I shan't worry you—"

"I'm not coming," said Joe.

"What on earth do you mean? You said you would."

"I thought it would be different. I thought that rich chap would support us."

"But he will! Look, he sent a cheque." Cato put Henry's cheque on the table.

"And I thought you'd still be a priest, and that would make it all right. You've no idea how bloody stupid you look in those clothes. All the—all the sort of—magic's gone—what made me care—Now you're just a queer in a cord coat. You're the sort of person I spit on."

Cato, in sudden utter panic, reached across the table and seized the boy's hand. "Joe, don't say that! It's me. You know me."

"I don't. That's the trouble." Joe drew his hand away, pushing his chair back a little. "If we went away together, Father, it would be muck—muck like you don't know about. And I wouldn't care a fuck for it, for anything that you could give me, or anything that you could do for me. There'd be no joy there, Father, only hell, the only point would be money. I cared for you once, Father, but I cared for the other you, the one that wore a robe and had nothing, not even an electric kettle."

"I've still got nothing."

"You've got a cheque for five hundred pounds from Mr. Marshalson."

"But I only got it for you, I only did everything for you, I didn't want you to suffer, I didn't want you to be poor!"

"Well, it's all spoilt now. I'm sorry, I was thick—"

"As for Mr. Marshalson's cheque, that's easily dealt with." Cato took the cheque and tore it into small pieces.

Joe looked at the fragments, then spread them out a little with his fingers. "That's sad. That's really sad."

"I can get another one—"

"I don't care what you do, Father, only you can't do it with me."

"But Joe, don't abandon me. I've got nothing now. I've given away everything so as to be with you, and you did say—"

"I was crazy. It could never have worked, like that anyway. I used to think there were two things in the world, you and somehow what you stood for, and the hell where nothing matters but money. Now I think there's only one thing in the world. The hell where nothing matters but money."

Cato was silent. He was trying to think. If he could only find the right words, only make the right appeal—In spite of Joe's rejection of him they were close, closer than they had even been before. He leaned forward and gripped for a moment between his fingers the cold thick sleeve of Joe's black leather coat.

"Joe, listen, just listen and don't interrupt. I impressed you because I was a priest but a priest is just a symbol. And I can't be that any more. But still it's true that there isn't just hell. There's love and that's real and I do really love you. And there's no need for you to think what does he mean, what is he after? I don't know myself, except that I want to help you. Isn't this something that you shouldn't just throw away? Are you so rich in love that you can refuse this gift? Why not at least try it? Let me be in your life. You know me well enough to know I wouldn't dominate you or interfere. I just want to help and to serve. I suppose that's all there is left of my priesthood. You asked me once if I wanted a love affair, and I said no. Now I say, why not? Of course I want to hold you in my arms, and now that I'm just a queer in a cord coat at least I can tell you the truth! If it happens good, if it doesn't happen, also good. You know I'll never let my love be a burden to you, I want you to be free, that's what love is all about. Can't you accept it all simply and let me help you to be happy? You talk about living in hell—well, why live in hell? If you go on as you're doing at present, playing at being a petty criminal, you'll end up as a real criminal, and you'll lead a hateful miserable frightened life which you won't be able to escape from. Surely you want to be free and happy? We can live together in Leeds and enjoy life. We won't be short of money. I'll work and you can learn something interesting—"

"I don't want to learn anything," said Joe, still looking down at the table, moving his hands a little to make shadows on the wood. "You're always on about learning as if people liked learning things. Well, maybe you do but I don't."

"You said you might like to be an electrical engineer."

"You said I might. I might like to be a pop star. But I'm not going to learn anything. Learning's finished."

"All right, we needn't decide at once what you do. The important thing is to get away, to know each other better and find a way to live and to work—"

"You want to be in bed with me."

"That's not important. I want to be with you, to live near you, to see you. We needn't even be in the same house if you don't want."

"You said we wouldn't be short of money, but you tore up that cheque."

"Look, Joe, I can get another cheque, I can get any money that we need from Mr. Marshalson. Anyway I'll have a decent salary and—"

"I don't want to know about your feelings and who you want to be in bed with, it disgusts me. It's no good, Father, it doesn't add up. I don't like you like this any more, it all makes me feel sick. When I said I'd go with you, I didn't think it would be like this."

"But I told you!"

"Well, I didn't understand then, I didn't think. I couldn't stand it, we'd end up murdering each other like queers do. Anyway, I'm not a queer."

"All right, I never said you were—"

"Yes you did, you implied it, and I resent that. I dig girls, I want to fuck them, even if they're bloody stupid cunts. You're just trying to bribe me and I think it's horrible. I don't want to see you any more ever again."

"Joe, dear heart, don't say that!" Cato moved his chair and put a hand onto Joe's shoulder. He tried to draw the boy towards him.

In an instant Joe had leapt up and was at the door. "Don't touch me!"

"I'm sorry—"

"You go away, go anywhere, just go away. And don't bloody come after me again or I'll smash you. You don't know me, you don't know anything about me, you don't know what it's like to be me, you've never bloody cared to find out, you've just imagined me the way you want me. I've had a lousy life, no one's ever really cared for me, and you don't either. My father hated me and my mother hated me and my brothers hated me and I curse the lot of them and I curse you most of all because you pretended to be different and you're not. You tried to catch me and trap me, but I can see you now and all your nastiness and what you really are, so don't you come near me again or I'll kill you. I'm in with the big boys now, I'm in a gang, I'm working on big things, and I'm nothing to do with you and your rotten lying ideas any more. I'm in with real people and I'm going to make big money. So it's good-bye, Mr. bloody Forbes or Cato or whatever you call yourself now. And leave me alone, I mean it. You won't find me anyway, I'm leaving. I'm going to be with *them*, I've found them at last like I said I would. So good-bye and you can make your own hell only I won't be in it."

Cato leapt up. Beautiful Joe flashed out of the door and banged it shut in Cato's face. The door of the yard banged.

Cato, after opening the kitchen door, closed it again and sat down slowly at the table. He started stroking the wood and making shadows on it with his hands, as Joe had done. He thought, it's perfectly true, I didn't know him. But I did love him. And not just in a selfish way. I loved him as well as I could.

He sat there for a long time, looking at his hands and twitching his shoulders about inside the unfamiliar garments. He felt that he wanted to cry but he could not cry. He felt shook. He thought, I deliberately destroyed my capacity to help him. But what else could I have done? I told the truth. Perhaps I should not have told the truth. And now he has gone to *them*. And perhaps it is my fault. Better that a millstone should be hanged about my neck and I should be drowned in the depths of the sea.

There is no point in going to Leeds tomorrow, thought Cato, I would have so much liked looking for nice digs for Joe, but now, I don't care where I live. I'll go up there when term begins and live anywhere. Maybe I'll stay on here for the present. But not because I think he'll come back. I'm sure he won't come back. Maybe after all I'll go home. I'll go to Laxlinden, to Pennwood. I have lost Christ and I have lost Joe. And Father Milsom is dead and I didn't even answer his letter. I have got everything wrong.

And he thought: I will arise and go to my father, and will say unto him, Father, I have sinned against heaven and before thee, and am no more worthy to be called thy son.

Dear Colette,

I have got your sweet touching utterly ridiculous and dotty letter. What a load of enchanting nonsense! Of course one is grateful for any signal of approval upon the harsh human scene, but this goes too far! Did you really expect me to take it seriously? Please return yourself to reality forthwith! These are schoolgirl day-dreams. And why pick on me for your "crush"? I am as old as the hills, embittered by my childhood, talentless, godless, rootless, and by now at least half American. Also shortly to be penniless. You may have heard that I am going to get rid of my patrimony. I gather the rumour is getting round, so if it was the Hall you wanted, forget it. What you need is a nice sensible English boy, young, fresh-faced (not all gnarled like me) with a respectable job (schoolmaster? solicitor? architect?) (what about Giles Gosling?) who will set you up in a safe cosy English *home*. (I am not being sarcastic.) Anyway you probably want your father to survive for a few years yet and he would certainly die of apoplexy at the prospect of me as a son-in-law. No, no, it won't do; as far as I'm concerned it's just good for a laugh, and I expect by now you are laughing yourself.

There is in fact a further reason why I cannot be yours, which is that I am engaged to be married to a dear girl called Stephanie Whitehouse, who is staying with me at the Hall. We are getting married soon and will then probably buzz off to America. So there! Thanks for your letter though. You must be the only person who ever preferred me to Sandy. Anyway it's all a girlish dream and will blow away as such. My very best wishes to you.

                                                                    Henry

My dearest Bell,

I am sorry I haven't written properly sooner. Everything has been, since I got here, awful and *mad*. An identity crisis I guess you and Russ would call it! I couldn't write because I didn't know who I was. I still don't. It occurs to me that I didn't in America either, only there it doesn't matter because there nobody knows who they are. (And I daresay they are the better for it!) Here I had lots of hats waiting for me to try on. I suppose I am still in process of rejecting them all. (Only the clown's fits!) You speculated so much

about how it would be with my mother and none of the speculations has been quite right. There's no row, no reconciliation, just a
dreadful blank. I didn't want it, I don't like it, but I may somehow
all the same have brought it about, or else we both did. It's all
abrasive and hurtful and basically cruel, on both sides. It's odd
that I can see this and describe it but I can't change it. And all the
old faithful psychoanalytical machinery which at this very moment
you are busy wheeling up won't do a thing either. All those would-
be deep explanations are so abstract and so simple when confronted with the awful complex thereness of a relationship which
has gone wrong. You thought she might weep over me, need me,
want me to become Sandy. Not a bit of it. Her feelings for *him*
remain totally private. I think I just *irritate* her, I'm not even a dis-
appointment! I haven't seen a single tear. My God, she's tough. I
suppose that women (I mean bourgeois English ones, not liberated
zanies like you!) learn pretty early on that they've got to be alone
and bear things alone, even when they're in the bosom of their
family. I daresay my father and Sandy were just the ticket, exactly
what she wanted, what she worshipped, but all the same they were
bloody ruthless egoists like all men are when they aren't positively
prevented from being so by exceptional women: hence that toughness, that solitude. I certainly can't get through to her, and given
that she hasn't shown me the slightest sign of tenderness or affection
since I arrived I'm not actually trying very hard! I think she expects
to be revered and accepted like a sort of monument, and that's not
my thing. And talking of monuments I have something to tell you.
I have decided (and this doesn't please my mother much either) to
see the Hall and all the land and all the property and all the stocks
and shares, the lot, and get rid of all the proceeds, give it away,
strew it about, get it absolutely off me, off my hands, off my neck!
I hope you're not shocked, saddened? I know it would be fun to
entertain you and Russ here, to get drunk together in the pseudo-
Grinling Gibbons library, after which you would want to dance
naked in the park or something! It would be nice to *épater* a bit
around the place! But these are childish pleasures. And honest,
Bella, I just *hate* it all, I *hate* it, I didn't know how much until I
saw it all again and my bloody mother doing the Duchess in the
middle of it. Faugh! I thought in my dreams that I might destroy
the whole set-up, but I didn't know that I'd be strong enough until
I actually saw it and observed myself reacting to it. My mother has
taken this final solution fairly calmly. She will be all right, she has a
decent annuity and will live in a nice little house nearby. Now I
know you're fishing after motives of which there are *hundreds* and

some of them may be disreputable (as if I cared) but mainly: I don't think I ought to have much when others have little and: I haven't the temperament to be an English country gent. I'd hate it and I'd become nasty. (O.K., nastier!) It's not just a spiritual burden, my dear, it's a bloody material practical one: walls, roofs, trees, servants, drainage, taxes ... God, the blessed simplicity of our life at Sperriton, and Christ how I miss it!

Well, that's bombshell number one, if it is one. (I wonder if you and Russ expected it?) Stand by, honey, for bombshell number two. I am engaged to be married. I am going to marry a sweet humble sexy totally unlettered kittenish beast called Stephanie Whitehouse whom I have inherited from Sandy—she is, you might say, part of the property. She is (literally) an ex-prostitute and was kept by Sandy secretly in London! (There's glory for you!) She loves me and she is the only woman apart from you that I've ever liked being in bed with! She has had a miserable life and I pity her intensely. She is not at all beautiful but very attractive, she warms and excites me and I feel safe with her. She is totally un-Laxlinden Hall, and I can't wait to get her away from the bloody scene here. Her age is thirty-four, by the way, as you'll certainly want to know that!

Bella, darling, don't be jealous. (All right, you'd clout me for saying that if you were here!) You know as well as I do that love (like other important things) is expansible—perhaps love is infinitely expansible, and the more the more. I can love poor Stephanie without taking any jot or tittle from my love for you. And listen: this has all become clear to me in the last few days. I feel that, in spite of all the horrors, I've been *thinking* like a cool little computer ever since I set foot on English soil, and I've only just come up with the answer. I want to come back to my job, I want to come back to you and Russ (*you* are my family), I want to bring Stephanie to Sperriton. I know we all said I'd come back, but did we all believe it? I'm not sure whether I did. But now: it seems to me that by some sort of deep unconscious ingenuity I've found the only woman who could fit the jigsaw puzzle. If I married an intellectual girl or even an ordinary English (or *a fortiori* American!) girl it wouldn't work, I couldn't come back. You understand. But little Stephanie is a waif and utterly not intellectual, she's gentle and sweet, and you'll like her and she'll fit. That at least is how I hope it and see it now. And I know that you will help me, and help her, because you are clever and good. I can't and won't lose you and Russ and it's now beginning to seem that maybe I won't have to. And quite apart from the jigsaw, I've got to come back to Sperriton anyway because I could never get a job over here or sell my enormous talents in England!

Please, Bella, understand all this and reassure me as you've always done. Receive poor Stephanie—she's a simple grateful girl and no sort of trouble-maker. And, you know something—since experiencing once again, from my dear mother, what English coldness can be like I value and yearn for, more than I can express, that American warmth, gentleness, and freedom into which you and Russ welcomed me and initiated me. Here I can feel myself getting colder every day—which is another reason why I must run. I've thought about you both so much since I've been here, and with such gratitude. I'm sorry I didn't write sooner, but I've been in such a *muddle*—and I'm glad I've written at last because a lot of things have become clear only since I started this letter! Show this to Russ and give him my love. Write to me soon, Bella darling—ever with so much love your (as you once called me) demon son

H.

"Careful," said Henry, standing back. "I don't want any strain put on it. You hold that bit up, Mr. Bellamy, while Rhoda unhooks those last rings. O.K. Now you can both drop it."

The tapestry descended with a loud plop to the floor and a cloud of dust arose. Rhoda and Bellamy climbed down from the tall ladders which they had erected at either end.

The sun had come out and the rain pools upon the terrace were little enamelled plates of radiant blue. A pale morning light reflected a subdued clarity in through the library windows. Now revealed upon the bare expanse of wall, an enigmatic vista of the past, was an old forgotten faded wallpaper with a trellis pattern enlaced with trailing roses. At the same time the library suddenly seemed much larger, much colder, as if the future had opened it up with rough chilling force. Henry went across to the tapestry and kicked it, eliciting another cloud of dust.

"Needs cleaning. Now could you fold it up and see if you can get it somehow into the back of the Volvo? No, don't do it here, take it out into the hall, could you, I'm suffocating."

235

Rhoda and Bellamy rolled the tapestry into a long clumsy sausage and hauled it out through the library door. Henry caught a last glimpse of Athena's powerful hand plunged into the hero's hair. He closed the door. Then he sat down at the round table and looked at the great blank expanse of wall, faded and pale and covered with little triangular cobwebs. He breathed deeply.

Gerda came in, wearing one of her long blue robes, the skirt swinging. Henry rose. She threw some papers down on the table with a gesture of violence. "Why did you do this without telling me?"

"I did tell you. I said I was sending it to Sotheby's."

"You didn't say you were going to do it today."

"Today or another day, what's the difference? You can't hang it in your cottage."

"This is hurtful, and on purpose."

"Mother, you don't understand," said Henry. "It's not on purpose to hurt, that would be ludicrous and petty. This business is bigger than you and me. It's a big financial transaction which in the end will benefit a lot of people whom we've never heard of and who have never heard of us. Do you imagine I'm enjoying this?"

"Yes."

"Well, you're wrong. I love that tapestry. I like it better than anything else in the house, and I like it more than you do because for you it's just a nice old accustomed wall-covering, while for me it's a work of art!"

Bird-headed Rhoda, expressively waving gloved hands, came in and said something.

"What's she saying?"

"She says it won't go into the Volvo," said Gerda, moving away towards the fireplace where a blazing log fire was disputing with the sunny light.

"Oh damn. Well, just leave it folded up in the hall, would you, Rhoda."

"Then why do you torment yourself," said Gerda, when Rhoda had gone. "And me. And your fiancée."

Henry followed her and stood stroking a garland of burnished chestnut brown acorns in the wood of the chimney-piece. "Mother, please, what has got to be has got to be. You've had your time here and I'm not going to begin. Be fair. Be fair to me."

"Why are you in such a hurry to sell the tapestry?"

"Because I want to sell something that I value and sell it quick. That will make the rest easier. When you thread a needle the tip of the thread must go through first and the rest follows. This is the tip of the thread. Mother, it's all going to disappear like Aladdin's palace. And we must now begin to believe that it will. I don't think you believe it yet. Perhaps in a way I don't."

"If you are so upset about it all," said Gerda, not looking at him, "and so unsure of what you want, oughtn't you to wait? And why are you taking your fiancée away now so soon?"

"I wish you wouldn't keep on referring to her as my fiancée. You know her name."

"Well, she is your fiancée, isn't she?"

"Yes, but you are being sarcastic."

"Why are you taking her away so soon?"

"Because you despise her."

"Henry," said Gerda. "Be sensible enough to have a little charity. I am trying to get to know her."

"You are trying to take her over."

"Oh don't be ridiculous! You resented our talking about Sandy after breakfast."

Henry turned and made for the door.

"Henry, wait, please."

Henry paused and faced her. "You snubbed me and needled me all through my childhood and you can't stop doing it now. You don't want peace. You want war. All right. I know you can't forgive me for being alive while Sandy is dead."

"Henry," said Gerda. "Stop tormenting yourself. You are fighting with yourself not with me. If you only knew how much I pity you."

Henry left the room softly closing the door behind him.

Gerda moved slowly back to the table and sat down. She sat there in a strained position, perfectly still.

A few minutes later Lucius came in, wearing his cloak, combing his wind-blown hair with his fingers. He said, "They've gone." Then he saw the desolated wall. "Oh my God! So that's what that great pile of stuff is out in the hall."

"It wouldn't go in the Volvo," said Gerda.

Lucius then saw the papers lying on the table, upon which Gerda had placed a large flat hand. He raised his eyebrows, then strolled towards the fire, where he stood humming pensively for a while, then turned cautiously to look at Gerda.

Gerda gave him her attention at last. "Lucius, what is all this stuff I found in your room? What is this, for instance? 'Dully her feet call up echoes that each time remember less. Clump, clump. The old girl.'"

"Oh—just poetry—"

"And this. 'Treading the paths of the house she misses the ways of the heart. Clump, clump. The old girl.' Am I supposed to be the old girl?"

"No, of course not, my dear—"

"And what is this, 'Her kitten warmth distracts me with a thousand women.' Who is this kitten?"

"No one my dear, it's imaginary—it's art—"

"Art! I can't tell you how impertinent and offensive I find this versifying. There's pages of it. 'Clump, clump' indeed! Here." Gerda pushed the pages at him.

Lucius gathered them, hesitated, stood up. "What do you—"

"If you were a gentleman you'd burn them."

Without any hesitation Lucius went to the fireplace. He threw the poems into the hot innards of the fire where they flamed up at once. He turned back to Gerda and sat down opposite to her at the table, regarding her with a mild quizzical expression and easing his cloak off onto the chair.

Gerda looked at him attentively, frowning. "So you are going to accept your pension from Henry?"

"Yes, my dear."

"Have you arranged to live with Audrey?"

"No. Rex won't let me."

"Where will you go then?"

"I'll find a little room."

"Where?"

Lucius sat looking at her with his bright mild face. "Somewhere near you, dear, if you don't mind. You're all that I've got left. All these things don't matter. I even think Henry may be right, I admire him, I wish I had his courage. We are getting old, my dear, you and I. If we lived in the East, we would be thinking of entering a monastery. Perhaps we ought really to give up the world. In a way, Henry is just making us do what we ought to do. We should live more simply at our age. All this stuff doesn't matter, this house, this furniture, those lawns and trees, it's all a kind of illusion, it's just a tapestry that can be folded up and sold. What matters is you and me, and we can get on better perhaps without them and all the care they represent. So I'd like to live near you, in a little room. I love you, Gerda, and I've given my whole life to loving you. I may have made a nonsense of most things, but not of that."

"All this is rubbish," said Gerda. "You've never 'cared' about anything here except strolling in the park and getting your meals served to you. You aren't fit to give up the world. And as for being old, speak for yourself. You're a good deal older than I am."

"I know, my dear, I was only—"

-"So you claim to be resigned?"

"Yes. The tapestry's gone. It will all go. I've said good-bye to it already."

"Well, I haven't," said Gerda. "Now go away, please, I want to think."

Lucius trotted upstairs to his room and poured himself out a little whisky and put on the second Brandenburg concerto. He began hastily to write out his poems again. He knew them all by heart.

Gerda sat thinking. She thought, *he* has made us old. Have I come to the end of being a busy active sensible woman, and am now to become a useless whining spiteful old hag? Then, staring at the wall, she started to remember the endless silly jokes that Sandy used to make about what was happening on the tapestry.

"Don't go on about it, Steph."

"And it's so unkind to your mother."

"It's a unique relationship."

"I wish you'd talk ordinary. You make everything into a theory. I don't know when you're serious."

"Almost all the time would be a good rule to go by."

"It's not a big house really and your mother runs it on a shoe-string, she was telling me—"

"You and she got on jolly well!"

"Aren't you glad?"

"Oh yes—yes—"

"I think she's a poor unfortunate old woman."

"I think that hardly describes my mother."

"You run her down, but you want to admire her all the same, I can see it all."

"You can't see it all and you never will. Don't try and understand, Steph. People who understand get murdered."

"Sometimes you frighten me. You were so rude to her, I could hardly believe it, and it's so awful that you're selling the house, it's a *nightmare*."

"Some men like to spend their lives playing with their property. I don't. I don't want to waste my time and yours bothering about trees and walls and drainpipes. My mother manages it somehow—"

"You think I couldn't?"

"I don't see why you should. I want us to be free."

"I don't want to be free. I'd *love* to spend my time on trees and walls and drainpipes. I've never possessed anything in my life."

"Lucky you."

"You've never known—"

"Ever since the world began, probably since Eden, men have been led by women into having material possessions. That's women's thing—having. I don't say it's their fault, it's their

240

nature, women have, men are. Well, thank God you're not going to involve me—"

"I wish I'd never seen the place."

"I didn't want you to see it. I wanted you to see my mother. Just once—"

"Why did you want me to see her at all then?"

"I wanted my mother to receive you and welcome you and recognize you and be courteous to you. I wanted to show you that it was possible."

"You mean because it would help me not to feel—"

"Yes."

The yellow Volvo rattled over the cattle-grid and turned left towards the village.

"You decide everything without me," said Stephanie. "You don't regard me as an equal."

"Very few men regard women as their equals," said Henry, "and if I do not regard you as mine that has nothing to do with your past. I just love you, and I regard you as my property. Not all those bloody trees."

Stephanie slid her arm along the seat of the Volvo behind Henry's back. She was wearing her black dress with the terrier brooch but had unbuttoned it at the neck. Her appearance had changed, so it seemed to Henry, since he had first met her. There was a brooding bafflement in her round eyes, a spirit of secrecy and thought which gave to her face intensity, almost beauty. She pressed her lips together, tasting her lipstick. "You're funny. I wonder if you mean anything you say? I never said good-bye properly to your mother."

"She was in a pet. Not about you."

"Will you buy me a diamond ring?"

"Oh, I suppose so."

"I'll believe anything you tell me if you'll buy me a diamond ring."

"You believe in magic. Well, naturally you do."

"Henry, please let us live at the Hall. You could sell everything else and keep the Hall. You *can't* sell it, you must be *mad*."

"Steph, I've got to drop it or it will destroy me. And if I just leave it to my mother it will get me in the end. Christ, is it me or the Hall you want? I hate the place with every atom of my soul. I can't tell you how pleased I am to be going back to London with you."

"I've been so deprived and miserable, I've had nothing—"

"I'll work hard for you, Steph. That will make sense. I want to live an ordinary life that makes sense."

"It's all because of Sandy."

"It's not because of Sandy!"

"It's because—"

"You and my mother had a jolly good talk about Sandy, didn't you?"

"Are you jealous?"

"Do you want me to ditch the car?"

Henry abruptly turned the Volvo into a lay-by and switched off the engine. They were almost in the village. Opposite to them was the sunlit wall of the park, the big rectangular golden stones glistening a little as the sun touched here and there the spiral patterns of the shell-fossils.

At that moment Henry saw the tall figure of Colette Forbes striding towards them along the road. He hesitated, reached for the switch, then sat back. She would have received his letter by now. He passionately did not want to talk to her.

Stephanie, turned with her back to the road, said, "What's the matter?"

Henry sat rigid, staring in front of him. The windscreen darkened. Colette walked round the car to Henry's side and Henry wound down the window. Colette was wearing a belted jerkin of green tweed and matching knee-breeches and a white shirt. Her long brown hair was looped up into a complex knotted tail which now hung forward over her shoulder.

"Hello, Henry."

"Hello, Colette. Stephanie, this is Colette Forbes who lives nearby. Colette, this is my fiancée, Stephanie Whitehouse."

"How do you do?" said Stephanie.

"Hello," said Colette, then, addressing Henry, "I got your letter about her."

"Well, there she is," said Henry, "as large as life. Thanks for your letter, I appreciated it."

"You appreciated it? That's a funny word."

242

"It was a funny letter."

"I'm glad it amused you. I think your reply was very stupid and very rude."

"Oh dear—"

"It was offensive and ungenerous and untruthful. You pretended to regard me as a child because you were afraid to face the challenge of a real relationship. You tried to make a joke out of something utterly serious and deep. You deliberately didn't treat me with respect. You can't have believed what you said, you were lying."

"Really, Colette. I think you are being stupid and rude! I wrote you a perfectly friendly, perfectly clear letter. After all, yours wasn't all that easy to answer! I hope at least you got the point."

"You were unkind and untruthful."

"What a cross peevish little girl!"

"What is this?" said Stephanie.

"May I say something to her?"

"No!"

Colette lowered her head to the window of the car. "Miss Whitehouse, I just want to tell you this. I am going to marry Henry Marshalson. I have known him and loved him all my life and he belongs to me. That's all. I am going to marry Henry. He is mine. Good-bye."

The tall figure whisked away. Henry caught a quick glimpse of Colette's long legs, clad in the green knee-breeches, swinging over the stile into the field which bordered the lay-by. He stared after her. Then he began to laugh. He started the engine. He laughed and laughed. The yellow Volvo sped away.

"How are you, Steph?" said Henry, after he had stopped laughing. He gave her a quick glance. The Volvo raced up a hill and turned onto the motorway.

Stephanie was shuddering, her plump legs drawn up under her, hunched behind her handkerchief, tears descending.

"Come, Steph, don't suffer from shock, I won't let you. That idiot girl is just good for a laugh. You didn't take it seriously, did you?"

"You were engaged to her, you were engaged to her—No wonder your mother was so strange—"

"I'm not engaged to her! She's just a naughty fantasy-ridden schoolgirl. I've only seen her twice since she was an adult."

"She said you lied to her, so you must have promised—"

"I tell you I've scarcely seen her—"

"Why were you laughing?"

"Because she always makes me laugh."

"But you said you'd only met her twice."

"Well, I laughed twice. This is the third time, and the last. If she upsets you she's not a joke."

"She's a witch. She wants you and she'll get you. She said 'He's mine' and it sounded true. She's put a spell on us, I can feel it."

"I'll give you a diamond ring to protect you."

"She'll draw you to her. You'll keep going back. You *must* have been engaged to her or she wouldn't have said those things."

"You don't know her! Now, Stephanie, stop it. I'll never see her again."

"Really?"

"Look, I haven't told you this, but when I've sold the house—"

"I don't want you to sell the house."

"When I've sold the house we're going to America. Back to my job there—"

"I don't want to go to America. Doesn't what I want matter?"

"It's so nice there, we'll feel so free and happy. I've got such a lovely little house—"

"I want to live at the Hall."

"If you lived at the Hall you'd be my mother's slave."

"I want to be your mother's slave."

"Oh, stop crying!"

"That girl will get you, she's a witch, I can feel it, she sort of attacked me, I feel I've been clawed."

"Stephanie, must you start this on the motorway?"

"I'm not strong enough to hold you against her, I know I'm not."

The yellow Volvo darted for an exit, rolled along the approach road into a suddenly quiet country lane, bumped on

244

a little way and came to a halt in the mud beside a five-barred gate. A lark was singing.

"Steph—look at me straight—don't hide behind the hankie—"

Stephanie looked at him, showing him her red swollen face shining with tears, her wet lips and drooping trembling mouth.

"Stephanie, hello, there isn't such a thing as a non-smudge lipstick, is there, yours is everywhere, you look a real gink, you look like a funny girl in a picture."

"You can't love me, it's impossible, you love her—"

"If I loved her would I laugh?"

"I don't know, you're so peculiar."

"You're my funny girl in my picture. And we're going to go to America and you're going to like it. You'll say I'm a male chauvinist pig, all right, I'm a male chauvinist pig. I've got to save myself, otherwise I can't save you."

"You love her, she's so young, I'm so frightened, she frightened me—"

"Stop whining, Stephanie, or I'll hit you. We've come together and it's fate, you were made for my situation and my problem. I asked the world a question and you were the answer. I've never been able to make love to a woman like I have to you. And don't say 'then it's just sex.' What do you mean, 'just sex'? Everything is sex, your hankie with the lipstick on it is sex, and the Volvo is sex, and that blue road sign and the moss on the gate and the silly old lark singing and the way I want to look after you. I've never wanted to look after anybody before, I've never had anybody to look after before, I've never had anything of my own since my mother took away my teddy bear."

"You just pity me."

"Of course I pity you. You pity yourself."

"You just want to annoy your mother with me."

"Damn all these justs. I could do that without marrying you."

"You won't marry me, you haven't even given me a ring."

Henry took off one of his driving-gloves and hit her across the face. She turned away and leaned her head against the window whimpering and biting her handkerchief.

"Stephanie, don't fret us to pieces. Look, do you love me or don't you? It's not just because of Sandy, is it?"

"No—"

"You don't feel you have to let me own you because he did? You loved him and I can't really see why you should love me. You know, you're not the only one with doubts. He was a tall handsome man and I'm a little skinny dark fellow. You don't have to have me, you can clear off. But if you do marry me, I'm the boss and we do what I want. O.K.?"

"O.K.—"

"Christ, I've got my troubles too, I'm lost, I don't know who I am, you're not the only one with an identity problem. Now stop crying. *At once*."

"I'm sorry. That girl frightened me so."

"Look, now there's lipstick all over my glove. Let's get out of the car. The sun's quite warm. Let's go into that field. I'll bring a rug. Come on Stephanie, quick, quick. Quick."

Later on the lark was still singing, an invisible point in the blue sun-radiant air. Flooding the sky with a song which, with little momentary ecstatic pauses now and then, went on and on and on.

"You do love me, Steph?"

"Yes, yes. Only it's like a dream, it's too good to be true, as if I daren't."

"It's the end of a story, Stephanie, and the beginning of another one."

"They lived happily ever after?"

"I don't know. I doubt it. But they lived together and trusted each other and helped each other and told each other the truth. Eh, Steph?"

"Yes."

"Listen to the lark."

"Give him his plate, and you go to bed."

Cato looked at Colette, so clumsy, so graceful, standing by the stove in her old green overall stained by garden mud, her looped hair tied back by a stringy ribbon, her face glowing and shiny as a boy's. He looked at his father, who was almost frowning in an effort not to beam, his grubby hands beyond leather-bound cuffs restlessly scratching the ridgy wood of the kitchen table. Cato looked into two pairs of eyes shining with love and welcome. And he thought, how lucky I am to be loved by such splendid people and how little they can do for me now, for all their goodwill. This is the first day of the new world wherein I must remake myself and as a duty search for happiness. How shrunk I feel, how thin and like a needle with deprivation and defeat and shame and the loss of all that gives me substance. He thought, I have lost my power, I have lost my stature and my dignity, and how unworthy it is to think of it in these terms as if that was what mattered.

"That's good. Now stop pawing him. Off you go, Colette."

"But, Daddy— Oh, all right. Good night, dear, *dear* Cato."

Cato thought, they are sorry for me. Love purifies their pity. Others will pity me less purely and I shall dwindle. I shall get used to being nothing after all except a queer in a cord coat. He began to eat the stew which Colette had warmed up for him. He had arrived home late.

"So you've got a job already? That's good. And in Leeds, a good place."

"It's only temporary."

"You might get into the university there, I know one or two people—"

"It'll take a bit of time to get back—as I haven't been studying lately."

"Pity you wasted all that time. At least earlier you were learning things. The last years have been a dead loss."

"Yes—"

"Well, you can settle down and study now. All your books are here. It'll be like old days, we'll both be working."

"Yes—"

"I thought you'd come to your senses in the end. It beats me how anybody can believe all that stuff. You must have felt you were in a false position. Aren't you relieved now it's all over?"

"Yes—"

"It's amazing how even rational people can deceive themselves. You're not the only one. God, I hated you in the black robe. Now you look like a man again."

"Yes, Dad—"

"Well, thank heavens you've pulled yourself out, and not too late either. We'll make you a career in the university."

"I doubt if—"

"In this day and age, well, it beats me—I suppose the thing has a sort of aesthetic appeal. Was that it?"

"Perhaps, partly—"

"Oh I can understand that. Religion has always been seducing art. And belonging to a big show, like joining the Communist Party, international brotherhood and history on your side and so on. That was the fashion when I was young."

"Only you never joined."

"Never tempted to. I saw through it straightaway. I was always too much of a craggy individual, never could stand bosses. Some people like them, there's safety in obedience, there's even thrills. Not for me. I was far too literal-minded. I always stuck to what I could understand. Truth is a pretty literal matter, it's a matter of details, what you can explain and get clear. I saw the danger signals. As soon as you start chasing after what's large and shadowy you get involved in lies, the lies in the soul, the things you can't quite see and can't quite work out but which you accept, because you're in love with the whole. Politically and morally, that's the road to hell. Any sort of metaphysics is a lie, anything big is a lie, it's bound to be."

"Yes, I think perhaps you're right," said Cato.

"You said I was a Philistine—"

"Good heavens, did I? I'm sorry—"

"Well, you said I was a spiritual Philistine."

"I only meant—"

"All right, I know what you meant. I don't believe in all those myths and legends and I think the notion of survival after death is the most morally debilitating idea ever invented, but I believe in the good life and in trying to be a good man and in telling the truth—I think that's at the centre of it all, telling the truth, always trying to find out the truth, not tolerating any lie or any half-lie—it's the half-lies that kill the spirit. You know, I'm not such a Philistine as you think."

"I'm very sorry I—"

"Your mother was a sort of saint. We were Friends when we were children, but religion passed out of our lives quite naturally. They knew a thing or two though, those old Quakers, there was something decent and honest there. The Inner Light, that's just truth itself. I saw that early on. I made my own sort of sense of it all. Not all that horrible theology, that sickly picturesque paraphernalia which appeals so much to your aesthetic sense, but just the humble business of living a life, earning your bread, helping other people, fighting against liars and tyrants. That's all there is to it, Cato, and that's enough."

"Yes—"

"You know, I never really let you have it—I never really told you what I thought and felt about that—"

"You said some pretty strong things."

"Nothing like what I felt like saying. I could see it was no use shouting at you. I abominate that bloody religion. It's got the cunning of the devil in it. Wherever it flourishes it kills honesty and thought and freedom."

"Dad, I'm knocked out, I think I'll go to bed."

"You're still half in love with that foul rubbish."

"It's not all rubbish."

"All right, go back to it then, I'm not stopping you. I thought you'd made up your mind."

"I have made it up. I don't believe in God any more and that's that, I'm through with the thing. Only please don't be angry with me and talk in that sort of angry tone. I'm glad to be home and I'm glad you're glad."

"Colette said I bullied you when you were children. I didn't, did I?"

"Yes, I think you did, but we loved you, and love is just as important as truth. I'm going to bed. Good night, Dad."

"I thought I was lecturing you. Now you're lecturing me. I'm so happy that you've come home. All right, all right, good night then, sleep well. I shall sleep well. I feel there is peace in the house at last. Good night."

Cato went upstairs to his room, the room which had been his ever since he could remember. The lamps were turned on. The patchwork coverlet on the well-designed light-oak bed had been folded back by Colette. There was a hot water bottle. The room had a sort of curious silence in it which Cato felt as an air wafted from his childhood, as if the room were still communing with the boy who had slept there and had read his books there night after night, and felt so happy and so quiet and so safe. The little neat landscapes of hillsides and cottages and trees which were obviously imaginary and obviously the product of innocent and artless minds hung still upon the walls in their shiny varnished frames. The dressing-table was covered with a blue and brown folk-weave cloth, upon which the ivory brush and comb set with his initials upon it had been carefully laid out, together with a silver-backed mirror which had belonged to his mother. His father had spoken of peace in the house, and there was peace, Cato could feel it round about him. It was a kind of plain peace, a peace of the woods and fields, not pagan even, ancient and blameless and simple. He felt it, he recognized it, but it could not enter him, it could not fill him, as a lost vanished peace had once done. "May the peace of God which passeth all understanding keep your hearts and minds in the knowledge and love of God ..." He sat down on the bed. Time passed.

Then he heard a little sound, a surreptitious sound like the sound of a mouse moving. His eyes became wide and alert and he listened. It came again. He puzzled, then recognized it as the sound of stifled sobbing. Colette was crying in the next room. After a moment Cato got up and tiptoed to the door.

His father's room was at the other end of the house, down a few stairs and up again. This end had always been the children's domain. Old memories came again to Cato as he scratched on Colette's door in a special way, then opened it noiselessly.

"Colette—dear—what is it?"

"Don't put the light on."

"I won't—what is it? Budge up, I want to sit on the bed."

"I thought you were asleep—you must be so tired—I'm so sorry—"

"Little Bear, don't grieve—"

"Big Bear, I'm so glad you're home. Oh I'm so stupid, so stupid—"

"So am I. Why are you?"

"I fell in love with somebody—he doesn't love me—it was a silly idea—I even sort of did it on purpose—but oh it hurts so—"

"Someone at the college, I suppose?"

"Well—someone I met—"

"But it's no good?"

"No, no, it's finished, he's going to marry somebody else."

"I bet he wasn't worthy of you."

"Of course he wasn't worthy of me, he's a perfectly silly man, but I just want him so, I want him more than anything in the world, I pine for him, all day, every minute, it's so *stupid*—"

"Did you go to bed together?"

"How calmly you say it. I suppose it's the confessional. No, of course not. I'm a virgin, I'm going to wait till I marry— only now I'll never marry because I just want *him* and no one else will do—I think I'd better become a nun after all—Oh Cato, I'm sorry you're not a priest any more."

"So you don't share Dad's glee at the end of this aberration. Why are you sorry?"

"It made a kind of place, an otherness. I can't explain. Not like magic exactly—but something precious and holy—even though I didn't believe—I wish you'd stayed there."

"I wish I could have done. Now stop crying and go to sleep. You know you'll get over this chap, you can even see he's not worth grieving over. Pull yourself together, Colette."

"You sound just like Daddy."

"I expect I'll get more like him every day now that I've left the Church. I could do worse. Think how lucky you are in a

251

world full of misery, and how young and free you are in a world full of people whose lives are done for. Just try to let cheerfulness break in. We'll talk of this tomorrow if you like. Now go to sleep. Think quiet thoughts. Go to sleep."

"'Think quiet thoughts.' That's what Daddy said Mummy used to say."

"Yes, I remember."

"Give me a blessing. I know you can't now, but give me some sort of blessing."

"May the spirit of love and truth and peace make its home in your heart, now and always."

"That's nice. What is it?"

"I just made it up. Will you go to sleep now?"

"Yes. Good night, Cato. I'll think: Cato's home, and go to sleep on that."

"Good night, Little Bear."

Cato went back to his room and sat down again upon his bed. He felt sympathy for Colette, then envy. How simple. How clean her pain was, and how soon she would recover. She would find a good husband and live at Pennwood and bring up healthy clever children who would become doctors and lawyers and teachers. She would achieve the central goals of humanity, a paragon of nature. And in the time to come he would be proud of her and glad of her and he would visit her happy home and feel envious and comforted and sad.

The new world, he thought, the new life, and how sad it is. I suppose I should be congratulating myself, it may even be that later I shall look back on *this* as heaven. I have escaped, I have got off scot-free from a stupid erotic entanglement and a big intellectual illusion. I am home again with my kind good father and my sweet loving sister. I have even got a job. But how worthless it all seems now. And in a great void he saw the face of Beautiful Joe beaming at him through those bright hexagonal glasses, with that deceptive air of untouched childish innocence, that utterly enchanting, utterly desirable boy-girl charm, that energy of life which shed its light upon all things. I shall never see him again, thought Cato, I must take that in as a certainty, perhaps my only certainty and the beginning of my truth. I could not help him, and perhaps I always knew this;

he simply, completely baffled me, he defeated me with a graceful demonic brilliance. He made a fool of me in the worst
sense. Lucifer, bearer of light. And Cato remembered how he
had once thought of Joe as a symbol of breakdown in his life,
as a significant temptation, even an emissary of the devil. And
he thought, no, that was just a consoling dream, a last attempt
to give sense to what in the end had none. Beautiful Joe is just
a passer-by, a little unimportant delinquent boy who will lead
a mean unhappy swindling sort of life, who will go to prison,
on some day when I am teaching a class somewhere in the
north or somewhere in America, and I shall never even know.
I loved him, but my love was a self-deception and a vanity, it
had no meaning and no saving strength. Men cannot help each
other, they cannot even see each other, nobody can be changed
or saved by the most extreme of loves. While I was gazing at
Joe in a dream it was all taken away, the high edifices of my
faith were dismantled: the three-personed God, the Fall and
the Redemption, the life of the world to come, *in saecula
saeculorum*. Now there is only sin and woe and no saviour.
Jesus was not the Son of God, he was just a victim, just a good
witty man with a delusion. And so my life has become tiny and
mean and incomplete and I must begin it again without comfort and without magic. It is the end of the story, and what
follows will be quiet and dull, and I am fortunate that it is so
and that I am not crippled and I will not even be miserable for
ever.

Part Two

The Great Teacher

"It's a very little diamond," said Stephanie.

"It's a very pretty ring," said Henry. "Don't you like it?"

"It's a very mingy little diamond."

"Well, it's all you'll get. You're lucky to get a diamond at all."

"Every bride gets a diamond these days."

"O.K., you've got one. Now shut up."

"I want to buy some more clothes."

"You've already bought enough to last you through a major war. The spare room is crammed with garments."

"I still need things, I need another coat and—"

"Oh all right, but this is the last instalment."

"A bus conductor would be kinder—"

"What on earth do you mean?"

"Nice ordinary men are interested in their wives' clothes, they make sacrifices so that they can have—"

"I'm quite interested in your hats."

"And you're rich and you won't even—"

"I'm not rich, that's the point, I don't want to start living like a rich man just when I'm going to become a poor one."

"You said we wouldn't be poor."

"Well, poorer."

"I so much want smart clothes. I've never had—"

"I'm not going to get my wife up like a society doll."

"I want to live at the Hall."

"Don't start that again."

"If only you'd wait a year, just see—"

"I can't wait, it's become an agony, Stephanie, can't you understand—"

"That's because you don't really want to sell, you don't really—"

"I do want to sell! I can't tell you how passionately I want to drop it all, to smash it all to pieces. I want it to be done and over with and then we can get away. I want to get home to America more than I've ever wanted anything."

"More than you want me."

"Take that look off your face. We're getting married and you're coming with me. We are getting married, aren't we, Steph?"

"Yes," said Stephanie, staring at him.

"You're not changing your mind, are you? I'll look after you, you'll like America. It's not like this crummy island—"

"I want to live at the Hall."

"Stop trying to madden me. The whole estate will be up for sale in a few weeks. We don't have to stay. When I've fixed all the details I'll leave it to Merriman. We can escape, fly the Atlantic and be free. We'll have fun when we're married, Steph. I'll see to that. We'll have lots of fun. We'll travel, my pay isn't bad. Bloody sight better than what I'd get here for being a mediocre hack. Cheer up. Aren't you ever merry and bright? You've got to be my fun girl now. Do stop looking the picture of misery because you can't have that bloody house. Shall I get you a mirror so you can see how disgustingly wretched you look?"

"No—oo—"

"Remember what I said I'd do to you if you started crying again? You do love me, don't you?"

"Ye—es—"

"Oh stop! You're making me into a sort of tyrannical monster, I don't want to be like that, you make me like it."

"I do love you," said Stephanie, staunching her tears with a paper table-napkin. "That's what's so funny."

"Awfully funny—yes—"

"But it's all so odd and I'm so frightened—"

"What are you frightened of, for God's sake?"

"I've never had anybody. I've never had a place or any family, and now you want us to be all alone in America just when I've seen how nice it could be here."

"Christ, do you want to live with my mother?"

"Well, I like her. I wouldn't mind."

"Oh *God*!"

It was breakfast-time. Half an hour ago they had been making love. Now the usual quarrel had started. Did Henry enjoy
the quarrel? He was not sure. He got up and went to the
window and looked out at the rain-washed dome of Harrods
glistening in the sun. He did indeed feel that somehow against
his will he was turning into a sort of bully. He had never
thought of himself as a bully. Invariably he had been bullied.
Russ and Bella had bullied him all the time. His pupils had
bullied him. His father and his mother and his brother had
bullied him. Was his curious passion for Stephanie, for it was
a curious passion, something to do with her unique attribute of
bully-ability? Was that what he had always wanted, a bullyee?

"It's odd," he said. "You said it was funny that you loved
me. I feel it's funny that I love you. You aren't like anyone
I've ever met before."

"You aren't like anyone I've ever met before—"

"I don't even know much about you. I don't want you to
talk about Sandy. And you won't talk about what went on
earlier."

"It was hateful—"

"Well, maybe you will talk later. Or maybe it doesn't
matter. I've lived in America with people who say every damn
thing. Maybe a silent relationship will be more restful."

Henry studied her. She was wearing a glossy expensive
négligé with a black and gold lozenge design and a collar
which seemed to be made entirely of black feathers. Since
leaving the bed she had made her face up carefully, more skil-
fully, she was learning something every day. She looked
handsomer, older, better kept. The lines beside the mouth
seemed less haggard. Good make-up, good food, happiness?
Was she happy? Was he? She was fated, necessary; happiness
was neither here nor there. There was no doubt that money
suited her. She had spent hundreds of pounds in a few days.
Henry had felt pity, generosity, a childish pleasure in her
pleasure, then annoyance. She could not see when enough was
enough. On the other hand, he thought, she might as well kit
herself out for her journey through life as Mrs. Marshalson,
Jr. He remembered her saying that Sandy had called her "the
femme fatale type." It occurred to him that she was the most

sensuous woman that he had ever seen, or was he going mad? Of course Bella was sensuous, but she was so clever and talkative and had such a piercing voice. And the girls had all been skinny with little breasts and glasses. He looked at the heavy jaw and the big round chin, the full mouth and the wide nostrils, the fine smudge of hair on the upper lip. Nothing fragile there, no intellectual pretensions, thank God. He looked at the large anxious moist eyes, a kind of blue with stripes of darkness. "You've got striped eyes," he said to her, approaching. What a painting Max could have made of that heavy sulky head. "Hello, Columbine."

Stephanie, reading his look, began to smile. "You haven't read your letters, darling. And there's a telegram." Her lightly accented voice was soft, pleasantly inaudible.

He sat down at the table and reached one hand across, pressing it down between the large breasts. She leaned on his hand, her pouting lips smiling. "I know what's in the telegram and the letters aren't important." He sighed, withdrew his hand and pulled his mail towards him. "Make us some more coffee, Steph."

There were the telegram and three letters. One letter was from Merriman, the second, forwarded from the Hall, looked as if it was from Cato, the third, also forwarded, was in an immature round hand with a Laxlinden postmark. Henry knew who that was from. He opened the telegram: GOT YOUR LONG LETTER WE ARE RIGHT BEHIND YOU KIDDO.   RUSSELL AND BELLA.

"Was that what you thought?"

"Yes," said Henry. "It's from some friends of mine in America. They're glad I'm marrying you."

"They don't know me."

"They're intuitive."

"Can I see?"

He handed her the telegram. He opened Merriman's letter. It was full of technical details about the sale. Mrs. Fontenay wanted to buy the copse that was adjacent to her farm. Giles Gosling had had a row with the borough engineer about extending the main drainage. A wall had fallen down. Henry skimmed through. Already it had all begun to seem blessedly unreal.

"Who are Russell and Bella?"

"Teachers at my school."

"School? I thought—"

"College. They're marvellously warm-hearted people. We'll all be warm-hearted together." He hastily opened another letter and glanced at it quickly.

My dear Henry,

Your answer to my letter was ungenerous and thoughtless. I am not a child. I think you think I am just because I'm a virgin. I don't think you understand me at all. Please see me and let us at least talk about this. I've known you forever and I love you so much. I feel, so strangely and so deeply, that just for you I am precious and mustn't be mislaid. Think about me. Don't just lose me out of carelessness. I feel so certain about this. I beg you to see me soon. You *will* marry me, yes, yes, you will.

Completely yours,
Colette

P.S. Of course I want the Hall, who wouldn't, and I want to be married in Dimmerstone Church, not Laxlinden.

Henry laughed and crumpled the letter up.

"Who's that from?"

"That mad girl."

"Let me see."

"It's just a schoolgirl rant."

"Let me see."

Henry handed it over and began to open the third letter. He watched Stephanie.

"Steph, now then—"

"Don't you see, she's a witch."

"She's a child."

"She's so young, and she says she's a virgin."

"So what, I hate virgins."

"You won't see her, will you?"

"Of course not, you dope!"

"She's put magic on you, you'll have to go to her, she says she'll marry you, she says she's certain—"

"Stephanie, shut up."

"You laughed because you were pleased."

"I laughed because it was ludicrous. Now just be quiet while

I read this letter. I've got a hundred things to do this morning. You go and shop since that seems to be all you can do."

Henry unfolded the third letter, which was from Cato. Cato's letter ran as follows.

Dear Henry,

What I am going to say will seem to you almost incredible, but please please believe it and please please do exactly what I ask. I have been kidnapped. I am a prisoner in a house in London, I don't know where. I was semi-conscious when I was brought here. Nor do I know who has kidnapped me, a gang of some sort, and I believe very bad, very determined people. I honestly think that my life is in danger. They want, quickly, a ransom of a hundred thousand pounds, in used notes. If they don't get it soon they'll start cutting me up. Please believe this, Henry, and please help me. And listen, don't tell *anyone* about this. For God's sake don't involve the police or any other person if you ever want to see me alive again. These people mean business. If you inform or bungle by telling anybody they'll kill you too. You are to come alone, next Tuesday, bringing the money in a suitcase, to the Mission at one o'clock in the morning, and wait in the little shed in the yard behind the house. Some-one will meet you there. This should allow time for you to raise the money. If you cannot come on Tuesday, for instance because of delay in receiving this letter, then come on Wednesday. Someone will be there every night at one until you come—but every day will put me in increasing danger of being maimed or killed, so please please hurry. And if you want to save my life, and your own, tell no one. And please make no mistakes. I am very sorry.

Cato

Henry's heart was beating violently and his face had become rigid. He tried to mask his emotion but he could feel his eyes staring wildly. Stephanie, engaged with the coffee pot, was not looking at him. He coughed and got up and went again to the window.

"What is it?" said Stephanie.

"I wonder if it's going to rain again? What's your view?"

"Oh I don't think so. What was in that letter?"

"Just business, about the sale."

"Can I see?"

"No. It should not be assumed that married people read each other's letters. The principle of mutual privacy should be established early in a marriage. I am establishing it now."

"You're upset. It's about that girl."

"Give over, Steph. I thought you were going shopping. I thought you wanted to buy a coat."

"I haven't any money. I want a bank account. I want an account at Harrods."

"Look. I'll sign this blank cheque. Don't drop it in the road. Now do buzz off, please."

After Stephanie had gone Henry sat down and read the letter through again, blushing and trembling with fear. It was a very strange letter in tone as well as in substance. Would Cato write such a letter, could Cato bring himself to write such a letter? Was it from Cato at all? It looked like his writing, in a rather wavery version. Henry wondered if he had still got Cato's previous letter somewhere. After a search he found not the letter but the envelope, crumpled in a jacket pocket. It was almost certainly Cato's writing. Or could it be a forgery? A joke? A confidence trick? And, he suddenly thought, today is Tuesday! What am I to do, how can I decide what to do so urgently, so quickly? Oh God, if only I can find out that Cato is perfectly safe and well and this awful thing is just a hoax.

Breathless with anxiety, he got the Pennwood number from enquiries and dialled it.

"Hello."

"Hello, Henry."

"Clever."

"I was expecting you to ring."

"Why?"

"You got my letter?"

"Oh, that."

"Let's meet, Henry. When?"

"Colette, just stop playing games, will you?"

"I'm not, listen—"

"Is Cato there?"

"No, he went back to London."

"When?"

"Oh several days ago. He only stayed here two days. Henry—"

"Where is he in London, at the Mission?"

"No, I think that's closed down. He may be with Father Craddock, you know, he's at the college—"

Henry rang off. He looked up the college number and in a moment was talking to Brendan Craddock.

"My name's Marshalson. I'm a friend of Cato's. Is Cato staying with you by any chance?"

"No, I wish he was. He's disappeared into the blue, I don't know where he is."

As Henry put the telephone down it began to ring again.

"Henry—"

"Bugger off, Colette."

"You hung up in the middle of a sentence, that's rude."

"It's rude to pester people by telephone. How did you know the number anyway?"

"I looked up A. Marshalson."

"How did you know Sandy had a flat in London?"

"Bellamy told Daddy."

"Fuck Bellamy."

"Henry, is it really true that you're going to sell the Hall?"

"Yes."

"You mustn't. Please, can't we talk?"

"No."

"You're in trouble, I can feel it, never mind about marrying me, just let me help you, you wanted Cato's help, please let me try, I'd do anything—"

"Good-bye."

He sat waiting for the telephone to ring again, but it did not. He thought, I'll go round to the Mission, but that won't prove anything. I suppose Cato wrote this letter, I suppose I must get the money—But I'll have to see Merriman and tell him some story and sign things and I can't possibly get it all by tonight, it'll have to be tomorrow night, oh God, oh *God*! And at the thought of that awful little dark shed in the yard his heart quailed and he moaned aloud. Could he, should he, tell the police? No, he dared not risk Cato's life, he dared not risk his own. His world was changed utterly. Bitter fear filled his throat and his mouth. He thought, I can't bear this alone, I can't bear it, and yet I must. If only I could tell somebody, somebody brave and strong, like John Forbes or my mother.

"How are you feeling, Father?"

"Terrible," said Cato.

"We thought we might have given you too much."

"Too much of what?"

"The drug."

"Brain damage," said Cato aloud to himself.

"Can you sit up?"

"Please don't shine it in my face."

Beautiful Joe put his hand over the torch, and his fingers made a luminous translucent pink-golden flower whose light dimly revealed a small windowless room. A cellar? It did not seem like a cellar. It was too square, too clear-cut, a cubical box, more like a prison cell; except that the walls were densely covered with some sort of dark all-over design. Wallpaper?

"Can you sit up?"

Sitting up seemed a far-off project. "I don't know." He looked up at Beautiful Joe's face, at the glossy hexagonal glasses which looked here like the appurtenances of some science-fictional spaceman, at the sleek blond hair neatly combed and parted, at the expressive (but of what?) slightly smiling mouth. He tried to remember.

He had come back to London after two days at Pennwood because he simply had to see Beautiful Joe again. He had no purpose, no plan, except to be once again in the boy's presence. He told himself that he had despaired too soon. He recited stories about "helping" Joe, about after all taking him away, about how, somehow or other, all might yet be well. He knew that these were stories. They might actually be true stories; but even this was unimportant, almost frivolous, compared with the simple need to see Joe again: a need single and metaphysical in its awfulness. If he did not see Beautiful Joe the walls of being would collapse; to save himself, to save the world, he had to go where Joe was. He had bought candles. That he remembered clearly and how symbolic an act it had seemed at the time. He had gone to the Mission and had set the candles in the window and lit them and waited there in the night for Beautiful Joe to come. And like a marvellous tiger-moth Beautiful Joe had come to him out of the night. Cato felt, in remembrance, that when he had heard those soft padding feet upon the stairs he had experienced the happiest moment of his life, a moment of absolute joy which like a magic jewel was worth all else, could perhaps redeem all else.

After that things were less clear. They had eaten or drunk something together and Cato had begun to feel very strange and confused. He could recall staring at Joe's face and seeing it shine with an unearthly beauty, as if Joe were a young saint revealed in glory, or perhaps a good wizard, some ageless being who wandered the world doing saving deeds, in the guise of a marvellously beautiful youth. Then they had walked together and the walking was joy, and the night sky of London was a brilliant rosy brown scattered with wispy pink clouds which gave light to the earth. And they had walked, it seemed, a long way; and then there had been a dark place with some steps, and Cato had fallen down the steps. Then he vaguely recalled a passage-way, then a sudden blackness and a door which he could not open. And voices, he thought that he had heard voices, far away, talking in some foreign language only he could not hear the words. Later there was something else. A candle, two candles, with motionless flames, glowing like some sort of heavenly luminous lard. And he had been writing a letter. The letter had been difficult, but it had come out somehow in the end, with clarity and ease, like a game of patience.

Cato was looking at Joe's hand, turned into a shining flower, the flesh transparent and bright, bright as the night clouds of holy London.

"So, Joe," said Cato, "we have come together again after all."

"Yes, Father. I knew we would."

"Yes, I knew too." Cato thought for a bit. He said, "I fell."

"Yes, Father, you fell and hurt your leg. How is it now?"

Cato felt, rather far away, a pain of which he had been aware, only he had not realized what it was. "It hurts a bit. I didn't break my leg, did I?"

"No, no, Father, it's just a bruise."

"People were talking, I remember, not in English. What language were they talking in?"

"Never you mind, Father."

"Joe, did you threaten me with a knife?"

"There was a knife, Father. I didn't threaten you."

"There was a knife." That was important. There had been a revolver once, only he had thrown it into the river.

"I wrote a letter," said Cato. He began to struggle up. He was lying on a low camp bed which had been placed against the wall in a corner of the room. The bed groaned and shifted. There was a pillow behind his head, a grey blanket pulled over him. He was in shirt and trousers. His feet were bare.

"Wait, Father, I'll fix the pillow."

Cato sat up uncomfortably, his legs outstretched, then he began to subside again. "I wrote a letter to Henry Marshalson asking for a ransom."

"That's right, Father."

"Oh, my God!" Cato lay for a moment. Then he said, "I must get up. Help me." He pushed against the creaking bed with his elbows, then with his hands. He moved his legs and bent his knees. The pain in his leg increased and a sudden pain smote him in the head like a swinging blow. He lowered his feet towards the floor and got into a sitting position on the edge of the bed, holding his head in his hands.

Joe removed his fingers from the torch and directed the beam at the floor. "Keep still, I'm going to light a candle."

Cato stared down at his bare feet. Then he pulled up his trouser leg and inspected an extensive bruise. He fingered the bone. It seemed to be sound.

A match was struck and a candle-flame flickered and then rose on the other side of the room. The light danced, descended. Joe had put the candle on the floor underneath a table so that it gave a restricted light. The walls were in darkness. Cato, looking up, was aware of two closed doors. The floor was covered in thick sound-looking red linoleum.

Cato tried to stand, then sat again abruptly. He fumbled at his trousers, then realized that his belt was gone and that all the buttons had been cut off. He considered the situation.

"Did you send off that letter?"

"Yes, Father." Beautiful Joe was sitting on the table swinging his legs, casting pendulum shadows across the red floor.

"I want to talk to one of your friends," said Cato. "I want this situation explained properly."

"You mean one of *them*?"

"Yes, one of them. Whoever 'they' may be."

"They won't see you," said Joe, still swinging his legs. "You know my face already. There's no point in your seeing another face."

"We could talk in the dark."

"No, no, Father, they wouldn't. And very much better not. I'm to look after you, and you're safe with me. They're not nice people. I'll see you don't get hurt. But you must promise to do whatever I tell you. And you could get me into trouble too. You understand?"

Cato pondered. Then he said, "Oh, Joe, Joe, the worst has happened, what I feared has happened, you're in the hands of the—"

"Sssh, Father—"

"So you're a sort of prisoner too—"

"I am not. I know what I'm doing. I'm free, really free like—"

"Free! When you—"

"I know what I'm doing. I just told you to be quiet for your own good."

"You threatened me with a knife."

"There have to be knives, Father. There are knives in the world. Fear is a knife. Look." Suddenly there was a flash. Cato saw a long glittering blade. Joe moved the blade, holding it low so that it took the full light of the candle. Then there was a click and the blade vanished.

"Have you ever stuck that into anybody?" said Cato.

"Yes. I carved a man's face. When I cut a face it stays cut. You didn't believe me before, did you? You kept telling me to be good and all the time you thought I was a little boy and that I'd be afraid of anything that was for real. You didn't believe the bad things, Father, you thought you did but you didn't. You didn't know real badness existed. You lived in a nice dream, you didn't see the world as it really was."

"Have you got the money yet?" said Cato.

"Never you mind. We're doing your friend a favour. He wanted to get rid of his money, didn't he? It was practically your idea, you kept going on and on about him. O.K., we'll bleed him whiter than white. What you said in the letter was just a first instalment."

"He'll go to the police."

"No, he won't. He knows who he's dealing with. He wants to keep you alive and to stay alive himself."

"I suppose when you've got the money your friends will dispose of me."

"I'll look after you."

"I think *you're* living in a dream, Joe."

"You won't tell, afterwards. You won't tell for your own sake. And you won't tell for *my* sake. *They* know that. It's part of the plan."

"I see ... Well, maybe I wouldn't tell, for your sake, but I don't see why your friends should take risks. Joe, is there a lavatory anywhere near here?"

"There's a bucket. I got it special. It's through that door."

Cato rose and, holding up his trousers, walked across to the door. His feet were curled and reluctant. In the confined space of what had doubtless been a lavatory Joe's torch revealed an orange plastic bucket upon the floor. Of the original fitments nothing remained except a length of piping which had led, perhaps, to a wash basin. Cato attempted to relieve himself but found that now he could not. He hobbled back to the bed and sat down heavily, feeling giddy.

"Are you hungry?"

"No." Cato felt he would never be hungry again. And he thought, any food that I eat will be drugged.

"You will be. I'll bring something later. I've got to leave you now. Don't try anything, if you don't want to get battered. There's a Negro chap who's a bit mental. I'm going to lock this door now. There are other locked doors, always someone about. This is a big place. Just sit still and mind you keep quiet. No one except them would hear you if you yelled. And they might get vexed and come in. Just do as you're told and I'll look after you."

"I don't see how you can," said Cato. He lay down again on the bed.

The candlelight swayed, then went out, and the torch was shone onto Cato's face. He closed his eyes. The light moved away and Cato opened his eyes again. Beautiful Joe was fitting a key into the other door. He saw for a moment in profile the fine intelligent girlish face, very intent. For a second Cato wondered if he should leap up and rush for the door. But physical fear had charge of his lower limbs and he knew that he could not.

"Good-bye, Father. Quiet now. Sweet dreams."

The door swung and closed again and he heard the key turn. Absolute blackness possessed the room. Cato sat up quickly, then held his head. He gasped, feeling suddenly faint. It was hard to breathe, as if the very darkness were stifling him, as if the room were cram full of black velvet. He thought, I mustn't panic. Courage. That is what I must use now. Courage. I have got it. I must use it. He breathed slowly and deeply.

After a while he got up and began to move, holding his trousers with one hand. Already the darkness had confused him and he did not know where the door was. He fell over the end of the bed, then he found the wall. His trousers fell to the ground. He fumbled for the bed again, then stepped out of the heap of fallen garments and put them onto the bed. It was cold in the room. He put his hand onto the wall and moved slowly until he felt the jamb and the crack of the door. He ran his fingers along the crack, which became a little wider towards the top, but not wide enough for leverage. He edged forward, leaning against the door, his hands noiselessly exploring the wood. He found the keyhole, then a metal handle. He pressed it carefully down and pulled cautiously. Locked of course. Moreover the door felt heavy and solid, no flimsy affair whose panels he could kick through, even if he had the courage to try. Then as he stood still, fronting the door, he had the weird feeling that someone was standing on the other side and listening. Listening to his movements. He stepped hastily away, cannoned into the edge of the table, and stopped. A moment or two later he heard a distant sound of voices, then a sound like a shutting door, and silence.

Cato felt he had already travelled a long way and spent a long time in doing it. His body retained no sense of the enclosing space. He had not expected the table there and had now no notion where the bed was. He explored the surface of the table, then, on all fours, the floor beneath, wondering if the candle and matches had been left behind, but there was nothing. He pulled himself up and bumped his head on the next wall. His outstretched hand encountered the lavatory door. He crawled round it and felt about thoroughly inside the lavatory. Occasionally he touched a soft elusive excrescence, perhaps an insect. The walls were cold, dry, smooth, without issue. He emerged, then moved on, knocking his questing knuckles at once against another wall. He slithered along it, then fell against the bed. He knelt down to explore under the bed. His hand searched for his shoes, but they were not there. He rose and after some fumbling about resumed his trousers and lay down again. He listened, hearing at first only his own breath. Then he thought he heard a faint brief distant rumbling, perhaps simply a vibration. A machine? The underground? The distant sound brought no comfort. It suddenly brought home to him that he was *somewhere*, hidden, caught, somewhere in London, in some fantastic, perhaps huge and labyrinthine hide-out, in somebody's terrible private prison. Whoever had made this room had made it, for its purpose, thoroughly. A windowless room, perhaps sound-proof, without a cranny into which he could even insert his fingers.

He lay looking upward into the thick stifling dark, and trying to control a moaning terror in his mind. He thought, when they have got Henry's money they will kill me and Beautiful Joe as well. He thought, I have reached the end of my road, and no one will ever know what happened to me or what it was like at the end. All I can do, my only duty now, is to hold onto myself, to keep a sort of fruitless dignity, something that relates only to me. And he thought, now there is only me left in the world, me and my relation to me.

And his thoughts began to swirl as if his mind were revolving and casting great coloured images onto the screen of the dark, and he saw with extreme clarity Brendan Craddock in his dressing-gown, sitting against the door and trying to prevent him from going away. And he saw, as if in a vision, his father sitting in his study at Pennwood, turning over papers underneath a lamp. And he felt a pure awful pity for his father. For those two days he had made his father so happy.

It was dark in the alleyway. Henry nudged the door with his foot and it jolted noisily back, making him jump. Sick with anxiety and fear and the explosive flutter of his heart, Henry stood still. Nervously he ran his finger along the top of the suitcase. He had tied it up with rope, but constantly feared it would somehow open, spilling bank notes. There was silence except for distant traffic. He stepped forward into the yard, feeling muddy earth and rubble underfoot. He did not try to close the gate but shuffled forward in the darkness. There was no light in the line of abandoned houses which rose above him against the reddish London sky.

He could now see the shed, its open door a darker darkness. It was just before one o'clock. Henry felt so sick with anguish he felt he might vomit. He did not dare to set the suitcase down. Throughout the journey he had felt certain he would be stopped by the police or else robbed by some quite unconnected criminal. He had taken two taxis, then walked, carrying the big case, a self-evidently guilty man. But no one questioned him, no one stopped him.

Desperate for help, living his life now as a hideous dream, he had told nobody. He went back to Laxlinden with Stephanie, enduring her puzzlement and her fear. "It's that girl Colette, you want to see her." Henry, morose with fright, was not able to console. "Well, think what you like, if you won't believe what I say!" Stephanie cried during the journey: and he, unable to speak to her, thought with an aching heart: I have made myself responsible for her and I will make her happy—but oh God how difficult and how dreadful my life has now become. How happy he had been a few days ago when he imagined he had problems! On arrival at the Hall Stephanie retired to her room with a headache.

It was of course impossible to conceal his distressed condition from his mother, only, seeing Stephanie's red-rimmed eyes, Gerda attributed it to a quarrel and asked no questions. Her bright pleased curiosity made Henry grind his teeth. Meanwhile, he had to see Merriman and inform that faithful discreet servitor that a large quantity of money must be produced in the form of bank notes, secretly and at once. Merriman, obviously amazed but asking no questions, settled to the task with fussy exactitude. He made telephone calls, explained, exhibited papers. Henry did not even try to understand. At last he took in that the money would be available for him in London tomorrow. He went back to the Hall. Stephanie was still upstairs and had asked for supper in bed. Henry went up to her.

"Steph, darling, what is it, are you really ill?"

"It's that girl, she's doing it."

"Oh rubbish! Look, Stephanie, you've got to be tough and brave and help me through life. I'm frightened too, every damn thing frightens me! We must help each other, you're fretting yourself into a fever."

"Will you come tonight?"

"No, it's impossible here. I won't be far off. I'll think about you. I'll try to dream about you."

"Oh darling—we will be married, won't we?"

"Yes, and I'll look after you forever. Only don't fuss stupidly about nothing. Tomorrow we'll go back to London."

Only when the morrow came Stephanie did not want to go with him, she said she wanted to stay at the Hall. Faint with fear before the day's programme Henry did not argue. He said he would come back. Gerda, taking charge, made Stephanie stay in bed, produced a thermometer, spoke of calling the doctor. Henry fled.

The business of actually acquiring the money proved, thanks to Merriman's labours, simpler than Henry had expected. In fact what Henry had picked up, and what the large suitcase now contained, was only twenty thousand pounds. This more modest sum was the outcome of such deliberate policy as

Henry, fighting against his paralysis of fear, had been able to formulate during the morning. Obviously he must somehow, intelligently, bargain. It would be foolish to hand over the full sum at once. He must give enough to prove his seriousness, not so much as to make his further co-operation of no interest. He must ask for proof that Cato was alive. He had to insist that the rest of the money would be forthcoming only when Cato was free. But how could he insist, how could he bargain, with such people?

At Laxlinden Henry had discovered in his waste-paper basket the fragments of Cato's previous communication. There could be no doubt about the authenticity of the handwriting. Henry had not in fact ever doubted the genuineness of the ransom letter. He had got to act. Nor did it seriously occur to him to inform the police. Henry's timid imagination had quickly grasped the imperatives in Cato's missive. He could not blindly put his friend's life at risk. Even more plainly he could not condemn himself to a lifetime of fearing some frightful revenge. In a way he could not earlier have conceived of, fear had taken over Henry's world and made him its slave.

Standing in the dark and looking at the silent black opening of the door of the shed he felt that he had been mad not to bring all the money. If he had only brought it all he could simply speechlessly have given it and then gone away having done all he could. A fear which was like guilt gripped him by the throat, a terrible sense of the present moment, poised on the brink of some hideously unimaginable future. Now he was perhaps inches, minutes, away from death.

He took another step forward. The silence seemed peopled, intolerable with menace. He stood rigid near the black doorway and tried to whisper something, but could not speak. He uttered a tiny noise. Then a torch flashed in his face. Henry dropped the suitcase and his hands flew to his neck.

"Come into the house," said a soft almost inaudible voice.

Henry reached down for the suitcase but jumped abruptly back when his hand encountered another hand. The torch drew a quick line upon the ground then went out. Henry followed the line and stumbled up a step and through a door. The door closed behind him.

The torch came on again, shaded by fingers, casting a little light. Henry saw the kitchen, the black curtains drawn, a single tall figure standing before him.

Then he recognized Beautiful Joe. He recognized the hexagonal spectacles, the limp fine girlish bobbed hair, the long thin delicate mouth. He made a noise in his throat.

"Sit down there."

Henry sat down.

"Keep quiet now, Mr. Marshalson. I have a gun and a knife, and a rather violent and impatient friend waiting outside." The torch flashed for a moment, showing a knife-blade, then shifted to the suitcase which was now open on the table. "Is all the money here?"

Henry thought, I have got to be brave like other men are. Oh why did I come here, why didn't I go to the police! I won't even be able to speak for terror. He said in a high shaky voice, "No—only—twenty thousand—"

The torch and one long hand scanned the contents of the suitcase. "Why?"

"I couldn't—get it all—I will soon—I promise—"

There was a silence as the quick deft hand sorted the packets of notes. "This is bad. My people don't like delays. They want to finish with this business. You must bring the rest tomorrow."

With a tremendous effort, Henry croaking, said, "I can't—I need more time to get it—I'll bring it Thursday or Friday—I swear I will—but I must know that Cato is—will be—all right —if I—" The words trailed into silence. Henry sat with his hands criss-crossed on his throat.

'We will let your friend go when you bring the money. If you don't bring the money, we shall send you a token. Your friend's ears perhaps or his fingers. But you *will* bring the money. Because otherwise he will suffer and die. And you too will suffer and die. And you know this. If you fail you will be listed, written down to be killed. A listed man might live a month, a year, not longer. If you fail you will never sleep at ease again. But you will not fail. We give you until Friday, here, at this time, and you must then bring the rest of the money. Then your friend will be released. We are not afraid of your speaking. Oh no, we are not afraid. Only bring the money and everything will be well. If you fail, or speak a word to any other person, you will die and so will he. You cannot escape from us. Now I am going. You are to stay here for half an hour. My friend outside will stay here watching, so don't try to leave for half an hour from now. Good night. Wait one moment though, I have something to give you. Hold your hand out towards me."

Henry stood up and extended his hand across the table. The room was so dark he seemed to be breathing darkness, indeed he could hear the staccato sound of his own gasps for breath. He felt Beautiful Joe take hold of his hand in a gentle firm grip, turning it slightly. Then a sharp searing pain ran across the back of his hand, just behind the knuckles. He could feel the quick agonizing jolt as the sharp knife-blade crossed the bones.

Henry gave a loud smothered whimper and sat down, jerking the chair back, clutching his wounded hand with his other hand and pressing it against his chest. He heard the scrape of the suitcase pulled from the table, then the door opening and closing quietly.

Henry sat in the dark and tears of terror and frustration and anger and pain burst from his eyes. He could not see his watch. He sat there trembling for nearly an hour.

Gerda, dressed in her chequered blue and green robe, was standing motionless beside the log fire in the library. Since Henry's long absences in London she and Lucius had reoccupied the room. It was nearly three o'clock in the morning. Henry had not returned. She could not now remember exactly what he had said. But she had understood that he was coming back that day. Stephanie had certainly thought so, and "doing her sick child act" as Gerda put it to herself, had kept on asking for him. Gerda gave her two sleeping pills, saw her take them, and said good night, Stephanie had no temperature.

It seemed to Gerda that Henry did not understand his future wife, was indeed quite unable to see her at all. This was not unusual and did not mean that the marriage would necessarily be a failure. About that Gerda felt quite open-minded. It could be that Henry, dominated by his mother, needed a woman whom he could dominate and look after. How much looking-after Stephanie would need perhaps Henry did not yet realize. Gerda felt pity for Stephanie, and guessed that pity, together with some weird feeling about her relation to Sandy, had been at least the beginning of Henry's interest. But then Henry was so strange. He seemed to Gerda like a little hard ball of implacable destructiveness and hostility. She had given up hope of reaching any understanding with him. He was destined simply to destroy her world and then disappear forever to America.

Gerda felt sorry for Stephanie, Henry had pitied her. Sandy doubtless had pitied her too. Gerda had talked to Stephanie a little about Sandy, but with none of the intimacy which Henry had suspected and resented. She had done this, not curiously, but out of some compassionate sense of propriety. She did not, confronted with Stephanie and with Stephanie's utterances, feel curiosity. She shuddered rather. That voice could tell her nothing about the real Sandy, but was capable of saying something that she would remember forever. Silence was better. And Stephanie, after her first outburst over the photographs, seemed to think this too. Gerda, ageing, realized that there were things in the world which she would never understand, and how Sandy could have cuddled that girl was certainly one of them. Gerda coolly suspected that Sandy had not cared about her very much. She would have forgiven Sandy anything and had no difficulty in forgiving him a certain callousness where Stephanie was concerned. She felt that, far above Stephanie's head, far above everything else, she met the calm eyes of her elder son, and they understood each other. No one knew, no one would ever know how perfect that relationship had been, although he scarcely spoke to her except about trivialities, and told her nothing of his life. Gerda had hoped, since she was resolved that he must marry, for an orderly respectable daughter-in-law, someone a little on the dull side. Later she suspected Sandy of being homosexual. It did not matter. She was joined to Sandy, now eternally silent, in a union which made nothing of these matters. So much so that she could even be fairly objective about poor Stephanie.

"I wonder if Henry has got a mental case on his hands," Gerda said earlier to Lucius. "Oh surely not!" shocked Lucius had replied. "Well, it's his business," said Gerda. She did not really think of Stephanie in this way, but she saw with exasperation the signs of a kind of weakness. Burke, Sandy, had been strong people. She was a strong person herself. How strange it now seemed that she had expected the home-coming Henry to exhibit weakness. He had been such a feeble weakling little boy. Perhaps the desire to expunge this image lay behind his present aggression. Her true strong ones had departed, and she was left with loyal spineless Lucius. With John Forbes, a tough sensible man whom she used to respect, she had quarrelled. And Henry's strength was mustered against her with, she increasingly felt, a kind of virulence which was poisoning her own soul with resentment.

One touching thing about Stephanie, and Gerda was touched, was that Stephanie, perhaps to her own surprise, had accepted Gerda as a mother. And Gerda had played mother. Of course she was able to do so more easily because the relation was temporary. Whether or not the marriage "worked" Stephanie would disappear, she would be elsewhere with Henry, in America, gone. Gerda had hated America. It seemed to her raw, ugly, vulgar, frightening, and curiously empty. She would certainly never go there again. She was prepared now to tend Stephanie, but physically she shrank from her. The moral weakness which Gerda sensed in her future daughter-in-law expressed itself in more corporeal ways. Stephanie had a lazy idle body. Henry had landed himself with a wife who would lie in bed till noon. She smelt of fat flesh and cheap cosmetics. Gerda did not like her attitudes or her underwear. She suspected her of being older than the age she had admitted to Henry. She felt, as a physical aura about this now helpless and pathetic being, a kind of cunning.

Gerda had promptly despaired of using Stephanie to persuade Henry not to sell the house. Stephanie could weep, but she would never persuade Henry of anything. Henry was a force of nature. Gerda recalled with detached amazement how she had once secretly hoped to tame returning Henry, to train him to love her, to be some shadowy feeble inadequate consolation for her loss. She had had, it seemed, some plan of redeeming Henry; but now Henry was clear as being unredeemable and one result of this was that she no longer cared whom he married. She just wished that it was all over and that they were gone. The scene that she loved was already being dismantled, and she was willy-nilly withdrawing her attachment. Bellamy had arranged to work for Mrs. Fontenay and John Forbes. In a few weeks' time the house would be up for sale.

Gerda stooped and put another log onto the fire. The bare untapestried wall behind her was like a chill-opening in the void. She shivered. She was waiting up for Henry not out of anxiety for him but out of a compulsive desire to exhibit her suffering. She pulled the skirt of the blue and green woollen gown back out of the hearth where the hem had become smudged with ashes. She shook it. She thought, even now I am far more beautiful than that girl, I am strong and clean. But what does it matter any more? An owl hooted from the big trees, with a repeated hollow fluting cry. The door opened quietly and bird-headed Rhoda came in, wearing her dark blue dress which looked so much like a uniform yet was not. In reply to her question Gerda said, no, she wanted no coffee, nothing to eat, nothing. She told Rhoda to go to bed. Her gesture of dismissal indicated, in the sign language of two women who had lived together for many years without ever speaking of anything except domestic trivia, her affection for Rhoda. She looked fleetingly into the huge eyes. She had not yet told Rhoda that she would have to go. No one indeed had told Rhoda anything, Gerda did not know whether Rhoda knew that the house was to be sold.

After a few minutes there was a creaking sound and a fumbling noise and Lucius came in, stooping, wearing his dressing-gown.

"Why are you up?"

"Gerda, dearest, go to bed, don't grieve over that bad boy."

"I hate the sort of words you use."

"I'm sorry. Don't grieve."

"I'm not grieving."

"How was poor Stephanie, did she get off to sleep all right?"

"Yes."

"Do you think she's really ill?"

"I think she's working up for a nervous breakdown, but that's Henry's problem."

"Gerda, you mustn't be against that girl because of Henry—"

"Do you imagine I'm jealous?"

"Well, it would be understandable—"

"Sometimes I wonder whether you are just stupid or whether you are really being vindictive. All this is so much larger and more important than anything you seem able to imagine. You have a mean petty imagination. I am not 'grieving' over a 'bad boy,' I am not 'jealous' of that wretched little neurotic girl! You understand nothing."

"Don't cry—"

"I am not crying!"

"Gerda, forgive me, I know I annoy you sometimes, I can't get anything right, but I do love you, you're all I've got, we will be together in the future, won't we—"

There was a faint distant sound, the sound Gerda had been waiting for.

"There's the Volvo. It's Henry. Go to bed, Lucius."

"Forgive me."

"Oh, you stupid, *stupid* man. There. Go."

Lucius padded away. He climbed slowly, laboriously, upstairs to his room. His heart ached in such a familiar way, and the very familiarity of it pained him. He had always thought of himself as a muddler, a sufferer, a victim. But what a cosy protected victim he had been. Gerda's irony, her little daily rejection of him, had hurt. But it had existed inside a kind of eternal safety, her continued tolerance and, however attenuated, her continued need. That Gerda really needed her last admirer had been his charter of survival. But now, in crisis, her gaze so easily passed beyond him.

He sat down at his table and drew his paper and pen towards him.

She looks into the mirror and sees her face.
I look into the mirror and see her face.
I look into the mirror and see empty space.

*

Henry came through the front door like a whirlwind. He shut the door, not noisily but abruptly, clattering the latch. The light was on in the hall, and as he strode to the stairs he saw out of the corner of his eye his mother standing in the library doorway. He would have ignored her and gone racing on up-stairs had she not said in a low voice "Henry!"

He whirled round, paused a moment, then walked to the library door and, passing her, went in.

"What do you want, Mother? It's late."

She was staring at him with horror. "You've hurt yourself."

"Have I?"

"Your face is all over blood."

"It's nothing," said Henry. "I banged my knuckles on a wall, they bled a bit, I must have rubbed my face. It's just a little cut."

"Show me. Where are you hurt?"

Henry had wrapped his wounded hand in a handkerchief. He put it behind his back. "No."

"Henry. Show me."

"*No.*"

They faced each other, suddenly raging.

"Henry——"

"Go to bed, Mother. How's Stephanie?"

"I expect she cried herself to sleep all right."

"Why were you waiting up for me?"

"I wasn't waiting up, I was thinking——"

"Well, I'll leave you to think."

"About the cottage at Dimmerstone."

"Did you go over and look at it like I asked you to? Giles Gosling says——"

"I've decided not to live there."

"Oh. All right."

"I shall live elsewhere. Not here at all. In a flat."

"O.K. I thought you wanted a garden."

"I'm too old for gardening, as you pointed out yourself. I've decided—"

"O.K. then. Do as you like. Good night."

"Henry, you have—"

"Oh leave me *alone*!"

He ran from her out of the door and she heard his light footsteps leaping up the stairs.

Gerda stood for a moment gazing at the pale bare cobwebbed wall. Then she turned out the lamps, and the room was in darkness except for the golden jumpy light of the fire. She pushed the fireguard forward into the ashes. Hot tears of rage and fearful misery spilled to her cheeks and fell onto her bosom. She could destroy herself before his eyes and he would not even care.

Upstairs in his bathroom Henry stared at himself in the glass. His face was streaked, almost as if striped, with blood. He turned away and began inspecting his hand. The handkerchief was stuck to the wound, stiff and dark with blood. His whole hand was swollen up to the wrist, hot and throbbing violently. A line of pain lay across it, a fierce probing pain as if nails had been driven through into his palm. Helplessly Henry put his hand under the tap. Hot water gushed over it and the pain stabbed fiercely, raced right up into his armpit. He turned off the tap, sat down on the edge of the bath and began vainly plucking at the handkerchief. It was stuck fast and the pluckings produced more pain. What was he to do? He could not go to bed in this condition. He must find a doctor, be seen to, comforted, looked after. He considered going to Stephanie, but she would be asleep, and besides she would simply be appalled. She would be, in his affliction, sorry for herself.

Under the bright light Henry sat there uncomfortably, nursing his hand and wondering what on earth was going to happen to him now. Had he really had any choice in the matter, had he chosen? Of course he had to try to save Cato's life, but was that what he was doing? He could not have ignored the letter, could not have failed to go to the rendezvous. Now he had in his head forever the idea of being "listed," the idea that if he were guilty of betrayal, even of failure, he would fear every strange man, every strange sound, for the rest of his life. Running to America would be no good, these people were everywhere. Fear had entered his life and would now be with him forever. How easy it was for the violent to win. Fear was irresistible, fear was king, he had never really known this before when he had lived free and without it. Even unreasoning fear could cripple a man forever. Perhaps unreasoning fear was worst of all. How here could he calculate, how defend himself in his mind? Perhaps if he went to the police he would survive, but he would never know, never be sure, never stop waiting for the blow. How well he understood now how dictators flourished. The little grain of fear in each life was enough to keep millions quiet. And he remembered a picture of Max's in which a kindly looking business-like torturer twists the arm of a screaming half-throttled victim while a figure resembling Lenin quietly pulls down the blind against the night. That was what it was like, essentially, in the background, in the end.

But what will happen, he thought, what will they do to poor Cato? If they get the money will they set him free? Will they not rather then kill him? With despair Henry realized he had already passed beyond this stage in the argument. No calculation and no act of Henry's could, in any light by which he could now see, affect Cato's fate one way or the other. Yet was it not for *this* that he had entered this dreadful machine? He was simply caught himself. And recalling the torch-lighted profile of the pretty boy Henry felt a vast miserable anger against Cato for having so stupidly made himself the vcitim of this vile little rat, the slave no doubt of other rats. Yes, I am simply caught, he thought, nursing the hot throbbing pain of his slashed hand. I will bring them the money, I will have to. But why should they stop there? They will want more, in the end they will want everything, everything I possess, everything my mother possesses. And I will give it to them, simply simply simply because I am afraid.

The darkness was total. Cato's eyes had not "got used" to it. Rather they had been filled with it, rinsed with it, so as to feel finally without the capacity of light. He kept his eyes open as he moved in the darkness, out of habit, rather than because they were any sensible help. Other senses however had become more informative and he had now a fairly complete idea of his surroundings. He had spent long periods listening and had twice heard again the strange voices, a murmur as of conversation taking place behind closed doors several rooms away. It still seemed to him, though he could make out no words, that the voices were not talking English. Apart from this there had been no sound except for the very faint noise or vibration which he took to be the underground railway, and an even more faint noise which it seemed to him that he had begun to hear as his ears, in the dark, became keener. This was a kind of scraping noise, as of digging happening a long way off. A very distant bulldozer, vibrating in the earth?

Cato had lost all count of time. Some while ago he had lain down on the bed and covered himself with the blanket, thinking he had better rest since there was nothing else to do, not imagining that he would be able to sleep. However he did sleep, and then did not know whether he had done so for minutes or for hours. And he had slept again since then, perhaps because of the drug, or because of some effect of the awful total darkness which seemed to be clouding his mind and taking away his sense of his own identity. He had never before realized how necessary the senses are to the whole business of thinking. Plunged in continuous darkness he felt strangely muddled and had to try hard to keep the most ordinary processes of thought from wandering aside into fantasy. It was not exactly like going mad, it was more like a gentle disintegration of a tentacular thought-stuff which had never, it now seemed, had much cohesion, and which now floated quietly away into the dark, into a sightless haze of wavering and dissolving connections.

When Cato felt the strange possibility of such a disintegration he tried with most deliberate will power to arrest it. He had never, he felt, really *experienced* his will in such a positive way before. And it was, to some extent, efficacious. His sense of touch, he found, now became a sort of life-line of significance. He explored his quarters again and again in the dark, feeling up and down the walls and along the floor. His cell seemed to be impenetrably smooth like a chamber cut out of polished rock. The only irregularity or point of interest, and Cato's fingers dwelt upon this, was the metal piping in the lavatory, which was a little more extensive than had seemed to him on his first inspection. A pipe emerged from the smooth crannyless wall, proceeded a little way, then divided in two at a joint. One section ran downward and ceased just short of the floor. The other continued, then at another joint turned abruptly upward and ended in a broken twist about the length of a hand. Fingering this twisted end it occurred to Cato that if he could somehow remove this last section of the pipe he would have a useful tool. He did not think of it as a weapon. He had no clear idea of what he might do with such a tool, but it might be worth possessing. The notion of tapping an SOS message on the pipe which entered the wall had already occurred to him, but with his bare hand he could produce no resonance. After all, pipes went somewhere and might carry a vibration a long way, if he could knock metal against metal. Or he might sometime use his tool to try to prise open the door. But more immediately, the twisted pipe, being the only oddity in the room, attracted Cato's attention because fiddling with it was something to do, a defence against the horrors.

He had already tried to break it off but this proved impossible. His arms were without strength and the fruitless effort brought bursts of pain in his head until he swayed giddy against the wall. He touched the joint gently trying to determine whether or not it was screwed on, but his finger-tips, when so urgently interrogated, sent contradictory messages and then became insensible. He swayed the pipe, tried to twist it, but was unsure whether, if it was a screw, he were not screwing it tighter rather than unscrewing it. Which way did screws screw? Without vision this instinctive knowledge was lost. After a while he gave up and went back exhausted to his bed and to the misery of remorse and the fear of death.

Sitting on his bed he fumbled for his trousers and pulled them on. Having been unable to devise any way of keeping them up, he had to take them off if he wanted to walk. For the hundredth time he searched his empty pockets, then slid his hands automatically down his trouser legs. His fingers touched the turn-ups of the trousers, his fingernails explored the fluff and dust inside the turn-ups. Then suddenly there was something else. His fingers, excited, sensitive, touched something, pinned it, grasped it. *A match*. Holding the match safely in one hand, he quickly explored for other ones. No. Only one match. But a match. Was it the kind that he could strike without a box? If so how could he use it? Should he preserve it for some future chance, or should he use it now to solve the riddle of the pipe in the lavatory? After reflecting he got up again and, holding the match very carefully, took off his trousers. He stood listening for a moment, then went back to the invisible piping, thrusting the now reeking bucket aside with his foot. He felt the position of the twisted pipe, then began to touch the wall above it. The wall was dreadfully smooth, but at last his fingers found a very slight granular roughness. After a moment's hesitation and with a violent heart-beat he drew the precious match firmly down the wall.

The sudden bright light was for a second almost an agony and he closed his eyes against it and nearly dropped the match. Then when he opened his eyes he seemed to be looking into a weird picture. The wall, very close to him, was a dark but rather radiant green, and Cato felt that he had never in his life seen such a wonderful colour. Then he saw that the wall was not plain, but was covered with the strange all-over design which he had noticed before in the light of Beautiful Joe's candle, and was also irregularly dotted with weird pinkish spots. Cato's eyes, struggling with the picture suddenly placed so close before them, found themselves *reading*. There was a name, *Jeff Mitchell*, and a date. A crude drawing. Other names. *Tommy Hicks, Peter the Wolf*. Other dates. *15 July 1942. 3.8.43. 20 January 1940. 17 April 1944. 11.4.41.* The whole wall was covered with names and dates.

The match burnt Cato's fingers and he dropped it, but just as it fell he looked down and saw the pipe and interpreted the puzzle which his fingers had failed to understand. There was a screw and he instantly knew which way it should turn. He leaned against the wall for a moment, breathing deeply. Then he took hold of the pipe and tried to turn it. It would not yield. He returned again to his bed. The match had revealed at least two other things. His cell was part of an old wartime air raid shelter. There were many such underground warrens, underneath government offices, or under buildings that had once been offices, some of which had disappeared during the war itself. He might be anywhere in central London, in some blocked abandoned honeycomb the entrance to which was a lost secret. He had read of such places. He had also, in his vivid flash of light, solved another problem, the origin of the sound which was so like a distant bulldozer. It was the tiny crepitation of hundreds of pinkish beetles, slightly larger relations of the ones in his kitchen at the Mission, which had made the place their own. He shuddered, stretching out his hands and seeming now to feel them everywhere, walking upon the bed, upon his shirt and naked arm.

He must not give way, he must take initiatives and try to save himself. It was a soldier's duty, if taken prisoner, to escape. But it all seemed so hopeless. If he was indeed in an air raid shelter the pipe on which he had intended to tap would not lead anywhere, to any neighbouring house or place of rescue. He would try to detach his "tool" because it was something to do. But he had no plan and no prospect of release, he was effectively buried. No one would miss him or look for him. His father would grieve over his absence but with proud arrogance would never seek for him, would assume he had run back to his "religious friends." Colette would be uneasy but would do nothing. What would Henry do? Would he, after that letter, go to the police? No. Could Henry easily be intimidated? Yes. Oh if only I had not written that letter, thought Cato, lying in the dark. It was such a dishonourable awful thing to do. I will write no more letters for these people. I would not have written it if I had not been so dazed. I must not let them drug me.

Some time ago (hours ago?) Beautiful Joe had come with some food. He had only stayed a moment, long enough to put the food on the table, and had then vanished in a flash of torch-light. Joe had seemed agitated, excited, nervous, angry, or frightened. Cato reflected fruitlessly on this enigma. The food, at which he groped, consisted of water, in a cardboard cup, two slices of bread and some sort of mashed-up fish (sardines?) which had been turned out onto a sheet of paper. He was very hungry. He decided that if the food was drugged the drug would be in the fish. He ate the bread and drank the water and rather reluctantly put the fish into the bucket. He now felt weak, hungry, but clear-headed. But what did he hope to achieve by keeping his wits about him? Did he really imagine that, even if he could achieve it physically, he would have the courage to charge out of the door into those awful rooms beyond where he would be killed like an escaping rat?

His eyes still boiled strangely from the shock of the sudden light, and lying in the blackness his head swam with images. He saw again and again, as if it had been printed on his vision, the green wall and the names and the wartime dates and the big pink beetles, moving quietly. He saw Colette in her green overall and the garden at Pennwood. He saw his mother, an almost imaginary figure composed out of now inaccessible memories. He saw Father Milsom saying mass, and Brendan's Spanish crucifix. He seemed to see somewhere, as a great black hump, his own death, and the fear of death turned and twisted in him with an anguish which was like the whining blubbering misery of a child. He pictured the face of Christ and wondered if he could pray. Strange words came to his lips. "Lord Christ, whoever you may be, if it please you to be called by this name, by this name I call upon you ..."

*

He had been asleep and woke. There was a pale faint light all about him, and the walls, scrawled with their patterns of graffiti, were a dark shadowy grey. A candle was burning underneath the table. He sat up, leaning against his pillow.

Beautiful Joe was sitting, as before, upon the table, quite

still, staring at Cato. He was wearing jeans and a shirt with the sleeves rolled up.

Cato felt a sick thrill of fear. His body, though scarcely yet his mind, had begun to know that each appearance of Joe brought him nearer to *that*. Joe looked different. Cato remembered that he must pretend to be drugged. In fact he felt so weak that no pretence was needed. He said, "I feel so strange."

Beautiful Joe continued to stare.

"Joe, Joe, speak to me—Oh God what a nightmare—"

Joe got off the table and came towards him, blotting out the light, his shadow falling on Cato. Cato cowered back. Joe sat down on the side of the bed. "You shouldn't have taken it."

"Taken what?"

"The gun. That was stealing. You threw it in the river. That was the start. That was what made me mad. I couldn't forgive you." His voice sounded odd, almost unfamiliar. He took off his glasses and rubbed his cheeks and his eyes looked huge and dark like the eyes of a skull.

"I did it to help you, to save you."

"You shouldn't have done it, and you shouldn't have gone on to me about Mr. Marshalson. You tried to buy me with his money. It's all your fault."

"Joe, are you all right? You look so strange. They haven't been doing anything to you?"

"They? No. They're not here just now except for the big chap on the door, that dotty Negro. He can break a man's neck just like that, snick."

"Have they seen Henry?"

"I've seen Henry. He brought some money. He was so frightened he could hardly stand. I'll make him go on his knees next time. We'll get the next lot tomorrow. Look I want to show you this." Something appeared in Joe's hand, flickered in the dim light. A knife. Cato wriggled back. "See those stains? That's Henry's blood."

"Joe, you haven't—"

"Oh, I haven't hurt him, I just nicked him to let him see I could. And I want you to know that I could too, see? Cato. Isn't that your name?" Joe wiped the knife on the sleeve of

Cato's shirt. Then he held the blade lightly, pointing it at Cato's throat.

"Joe, put that knife away."

Joe advanced the blade and Cato felt the light touch of the point on his neck. Then there was a click and the blade vanished. Joe put the knife in his pocket. "You wouldn't believe how cruel these men are, they're real cruel people. They're cruel just because they like it. So you better keep quiet, you know. They could just lock you up here and go away. You could scream. No one would find you for years. Christ, that bucket stinks. I wonder if you'll suffocate."

"They'll hurt you too—"

"No they won't. One of the top chaps fancies me. He's going to take me away with him to—never mind where. He's going to take me away like you wanted to once, Cato. Such a long time ago. It seems years ago, doesn't it. Did you really mean it?"

"Oh God, if only you'd come—"

"And we'd have lived together—up there—"

"In Leeds."

"And you'd have done your teaching stuff and I'd have learnt things like you wanted—read books maybe—I'd like to learn philosophy—"

"Yes—"

"I think I'm a bit of an existentialist, Cato."

Cato thought, he is drugged or drunk. But the idea of escape could not now move him even to twitch a limb. It was hopeless, the knife here, the big crazy Negro beyond the door. Cato put a hand to his throat where he could still feel the point of the knife. Only a willed rigidity kept him from trembling.

"Joe, if we could only get out of here it could all come true even now, like you said. Henry would give us money, we could live in the north, you could do anything you like, study philosophy, why not—Joe, can't you get us out somehow? You can't want to stay with these awful people, you can't—"

"You better be careful, Cato. That's not a way to talk. Do you want me to tell on you? They'll be back soon. They got other things to do. You're not important. I just got to look after you, that's my job, you were my idea. Then I'll be away in the

290

big time, in the big world, out of this shitty little country. So don't you talk. You lie still, or I'll break you myself. It's all your fault, I told you. You shouldn't have taken that gun."

"I'm sorry—"

"You said you loved me—"

"I did, I do."

Beautiful Joe was sitting close to him on the bed. Cato could feel the warmth of the boy's body and now a slight movement brought Joe's bare arm into contact with his own. Joe's face, without his glasses, with the huge skull-eyes, looked older, vulnerable, wild, the face of a stranger. His girlish bob of hair was tangled. He looked for a moment like a mad old woman.

Cato, who had been reclining, rigid and cold, now, as he felt the touch of Joe's arm, scarcely that, the hairs on his arm touching the hairs on Joe's arm, felt a kind of abstract pang of desire, as if his body was vainly yearning to distract him, or perhaps did not even know of his fate.

Joe, slowly, almost awkwardly, rubbed his arm against Cato's with a sort of intimate animal gesture, then his hand moved and took hold of Cato's hand.

"Joe, darling, get us out of here."

"You shouldn't have done it, Cato. You shouldn't have chucked the priesthood, that was the end. You deserted me. You gave up trying to save me. No wonder I got desperate. No wonder I felt I was all alone. When you were telling me yourself there wasn't any God. I'd have gone with you if you'd still been a priest, if you'd ordered me to go, I'd have done anything. You didn't know your power. You've thrown it all away. I loved you, I still do, but it's no good any more. You're nothing now. I'm sorry for you. I hate to see you here, I hate to see you shitting with fright."

"You brought me here."

"It was fate, that's what. Oh if only you were different, you, but different—you're the only person I've ever really—Father, put your arms round me." Suddenly the boy was lying beside him full length, burying his head in Cato's shoulder. Cato moved and took him in his arms. Joe was shuddering, and now he had taken hold of Cato's shirt in his teeth. Cato could feel the dampness of his lips, perhaps of his tears.

"Oh my dear—" said Cato. Distraught with fear tenderness and desire he put his hand into the tangled hair and cradled the head which felt hot and throbbing to the touch.

With a violent movement Joe jerked away. He stood up and tucked his shirt in. He put on his glasses. "Don't maul me. Poor bloody queer, that's all you are. That's all your religion ever was. A way of being a queer."

"Joe—"

'I came to tell you something, Cato."

"What?" Cato slowly sat up and put his bare feet to the floor.

"You got to write another letter."

"I won't."

"Don't be daft. You will. You don't want to be maimed do you?"

"I wrote one letter, that's enough. You can write your own letters now."

"You got to write another letter. They want your sister to bring the next lot of money."

"My sister? No, no, *no*—"

"Your stuck-up sister. The girl you thought was too good for me. She's got to come. And you got to write and tell her to come. See? Cato."

"No," said Cato. Rage obstructed his tongue and he could hardly articulate as if his mouth was filled with rags. "No. Leave my sister alone, leave my sister alone, leave her alone, leave her out of this—"

"Too grand for me, your precious bloody sister, eh?"

"No, no, no—oo—" Cato wailed. Then he cried out again, as he received a violent blow on the side of the head. He fell back on the bed. The light was blotted out.

Dear Henry,

They want the rest of the money quick, but don't come yourself, Colette is to bring it. No one else must know. Tell her to come to the same place. There will be someone there at one o'clock for the next three nights. Keep well away yourself and tell no one else if you want to go on living. Don't go near the police or it's the end. *Colette must come.* Otherwise they'll start sending pieces of me. Believe this.

Cato.

"What's the matter?"

"You're dropping cigarette ash on the sheets."

"What's the matter, what's the matter?"

"Nothing."

"You're thinking about something."

"A man can think."

"What is it?"

"Nothing, nothing, nothing."

"I'm so unhappy, nobody tells me anything. You won't stay with me tonight and I shall have nightmares again."

"I can't here, how can I, everything's horrible."

"It wouldn't be horrible if we lived here."

"Well, we're not going to live here. We're probably not capable of living anywhere."

"What do you mean? Are you going to leave me? What do you mean?"

"Of course I'm not going to leave you. But some married people just live in a suitcase all their lives. We're like that. We're just suitcase-size."

"You do love me, don't you? You will look after me, won't you?"

"Yes, yes, yes, but for God's sake stop whining and moping. The doctor said there was nothing wrong with you."

"Well, there is. You don't know what it's like when things are terrible in your mind. You don't understand, your mother doesn't understand, you're healthy people. Oh if only we could stay here in this house forever, I feel safe here, it's all so big and so real, I don't want to go back to London, that flat's like a tomb, I'll go mad there, oh I so much want to stay here. You don't know what it's like to be me, you don't know what it's like to be all tattered and destroyed inside—"

"I wish you'd stop smoking," said Henry. "This room is like a bloody gas chamber."

It was after eleven o'clock at night. The letter from Cato had arrived by the late afternoon post. Henry felt as if a bomb had exploded in his mind. He could not act or think. He had been carrying on a mechanical conversation with Stephanie for nearly an hour simply to pass the time.

Stephanie had spent the day in bed. The doctor had visited her and pronounced her fit. He had prescribed some tranquillizers and Gerda had fetched them from the chemist in Laxlinden. Stephanie was lying in the big brass bed in the cherry blossom room, which had remained unchanged since Burke's father's day, and which smelt of the past, a mean musty powdery pompous smell which made Henry shudder. Better life in a suitcase. The shutters were closed, pale green and faded between huge looped-up billows of lace curtains. A similar mountain of lace crowned the bed, wound about like a turban, yellowing with dust and age. The cherry blossom wallpaper, depicting Japanese scenes, had faded too and retired behind a spotty pale brown haze. Upon a slope of pillows very white by contrast, Stephanie lay with an almost ostentatious awkwardness. She was breathing quickly and her face was flushed. She was wearing a frilly pink night-dress, tight in the bodice and a little too small for her. A frilled shoulder-strap cut into the flesh making it bulge on either side. She kept jerking and twitching with nervous irritation, lacking the will to move and make herself comfortable. Henry roved about. His hand, which he had not shown to the doctor, was hurting. He looked down on Stephanie with a mixture of pity and annoyance and possessiveness and sheer blank responsibility which seemed to make up his love for this odd untidy woman. Yes, untidy, physically and spiritually untidy. Her big heavy chin was greasy, her almost round eyes were moist and glowing, hot with some kind of secretive emotion. A subject for Bonnard,

Vuillard, better still Degas. A large overflowing ash tray was balanced on her stomach while her hand, holding a lighted cigarette, trailed about like some sort of independent distracted animal. Even in his distress he found her exasperating, attractive. Only the centre of his mind, where it was all blown away, was occupied with Colette.

"You're thinking about that girl Colette."

"I'm not. Take your sleeping pills."

"I wish I had a hundred. I don't want to go to America. Please, darling, try to understand. I know you've got to be you. But I've got to be me too."

"I daresay that's a tautology."

"And there's all sorts of things I ought to tell you—"

"You mean about the past, about Sandy and all that—"

"Yes."

"I don't want to know. Sandy doesn't matter. He doesn't exist any more."

"You speak so cruel, it hurts. I know you don't mean to. You think that I'm just weak like a coward is. But I'm so unhappy in my mind and I can't do anything to stop it."

"Look out, you're burning a hole in the sheet."

"Your mother thinks I'm just a—"

"Look *out*—"

"I don't care, and you don't care since you're giving it all away—"

Stephanie jerked up and strewed the contents of the ash tray together with her glowing cigarette all over the early-nineteenth-century patchwork counterpane.

Henry lifted the ash tray and began to brush the glowing sparks and ash off onto the floor where he trampled them into a grey mess on the Persian carpet. He looked down with exasperation at Stephanie's hunched shoulder and at a large round dark-rimmed hole in the sheet. Then he reached down and grabbed one of the frilly shoulder-straps with both hands and snapped it. Stephanie's flushed face became suddenly smooth and bland and she relaxed, lying back among the pillows and gazing up at him with her hot eyes.

Henry touched her cheek. Then put the ash tray carefully on

the glass top of the dressing-table and then left the room closing the door quietly. He went downstairs.

*

"What is it?" said Gerda.

Henry was standing in the doorway of the library. A television programme was on, showing a picture of a hijacked
aeroplane standing on the tarmac at an African airport. Gerda,
dressed tonight in a dark red robe, was sitting in an armchair.
One lamp was on. A last yellow flame flickered in the grate.

Henry said nothing. He turned off the sound of the television, then came forward and sat astride on the club fender,
one foot dabbling in the ashes of the log fire, the other rucking
up the red and brown Kazak rug. The rug was covered with
little burnt patches where hot embers had leapt onto it from the
fire.

Gerda stared at her son as he sat there, pale faced, small
headed, curly haired, dangling his long legs and poking the
ashes intently with his foot. She said, "You've decided not to
sell the house?"

"No," said Henry, kicking up a cloud of ash.

"How is your hand? I wish you'd let me—"

"It's all right," he said after a moment, not looking at her,
gazing down at his ashy shoe. "What did you mean about not
living at Dimmerstone? Wouldn't you like to live at Dimmerstone?"

"No."

"Why not?"

"A man may do what he likes with his own," said Gerda,
"and I cannot complain since I am, as you say, old and have
had my time, but I do not want to stay here and see what is
done to this place which I love. When the house is sold my life
here will be over and finished. I shall leave and not come back."

"O.K.," said Henry, after a moment. "Where will you live
then?"

"In a flat in London."

"O.K. They're jolly expensive now, you know. You'd better
have Sandy's. I don't want it. There's a view of Harrods."

Gerda was silent, staring at him. She was wearing a white

flannel night-dress under her red robe, and had pulled the collar of it up around her neck. Her large magisterial face seemed smooth and unwrinkled in the dim light. Her dark hair, a little tossed and unkempt, was piled inside the white collar. She said again, "What is it?"

Henry took Cato's letter out of his pocket. It was a little crumpled and he smoothed it down. He handed it to Gerda.

Gerda read it, frowning. "Whatever is this?"

Henry swept his leg over the fender and sat facing her. "Well you may ask."

"What does it mean?"

"Listen," said Henry. "Something absolutely awful has happened. I've got to share this with somebody, especially now. Cato has been kidnapped by some gangsters. I think it was the idea of a delinquent boy, one of his flock. This boy got wind that I had a lot of money, and now this gang have got Cato and are blackmailing me. I've given them twenty thousand and I'm supposed to give them some more. But now this has come. I don't know what to do. I can't send Colette to those swine. I daren't go myself now. I daren't do nothing in case they start maiming Cato. I don't know what to do, I think I shall go mad."

Gerda read the letter through again. "You're sure this is genuine?"

"Yes. It's Cato's writing. And I've met the boy. It's genuine all right."

"What an extraordinary letter to write," said Gerda. She returned it to Henry. "Who have you told?"

"Nobody. You."

"You haven't told the police?"

"No! How can I?"

Gerda reflected. She said, "Wait, I'm going to change. I think we should go and see John Forbes."

*

Henry was sitting at the big scrubbed kitchen table at Pennwood, his elbows on the table and his face in his hands. He felt a mixture of profound relief and pure terror. Gerda and John Forbes were talking. "It's a matter of eliminating possibilities," John was saying.

John Forbes had expressed no surprise when Gerda had tele-phoned just before midnight to ask if she could come over to see him. He had shown only the briefest flicker of emotion at the news that his son was kidnapped and his daughter on de-mand by gangsters. He had blushed as a man might when he was insulted. They had arrived to find the lights on in the kitchen, the stove radiantly hot with open doors, the room, which Henry had not entered for so many years, tidied for visitors. He read Cato's letter, and then, while Henry was tell-ing the rest of the story, offered tea, coffee, beer, whisky. Chocolate biscuits. Gerda refused refreshment. Henry accepted whisky. He thought, I never realized how free I was before this fear came. Even if we get Cato out I'll be afraid now for the rest of my life. Oh God, why did this have to happen. Stupid bloody Cato, it's all his fault. He drank some more whisky. He had answered many questions and now left the discussion to the other two.

"It's just as well Colette isn't here," said Gerda. In spite of the warmth of the room she had kept her tweed coat on.

"Yes. She went to London this afternoon to see her Aunt Pat. You know, Ruth's old friend, Dame Patricia Raven. She'll stay the night there."

"I agree with you," said Gerda, "there just aren't any other possible moves."

"Obviously we can't let Colette go to those men, either alone or with an escort, we agree on that, don't we? If Henry goes he may be in danger. There was perhaps some point in Henry playing for time by giving them some money and promising more. I don't blame him for doing that. After all, the situation wasn't even clear till then. But I don't think there's any point in feeding them more money now. That won't ultimately save Cato's life. Now they've got some they'll probably be prepared to wait and bargain a bit. This boy that came, Henry, the one you'd seen before with Cato, you said you thought he was just a sort of pawn?"

"Cato said he was a petty criminal," said Henry, lifting his head. "He's very young. I suppose he's just got into the clutches of those people."

"Exactly. Now it's absolutely no good our trying to play the detective about this on our own. We've agreed on that too. We've nothing to go on. This place where Cato is may be anywhere. The postmark is certain to be misleading and this letter gives us no clue."

"I can't think how he can have written such awful letters," said Gerda. "It's a terrible thing to do, to involve other people like that. Henry might have got hurt."

"I did."

"A pity you destroyed the other letter."

"There wasn't any more clue in the other one," said Henry sulkily, his chin nearly down on the table.

"No, this tells us nothing," said John Forbes, inspecting Cato's letter. "The only positive thing that can be done is to lay hands on this boy. You said he had someone with him, Henry?"

"Yes."

"Did you see the other man?"

'No, but he said there was someone outside and it stands to reason he wouldn't come alone."

"These people must be ambushed. Henry must go once more and—"

"I don't see why Henry—" said Gerda.

"Neither do I," said Henry.

"Anyway this is a question for the police," said John Forbes. "It's a technical question, a question for experts. I think Henry should be prepared to—"

"If we agree to tell the police then let's do so at once," said Gerda. "I wanted to ring them immediately. Where should we telephone, here or London?"

"There is a risk in telling the police. I wanted to satisfy myself—"

At that moment the telephone began to ring in the hall. John Forbes got up and went out, leaving the door open. Henry lifted his head and looked at his mother. There was a slight shudder of emotion but neither of them moved. They could hear John talking in the hall.

"Hello ... Oh hello, Pat ... Yes ... What? But I thought she was with you, she said you'd rung up ... Oh my God. Yes, read it, read it ... Oh my God ... No, no, it's not your fault

... Oh *Christ* ... Look, Pat, I can't talk now, I must telephone the police ... Yes, yes ... yes, I'll ring you back later on tonight."

John Forbes came back into the kitchen and sat down heavily at the table. He was flushed again. He put his hands to his face.

"What's happened?" said Gerda.

"Colette's gone. She's gone. She's gone—there—to those men—"

"How—?"

"She said Aunt Pat had rung up and that she was going to see her. I was out all afternoon and when I came back she told me and then she went off to the train. But Pat didn't ring and she didn't go to Pat's. She just dropped a letter in there addressed to me with 'Please forward' on it. I expect she thought that Pat had gone to bed and wouldn't get it till the morning. But Pat came in late and picked it up just now and thought it was so odd she opened it—"

"And what—?"

"There was a letter from Cato inside addressed to Colette, telling her he'd been kidnapped and that she must come to the Mission at one o'clock if she wanted to save his life. And there was a note at the bottom from Colette just saying 'I've gone.'"

"She must have got that this afternoon," said Henry. "It must have come by the same post as mine."

"What's the time?" said Gerda.

It was a quarter past one.

Awkwardly, dragging at her hair which had become entangled in the knot, the boy took the bandage off her eyes. Colette automatically helped him to undo it and he left it in her hand. She was trembling so much that she almost staggered. Walking blindfold had disturbed her balance, and now an ague of physical fear seemed to rattle her whole body. Her teeth clicked together. She blinked and turned her head away from a

300

globe of bright light which was shining near her face. She was in a small room which was lit only by a candle standing on a shelf level with her eyes. Beside the candle was a small square box with a latticed metal front, perhaps some sort of microphone or speaker. The dust on the shelf was scrawled with circling tracks. She stood there staring, her hands to her face, the bandage trailing, her handbag hanging from one arm.

"Don't make a noise or they'll come. Sit down."

She half turned and saw the edge of an iron bedstead and sat down on it. She dropped the bandage and put her handbag behind her. She wanted to speak but could not. A strangled wavering sound, the very utterance of terror, came into her mouth and died there like a little mouse. Her hands returned to her face and she could feel her mouth trembling. She pressed her fingers against it to stop it. Shocked and helpless, she experienced her terror with a kind of surprise.

"What's the matter?"

"I'm frightened," said Colette. Saying it might help, and she could think of nothing else to say. She was able to articulate the words but her voice sounded cracked.

"Sssh, they'll hear. Sit quiet for a while. Don't tremble so. You'll make me feel frightened too."

The boy was sitting on a chair looking at her. Colette had recognized him as soon as he appeared out of the darkness of the alleyway behind the Mission, just as she was opening the door of the yard. He shone a torch into her face and by the light of the torch she had glimpsed the odd hexagonal shape of his glasses and the neat cut of his straight fair hair. He had stood for a moment shining the torch on her. Then he lowered the torch and had shown her his other hand, which was holding a knife. Neither of them spoke. Colette walked by his side, her mouth slightly open, her eyes staring, her body tethered. He did not take her arm, but she walked beside him through a kind of telepathy, twisting and turning with him through small ill-lit empty streets. Then when they came to an open space where there was nothing but blackness ahead he stopped and blindfolded her. Colette could not understand for a moment what he was doing, but stood there paralysed, then let him lead her on over uneven ground. He still did not take her arm but pulled her lightly by the sleeve of her coat, and still tethered she followed him by telepathy. They climbed over some obstructions and sidled past other ones and descended a ramp and then some steps and entered a place that echoed. Then her hand knocked hard against a wall and they halted and he undid the blindfold and she saw the candle burning.

Colette was for the moment almost entirely concerned with a sort of physical struggle with herself, as someone might be who was determined not to drown or fall. After she had, home at Pennwood, received Cato's summons she had felt weak and flimsy with terror. Then, coming to her like a long cool breath, came courage, the sudden extraordinary ability to lie to her father, to leave the house, to catch the train, to endure, sitting in a café at the railway station, later in a pub, the awful interval. What chiefly upheld her during this time was the absence of any alternative. Cato had asked her to come, somehow to help him, somehow to save him, and she had to come, just as she would have run into a burning house if she had heard him calling. Still stiffened by courage, and even with relief, though her heart beat so terribly, she had come to the Mission. She had, putting herself deliberately into a kind of daze, endured the weird telepathic walk through the strange streets, feeling herself, a girl walking with a boy, to be invisible, her crazed mask invisible. But now suddenly there was no more courage, no more purpose, only this shuddering and a mute scream lodged in her throat. Shaken by her collapse into fear, she fought with herself.

Deliberately she looked about the room, not at the boy. She was in a small grey cubical box with pitted concrete walls. The bright candle-flame wavered slightly. There was a slight draught and a watery muddy smell. Conscious of the boy's eyes, or rather of his glasses, which she could see without looking at them, she inspected the rest of the scene. There was the bed, the chair, and a lowish table which suddenly looked to her like an altar. Upon the altar, touched with a moving glitter from the candle-flame, lay the unsheathed knife. Underneath the table was a suitcase, with packages of papers piled on top of it and round about it. She pressed her hand against her mouth and took her lower lip between her teeth, then flinched as the boy suddenly moved. He leaned down and picked up one of the packets, pulled and snapped the elastic band that held it, and threw it onto Colette's lap. She gave a little smothered cry, and then stared down at the coloured faces of five- and ten- and twenty-pound notes which were falling about on her skirt and raining to the floor. The boy laughed, and kicked at the notes as they fell.

"Can you remember my name?"

At the shock of his movement tears had leapt into her eyes. She rubbed them away with her hand and with the same movement lifted her loose hair back behind her shoulders. Somehow the quick tears steadied her, softly breaking some tension which had seemed as if it could only break with a scream. "Beautiful Joe."

"Don't cry. I won't hurt you."

"My brother—" said Colette.

"He's all right. So far. Don't cry."

"Is he here—?"

"No. Don't talk loud. There's no one here now but the big Negro who keeps the gate, but I don't want him to come. If you screamed or anything he'd come. He was reading his comics when we came in. The people I work for are very cruel people. But if you're quiet and sensible I'll look after you."

"But my brother—what is this money—?" Colette shook the rest of it off her skirt onto the floor.

"Ransom."

"For him—who paid it?"

"Someone."

"But what's going to happen, what will they do to him?"

"He'll be all right if you do exactly what you're told. I'm telling you the truth. If you don't something bad will happen. Look, I want to show you something. Never mind the money, get up, stand on it, stand on it."

Colette rose and stepped onto the scattering of bank notes.

"That's good, that's nice. You've got such—pretty shoes." The candle moved and shadows rushed about in the room. She now looked at the boy's face, but without seeing it clearly, though the lifted light was making it golden. The golden bristles about his lips and chin were glittering and shifting like the scales of a fish. His curling lips lengthened and she could hear his fast breathing. There was a faint vibration in the pitted wall. Colette covered her mouth.

"Look at this. I bought it for you myself. Today. Yesterday."

The candle dipped and she saw, under the foot of the bed, an orange plastic bucket, quite new, with triangular paper labels still upon it.

"That's the toilet. It's all yours."

Colette looked at the bucket. Then for a moment it seemed that something hot, some strengthening cordial, anger perhaps, had been injected into her blood. The sight of the brand new orange bucket somehow filled her with intense annoyance. "Look here," she said, "what is all this, I want to see my brother, I want an explanation."

"Your brother isn't here."

"Is he all right? Why do they want me?"

"You'll see."

"Why—?"

"Shut up. Be glad you're still alive. Life is cheap around here. I've got to go now. You can't get out, so don't try. You'd better lie down and sleep, I mean it's still night-time so you may as well. Don't make a noise or the Negro will come. He's subnormal, he likes hitting people. I don't want to come back and find you with your face all smashed. I can look after you if you're good. If you're not they'll take you from me. See?"

The candle moved towards her face and Colette backed away, stepping back over the carpet of bank notes, seeing the low table and the unsheathed knife. The bed touched her legs and she sat abruptly. She saw Joe's hand descend to pick up the knife. The candle moved to the door and disappeared through it. The door closed and a lock turned. A further door opened and closed, there was a rattle and a click and then silence.

The darkness was thick and total, the absolute dark against which ordinary darkness would show as grey or blue. Colette sat quiet on the bed, both her hands holding her throat. She sat absolutely still for a very long time, her body tense. Then muscle by muscle, limb by limb, she began to relax. She felt behind her for her handbag and found it. It was company, like a dog. It did not occur to her to grope about and explore her prison, she knew that she could not get out of it. Nor was she tempted to shout or scream. If she did that the violent men would come and silence her. She concentrated on breathing deeply and steadily and she tried to think. Cato had said in his letter and underlined it, "Tell nobody." Colette had intended to tell nobody, but out of the misery of it and a desire to share her anguish she had dropped the letter in on Aunt Pat who would find it in the morning and send it on to her father. But if her father had paid that ransom money, which even now was strewn all over the floor around her bed, he must know already? But that was impossible. He could not have acted to her, could not have concealed his distress. Somebody however must know, somebody else, who had paid the ransom? Where was Cato now and was he even still alive? Her loving will, so bent upon her brother ever since she had received his letter, now felt checked and desperate. Tears came out in the darkness and wandered on her face. She felt her cheeks and they were blazing hot.

With an effort she decided to take off her shoes. She lifted her feet carefully out and put the shoes neatly together under the bed. She did not take off her coat, but lay back and pulled the blanket up over her. She became aware how cold the room was. Stiffened and aching now with cold she lay controlling her breath and listening. She told herself, I can do nothing now but wait, I have done what Cato asked, I have done right. Now I must simply wait. And as she lay there it seemed that something odd was happening to time, and it was as if her whole life up to now were a sort of present moment which had just gone by, and the present moment in which she now lay, as in a great cup, was of equal length. And she looked at her life and seemed to understand it and to grieve over it as if it were already over, although she did not clearly formulate the idea that she was about to be killed.

I thought I was coming to Cato, she said to herself, I thought I was coming to help him, but this makes no sense now, nothing makes sense now. I don't know what I've done, and perhaps I shall just disappear and no one will ever find out what happened to me. And I don't even know whether I've been brave or whether I've just been stupid. And an awful pain of remorse

305

began to grow inside her. Her father had so often scolded her for doing stupid things in a hurry. Here was another of them and perhaps the last. Why had she come running because Cato had written a letter asking her to do something which perhaps he did not want her to do at all?

She lay stiff and in anguish, and then, quite suddenly, with a part of her mind which was not yet in bondage, she began to think of Henry Marshalson. She had loved Henry so much when she was a small child, only no one would ever believe this or even hear about it now. That love all belonged to the elapsed moment. She recalled the strange lurid evening in her little room in college when she had sat holding her father's letter telling her of Sandy's death; and she had felt such a violent jolt of love and certainty, and had understood in a second so many implications and had seen so many visions. And as now she had rushed towards Cato because of his letter, just so compulsively and so blindly had she fled from the college, back to Laxlinden simply and solely to see Henry again, to be with him and to worship him with her love. She turned on the bed, bringing her knees up and bowing her head and screwing up her eyes in the dark. She thought, I *ran* to Henry, I had to. And she saw his quizzical laughing face framed in the dark curling hair, and his dark glowing eyes looking at her, and she wished for physical desire to distract her from her misery and terror, but it would not come. And she felt with a sadness that she had lost him, not because he did not want her, but because she did not any more want him. In this darkness Henry gave no light, he was just a young girl's silly empty dream.

"I've got to sleep," said Henry. "I've *got* to, I have to go to London tomorrow to see the police there, they want me to go to that place tomorrow night."

"You'll be killed."

"No, I won't, the police will be watching."

"When they see the police there they'll kill you."

"They won't see."

"How do you know they won't see?"

"Oh stuff it, Stephanie, I'm quite bloody scared enough without your laying it on—"

"So you *do* think you'll be killed."

"No, I don't! The police will be inches away. Look, clear off for Christ's sake, I've got to sleep, I've got to rest, with any luck I'll become unconscious and have a nice dream. I was having one when you arrived."

"Why didn't you come to me?"

"I thought you'd be asleep."

"Let me stay."

"If you stay I won't sleep. Christ, I want to *sleep*, is that so odd?"

"I don't believe that story, it's all a hoax, why do you believe it when there isn't any evidence?"

"Oh do *stop*—"

"It's all a plot and a pretence, it's all invented by that girl to make you sorry for her, to make you fall in love with her, it's all magic."

"Well, if it's pretence it's not magic," said Henry, "and if it's that kind of plot then I won't be killed. You can't have it all ways."

Henry had been suddenly awakened from sleep. He had been dreaming that he was at home at Sperriton and Russ and Bella were with him in the garden which had become very large, and in the garden there was a lake and on the lake was a toy yacht with white sails. Conscious of the strong approving presence of his friends, looking at the white sails, Henry had felt a deep joy.

In the moment of waking he had experienced first happiness, then, intensified by the contrast, misery and fear. He dreaded the police trap in which he had felt bound to say he would co-operate. The police seemed to think that since Cato's second letter about Colette had simply demanded her and not the money, the gang would be waiting for Henry to bring the rest of the ransom as previously arranged. Henry pictured the awful darkness, the hidden ruthless men. He was sure that the gang would realize that the police were watching and would instantly kill him. He felt in his body all the terror of imminent violence, just as vividly as if he could actually see the gun or the knife which was about to maim or kill him. And even if he survived that terrible meeting he would be scarcely better off since he would be black-listed, marked down as a traitor, a man to be eliminated later. All the innocence and pleasure of life had been taken from him, as if he had actually been suborned by his foes, as if he too had become criminal. Indeed if it had not been for one thing, Henry Marshalson would now have been simply a single quaking mass of solipsistic dread. The one thing was the thought of Colette.

In fact Henry had agreed to act as a police decoy, not because of Colette, but out of some old primitive sense of duty, or sense, more simply, of the "done thing." He did not see how he could get out of agreeing and it did not seriously occur to him not to agree. The thought of Colette was something extra, an extra pain, an extra grace, and though Henry was not then capable of thinking of it that way his anguish for Colette helped him a little by diverting his attention from himself. He imagined himself gunned down, hit on the head, made imbecile by brain damage. He also imagined her, and what might now be happening to her; and somehow beyond these imaginings the image of Colette and the thought of her wholeness and her courage entered into him like a spear, like a hard line of pure non-Henry in the midst of the humiliating jelly of his personal terror.

"I won't be able to sleep, I'm so frightened."

"I'm frightened too, but I propose to sleep."

"You said you weren't frightened."

"I didn't, I am, never mind, just get out, there's a good creature."

"You don't love me. You're thinking about that girl."

"Oh shut up, *shut up*, can't you see I'm frantic, I don't want to chat with you, do you want me to scream?"

"You don't need me. You're in trouble and you don't need me."

Henry had woken up to find the lamp turned on and Stephanie sitting on the end of his bed. She had heard the car

308

depart, taking Henry and Gerda to Pennwood, and she had come to the just returned, instantly sleeping Henry to ask where he had been. Though Gerda had advised him otherwise, Henry had felt himself bound to tell. Stephanie seemed determined not to believe him and indeed the tale sounded mad, and to Henry's now hazy mind it was far from clear on what evidence so much terror rested. But the terror was real.

Stephanie was sitting hunched, wearing the *négligé* with the silver and black lozenge pattern and the feathers. Her bare feet were tucked under her and her head was sunk between her shoulders and her hands were crossed under her chin. Her hair was tousled and her face without make-up was puffy and pale, the harsh lines on either side of her mouth deeply shadowed in the lamplight. She looked old, and, for the first time since Henry had met her, utterly indifferent to her appearance. It looked as if she had been crying. Henry felt, together with his exasperation, the familiar possessive loving pity. Then he turned from her, stretching out his body and groaning, hiding his face in the pillow. He was conscious of himself, as if he could see himself, slim and taut inside his blue cotton pyjamas, strong, intact, young; and this time tomorrow likely to be maimed or dead.

"I want to ask you something. Why do you love me?"

"I've taken you on," said Henry. Sleep was now impossible. "I love you because I've taken you on."

"That's a funny answer."

"You're a funny girl."

"Why have you taken me on?"

"Because I'm sorry for you. Because of Sandy. Because I was able to make love to you. Because of your turned-up nose and the fact that however hard you try not to you dress untidily."

"Because of my past."

"Because of your past, because of your eyes, because you were grateful. How can one say why one takes somebody on? I'm a funny chap myself."

"I've got something to tell you, Henry, listen. I told you some lies."

"All right. Does it matter?"

"Henry, darling—I was never a stripper, I was never a prostitute—none of that was true. Do you mind?"

Henry sat up. Stephanie, hunched in a ball at the foot of the bed, was like an old bedraggled bird. "What do you mean?"

"Just that. I invented it all. I was never like that. I was respectable, I was a typist, I wasn't a tart. I just said that."

"Oh," said Henry. He stared at her. Tears came quietly from her eyes. He had never seen her look so pathetic and so ugly. "Why?"

"I thought it would interest you and make you sorry for me."

Henry considered this. "Fair enough. It did."

"And it doesn't matter?"

Henry considered, looking at her tears. Wrenched from his dread, he concentrated. He felt he had been made a fool of, he felt a deep bewildered anxiety. "I don't think so. It makes me feel a fool and somehow sick, but I don't suppose that matters. You are a liar and I am a fool, that's all."

"And you forgive me?"

"The question doesn't arise. Well, yes, of course. So when you ran away from your family you became a typist not a stripper. O.K. O.K."

"But I didn't run away. I lived with my family until I was twenty. They're still living in Leicester. I was there at Christmas. My brother's in computers."

"Congratulations," said Henry. "A secure job. So it looks as if I was wrong to feel sorry for you. O.K."

"No, no, you were right. You see—oh do please try and understand. My life became awful, just gradually and not for any reason. You've never known that kind of awfulness. I could never manage my life. The only thing I ever learnt was typing and I was no good at that, I kept losing jobs and then, when I had no references, it got harder and harder to get other jobs. You don't know what it's like, what the despair is like, when you just sink and sink. I tried to be a clerk but I couldn't do that either, I couldn't do anything. I started to live on national assistance—"

"I'm beginning to feel sorry for you again."

"Of course I wanted to get married, it seemed the only hope, and there were one or two men I met in pubs, but they were

310

horrible and just wanted sex, and nobody was ever kind to me
or cared about me as a person, and I never managed to make
any woman friends and I just went on trying and failing at
everything, and I used to sit alone in my room and cry for
hours, and no one cared, and then at last just out of loneliness
and not having a job I had a nervous breakdown and went into
a hospital and they gave me drugs and electric shocks and I
lived there for nearly a year and it seemed impossible that I'd
ever get out, and I didn't even want to get out—"

"Why didn't you tell me?" said Henry.

"I thought you'd go off me if you thought I was neurotic or
mad or anything. A girl in the hospital said, never tell anyone
you've had a breakdown, if you ever want to find a job or a
husband. And then I came out, they made me come out, and
I went on living alone—"

"So you weren't anybody's *femme fatale* after all," said
Henry, "except Sandy's and mine. Where did you meet Sandy
then, if it wasn't in the strip club?"

"This is what I've got to tell you," she said, and her mouth
was wet with tears. "It wasn't true. I wasn't ever Sandy's
mistress. I didn't know him at all. I was just the charwoman."

"*What?*"

"I went cleaning houses, it was the only thing I could do. I
cleaned the stairs at those flats and then one of the ladies asked
me to clean her flat, and she recommended me to Sandy and
he left his key for me in an envelope, and I used to come in on
Mondays, only he was never there on that day, he used to leave
notes for me and the money, I only saw him about twice, on
the stairs, and I wasn't even sure if it was him and he didn't
know who I was, and then I saw in the paper that he'd been
killed—"

"But—wait—wait—you mean you weren't Sandy's mistress,
it was all a lie?"

"Yes."

"But that's impossible, really, you must be mad, you knew
all about him, you knew all about *me*, you recognized me as
soon as we met—"

"No, I knew nothing. I looked in his desk, but I could find
out nothing—"

311

"But you recognized me, you knew he was called Sandy, you—"

"You told me who you were. You told me his name. I just waited and it all came out, *you* told me—"

"But, Stephanie, you said you were Sandy's mistress, you said it five minutes after we met—"

"Yes—"

"My God. So you'd got it all ready, the lie, for whoever came?"

"For whoever came. But it was—oh I can't explain—it wasn't like that, it wasn't sort of cold-blooded, it sort of happened—"

"How did it sort of happen, for Christ's sake?"

"I had a sort of day-dream about Sandy, a sort of fantasy, I had these fantasies about lots of people, any man I saw practically, how he'd love me and marry me and turn out to be rich, and I imagined it all, how it would be with Sandy, and how I'd tell him that I ran away from home and became a stripper and he'd be sorry for me and he'd look after me—"

"God!"

"Then you see when he died and nobody came—weeks and weeks went by and nobody came and I kept waiting and waiting—and I used to come in every day and walk around the flat and it was so odd, all empty and nobody there but me—and then I lost my room and it seemed like a sign—and I moved into the flat, like just for emergency—and then I had a sort of day-dream that no one would ever come and I could just take over the flat and live there—And then one day it occurred to me that if someone did come at last and if I pretended I'd been Sandy's mistress, then even if they were cross they'd give me some money and I had a fantasy that they might even give me the flat, and after all I might have been Sandy's mistress—"

"Yes, you might, mightn't you, so that makes it very nearly true. I think you're a genius, those electric shocks must have done you a world of good. And then I appeared."

"And then you appeared and—I pretended—and you told me everything, who you were and everything, and I just had to pretend to know what you told me, and I hoped you'd give me the flat, at least at first I did—"

"And then you began to see that you could scoop the pool."

"Well, then I—then I—loved you—"

"Another fantasy. At any rate my money was real. So all that touching stuff about how Sandy looked down on you—and about the child and so on—all invented—Christ, you ought to be a novelist. And I swallowed the lot. You must have been amazed at your luck."

"But Henry, I do love you, I do, it's not a fantasy—and I've told you the truth and I didn't have to and it's been hard, and I'm so terrified that you'll feel different now, only I couldn't go on lying. I had to know you wanted me as me, and not just because of Sandy or because of the stripping or something, so I have been brave, haven't I? Oh please understand and don't see it as something awful. I had to try, I had to fight, I've always been by myself, and no one ever helped me or bothered with me or ever liked me very much, I had to fend for myself, I had to make plans—"

"What other plans did you make? I'm fascinated—"

"Oh nothing like that—nothing ever worked for me—only I was getting desperate—you see, I'm getting old, I felt it was my last chance—"

"How old are you?" said Henry.

"I'm—well—I'm a little older than I said—I'm—nearly forty—oh dear, oh dear—please understand—I just had to look after myself, nobody else would—and then you came and you were so *kind*, you called me Miss Whitehouse and you were so respectful and so polite and you didn't treat me like dirt like everyone else did and you *noticed* me and you thought I was attractive—"

"It sounds as though I was your first bit of luck."

"Yes, yes darling, you were my first bit of luck, the first good thing that had ever happened to me—but oh I haven't spoilt it all by lying to you, have I? You do forgive me—" Stephanie slithered onto the floor and edged up towards him on her knees, pushing the rug before her on the wooden floor. She put her hands up to him like a begging dog. Her hot damp fingers tugged at the blue cotton sleeve of his pyjamas.

"No wonder you laughed so when I proposed. You needed me and you invented me. Yes, you're a genius."

"Henry, please—"

"So you're not a *femme fatale* after all, you're just the char. You're just a comic, a comic charwoman."

"Yes, yes, a comic, your comic, aren't I? You do forgive me, don't you, say that you forgive me. You said you were sorry for me, you said you loved me because you were sorry for me, but you still are, aren't you? I've had such a miserable life and I've been so lonely, and you can't leave me just because I've told you the truth, I had to tell you the truth because I love you—you can't leave me now, you said you'd taken me on, that hasn't changed, has it, just because—"

"That hasn't changed," said Henry.

"Oh—thank you, thank God—" she continued to kneel, giving little shuddering sobs, and holding his hand against her wet lips.

Henry looked down at the disordered hair and the absurd feathered collar and Stephanie's heaving shoulders. He thought, she admits to forty and is probably more. He said, "Hi, Steph. Hello."

"You are so good, so kind, the only person who was ever kind—"

"Do get up, Steph, these transports are most improper, no, I don't want you, go and sit in that chair, please. Here, have my hankie."

Stephanie got up and went to the chair, mopping her face. "So it's all right, it's really all right?"

"Yes, it's got to be. Steph, I can't chuck you, I won't, I just feel I don't know you very well, you don't know me very well, and there we are, we seem to be each other's doom. I expect we'll be O.K., we'll look after each other O.K. Now please go away, no, you can't sleep here, there isn't room and I'm as cold as ice. Yes, yes, I forgive you, but please go."

"Henry, don't go to that place tomorrow."

"I've got to."

"If you were killed tomorrow I'd have nothing—"

"Oh, Steph! All right, I'll make a will leaving everything to you!"

"I didn't mean it that way."

"You don't know what you do mean. You're my comic girl

friend. But look, you must do as I tell you, I mean if I survive as I certainly intend to, you must come to America with me and be an ordinary person and not a rich lady. Please no more fantasies."

"I'll do whatever you—"

"Now please go, *please*."

"And it's—"

"Yes, yes, yes."

After she had gone Henry got up and drank some water. Then he washed his hands. He turned out the lamp and pulled the window curtains back. The dawn was breaking.

Cato had been jerking the pipe to and fro for a long time now, perhaps an hour, his sense of time had become very vague. He was kneeling on one knee, leaning his shoulder against the wall. His arm ached, his hand felt wet, perhaps it was bleeding. The pipe had unscrewed to a certain point, then stuck. Cato moved the loosened pipe to and fro because it was an occupation, like turning a prayer-wheel. It was the only thing he could think of to do for his salvation. His open eyes were filled with blackness, useless as if atrophied. His body lived through his sense of touch and already seemed as if it had always done so.

Prolonged darkness and hunger seemed to have radically altered all his senses. He experienced himself in relation to his surroundings through a sensibility which lived in his feet, his fingers, and the flesh of his face of which his blind eyes now seemed an indistinguishable part. When he was still, lying or sitting on his bed, he felt himself to be both narrowed and enlarged, as if his body had become a big tight uncomfortable barrel within which his soul or his will or something lived as a thin flexible line. He felt at the same time solidified and hollow, weak and yet frenzied with useless power. His body was a burden to him, a source of disgust, and yet his sensitive fingers, like long long antennae, had learnt new tricks, a new sense of space. He could move noiselessly, lightly, confidently about his

315

prison, yet at the same time he was a toad and he could smell the horror of his breath.

It was now some time since Joe had paid the last of his flying visits, bringing him bread and water. Very hungry, Cato had eaten all the bread. Later on, drugged or again hungry, he had begun to feel giddy. He had still seen no member of the gang except Joe, and this in itself had become a source of dread. He felt a crazed lonely curiosity, as if even the most horrible person would have been welcome company for him. Only still, fearing for his own safety and for Joe's, he did not dare to shout and knock. He had heard once more, but not lately, the odd distant gabble of voices, and sometimes footsteps. Now, obsessed with detaching his piece of metal pipe, he had ceased to listen. He had no plans for his tool, he just wanted to have it. Now, growling very softly, after a short rest, he shifted to the other knee and set to work again.

The time of writing the first letter to Henry was now immensely distant. It was, he supposed, days ago, and seemed by comparison a period of ignorance or even innocence. When he had first addressed Henry he had done so, it now seemed in retrospect, with a certain sense of absurdity and without any very lively realization that he was leading his friend into serious danger. Yet of course he knew that he ought not to have written that letter, and he could not remember having been then so afraid that he could not have refused to write it. Extreme fear, it seemed, had come later, had come with physical weakness and mental confusion. Yet it was the fact that he had written the first letter that had made it that much easier to write again, to Henry, and so shamefully to Colette. He had written in fear of Joe, of Joe's anger and his craziness and his viciously playful knife, and in fear of *them*, to whom he was to be delivered for punishment if he failed; whose victim also Joe would then become. It was all so incalculably complicated. Cato had felt so weak, so sick, so tired, so unable to fight, so unable to think, to resist, even to delay. And he had let himself be consoled amid the horror of his treachery by the thought that Colette would tell his father and his father would tell the police. Colette would not come, that never. Only now he was not so sure.

There was a sudden cracking sound and a pattering shower of fine debris and Cato sat back abruptly on the floor holding the section of piping. He sat there for a moment exploring his trophy. The pipe was heavy, about nine inches long, and had a jagged tongue of metal at the end projecting perhaps four inches. Cato sat touching it, playing it as if it were a silent instrument. Then he struggled up, stood giddily for a moment, and made for his bed. He lay down holding the piece of pipe against him as if it were something cherished and precious. He even felt its shape against his cheek. It was dear to him as an indubitable thing, something outside his body and his mind, a talisman, something for which he had toiled and which he now possessed as some kind of evidence or proof.

Cato listened. There was total silence. The intermittent vibration which he interpreted as the underground railway was absent, so it must be night, perhaps two or three in the morning. Night. His father and Colette would be safely asleep at Pennwood. Silence. He tried to think about Henry and to wonder whether Henry had brought the rest of the money, but Henry and the money seemed unreal and shadowy, could not possibly be part of the story. He thought, I shall stay here and starve, stay here and die. I shall scream in the end, but there will be no one to hear. Perhaps they have all gone away and Beautiful Joe is already dead. I shall scream in the end. No one will ever know where I am or what happened. Silence. Night. Colette is asleep.

Then, clutching the pipe, he turned over in anguish and then sat up. He had written that letter to Colette, that terrible craven fatal letter. He had not fought, he had scarcely even argued, he had tried to purchase his survival with his sister's safety, perhaps with her life; with her honour, with his honour. He thought of other prisoners, brave men imprisoned by tyrants for speaking the truth. He was not of their company. Cato sat open-eyed, light-headed with misery and shame. He now saw that of course Colette would come, would come like an arrow to him, for him, as she thought. She would tell nobody, she would simply come.

He sat listening to his breathing and to the beat of his heart. He sat upright, straight-backed, legs slightly apart, and the attitude suddenly brought back memories of his earliest days as an ordinand when, sitting in what had then seemed like darkness, he had passed long periods in meditation. No one had told him what to expect, scarcely even what to attempt to do. Should I see images? he had said to Father Bell. Do what you please, he was told. Kneel. Sit. Stand. Kneel. Sit. Stand. Kneel. Automatically Cato canted forward and knelt on the floor. He laid the piece of piping down carefully and noiselessly beside him and he looked into the perfect darkness. He saw Colette looking at him with a look of immense tenderness, and then with an air of sadness turning her head away. With an intense concentrated quietness of transformation, Colette's face had become the face of the Redeemer, and the Redeemer had huge eyes luminous as a cat's, staring at him out of the darkness, yet there was a bright light all about. And Cato could see the tendrils of hair that flowed about the beloved head, and the way the beard grew. And he had a most intense sensation of not being alone.

Cato knew that these images were simply hallucinations. He had never so clearly felt and known the emptiness of such imagery, the falseness of that consoling sense of presence. He had betrayed his sister. He might soon die, or else live in shame. He had written a letter, he had performed an act, there was evidence against him. Some words came to him: God is the author of all actions. And he thought, but there is no God. Only those images, only actions and their consequences, and death. Lord have mercy. Christ have mercy. Lord have mercy. This is not prayer, he thought, and I have never prayed. There is only sin and nothing to alter it or to change it, only our sin which is more foul than anything which we can understand or know, because we are made of lies.

He reeled, steadied himself with one hand on the ground, and went on kneeling. There is no God. I have nothing. I am nothing. God is the author of all actions. There is no God. Lord have mercy. I am a criminal. There is no hope. There is no one here. There is an abyss. He reeled again. Then, placing his hands on the floor, let himself fall forward until he was lying prone. There is no God, he thought, and he felt that it was the first time that he had ever really experienced the positive truth of this; and with the experience came an extra-ordinary breaking as if all the strings and tendons of his body had been cut, and he lay there limp as one to whom death has come unexpectedly.

The candle was burning on the shelf, moving slightly in the draught, like an almost motionless dancer who quietly shifts one foot. Colette and Beautiful Joe were sitting on the bed.

"Colette," Joe reached out his hand and held it open towards her. Then he let it fall gently to touch her knee. She shuddered. "Let me touch you. Call me 'Joe' will you?"

"Joe."

"Are you afraid of me?"

"Yes."

"Are you afraid of sex?"

"Yes."

"You've had sex?"

"Never."

Joe withdrew his hand. "I've never met a bird like you. You're—you're—precious."

"Joe," said Colette, "I want Cato to be all right. I want him to be set free. There's no need for them to keep two of us. I came so that he should be set free. Won't they do that? Surely whoever paid them money would pay it for me."

"Henry Marshalson. You reckon?"

"Henry paid that ransom money?"

"Yes, and he's going to pay a lot more before he's through."

"But can't Cato please go now? I'm enough for ransom."

"You aren't here for the money," said Joe.

Colette looked away from him. She looked at the low table where Joe had once more laid down his unsheathed knife. The knife glittered amazingly as if it were made of some magical metal which was a source of light. The blade shone like a flame. The strewn bank notes were still carpeting the floor.

"Colette," said Joe. "I want you to give yourself. I don't want you to fight me."

"Give myself—to you?"

"Yes."

"Not to—anybody else—I mean?"

Joe was silent for a moment. Then he took off his glasses and put them on the table beside the knife. His face now showed weariness. "Sex is so nice, Colette. A woman's body, the way it moves—"

"If I give myself to you, will Cato be set free?"

"Maybe. Yes, it'll help. I could get mad, I could force you, you're frightened of me. Some men like that. Don't make me mad. I'll try to help your brother. But you've got to give. After all, you're helpless, you're a prisoner. I could force you, anybody could. You're just a girl. You don't want to get messed up, do you? You don't want your face to get messed? I could slash you with that knife. I know how to slash people so they stay slashed, the scars never go. You know?"

Colette made the effort to turn and look at him. Without his glasses he looked so tired, so young, a boy. He narrowed his eyes, staring back, then smiled a little, acting, tossed his neat head of hair. "It's Beauty and the Beast, isn't it! I know I'm Beautiful Joe, but compared with you I'm a beast. Do you like me, Colette?"

"I am very sorry for you," she said.

"I don't want your bloody pity. Won't you take my hand? Look, I'm offering it to you again."

Colette took his hand and then gasped with pain. He had twisted her wrist violently. Tears came into her eyes, tears of pain and helplessness and fear. She had for some time now had one idea clear in her mind. She would be raped in any case; but if there was any chance of making some sort of bargain, making of her surrender a significant action, she must find it and use it. She still had a last measure of freedom and must exercise it intelligently. Had Joe any power to help Cato? If she hastened to do what Joe wished would she buy his friendship, would she not just be passed on, a despised acquiescing slave, to one of Joe's masters? Her body curled and shrank, but she knew that she would not resist the knife. A little pain, and she would be a blubbering idiot, unable to think, unable to bargain. She said, "Listen, Joe, I will give myself, if you will let me see Cato first. I want to be sure he's all right."

Joe hesitated. "He's not here."

"I don't believe you. I want to see him."

"You can see him after."

"No, before."

"You can't make conditions," said Joe. "Take your tights off."

"Please. Not yet. Joe, talk to me. I don't know you. Let's be friends."

"Do you mean that? I'm sorry I hurt you just now. I didn't really hurt you, did I? I was just mad because you wouldn't take my hand, as if you looked down on me."

"I don't look down on you. But I wish you weren't with these awful people. Joe, can't you get us out, rescue us, Cato and me? I'd do anything that you want."

"You're going to do that anyway. May I kiss you—Colette?"

Colette sat rigid and let the boy lean over her. His hot wet lips, trembling slightly, touched her mouth, withdrew, then came back and his arm went round her shoulder. Colette closed her eyes.

"You're stirred," he said, withdrawing again. "You want me. Let me touch you here, just touch. Have you ever wanted a man?"

"No."

"I won't force you. I want this to be proper, I want it to be perfect. I've got to have you, Colette, now, tonight. When a man starts he can't stop. But we won't hurry if you don't want. It's better that way. I just like touching you like this. You're lovely, lovely—I've never had anyone like you—Colette, you do want me, don't you? Can't you feel it, it's sex, can't you feel?"

Colette breathed deeply. The motionless dancer was moving, the room was vibrating, soundlessly drumming. A sigh came from her out of a depth of physical being which she had never felt so poignantly before. She was repelled, disgusted, horrified, frightened, excited.

"Let me touch you here."

"No."

"Don't fight me. Let me see your breasts, you don't mind that. You'll be as keen as I am soon."

"Joe, let's be quiet together," said Colette. "I want to be friends with you, I won't fight you, only don't—just yet—Joe, will you promise to get Cato out?"

"Yes."

"You promise?"

"Oh damn Cato. Yes, yes. Oh, you're marvellous, you're heaven. That's nice, isn't it?"

She had let him open the front of her dress and wriggle one hand in onto her breast. Reaching back she undid the brassière.

"That's better. Wait. Oh Colette—" Joe jerked away and pulled off his shirt. He unzipped his jeans. Then very gently replaced his hand. "You see, I can be quiet. I'm not a wild beast, not yet, you know. That's nice, isn't it? Put your hand here. All right here." He led her hand to his front and she felt, amid the mass of golden hair which ran down his body to his waist, the hidden nipples and the violently thudding heart. "You can feel my heart, I can feel your heart. You're excited."

"Joe, where is Cato? Joe, dear Joe, you will help us?"

"I've said I would. You called me 'dear Joe.' Do you like me?"

"Yes," said Colette. It was true. She felt irresistibly sorry, irresistibly moved.

"I'd like to tell you about my life, only not now. Afterwards. It's nice afterwards, Colette, when you feel you've been in heaven and then you feel so soft and limp and yet so wonderful and you lie together and it's so tender—"

"Won't you tell me about your life—now—I'd like to know—"

"My father beat me, my brothers beat me, and my mother— God, women are muck—I don't mean you—Colette, darling, take off your tights, just to show me that you will. I won't hurry you, I won't force you, I know it's the first time. I wouldn't believe any other girl, but I believe you. Colette, you know it hurts a bit, don't you, the first time?"

"Yes." Slowly, Colette kicked off her shoes, then began to

wind down her tights. She was trembling violently now. She dropped them on the floor, then pulled the skirt of her dress down over her knees.

"You're like a little girl."

"Joe, the other people, the other men here—will they come? Oh Joe, I'm so frightened, I'm not frightened of you, I'm frightened of them."

"Them? Oh, them! Colette, listen, I'll tell you a secret. Then we make love, yes. I want you to be happy. There isn't anybody else, there's only me."

"Only—you—?"

"Yes, I made believe it was a gang. I just said it and they believed it. God, how I laughed. It was so bloody easy. There they were all shaking in their shoes. Henry Marshalson bringing all that money, and your brother scared stiff and sitting there like a petrified mouse! God, people are such bloody cowards. You just show them a knife and they'll do anything."

"But—you mean—there's no gang, no other people at all, you mean you've done it all alone, captured Cato, made him write that letter, got all that ransom money—?"

"Yes. Aren't I great?"

"But the Negro, you said—"

"There isn't a Negro, there isn't anyone— See that transistor set, I put it on sometimes, on the foreign programmes, so it sounded like people talking. God, I laughed!"

"So it's all a hoax, a joke?"

"I didn't say that—"

"But where's Cato? You must tell him, you must let him out at once—where are we—?"

"Later, later, don't make me angry, I can be angry, you know I can."

"You must give the money back and—"

"Stop, honey, don't yap. Of course I'm not going to give it back, and he'd better bloody not ask for it. I worked for that stuff. I'm big now, I've made myself big, and I done it alone. It needed some bleeding nerve, I didn't know it would be easy. I'm dangerous, and he can spare it, can't he? I'm free and I'm going to stay free and have things my way."

"Joe, you haven't hurt Cato? Oh do let me see him—"

"No, no, just scared him green and silly. How damn stupid people can get. I had to pay him out because he stole my gun, he threw it in the river, that started it all. But I didn't know he'd be so dead easy to push around. If he'd shown a bit of fight I'd have told him, I wouldn't have hurt him, I like him, he's my friend. But he was so stupid and so quiet, he was as meek as a sparrow. I made him write to Henry to say send you with the money, and then I thought I just couldn't wait for you, so I made him write to you and you came at once, I knew you would! You see you're more important to me than the money. Do you understand that? Colette, take those things off, dear, dear—and look at me now, look. That's what it's about. That's right. Colette, you will be my girl, won't you? I'll be kind to you, I'll work for you. He wanted me to go with him to the north, let's all go and live on the money, why not, and you be my girl."

Colette closed her eyes and lay back on the bed. Her dress dragged, then tore.

"Colette you will be my girl, won't you, honey, honey, say yes."

"Yes."

"And we'll go and live in the north, and I'll work, I'll learn things like he wanted, I'm smart, I'll do anything for you—"

"Yes."

"Relax, relax. Look at me. I want you to see it."

Colette opened her eyes. Her body was stiff with repulsion, she felt as thin and as dense as a rod. She saw Joe's face flushed and grimacing, his wet mouth hanging open, his eyes glaring. "Colette, oh Colette, darling, quick—you promise you never did this with anyone before?"

"Yes."

"Relax, damn you, don't fight me, do you want to get hurt?"

Colette was suddenly whirling beneath him. Her knee came up into his stomach, her hands grasped his hair, trying to pull that hot dribbling face away. His arm came down heavily across her mouth and she bit into the flesh. She saw above her the sudden flashing arc of the knife-blade, and a strange dead line was laid across her cheek like a thread, followed by burning pain. She began to scream.

Cato had got up and was sitting on the bed. He had lain on the floor for a long time. There was an ache in his jaw where he must have been resting it on the ground. He was shuddering with cold. Automatically he pulled the blanket over his shoulders. There was blackness. All previous blacknesses had been grey. There was nothing. All other nothings had been full of secret life, all other voids crammed with debris. Now all was destroyed or surrendered and there was an emptiness that was not even space. Cato sat, breathing. He sat, and the last spark of active spirit in him attended, waited. He was taut, vibrating, strained as if across a whole galaxy of being, in order to be so empty, so quiet, so here.

Then there was a flash of light, only he knew instantly it was not light but sound. Somewhere, not very near but clearly audible, a woman was screaming. Without any act of recognition he knew that it was Colette. He jumped up, suddenly clumsy, stupid, frantic, uttering wild words to himself. His trousers fell about his knees and he kicked them off. He ran to the door, banged on it, pulled at it, and for the first time since his captivity, *shouted*. He clawed at the door, rattling the handle, then trying to find a crack for his fingers. He ran back to the bed desperately searching for his piece of piping, but he had left it somewhere on the floor. He stumbled over it, picked it up and rushed back to the door still shouting, roaring, not now with words, but with the crazed rage of an animal. He banged the lead pipe upon the lock, pounding the lock and the wood all around it. Then thoughtlessly, frenziedly, he dug the narrow broken end of the pipe into the crack between the door and the jamb and heaved. His weakened body strained with the leverage and a cramplike pain shot through his entrails. He fell back, then returned, driving the thicker end of the pipe back towards the wall. There was a rending sound of splintering wood and he felt that the locked door was beginning to pull the jamb out of the plaster. He drove his tool further into the opening space, found a purchase for his fingers, and the jamb and part of the lintel came away, carrying the door with it, lock and all. Not shouting now, but wailing with anxiety and fear, Cato scrabbled, but still could not get out. Plaster was falling about his feet. He drove his shoulder, then his leg into the gap between the wood and the wall. There was a further rending of the lintel above him, the gap widened and he struggled through. Still holding the pipe, now by its thinner end, he stumbled forward through a darkness which was already less intense. His hand touched a corner, he swung round it, and saw a long way off a source of light. Colette screamed again.

When Cato reached the room he saw first a weird long panel of spotted grey which he could not interpret, which was the wall seen through the half-open door. Then the light of the candle appalled his eyes. He half fell, saw before him a kind of pulsating pink globe wherein two human bodies were struggling and writhing. He saw Colette's face covered with blood, her mouth open in a cry. Someone was screaming, he was screaming. He saw a man with a knife and was never sure afterwards whether in that moment he recognized him. He brought the thick end of the metal pipe down with all his strength upon the back of Joe's head. Then he fell to the floor.

"By the way, I found those Landseer sketches," said Henry. "They were in the chest in the gallery. I've put them in the portfolio with the Orpen stuff."

"Good," said Gerda. She ticked the paper.

The sun was shining into the ballroom, where Henry and his mother were sitting together at a table. The room was filled with an orderly jumble of stacked-up pictures, rolled-up rugs, articles of furniture, several dinner service and a mass of small *objets d'art*.

"And the *netsuke* are all in that box."

"You wrapped each one separately?"

"Yes. Don't you want any of them, Mother?"

"No, thank you, Henry. Almost everything is numbered now. You've got the lists there?"

"Yes, in triplicate."

"You'd better give them to me."

"You're marvellously efficient, Mother."

"The vans for Sotheby's should come on Tuesday, then all the rest stays here for the auction. The garden tools are all in the stables. You'll be here tomorrow morning, won't you? The auctioneer's men are coming over again."

"Yes, I know. They still haven't got out the brochure for selling the house. Don't you want more of this stuff, Mother? I know you've got enough furniture, but what about the little things, those rather nice Meissen animals, and those glasses—"

"There's not much space and I think a simpler scene is more suitable. We always had too much in this house. After all, I won't have Rhoda to dust for me."

"Oh yes—Rhoda—so she's not—?"

"She's gone into service with Mrs. Fontenay's daughter, you know, over at—"

"You mean—she's already gone?"

"Yes."

"I meant to give her something."

"Well you still can."

"Who cooked the dinner last night?"

"I did."

"I'm glad you decided to go to Dimmerstone after all. Wouldn't you like to take some plants from the garden? I'm sure Bellamy—"

"No, I'd rather start from scratch. It will be an interest for me."

"When would you like to move? I'll fix a van."

"It's quite all right, Giles is going to move me with his lorry, some of the builder's men will come and help."

"Giles? Oh—you mean Gosling."

Henry got up and mooched over to the great arched window which faced south. Directly opposite to him across the little valley the black granite obelisk was sailing in a blue sky against a fast procession of small gilded clouds. A brisk wind was stirring the woods beyond where the varied greens were tossing and shifting. As in a picture by Claude, two little figures were wending their way along the radiant grass beside the white flicker of the descending stream: Lucius and Stephanie. Henry returned with dazzled eyes towards his mother, knocking over a stack of Cotmans. "Damn!"

"I think you should go over to Pennwood and see Colette—"

"I haven't time," said Henry.

"You needn't stay long. It seems to me just a matter of politeness."

"Colette's all right, isn't she?"

"Yes, of course. Except that she's got a scar on her face that will be there forever."

"Well, I suppose that doesn't matter too much."

"It might to a young girl. And being raped cannot be a pleasant experience."

"She wasn't raped."

"Anyway I imagine she's suffering from shock."

"So am I. You've no idea how awful it was that night, standing in that ghastly place in the dark and listening, and then nobody came, and the police said—"

328

"And I think you ought to see Cato too."

"He's in London. Anyway I doubt if he wants to see me. I wouldn't if I was Cato."

"You know that wretched boy died?"

"Yes."

"Who told you?"

"Lucius. Who told you?"

"John Forbes. I suppose John told Lucius. Henry—"

"Yes."

"Do look after Stephanie a bit more."

"Mother, please leave Stephanie alone."

"I am doing so. I just think you should be kinder to her."

"I haven't time."

"You don't seem to have time to be kind to anyone."

"Well, I am kind to her. An outsider can't always see how kindness happens. Stephanie knows I care, she's all right, she's tougher than you think. You don't realize how much strain I'm under. All that awful night waiting in the dark, and the police said—"

"I think you ought to go over to Pennwood."

Henry saw his mother, large and calm and ostentatiously bland, looking as he had so often seen her in the past. He saw that image going back and back as images in opposing mirrors. His mother, cool, invincible, always in the right. Gerda, dressed today in a coat and skirt of blue and black tweed, her heavy dark hair loose to her shoulders, carefully combed, her large face so pale and smooth, pouting a little with the will to be calm which lent an air almost of self-satisfaction.

Gerda saw her son, so slim and so tense, one leg twisted round the other, one shoulder hunched up to the chin, his mouth sneering with hostility, his burning dark eyes surrounded by wrinkles of mistrust, his curly hair plucked over his brow with tiredness and irritation.

"Look, Mother, I don't want to go to Pennwood. I've got things to see to here. I'm leaving soon, just as absolutely soon as I can!"

"Oh, all right—"

There was a moment's silence, during which Henry viciously kicked the trim foot of a Sheraton commode.

"Has Lucius decided what stuff he wants out of his room?"

"Yes, I think so," said Gerda. "I've got his list here."

"What's he going to do?"

"He's going to Audrey's for the present."

"Oh."

"What happened to all that money, by the way?" said Gerda.

"Which? Oh, the ransom money. It's in London, at the flat."

"Hadn't you better put it into the bank?"

"Yes, yes, yes, I can't think of everything."

Henry had gone back to the window. Suddenly close to now, he could see Stephanie's big flowered hat appearing on the terrace. Puffing, red-faced, after having climbed the steps from the lawn, unconscious of being observed, she settled her hat, then plumped her shoulders and moved with a little springy swagger towards the drawing-room windows. Watching her, Henry knew that Gerda, watching him watching her, imagined that he felt for his fiancée something like contempt.

"Here's Stephanie, I'm going to be kind to her."

"I wish you could persuade her to smoke less. And to dress more simply."

The door closed behind Henry.

Gerda, still seated, straightened out the papers on the rosewood table before her. Then she laid her hands down on top of them, one above the other. She had meant to give Rhoda some of her jewels, but she had not done so. She had meant to kiss Rhoda when they parted, but she had not done so. She and Rhoda had been together for so many years. And now she would never see Rhoda again because Rhoda was a servant and not a friend.

"Hello, Steph, I like your hat."

"Oh good—"

"It's new, isn't it?"

"Yes, I bought it yesterday in Laxlinden."

Stephanie bought some article of clothing every day.

"I'm not sure it goes with the dress, but it's awfully nice."

Stephanie took the hat off. She was wearing a peacock blue crochet dress which showed off her round breasts and seemed to reflect purple streaks into her round eyes. She had evidently also had her hair done and re-dyed in Laxlinden yesterday.

"Had a nice walk with Lucius?"

"Yes. He's so nice."

They sat down on the seat up against the yellow ironstone shell-studded wall of the house out of which the sun's warmth returned to them. Henry put his hand back and touched the wall. The thyme upon the terrace was already covered with little pinheads of pink buds. A few healthy young nettles had rooted themselves among the stones. He looked sideways at Stephanie, at her wonderfully expressive *retroussé* nose and small protruding mouth. She was blinking serenely in the sun like a cat. Shall I ever know her well? he wondered. Shall I ever know anyone well? Does anyone ever know anyone well? Did he really know Russ and Bella? Of course, they were Americans, total foreigners, enigmas, it was impossible. He got on with them perfectly but they did not know each other, did not look into each other's eyes and *see*. Cato? No.

"You're sighing."

"I'm wondering if I'll ever know you."

"Oh dear, you're not—"

"Don't be tedious, Steph."

"Do you think we'll be happy?"

"Happiness is not my aim."

"Will it really happen?"

"Our marriage? Yes, I have initiated the arrangements."

"I can't see the future, it's a blank. It's like looking in the crystal ball and seeing nothing, as if one will be dead."

"There's nothing to see in crystal balls except one's own reflection. I can't see the future either, but it doesn't matter. Marriage is like that, Steph, it's a weird business. One hasn't the faintest idea. I expect everybody getting married feels it's unreal and practically impossible."

"I'm so frightened of Russell and Bella."

"Don't be. They'll adore you. Bella will boss you. You'll like our little house. We'll live simply. You'll see, you'll understand. All this has got to be, Steph. I haven't the guts to live like a saint and anyway the question doesn't arise, but I can avoid the grosser temptations, thank God. We'll be poorish and ordinary."

"You aren't ordinary. You're a pixie. I'm ordinary. I can't think why you like me."

"I don't like you, I love you. You're a portent for me, a sign. I've always lived by signs. I never had any luck with the girls I ran after. You just happened to me, you fell from heaven."

"I wish I wasn't ordinary, I don't want to be ordinary, I want—"

"Well, you'll be married to extraordinary me, won't that do? Most women are content to live through their husband's achievement."

"You think I'm stupid."

"You said you were ordinary. I was just pursuing the idea. Don't you understand irony? Oh Steph, aren't you ever cheerful, don't you ever laugh or make jokes? We're like two dead people together."

"You think I've got no sense of humour, and you do think I'm stupid and you only like me because I'm a sort of simple person. You know you can't argue with me like you would with—"

"I am arguing with you, you dope!"

"No you aren't, you're just prodding me as if—as if I was an —insect."

"I don't go around prodding insects. Look, would you like to see them again, shall I show you?"

"Oh, yes please—"

Henry drew an envelope from his pocket and took out two long red aeroplane tickets.

"See? To St. Louis via New York, Mr. and Mrs. Henry Marshalson. That's proof, isn't it? The future's there, we've got it under contract. By the time that aeroplane takes off we'll be married. You'll like New York, Steph. You'll like St. Louis, it's a strange city and so beautiful. Don't you want to see the Mississippi?"

"No. Oh darling, I do wish—"

"Oh, do stop, Stephanie, I'm so *tired*, I had such an awful night of it waiting in the dark for those crooks, I haven't got over it yet. I haven't told you what it was like, the police said—"

"Henry, please, you won't ever tell anybody else that I wasn't Sandy's girl, you won't ever tell Lucius or your mother?"

"No—"

"Or Russell and Bella?"

"They don't matter. When we get to America we'll be different people, all this will be gone."

"You're sure that you don't mind that I wasn't Sandy's girl?"

"Oh don't go on. In a way, Sandy did give you to me."

"You feel that? I'm so glad."

"I don't see why. Everybody around here seems to regard Sandy as the sole fountainhead of significance."

"You do still find me attractive, don't you?"

"Yes!"

"Kiss me, then."

Henry kissed her. "You've got navy blue eyes, and your lips taste of tobacco."

"Good. You know I feel so awkward, I feel everybody's laughing at me."

"Nobody's laughing here—"

"Henry—"

"Yes, Stephkins?"

"You won't see that girl, will you, that girl Colette, before we go, you won't see her, will you?"

"No, no, no."

"I know it's awful about that boy—"

"Steph, look, I must go over to the stables, I've got to check the list of the garden tools."

Stephanie walked with him to the top of the steps, swinging her hat by its ribbon. "It's all so beautiful here, so perfect, it just breaks my heart—"

"Stow it, Steph. Listen. Our bird's singing our song."

The little round clouds had gone away and the sky was an untainted blue out of which sunlight blended with the song of an invisible lark was radiating in glittering pulses of energy. The lake was a long flake of azure enamel and the green dome of the folly beyond was lightly splashed with silver. From the lakeside, hazy with feathery willows, the plump green slope of the hill rose towards the wood. The wind had dropped and over the rounded heads of the now quiet trees rose the radiant pale grey tower of Dimmerstone church. Henry looked at it all, and it was like looking at his own mind, his own being, perhaps his only reality. So much the worse for reality then, he thought; and an old favourite Latin tag came to him out of his boyhood. *Solitudinem facio, pacem appello*. No, no one at the Hall was laughing, Henry had seen to that. It must all be destroyed, all rolled up like a tapestry. No wonder he could not communicate with Stephanie. For the present, for the duration of this *work*, he was solitary and damned. Then he thought: how I wish I'd been a hero, how I wish I'd rescued Colette. I really was very brave, but nobody knows or cares.

"Who's driving the Volvo?" Stephanie had turned round towards the stable, whence the yellow car could be seen disappearing up the drive.

"I've sold it. Oh Stephanie, don't take on. Stephanie, don't cry. It's just a motor car!"

"You never asked me—"

"I didn't know you'd mind!"

"You never asked me—it was ours, it was like our house—I loved it so—"

"Oh be quiet, here's Bellamy."

Bellamy's battered trilby and then his reddish-brown weather-beaten face rose, as upon an escalator, from the steep terrace steps. He kicked, instinctively perhaps, at the clump of nettles, then came forward touching his hat. "Oh, Mr. Henry—"

"Hello, Bellamy, lovely day, isn't it."

"I've got a letter for you, sir."

"Thank you, Bellamy."

Henry took the letter and opened it quickly. Bellamy descended again out of view. Stephanie was touching up her tearful face in her make-up mirror.

"Who's it from?"

"It's from the architect," said Henry. "I've got to see him about something. Excuse me, I won't be long." He went in

334

through the drawing-room window and on through the library and out onto the terrace on the north side. Then he read the letter properly. It was from Colette and it read:

Dear Henry, I must see you, please, at once, please come to Pennwood, there is something I have got to say to you, come and see me, *please*.

C.

*

About fifteen minutes later Henry, having run along the north drive and climbed the gate, was panting outside the door of Pennwood. He was sweating and had a violent stitch in his side. He wished passionately that the girl had not written to him. But of course he had to come and see her, see her and get it over. Oh damn *damn*. He stood at the door, trying to stop panting and gasping before he knocked.

John Forbes opened the door and seemed surprised and not very pleased to see him. "Oh—good morning, Henry. What can we do for you?"

"Could I see Colette?" said Henry.

"Well—she's a bit knocked out."

"Could I see her, please?"

"I'll ask her," said John Forbes, leaving Henry at the door. He returned in a moment, pointed towards the sitting-room. "Don't stay long."

Henry knocked softly, then entered.

He had not seen the room for many years. It was exactly the same as when he and Cato used to sit there eating crisps and drinking Coke. He recalled the dove-grey room, the grey photographs of Greece, the grey Copenhagen china and the artificial flowers in the fireplace. He saw in a vision what a quiet sweet innocent room it was. And there in the window, lying in an armchair with her feet up on a stool, half covered with a blue and white check rug, was Colette. She looked very strange, older, very pale, and at first Henry thought that her hair had been cut. But it had just been severely pulled back and plaited, and the plait stowed away behind a cushion. Her prominent brow was wrinkled, pitted almost, with strain, and the pupils of her eyes were dilated. She was wearing a sort of plaid dressing-gown jacket and a striped shirt underneath it. One hand was at her face when he entered, and when she lowered it he saw that one cheek was covered by a bulky dressing kept in place by sticking-plaster.

Colette did not smile and neither did Henry. Her mouth drooped and he felt his droop, as if he were looking into a mirror. She was sitting with her back to the window and he seemed to feel rather than see the huge anxiety of her eyes. He felt an extraordinary combination of anguish and of something within him relaxing as if an exhausted man should find relief in falling. He came to her and took her outstretched hand. They shook hands.

"Thank you for coming so soon."

"Not at all."

"Do sit down."

Henry pulled up a chair.

"It's not too hot in here? Shall I turn the fire off? I can't seem to get warm any more."

"No, it's fine. How are you feeling?"

"Oh, all right. Look, I wanted to talk to you."

Henry sat stiff, scarcely breathing, gazing.

"It's about Cato."

"Oh." Henry looked away, inspected a photo of the Parthenon. He heard his breath emerging in an absurd puff.

"I must talk quickly, otherwise Daddy will come in—you see—oh I don't want to be a nuisance—you're the only person I can talk to, I want you to go and see Cato."

"Of course," said Henry, "I'll do anything you want me to do."

"You see—I'm afraid Cato may go mad."

"Oh come—he won't do that."

"You know that Joe died?"

"Yes."

Colette was silent for a moment biting her lip. Oh don't cry, Henry thought. Then he thought, yes, cry, cry bitterly, and I will cry too.

Colette did not cry. "It's not that Cato has broken down, not yet anyway. He's been wonderful. Do you know that he went to see Mrs. Beckett, and he *told* her?"

"Mrs. Beckett?"

"Joe's mother."

"That was good of him."

"Yes, wasn't it? But I'm so afraid—"

"Where was this place where they kept you prisoner, what was it like when—?"

"It was underneath that wasteland by the Mission. I thought it was miles away, we must have walked in a circle, then he blindfolded me. The bulldozers had uncovered the entrance but they'd closed it with corrugated iron. It was part of some top-secret place during the war—"

'But how did you get out, and how—Your father told Lucius a bit and—"

"He doesn't know it all, and the newspapers just mixed it— oh, at the end Cato was lying in some sort of faint after he hit Joe—and Joe was unconscious and I—put some clothes on—"

"God."

"And ran out and found a telephone box and then the police and the ambulance came and—But that's not what I wanted to tell you. You see, it's about Cato, I'm afraid he'll find out, or that he may have already, and that will drive him mad—"

"Find out what?"

"What really happened. You see, the police were wonderful, they were so kind, and they understood—"

"Colette, do be calm, what is this all about?"

"The police didn't tell him, or they said they wouldn't, and I want you to see him and—of course you can't ask—but I do want to be sure that he doesn't know—"

"Doesn't know *what*?"

"That there wasn't any gang—it was all—oh almost a joke— there was only Joe—oh I know it was awful because he made you come and bring all that money, and he somehow terrorized Cato, but he said if Cato had only resisted he wouldn't have hurt him, he'd have told him the truth and laughed—"

"Wait, wait, you mean it wasn't the Mafia or—?"

"No! There wasn't anybody but Joe. And—oh Henry—it was all my fault, that's what's so awful awful awful, and I've got to live with it forever and tell nobody." Tears now came, not frenzied but in a slow stream.

"Colette—my dear—stop—"

"I won't cry. I mustn't. You see he was kind and sweet and —not awful at all—I was so sorry for him—and he *told* me, he told me he wasn't going to hurt Cato and it was a sort of hoax all the time—"

"That mightn't have been true," said Henry. "You resisted and he hurt you."

"Yes, but that was different—"

"And mightn't that have been a lie too, about it being only him, just a cover-up for the others?"

"No, no, it was true, it was true, the way it came out, and there was never any evidence of any others, and I saw at once, afterwards, that Cato must never know, and at first I thought I wouldn't tell the police what Joe had said, but then I saw I must tell them because otherwise they'd be looking for accomplices and a gang that didn't exist, so I told them everything but I asked them not to tell Cato—"

"Well, I'm jolly relieved to hear there isn't a gang," said Henry. "I thought they might have it in for me for telling the police. Wouldn't Cato be relieved too?"

"But then, don't you *see*, he'll think he killed Joe for nothing, he'll think if only he'd been braver—but really it wasn't his fault, it was my fault, if only I'd been more intelligent, if only I hadn't screamed—"

"What did happen exactly?"

"Joe was—oh he was talking about how we'd all go to Leeds—"

"All go to *Leeds*?"

"Yes, you know Cato's got a job there, or had, and he wanted Joe to go with him only Joe wouldn't, and then Joe said to me we'd all go and we'd live there on your money and I'd be his girl—"

"Oh *Christ*."

"And he said would I and I said yes—"

'But you didn't mean it?!"

"No, well, it was all mad, but I felt so sorry for him, I pitied him so much, and somehow he was sweet, really sweet, and he was talking about how we'd live together the three of us—He could have been saved somehow, anyway I don't think he was

338

really a criminal at all, and he did love Cato and Cato loved him—Perhaps we could all have been friends—I know this sounds crazy, but you must try to love people even when it's hard or awfully odd—and now he's dead and I can't help him any more."

"Colette, don't be sentimental, that boy was a *rat*—"

"That's what Daddy says, but it isn't so—And then all the time he was saying would I only let him make love to me and then he'd let Cato go and of course I said I would let him—"

"And you did?"

"I meant to—oh God, if only I had. I should simply have loved him and let him do anything. I think I did sort of half love him, but it wasn't enough. And then at the last moment just out of stupid sort of—cowardice—and female instinct—I started fighting and screaming, and then Cato broke open his door and came and—killed Joe."

"But Joe was knifing you—that's what I heard."

"Well, I hope that's what Cato thinks. I let him think that he'd really rescued me, saved my life. That's what he *must* think, otherwise he'll go mad. You see, Joe had the knife in his hand, but I'm sure he didn't mean to hurt me, it was an accident, only I was struggling so and he was so excited—oh if only I'd been sensible enough to just let him do it, and kept *talking* to him, but I lost my nerve and—oh if only I hadn't screamed, if only Cato hadn't managed to get out—"

"Hold up, Colette. You can't know Joe wouldn't have killed you or Cato in the end."

"I know he wouldn't, I *knew* him in that time we were together. But now you do see what I want, I want you to see Cato, don't say I told you anything, just see what he says and see what he's *like*. He's so fond of you, I'm sure he'll break down and tell you *everything* and then you'll know if he knows. I'd be so relieved if you'd see him anyway, it would make me feel better. I'm sure he doesn't want to see me, he feels—you know—that he can't face me yet—that's why he hasn't come home—and he can't face Daddy. And I know he feels *awful* about having written those letters—"

"Does your father know exactly what happened?"

"Not exactly. He knows there was no gang, the police told him that, and he won't tell Cato. But I haven't really told him, like I told you, I *can't*—Oh Henry, it's so awful, I've never been inside such a nightmare in my life, I've never imagined such a nightmare, it's like torture, it's like a machine, and I keep going over and over everything that happened and thinking if only I'd done differently I could have saved that poor boy and not driven Cato mad—"

"Steady, steady. You won't break down, Colette."

"No. I know I won't. But Henry, you will see Cato? He loves you and he'll tell you everything."

"I'm not sure about either of those propositions."

"Oh—and—Henry—"

"What is it, my dear?"

The bright sun, reflected from the white wall of the garden, made a clear soft light in the dove-grey room, and Colette's face was illuminated with a soft intense clarity. She looked, thought Henry, like a boy on a ship, a young gunner of Nelson's day, a child who yet had seen blood. What an odd image, he thought, and he thought, how beautiful she is.

"When are you getting married?"

Henry looked out at the sunlit garden, neat as a room. "In a couple of weeks. In London."

"Ah. Good. And then to America?"

"Yes."

"I hope you'll both be very happy," said Colette, and her words were a farewell. She shifted, patting her bandaged cheek, sitting up a little and pulling out her plait, and Henry shifted, made to rise, and rose. He stared down at her, willing her to look at him, but she would not.

"Henry. I must apologize for that lunatic letter I wrote to you and for saying all those dotty things to Stephanie that day in the car. Of course it was all nonsense and I didn't mean it, I realized that later. I was just a child then. I'm sorry—"

"Not at all—"

"I thought—I felt—it might relieve your mind to know I'm not in love with you—I never was—I didn't know what the words meant—"

"Well, of course it does, it's good of you to tell me—"

"It's so tiresome when you think that somebody—anyway—that's that—So the Hall is to be sold?"

"Yes."

"And your mother will live in Dimmerstone. Give her my love. I hope I'll see her, well, of course I will—"

There was a moment's silence. Colette, who had been fiddling with the tassels of the rug looked up quickly, then they both spoke at once.

"What— Sorry?"

"I— No, you say."

"I was just going to say—well—what's Cato's address in London—"

"Oh yes. He's at Brendan Craddock's flat, Father Craddock you know. It's in the telephone book."

"Thanks. I'm afraid I may not be coming back here after I leave, but I'll make sure to see Cato and I'll write and let you know how he is."

"How kind—"

"Well, good-bye, Colette. I don't suppose we'll meet again. Unless maybe—you'll look us up if you're ever in Illinois."

"I'll do that. Good-bye, Henry, and thank you."

She gave him a firm handshake, looking him now in the eyes. Henry shuddered for a moment with the possibility of kissing her hand. Then it was too late, and he turned away, went to the door, waved nonchalantly and went out.

He made straight for the front door and let himself out. As he was closing it behind him a shadow fell, and Henry, for whom the external world had been momentarily invisible, cannoned into Giles Gosling.

"Oh hello."

"Good morning."

"Lovely day, isn't it."

"Lovely."

They sidled round each other. Gosling knocked at the door and was admitted. Henry walked slowly along the lane and along the road until he came to the iron gate. He leaned against it for a long time, looking through at the weedy driveway where the tree-filtered sunlight was making shifting patterns upon the gravel.

"I've never known anybody famous," said Stephanie.

"I was quite famous once," said Lucius.

"I'd like to know some celebrities, pop stars, film stars like."

"Yes, I was famous once. Not any more."

"What's that big bird?"

"A heron."

The heron, which had been walking with long strides in the shallows beyond the rushes, now rose with a careless slowness and wheeled over the water, then came down with an air of fussy precision on the other side of the lake. Nearby, a bright-eyed blackbird stood, its head on one side, upon a heap of mown grass, listening for the crepitation of insects. A magpie passed in trail-tail helicopter flight. A pair of collared doves fluttered and wailed. The continuous song of the lark spread out over the surface of the sky. Henry had gone to London to see the people at Sotheby's. It was another sunny day.

"I've never had a friend," said Stephanie. "Some people are like that."

"Oh come. You must have had women friends."

"No, they all hated me."

"Well, I'm a friend."

"But I'll never see you again."

"Then let us live in the present."

"I don't think women have friends."

"I used to have lots and lots—"

"I had a dog as a child, he was my friend."

"Do you mind if we sit down? I feel a bit funny again."

"It's the heat. I so much don't want to go to America."

"Henry will look after you."

"He's got a woman friend there called Bella. She's clever, she's a professor."

"Everyone in America is a professor."

"Henry will go off with someone clever."

342

"No, he won't. Henry is a gentleman. He'll do what he has undertaken to do."

"I'd feel safer if we were being married in church."

"There are sacred vows outside churches. Henry will be loyal. Come, you know that."

"He thinks I've got no sense of humour."

"Married people have to learn each other's sense of humour. It takes time. Look, there's a kingfisher."

"Where?"

"Gone."

"I do like it here. I've never really been in the country before. Henry says there is no country in America."

"Henry talks nonsense sometimes."

"I suppose it was a joke. I don't always know when Henry's making a joke. That's why he says I've got no sense of humour. He's always getting at me."

"An aspect of love."

"I don't know what I'll do with myself in America."

"You might get a job."

"I couldn't. Once you've had a breakdown it's finished."

"You needn't tell anybody."

"I wouldn't want a job now anyway."

"You might try having a baby."

"Oh I couldn't cope with a baby. Anyway I'm—No—"

"All right, no baby. But what do you like doing?"

"I wish I'd had a baby—"

"You must like doing some things."

"I like buying clothes."

"Well, that's something."

"And I like eating and drinking."

"What ye shall eat and what ye shall drink and what ye shall put on."

"And I like going to sleep if I'm not worrying, but then I'm always worrying."

"So that cuts that out. What about religion, God?"

"I've never understood religion. My mother was a Christian Scientist, but Dad never let her talk about it."

"Do you like any art?"

"Do I like what?"

"Any art. I mean, do you enjoy music or reading or—"

"No."

"You could learn."

"I'm not clever. Henry won't understand that. I'm like lots of people really. You make it sound as if I don't enjoy anything, but I do. I like animals and sunshine and places like this and—"

"Look at that enormous bumble-bee, he's like a flying puppy dog."

"He's gone into the ivy."

> "He will watch from dawn to gloom
>   The lake-reflected sun illume
>   The yellow bees in the ivy bloom,
>   Nor heed nor see what things they be,
>   But from these create he can
>   Forms more real than living man,
>   Nurslings of immortality."

"Did you write that?"

"No. I wish I had."

"I liked some poetry when I was at school, but I've forgotten it now. It's nearly lunch-time. Gerda won't let me help in the kitchen."

"You go on up. I'll wait here a little. I can't go fast up the steps."

Stephanie tripped away and Lucius watched her go. She had changed in his eyes since his first vision of her as a mysterious plump charmer. He thought now that she was one of the most purely simple-minded beings with whom he had ever conversed at length and one of the most touching. With what experience, what abysmal innocence. He felt curiously proud of his ability to communicate with her so easily. He had never so *chattered* with anyone. There was something rather absurd and precious about her. He pitied her, and he saw Henry doing so. Gerda saw Henry's love for Stephanie as perverse, almost weird. But Lucius understood.

He sat quiet on the wooden seat, staring across the lake at the grove of willows and red dogwood on the other side. He dreaded the steps now. He was so hurt that Gerda had not asked him to stay near her. She seemed to take it for granted that he would just go away. She had ceased to talk to him or to show him any of her heart. Perhaps, he thought, she is suffering too much and wants no witnesses. She was always a proud woman. Oh, if only I could comfort her! But against that judgement there was no appeal. He was to go to Audrey's. That would not serve; and anyway, and perhaps it was just as well, Rex would never let him settle down there. I shall go to London, he thought, and find myself a little room in Soho, and sit every day in the literary pubs, there must still be some. And he pictured himself there, a venerable picturesque white-haired figure in a large black hat, sitting in his accustomed corner and writing, pointed out to visitors. Henry had offered him money, but it was not enough. Surely someone will support me, he thought. The Royal Literary Fund? The Arts Council?

He looked across the lake and resolutely thrust away the panic that was always close to him now. Wakeful at night he saw himself destitute, abandoned, old. If only, he thought, art does not finally fail me. If I can only go on writing *something* I shall be all right. Perhaps I could write my political autobiography as an epic poem? God, how the time has passed. How can a whole lifetime pass so quickly with so little done? I thought I would achieve wisdom in the end, and now it is the end and I am still a fool. Well, there's life in the old creature yet. He took out his notebook and wrote.

> The old grey heron
> Seeks among the streams of his youth
> For one pure source.

Henry rang the bell. A man opened the door.

It took Henry a substantial number of seconds to recognize Cato. What he saw at first was an elderly man in a dirty white open-necked shirt and dark trousers with a round rather puffy blotchy face and staring eyes.

"Oh—come in—"

"I see you're in mufti," said Henry desperately, trying to account for his amazed look.

"Oh yes. That's all over. Brendan's at the college. What can I do for you?"

"I hope you didn't mind my ringing up?"

"No, no. What can I do for you?"

It was midday on the day following Henry's meeting with Colette. Once the task had been laid upon him he had felt unable to put off seeing Cato. He was glad that she had asked him, but the gladness was also a source of pain, and he wanted to finish with the bond which this duty established between him and the girl. He would send his report promptly in a letter. After that, thank God, America. He had not told Stephanie about his visit to Colette or about his mission to Cato, but had made another excuse about going to London. To spare himself anxiety he had not tried to think too much about Cato beforehand and about the awful thing that had happened to him. But now looking at that staring unsmiling face he saw what Colette had meant when she feared that her brother might go mad. Cato looked, in some way which was hard to define, very ill. His face looked swollen and greasy and there was a dark purplish ring round each eye. He kept opening his mouth, then closing it, then pursing his lips and wrinkling his nose in a quick nervous movement. His eyes roved constantly, avoiding Henry.

The sitting-room of Brendan Craddock's flat was rather narrow and dark with one window which looked out onto a wall, and even though the sun was shining outside the room seemed almost in twilight. Cato made no move to put on a light, probably not noticing the gloom. Books lined the walls. There were some black velvet hangings and rather too many rugs. Henry sat down gingerly on some sort of embroidered chair. Cato stood leaning against the books, took a pace or two carefully brushing them with his sleeve, then leaned again, gazing at the window. After his query he seemed to have forgotten Henry.

"I wondered how you were," said Henry.

"Oh, all right." Cato moved along the bookshelves, skirted the window and returned along the shelves on the other side, keeping his arm against them as if this contact were necessary to his safety. He reached the door, then returned using the other arm, now pursing his lips up with an air of scrupulous exactitude.

"I wondered if I could help in any way," said Henry. The words, in this scene, sounded flat and impertinent.

"I don't think so, thank you."

"I was—so awfully sorry—to hear about—"

Cato said nothing. He pursed, scrutinized the books as if searching for something, then began to move again.

Henry said, "I had an awful time too, I waited at the Mission, you know, with the police, I waited all night, only nobody came—and—"

Cato was silent.

"Well—so—you're leaving the priesthood?"

"Yes."

"I'm sorry."

"I don't see why you should be sorry," said Cato, frowning slightly, "seeing that you don't believe in God."

"You don't know what I believe," said Henry petulantly. He hoped that Cato, who had shown a faint sign of feeling at last, might reply to this, that some kind of conversation might begin; but silence followed. Cato gazed about, not at Henry. Henry turned round and contemplated the books behind him. The *Summa Theologica*. The complete works of Nietzsche in German.

"Look, Cato, for Christ's sake stop walking up and down. Is there anything to drink here?"

"I don't think so."

Henry got up and investigated a cupboard which was set in the bookshelves. There was a bottle of whisky, a decanter of sherry, glasses. Henry poured himself out some whisky.

"Would you like a drink?"

"No, thank you."

Henry sat down again. Cato paused again, studying the books, then gave a deep sigh, the sort of sigh which a man gives when he is alone.

"Cato—please—talk to me. What are you going to do with yourself now?"

"I have a teaching job in Leeds. I shall go there."

"Will you go back to Pennwood first?"

"Only if I think I can tell lies." Cato selected a book, opened it and examined it intently.

"Lies—what lies?"

"Suitable ones."

After a moment Henry said, "I saw Colette."

"Did you." A look almost of malevolence twisted Cato's puffy face, but he continued to peruse the book.

"She—she—seemed none the worse for her ordeal."

"None the worse. That's good."

"Cato, do sit down, do talk properly, please."

Cato, grimacing, turned the look of malevolence onto Henry. Then he dropped the book noisily onto the floor.

"Did you ever think that perhaps I might marry Colette?" He wanted to startle Cato into some real speech.

"You? Marry *Colette*?! No!!"

Henry flinched at the quick force of spite in the reply. "All right I never wanted to—I mean—"

"Colette will marry somebody distinguished and good. If she marries."

"Why shouldn't she marry, or do you think she'll become a nun?"

"It's up to her," said Cato, his voice blank again. He leaned back against the shelves and looked at his watch.

"Cato, don't be angry with me."

"I hear you're marrying some whore."

"Yes," said Henry, "I am."

"And then, having vented your vindictive resentment on your mother, you are returning to America."

"That's right. I know you were against the sale—"

"Oh, I'm not," said Cato. "Not at all. I'm for it. Sell the place up, excellent. And those old houses are much better made into flats or bloody conference centres, and all those useless acres built upon. There's a housing shortage here, you know."

"Cato—hadn't you better see a doctor?"

"Why did you come here?" said Cato, staring at Henry again, speaking very incisively but softly.

"I came out of affection for you."

"You came out of curiosity."

"I came because we're old friends."

"You came as a tourist."

"Cato, stop."

"Did you ever kill a man?"

"No."

"You should try it some time. It's a funny feeling. It's so easy to end a man's life. Once you've done it you feel you might do it again. Why not go around killing people?"

"Cato—is Brendan coming home soon?"

"Are you frightened of me?"

"No—but—I feel you shouldn't be alone."

"Do you imagine I'll kill myself?"

"No, of course not—"

"After one has committed a murder—"

"But you didn't!"

"One realizes that there are no barriers, there never were any barriers, what one thought were barriers were simply frivolous selfish complacent illusions and vanities. All that so-called morality is simply smirking at yourself in a mirror and thinking how good you are. Morality is nothing but self-esteem, nothing else, simply affectations of virtue and spiritual charm. And when self-esteem is gone there's nothing left but fury, fury of unbridled egoism."

"Cato—you're suffering from shock."

"You came here as a tourist to view the ruins."

"I didn't—Please—"

"Sorry. Sorry. You'd better go. I'll be all right. I don't need a doctor. Please go away. And don't tell them anything at Pennwood. I just hope and pray for you—may you never see what I see now, never know what I know now, never be where I am now!"

"Cato—"

"Oh get out, get out, get *out*!"

Henry fled to the door and half fell down the first stairs. The door closed behind him. He paused, and heard again that awful lonely sigh, now prolonged into a kind of quiet moan. He ran down the remaining stairs and out into the street and hailed a taxi. "National Gallery."

*

349

Twenty minutes later Henry was sitting in front of Titian's great picture. His violently beating heart was slowly calming a little. He kept his eyes fixed on the picture as in an activity of prayer.

He thought, I can never tell *that* to Colette, or to anyone. I've somehow run myself into hell. There must be many entrances. I won't write to Colette. I'll send her a little air letter saying nothing, from Sperriton. Oh God, he thought, three weeks from now I shall be home in Sperriton and I shall be married and this whole nightmare will be over. I shall be with Russell and Bella—and Stephanie. And my life will be simple and I shall have simple duties: to make Stephanie happy, to live at peace, to teach my pupils, to drink martinis with my friends and tear along the freeway in my automobile. All the violence will be over. I shall be back again with the innocent ones, in the land of innocence, thank God.

He stared at the picture and his heart became quiet. How different it is, violence in art, from the horror of the real thing. The dogs are tearing out Actaeon's entrails while the indifferent goddess passes. Something frightful and beastly and terrible has been turned into one of the most beautiful things in the world. How is this possible? Is it a lie, or what? Did Titian know that really human life was awful, that it was nothing but a slaughterhouse? Did Max know, when he painted witty cleverly composed scenes of torture? Maybe they knew, thought Henry, but I certainly don't and I don't want to. And he thought of Cato now with a horrified pity which was a sort of disgust, and he gazed into the far depths of the great picture and he prayed for himself—May I never see what he sees, never know what he knows, never be where he is, so help me God!

"I've decided to write my autobiography in the form of an epic poem."

"Any furniture you want to keep can go into the barn with my trunks."

350

"Just the table and the chest of drawers."

"I'll tell the men."

"I can't believe it's all ending."

"Look about you, doesn't it look like the end?"

"Who'll look after me when I'm old?"

"You are old. We are old."

"Audrey I suppose. Except Rex won't let her."

"You said you wanted to live in London, you said you felt caged here."

"Gerda, don't send me away. You cared about me once."

"You loved me once. You wrote poems for me. Now there's nothing left but 'Clump, clump, the old girl.' "

"Can't we start again?"

"We are starting again."

"But together? Can't I live with you at Dimmerstone?"

"There isn't room."

"You're just punishing yourself, you want to pull everything down, you don't want me at Dimmerstone because you don't want me to see you defeated."

"I wouldn't mind you as a witness any more than I'd mind Bellamy's dog."

"I am your dog. Gerda, don't abandon me, I feel death is near. Let's stay together."

"You never helped me, never supported me. Don't start crying now."

"I love you, I've always loved you. Gerda, marry me. Let's spend our last days together. It isn't too late, darling, is it? Marry me, Gerda."

"If you'd said this long ago it might have meant something, but you didn't. Now you just want a room and a nurse."

"But I did say it long ago."

"You may have thought it but you didn't say it."

"I did—You mean you would have married me?"

"Oh, I daresay."

"Gerda, I shall go mad!"

"If you had really loved me you would have insisted on marrying me and I would have consented. You just didn't love me enough, Lucius. And nothing is more absolute than that. One gets justice from life really."

"You mean you loved me?"

"As far as I remember."

"But Gerda, if you loved me then you can love me now. Forgive me and marry me, you *must*. Let us salvage something, don't let it all be lost. Don't just refuse me now out of pique."

"Pique! Oh you are a *fool*."

"Gerda, darling, forgive me, marry me, I love you with all my heart, everything there is of me is yours, I've given you my life, it's all yours. You can't be so ungrateful as to reject me now."

"You rejected me."

"I asked you to marry me, I'm sure I did!"

"You didn't. Never mind."

"Then it must have been because you made it clear you didn't want me."

"If you had been more passionate you might have been more successful. You only cared about yourself. Did you want me to run after you and beg you?"

"So it was just pride then. And it's just pride now."

"Oh Lucius—Never mind."

"I am a passionate man, I am, I am! I'm not going to leave you, I won't, I won't!"

"All right, call it pride. I do want to be alone at last and without witnesses. You belong to the past, Lucius, as far as I'm concerned you're a ghost. Oh you are so stupid! You are stupid, so is Henry, so was Sandy, so was Burke. Oh God, why was my lot cast among such stupid stupid men!"

"Do you mind if I sit with you, Mother?"

"Of course I don't mind."

Henry perched himself astride on the club fender. It was late in the evening and the log fire in the library had subsided into a mobile mound of twinkling glowing embers, resembling a hill city at night. The carpet had been removed and some of the furniture, including the round table, had gone to the ballroom on the way to Sotheby's. The room echoed. Gerda, who had pulled an armchair up near to the fire, was sewing a button onto her tweed coat.

"How quiet it is. Except for the owls."

"Yes."

"I suppose this is sort of the last sort of moment."

"I suppose so."

"What was Lucius so bothered about this morning?"

"He'd just proposed to me," said Gerda.

"For the first time?"

"Yes. He thought he'd proposed before but he hadn't."

"A muddled man. Did you ever love him, Mother?"

"Oh yes, I think so. He was a charming and romantic figure when he was younger."

"I remember him. All that wild hair. Did you accept him?"

"No, of course not."

"I'd like to feel you had somebody to look after you."

"Lucius needs somebody to look after him."

"Well, shouldn't you?"

"I've been doing so for years. I want a change."

"I can imagine that. I've never had anybody to look after."

"Did Stephanie get up?"

"She trailed around in her dressing-gown."

"She needs fresh air, a brisk walk."

"I wish she'd do something, even if it's only reading a novel."

"In my opinion—"

"She'll be perfectly all right once we're in America and out of sight of these faded glories."

"I hope you are right."

"Mother—"

"Yes?"

"I feel I should tell you. Stephanie wasn't ever Sandy's mistress."

"I know."

"How did you know?"

"Because of the way she talked about him. It simply sounded false. Then I laid a trap for her."

"What sort of a trap?"

"Well it concerned—a scar—"

"So you knew. Why didn't you tell me?"

Gerda was silent for a moment. "I thought it would make no difference to your plans and I found it all so—"

"Disgusting?"

"Upsetting. I preferred not to go into the matter. She told you?"

"Yes. She never knew Sandy—she was the charwoman."

"She is in her way an ingenious little person."

"You seem to have been quite ingenious too."

"I wonder if you will be happy with her."

"When was I ever happy, Mother?"

"Oh don't be stupid, Henry."

"One can't whistle up happiness. It's a gift of nature and I haven't got it."

"Why do you want to marry her?"

"How can one say? It's the way the universe is flowing. I'm not a lucky person who makes radiant decisions which are obviously right. Perhaps it's sheer self-importance that makes me feel so responsible for Stephanie. Of course there was a lot of illusion involved, there probably still is, and of course it was partly because of Sandy. I don't mind her having lied, there was something heroic about that. She's so frail, and yet she fought back against life, against rotten luck. She's got a strange charm, I know you can't see it. Perhaps it's just that she's so awfully touching and I'm sorry for her—and I've *got* her, and this has never happend before. It's the first serious thing that has ever come about in my life and because I'm me I've no idea how it happened or why. I see through the illusions, or some of them, and I love her like God loves her, I guess. Maybe I've been swindled into it, swindled into seeing her as God sees her and loving her as God loves her. Well, of course I don't mean it about God. I just mean I can see what a mess she is but she's mine and I feel fatalistic."

"I rather hoped you'd marry Colette," said Gerda, snapping the thread and sliding the needle carefully back into the pink cushioned lid of her work box.

"Oh Colette. You know she proposed to me. It must be proposal time."

"And you refused her."

"Yes. I couldn't—see her—" Henry was intently lifting up some warm ash on his shoe.

"But you can now?"

"Oh I don't know. She took it all back later, she isn't in love with me. Anyway she's a kid, a schoolgirl. No, Colette isn't my fate."

"Why do you think you haven't got the gift of happiness?" said Gerda, after a moment or two. She was now sitting in repose, her hands folded, watching Henry twisting his leg round one of the bars of the fender.

"Because you and my father stole it from me when I was an infant."

"So you think you had it earlier, in the womb perhaps?"

"You're smart, Mother. Maybe. But consciousness doomed me. My confidence was broken before I was six. Everybody combined to put me down. Sandy bullied me, my father mocked me and discouraged me and contradicted me. He jeered at me and encouraged you and Sandy to jeer. You should have protected me. All right, you much preferred Sandy, but you could have stopped Father from crushing me. You didn't—you were his ally and his agent. Because we were taught to be so bloody tight-lipped and stoical you probably have no idea how much I suffered as a child, how absolutely my will was broken. Every little project that I ever made for myself was somehow destroyed by Father, shown to be petty and laughable and worthless. You both waged war on me. Of course Sandy joined in. I spent my childhood concealing my misery, concealing my tears. No wonder I've never wanted to do anything since except run and hide."

"This is unjust, of course," said Gerda, sitting very still with folded hands.

"All right, it's only my impression. But people are responsible for the impression that they make on children."

"I think you were often happy."

"O.K. Forget it."

"Your father was an impatient strong-willed man."

"A bully. Yes."

"Yes."

Henry tapped the ash off his toe and looked at his mother.

"You accuse me of being his ally," said Gerda. "Perhaps I should have fought him, but the cost would have been too great. I had to submit. Of course he absorbed me and domin-

355

ated me as the years went by. I had to attend to him and not to you. I loved him and I tried to make him happy and be happy myself. It wasn't easy, perhaps it wasn't possible. I kept on sacrificing my will to him, and I kept on thinking that I had come to the end of my will and the end of the sacrifice, but there was always something more that he wanted from me that was hard to give. He loved me and it was one sort of way of having a satisfactory marriage. But I couldn't deal with both you and him. Sandy was all right, I think he sort of understood, and anyway he was independent. I hoped you'd be. You weren't. You were demanding, then you were terribly hostile. A child's hostility can hurt too. I couldn't reach you. I had my own fight, and my own tears. It was partly just a matter of energy. I liked Lucius because he was so absurd and sensitive and gentle. And then when Burke died Lucius was somehow useless, he didn't seem to care enough, at any rate he didn't assert himself enough. Lucius and I mislaid each other because I had lost the will to happiness, I had lost the key. I ought to have taken hold of Lucius then, but my strength was gone and I stood there coldly and waited for him to take hold of me. And now there's nothing left of that either. I let him become a dependent, a figure of fun, a silly idle man. I almost made him inferior because he had failed my hopes. Sandy was the only thing that gave my life any pure sense and any pure joy, but I never talked to Sandy. I never communicated with Sandy. I never told him what I've just told you. I never touched him or kissed him after he was twelve." Gerda's voice was perfectly steady, only her immobility conveyed emotion.

Henry, who had been holding his breath, gave a little whistling sigh. "You're a cool customer, Mother. Maybe we're a bit alike after all. You know—I hope you don't think I'm selling the property just for revenge."

"Not just for revenge. I think your motives are mixed up. I think you are mixed up. I don't like what you are doing or the way you are doing it. But perhaps one day when I am living at Dimmerstone I shall be grateful to you."

"Ah—you are—yes—thank you—"

Gerda was very still. Henry was now standing in front of her. He went on after a moment, "I don't know you very well. I feel now that I don't know you at all. I'm so grateful that you —talked to me. This is the first real conversation that we've ever had. Yes, you are a cool customer. I wish—oh, I wish—I wish—"

"Don't wish, Henry. We've both got to accept what you called the way the universe is flowing. Go to bed now, my dear, it's late."

"Oh Mother—it's as if—as if—"

"Good night, Henry."

Henry stood stiffly, then twisted and took a step away, then came back. Gerda lowered her eyes and slowly put her hand out towards her work basket. The moment passed. Henry turned again and his swift steps echoed in the room, in the hall, upon the stairs. Gerda closed the work basket and fixed its catch. She checked tears and gazed, frowning thoughtfully, into the now pale remains of the fire.

"Oh stop crying, Colette," said John Forbes, exasperated. "It's just nerves. No one can sincerely go on and on crying."

"I can," said Colette. She had removed the Copenhagen animals and was sitting on the ledge by the window, looking out into the garden.

"He'll see you there."

"He sees nothing."

Cato was outside in the garden weeding the flower-beds. It was raining slightly. He was without coat or hat.

"I've been watching him for an hour," said Colette.

"I hope you haven't been crying for an hour, you'll damage your eyes. God, girls are so stupid."

"He isn't seeing. I've been watching him. He picks the weeds out all right, but it's as if he was blind. I've never seen anything like it. Just look at him."

"I won't look at him," said John Forbes, and he turned away from the window, clenching his fists. "He's getting wet. I'll tell him to come in."

"Better not, it'll be like waking someone from a trance, he might die. Anyway it's stopping. Look, there's a rainbow."

"I wish he'd do something else."

"He can't. Well, he could wash up, I've left him some. He can't go for a walk or read a book or talk to us. He's in hell. I've never seen anyone in hell."

"Don't talk nonsense, Colette. You know nothing about hell. He's suffering from shock. I wish he would talk though."

"It's impossible. He feels ashamed. And for him it's terrible, terrible, not like it would be for us. Have you ever felt ashamed, Daddy?"

"Yes, of course." But John, who was embarrassed by the question, could not recall any very convincing instances.

"I think he's dying of shame."

"Stop crying, Colette."

"All right, I've stopped. It's cold in here. Can we have the fire on?"

"Don't watch him."

"All right."

"I only hope this ghastly business won't send him running back to the Church."

"I hope it will. He's got to get help somewhere and we can't give it to him. I wish I could pray for him. I almost feel I could learn to pray, just for this time, as if I could invent God simply to save Cato."

"Don't you start! You exaggerate everything so, Colette. You're so absorbed in your own feelings, you make a sort of metaphysical crisis out of every disaster."

"He loved the boy. He killed him."

"Of course he didn't love him! And he killed a dangerous violent criminal. No one dreamt of blaming him. I know it must be terrible to kill someone. Thank heavens the war spared me that experience. But one must be man enough to deal with it. It's a hard saying, but it's one's duty not to have a breakdown."

"He's not having a breakdown. He's in hell. It's different, it's worse. Don't you see how his face has changed?"

"Yes." John Forbes had felt terror when he saw that changed face. "What I can't understand is why he wrote those awful servile letters, and how it was he didn't make any serious attempt to get out until the very end. We were taught it was an officer's duty to escape."

"Cato's not an officer."

"What on earth do you mean by that?"

"I mean it's different. Daddy, you won't ever say that to Cato, will you, about the letters and his not trying?"

"No. But he ought to be able to stand it if I did. I certainly wish I could understand."

"Please don't say it, and please don't think it either, it's somehow disloyal to Cato."

"I propose to think what's true, not what's loyal! I'm not hurting him by thinking, am I?"

"Yes, you are. We can't talk to him now or even touch him. I touched his arm this morning and he shuddered and gave me a terrible look. What we must do is hold him in our thoughts very sort of tenderly and lovingly—"

"Colette, please don't be sentimental. All this hypersensitive brooding over him won't help. He'll have to be robust and realistic about it in the end. I'll have a talk with him tonight."

"Daddy, please don't, please. You'll only drive him away. I feel he's—it's as if he's just being *polite* to us. He's pretending all the time. He'd like to pretend to be calm, only it's absolutely unconvincing, he's screaming inside. Look at him now, look at the way he's bending, he's physically different, he's like a marionette."

Cato, bending rigidly from the waist, dropped his head and stretched out a poised hand. He plucked a piece of groundsel, then stood up throwing his head back. He tossed the groundsel, without looking, onto a heap, took a step to the right, drew his feet together, then bent again.

"I can't bear to see him like that," said John Forbes. "If only he hadn't written those letters, that's what I can't understand—"

"In an officer and a gentleman! You despise him and he feels it, he feels everybody does. He feels ashamed and disgraced. I think at the moment he hates us."

"Oh nonsense! I hope he'll stay here till his term starts."

"I don't. We can't help him, Daddy. We haven't got the machinery to help him. He'd far better go back to London to

Father Craddock. He will go back, I know, as soon as he feels he's been polite enough to us."

"Polite! Colette, go and wash your face, you look a sight. Suppose Giles Gosling calls and sees you like this?"

"I don't care."

"You will go to the dance with him, won't you?"

"I haven't got a dress."

"Then you must buy one. Why not go to London tomorrow morning? What does a nice dress cost now, ten pounds?"

"Daddy, you're living in the past!"

"Well, twenty pounds, thirty pounds. Colette, do go and buy yourself a dress. I want you to go to that dance with Giles and I want you to be the prettiest girl there. Forty pounds?"

"Daddy, you're bribing me to be happy!"

"It's all fixed," said Henry, just returned from London at tea-time. "The vans for the stuff for Sotheby's are arriving at eight on Tuesday morning."

"The men from the auctioneers were here," said Gerda. "Lucius, don't you want a crumpet?"

"I shall never eat a crumpet again," said Lucius.

"Why not?" said Henry, helping himself to one.

"I hear Cato Forbes has gone back to London. I'm very sorry you didn't see him, Henry, I'm sure you could have helped him."

"Because crumpets belong to happiness."

"Oh, come," said Henry. "I hear you're going to write your autobiography in rhyming hexameters."

They were having tea in the dining-room which was still intact, since the big mahogany dining-table and set of Victorian chairs were to be sold *in situ*. White numbered labels had already been stuck on. Meals, never elaborate since Rhoda's departure, had now been reduced to a basic simplicity. Scattered crumbs were not always removed. Lucius was wearing his cloak with the collar turned up, although the day was still very warm. He sat sideways to the table, staring at the wall, his legs thrust straight out in front of him. He seemed to be already remote, grey, deep in a dream, no longer seriously attempting to arouse sympathy. Gerda on the other hand was in a nervous bright mood. Henry had attempted in vain to restore the communication between them. She evaded his tacit advances and refused to meet his eyes. She had put on a summer dress and appeared alert and young.

Henry, looking through the window at the sun caressing and celebrating the red brick wall of Queen Anne, covered on this side with budding wisteria, felt as if he were waking from a dream. Or rather as if he had had a nightmare and then found it real. Had he not known, not understood, what he was doing till now when he saw the white labels pasted on the furniture and Lucius too miserable even to pose? Ever since his return home he had been having, for the first time in his life, an orgy of will. He felt as if he had never before really positively done anything, never stretched out a strong imperious hand and altered the world, never until now. Now he had courageously done so, hoping to have life more abundantly. But he felt rather as if he had killed himself. He had destroyed the house of his ancestors, he had exiled his mother and uprooted that silly pretentious harmless old man. Had he done it to prove his pluck or out of a sense of duty or for a revenge? He could not have endured property and riches and to be corrupted by them, and did not all else flow from that? Was not this moral courage and the drawing of consequences?

Lucius had accepted money and his mother would certainly survive. And he would be married and would return to America with the dear helpless woman who was now and forever to be his task. How was that for will power? And if it all seemed at the moment like a desolation, had he not willed it and was it not his as nothing had ever been before? He had won a kind of liberation, he had won a kind of Stephanie, and out of these he would create the future, his right decision and his wife. Yet he felt an awful remorseful anguish which he connected somehow with that talk with his mother when, for the first time since his childhood, they had really, just for seconds perhaps, communicated with each other. And by that communication some deep rift had been made, some old capacity to love his mother had been touched and wakened. There was a love in him still which did not know of her crimes or could ignore them. Only now there was no time left, and Gerda had closed herself again and armed herself with an awful glossy cheerfulness. Henry stared at her, but she refused to look. He wanted to touch her hand. He stretched out his fingers and moved some crumbs upon the table, wondering if she was aware of his movement and what it simulated.

"Well, have some bread," said Gerda to Lucius.

"I shall go to Audrey's before the auction."

"You can't forswear bread for ever! And there isn't much for supper."

"I'm to have Toby's bedroom. I know what that means."

"What does it mean? More tea?"

"Where's Stephanie?" said Henry, who had not seen her since his return.

"Either in bed I imagine or gone out for a walk."

"I hope she's gone for a walk," said Henry, "that will do her good." He hoped so much that she had gone for a walk. Each return to her now compressed his heart with pain, like a return to the cage of a sick animal. He dreaded going up and finding her lying in bed, dropping cigarette ash on the sheets and looking at the room with what seemed to him a simulated hollow stare. Christ, he thought, she's going to marry me and that's what she feels like! And that's a bit what I feel like too. I expect everybody feels rather doomed when they get married. But when we are right away from this mess, when we are in Sperriton, it will be all different. And the prospect of seeing Russ and Bella lit for a moment like a golden spark.

"Go and see if you can find her anywhere," said Gerda. "Ask her if she'd like some tea."

Henry got up and went out into the hall. He saw on the hall table a letter from America, in Bella's huge handwriting, and he put it into his pocket and walked out through the front door onto the terrace. The westering sun was striking full onto the façade of Queen Anne and was blotching the green slope to his right with the long rounded shadows of the big trees. The lake vibrated with blue and the warm air was spiced with flower smells and jumbled bird-song. Henry looked about anxiously hoping to see Stephanie crossing the bridge or lingering beside the lake, wearing her floppy sun hat and carrying an ancient parasol which Henry had found for her and which had seemed to give her pleasure. Perhaps today she had, like his mother, put on a summer dress. But there was no sign of her. The great expanse of grass was empty, except for a few bounding squirrels. A trio of magpies was flying towards the wood, seeming like an omen. Now he must go and look for Stephanie upstairs. If only he could persuade her to open a window. Was that awful smell just cigarettes? In order to delay a moment longer he pulled Bella's letter out of his pocket and began to read it.

Honey, listen, and don't think we're pigs. A hell of a lot has happened in the last few days. To put it in a nutshell, Russ has got a job at Santa Cruz, and we're going at once. One of the faculty there killed himself accidentally with drugs, bless his heart, and they wanted someone at once and they rang long distance and asked if Russ would come and they more or less promised him tenure if he would and there's even a house (not the deceased's) and we had to decide instantly, and of course we just had to say yes and we sure do hope you'll understand! So we'll be gone when you get back to Sperriton. We've left your keys with Paul and May Horowitz and they'll be sprucing up the house for you and your bride, and we're hopping mad that we won't be there to welcome you and of course we're *dying* with curiosity—but we'll see you before long won't we? You must come to Santa Cruz soon with Mrs. M. and be our guests. Our new home faces the ocean and there's a jungle garden and a Roman emperor-style swimming pool! You got to come, and soon, that's for sure, or we'll suspect you don't forgive us! And of course we'll be beavering away like crazy to find a job there for you. Write us soon, honey, we're thinking of you all the time. You should have told us exactly when the great day is. And, darling, if you're wondering if I'm jealous, of course I am! Write soon, care of the philosophy department, we won't be in the house at once. (It's heavenly Spanish like we always wanted, there's a *fountain*). And don't forget we love you and you belong to us, married or not. Much love.   Bella.

Russell had scrawled at the bottom of the page.

Sorry kid. We love you but I guess we love ourselves more.

Henry crumpled up the letter and returned it to his pocket. A cloud of blackness had formed before him and was slowly enveloping him. He stared at the sunlit scene and was blind. Everything, he now realized, to do with taking Stephanie to Sperriton had been touched and enlightened and made possible by the idea of Russ and Bella. How unfair to Stephanie. And yet that had been the reality of the matter, perhaps its main reality, and not a bad one. Because Russ and Bella were brave and good they would all have been saved somehow. Only now —however bravely Bella talked it was over and things would never be as they were. In Sperriton, Russ and Bella could have swallowed Stephanie, swallowed her right down. At a distance of eighteen hundred miles Stephanie would be a curio. She would be a stranger, and he would soon become one. Russ and Bella would inhabit another world, make new friends, love and be loved elsewhere, adopt another Henry. When he and Stephanie went to visit them there would be parties and cries of joy and Bella would show off her new world and Henry would suffer agonies of jealousy and deprivation. As for getting him a job at Santa Cruz, they might as well try to get him a job as an astronaut, and they knew it. It was the end of the road with Russ and Bella : and there was no substitute, not May and Paul, not Franz and Rosina, not Bill and Emmy, not Ann and Minio, no one.

Henry turned round slowly and entered the house. He felt cold and there was an itchy stirring in his eyes as if he might cry. He thought for a crazy second of going to his mother, but turned towards the stairs. If only, in going now to Stephanie, he could feel that he was going where he could be held, not where he had to hold.

The house echoed oddly. The stored furniture had been removed from the gallery and the rugs were gone from the upper landing. Henry said "Hello" and entered Stephanie's bedroom but found it empty. He went across to the window and looked out towards the north to see if he could discover her anywhere on that side of the house. He scanned the overgrown drive which wound away into the conifers, hazy with weeds which were now in flower. He looked for Stephanie's little figure, lingering near the shrubbery or emerging slowly from the birch wood. She always wore such unsuitable shoes and walked so maddeningly slowly. Thinking of her shoes it occurred to him that it was now many days since he had made love to her. The sprouting tops of the conifers merged with a reddish sheen into the sky. Looking away up the drive Henry sighed. The room was stuffy and smelt of tobacco smoke and cosmetics and of some other emanation of humanity, sweat, or underwear or something. Henry opened the window wide and smelt the warm spicy air and sighed again. He turned back, dazzled by the bright light, towards the room. Stephanie's bed, a little tumbled and humpy, had been roughly pulled together. There was a white patch upon the counterpane on top of the pillow. Henry moved forward blinking and saw an envelope. A letter addressed to him.

As soon as Henry saw the letter he felt a prophetic ray of pure fear pass into his heart. He seized it and opened it.

Dear Henry,
  I expect you will not be surprised to hear from me in this way, you must have expected it and wanted it and I feel you have not behaved squarely by me, you drove me to it yourself you know you did. You love somebody else, as I have reason to believe, and you have never considered what I want only what you want. There should be equality in marriage and you have rushed me into this. I wanted to live at the Hall and not go to America only you would not hear of this, you would not discuss it with me as an equal. I have been unhappy all my life and I thought when I met you I would be looked after and happy but it was not to be. I am so miserable as I write this and I do wish you would change your mind and make everything well so we could live at the Hall, and not go to America where there is this woman, you have expected me to put up with a lot and when I wanted to talk of it you just made jokes and I happen to know that you think I have no sense of humour. The only person who was really kind to me was Lucius, your mother did her best but she did regard me as inferior, as I think you do too. You don't know how much you hurt me by your attitudes and by always laughing at me. I have gone back to London to think it over, but if you still want to sell everything and go to America I feel we are not right for each other. I wanted to live at the Hall and this was what I understood we were to do at the start when we were engaged. I know you think I am stupid and of course I have always

365

had bad luck and have been deserted and abandoned and other people have their own affairs and will not stop to help. You were only interested in me because you thought I was an easy woman and because of Sandy. I wish I had got to know Sandy properly as I would have done if he had not died, he was such a nice man and I feel we might have got on, at least it was a dream. If you want to see me and talk things over, I shall be at the flat, by the way you did say I could have the flat, anyway, you did say that at the start, but I don't want to see you unless you are to keep the Hall and be as you ought to be in England. You know we have never really got on and I feel I could do better with somebody who understood me and really cared. I cannot face being hustled into marriage and taken away where I am not used to and your clever friends would laugh at me, I have had enough pain. You have never really tried to see me as I am, I feel you have used me. I am so sorry, Henry, but I have been so unhappy I thought I would die and you did not help me and I have got to run away, but do think about staying in England please, but I think it is best that we part if you will never do what I want.

We did like it in bed anyway and that is always something. Please try to see that I have to be myself and not just what you want. Oh I am so unhappy. Yours with love

                                                            Stephanie

Henry was sitting on the bed reading the letter. The northern evening light made the room glow with a radiant clarity. The house was silent against the song of the birds. Henry felt a very pure strange pain, like an unmixed repentance pain such as one might feel when compelled to review one's sins in the presence of God. It was not that there were no more concealments or illusions, but just for a moment there was for Henry a very narrow and clear vision of what he had been doing. Of course he had used Stephanie, of course he had been indifferent to her wishes and had expected her to obey him, of course he had not regarded her as an equal. He had expected her to be grateful for his notice. He had not imagined her. *I have had enough pain.* Of course he had known very well how much sheer incoherent muddle he was embracing when he embraced her. But in his orgy of will he had imagined that somehow if only he could rush along fast enough all would be well. Would he now pursue her to London? Quietly and clearly the answer formulated itself: no. In its funny way it was a brave letter. In her funny way she was a brave girl.

He sat still, dazed, breathless with emotion, entertaining that pure pain of loss and self-reproach. Funny little dear little Stephanie had gone, with an inventiveness, sheer strength of self-preservation with which he would not have credited her. She had escaped; and now he would never look after her and educate her, never toil to make her happy and to compensate her for her rotten life. Had he ever really thought that he would? Henry sat rigid, holding on to the purity of the moment and blindly checking something that was also present: a profound sense of relief. He felt pity, that old familiar friend that had joined their hands together. "Poor old Steph," he said aloud, "Poor Steph, oh poor Steph." His love for her was with him, burning him, but condensed into a small awful ball, outside which he was quietly and disgracefully expanding. How absurd, he thought. I am absurd, she is absurd. I would never have left her, never. Yes, I am sure that's true and it's important. But now she has left me and ...

He got up slowly, noticing everything in the room, the striped face-powder dust on the empty dressing-table, the grey cigarette ash marks on the sheets, a pair of Gerda's slippers which Stephanie had borrowed. He walked slowly to the door, dropping Stephanie's screwed-up letter as he went, and crossed the echoing landing to the stairs. Leaning hard on the banisters he marched down the stairs two at a time, then crossed the hall into the library. One of the tall windows was partly open and he ducked under it, raising it with his shoulders, and strode over the terrace, leapt from there onto the grass, stumbled and began to run. It was slightly uphill and by the time he reached the north drive he was panting. He ran along the drive, the gravel was invisible, it was like running on a flower-bed, and the wild-flowers twisted round his feet. By the time he reached the conifers he had to slow to a walk. The iron gate onto the road was still padlocked, he had never remembered to ask Bellamy to open it. He pulled himself up onto the central bar and put one hand on the wall and thrust a long leg over the top. A spike pierced his trousers and there was a little rending sound. He felt the sun-warmed iron on his leg, detached himself and leapt down, slipping and jarring his hands on the stony edge of the road. He turned to the right towards Penn-wood, dusting the pebbles off his palms and pulling down the tail of his jacket. As he came near to the turning he walked a little more slowly, attempting to think.

At that moment Colette emerged from the lane and turned towards the village ahead of him, walking slowly and not noticing him. Henry walked for a while quietly behind her at a distance of about twenty yards. The road was straight here, bordered on one side by the elders and on the other by a wide grassy verge and a line of elm trees. Among the elders and the foot of the trees a great many primroses were still in flower. Henry's catlike footsteps were silent. The westering sun laid his long shadow down before him. He now increased his pace until his shadow-head reached Colette and then passed her. Seeing the shadow at her feet Colette turned round, then stopped. Henry too stopped instantly and stared at her in silence.

"Oh—hello, Henry."

She was wearing the green knee-breeches which she had had on when she had spoken to Henry and Stephanie in the Volvo, only now instead of the tweed jacket she was wearing a light brown Russian-style shirt open at the neck. Her sea-brown hair was piled up behind her head, cunningly rolled under and pinned. She was carrying a basket. The bandage had been removed from her cheek revealing a long livid furrow.

"Hello," said Henry. But he stood still.

Colette, who had not smiled, stared at him for a moment. Then when he did not speak she gave a vague wave of her hand and turned and walked on. Henry began to walk too, padding about ten yards behind her. A car passed them.

Colette stopped again and turned, stepping onto the grass verge. Henry stopped too, not yet near her. She looked at him frowning. "What's the matter?"

Henry advanced a pace or two in the long grass. "Where are you going?"

"To the village."

"What for?"

"To get some beer and tobacco for Daddy."

As Henry said nothing she began uncertainly to turn away.

"Wait a moment," said Henry. He stepped through the grass until he stood before her. "Colette, listen. Last time I met you wearing those totally absurd but I must say rather fetching trousers you told me that you loved me. Later on you denied this proposition. I find it hard to believe however that you really changed your mind. Your first statement carried conviction, your second did not. Do you, please, still love me?"

Colette looked at him, narrowing her eyes against the sun. Then she threw her basket sideways into the grass. "Yes, of course, I still love you."

"In that case," said Henry, "we shall get married, because I love you too—Colette—"

"Don't you mind—my face?"

"Oh *God*," said Henry, "you *idiot*!" He took another step and fell on his knees at her feet in the long grass. As he stretched out his arms to the green breeches and the embroidered hem of the brown shirt she subsided towards him and he took her swaying shoulders and keeled over with her among the primroses. "Colette—forgive me—this is true, isn't it—this is it—you do love me, don't you? I know I don't deserve it—but I couldn't bear it if you didn't any more, I should die and you'd have to shovel me into the ditch."

"I do love you, oh Henry, I've cried so about you, I thought I'd lost you—I only said I didn't love you because—you know —what was the use—and I wished so much I hadn't said that stupid thing about wanting the Hall, I don't want the Hall, I don't care about anything, I don't want anything, except you, I'll go with you anywhere, I don't mind how poor we are—"

"You don't rate my earning capacity very highly," said Henry, holding her rigidly and looking into her face, his head pillowed on her arm.

"I'll go away with you anywhere—"

"Whither I go thou wilt go and my people shall be thy people and my God thy God?"

"Yes, yes, yes."

"And you don't want to marry that bloody man Giles Gosling?"

"No! But what about—?"

"I'll tell you about that later," said Henry. "I'll tell you about everything later, everything that I know, and you shall explain me to myself. I shall empty myself and your grace and your truth will fill me. May I kiss you?"

"Yes, Henry."

He pulled her closer and kissed her, gently, carefully.

"Your lips taste of apples."

"Oh Henry, I love you so much, I'm so happy—"

"This grass is bloody wet," said Henry. "I suppose it's the dew. Is it the dew?"

Gerda, who had heard Henry's rapid descent of the stairs, and who had followed him noiselessly into the library to observe his exit and leap from the terrace, watched him as he ran fast, long legged, across the lawn. She watched him until he had disappeared, still running, round the corner of the drive. Then she returned to the dining-room. She opened a cupboard.

Lucius came in still wearing his cloak. He took his top teeth out, scrutinized them, and put them in again. He said, "I don't know what to do about that trunk I put my manuscripts into. If I leave it here it may just vanish, but it's too big to go into the taxi. Perhaps I'd better unpack it and divide the stuff—"

"I shouldn't worry too much," said Gerda. "Look, I'm sorry I made you burn those poems."

"Oh that doesn't matter," said Lucius. "I know them all by heart so I just wrote them out again."

" 'Clump, clump, the old girl.' I wasn't really angry. But I wish you'd write me something a little more romantic."

"Do you really? Well then I will! Oh good, oh Gerda, can I—what are you doing?"

"Lucius, could you just help me to open this bottle of champagne?"

Do you consider yourself to be sexually experienced? Stephanie considered this question.

She was sitting in the kitchen of her flat, wearing her new Japanese house-coat with the slit sleeves and the yellow embroidered dragons, and she had just made herself some more coffee. It was eleven o'clock in the morning and the sun was shining brightly onto the vegetable dome of Harrods. The flat and its contents were now legally hers, the papers had arrived by post that morning. So that at least was settled. She had been a little anxious.

Are you confident with the opposite sex? No, she thought, I am not confident, and I am not sexually experienced either, I am like a young girl in these matters, a shy innocent person really. Isn't it strange that I feel so young, as if I were always at the beginning of things. I suppose that is what they call being young in heart. She sat picturing herself. She remembered what some men had called her. Men were horrible. She had been so unlucky.

Stephanie would have been entirely unable to resolve what had become for her a truly agonizing dilemma had it not been for the sympathetic assistance of Gerda. Stephanie would have collapsed and let the old familiar demons of her life take her over, only Gerda had forced her to think and act. She had seen quite a lot of Gerda during the times when Henry was away on his own private business. Gerda had attended carefully to Stephanie, had sought and gained communication with her, and Stephanie had responded with a kind of gratitude, a kind of trust. Gerda had told Stephanie frankly that she thought that Henry was really in love with Colette, whom he had known all his life. She said, and Stephanie had to agree, that Henry knew very little about the real Stephanie and was not seriously attempting to find out more. "That's right, he treats me like a child, like a toy," said Stephanie indignantly. According to Gerda Henry had only become engaged to Stephanie out of some sort of a sense of duty. "Yes, he pities me." Gerda said that Henry had only been seriously interested because of Sandy, and had not got over the shock of learning that Stephanie had lied about Sandy. "He told you?" Stephanie wept. So she had lost by truthfulness what she had won by lying. She had felt so virtuous and heroic when she told him the truth. It had seemed to her then, in a confused way, that some reality which had always eluded her was suddenly within reach, she could stretch out and touch it, the real thing at last, not the dream. And Henry's apparent forgiveness had seemed the guarantee of ultimate safety. Only this too, like everything else that she had ever trusted, had proved unreal.

Gerda went on to point out that Henry was, as Stephanie could plainly see, determined to be penniless. This was Henry's form of romanticism, very charming, very inconvenient. Gerda could understand and shared Stephanie's horror of America. And was there not a woman there in whom Henry was supremely interested? "Of course he won't abandon you," said Gerda. She paused. "I feel sure of that." Stephanie replied, "The trouble is that when he's not here I don't really believe in him at all." If only he had stayed with her all the time as a lover should she would never have had these terrible doubts. Why had Henry gone away, where was he now, with whom? Gerda professed not to know. Henry was always going away. Stephanie pictured America, she pictured Bella. "What do you really want?" Gerda asked her.

What did Stephanie really want? In a supreme spasm of self-knowledge Stephanie decided that what she really wanted was London. This was what she had always wanted during those awful years in Leicester about which she would have told Henry so much more if he had only cared to ask. Her lie to him had effectively blocked that channel of communication. He wanted her to be something which he had just invented, and which he possessed here in the present. He did not want to know about her past, about why she had had to escape from her parents in order to be free. She had wanted freedom and freedom had meant London; and with Gerda's help it became clear to Stephanie that what she wanted now was the London life which she knew so well, the life of shops and pubs and adventures: that, with the addition of money. Stephanie did not believe that reality existed except in London. "So you wouldn't have liked it here," said Gerda, smiling. In the end Gerda offered, and Stephanie tearfully accepted a considerable honorarium. Gerda advised her how to invest it.

Back at the flat, in the frightfulness of the old solitude, Stephanie had spent days of anguish, uncertain once again about what she really wanted. Did she want Henry to pursue her, and would it not be terrible if he did not? If Henry were to say, all right, then we will live at the Hall, would not this be the best thing, the thing which by her flight she had attempted to bring about? She had certainly felt, in writing that letter, that either way she had nothing to lose. As the days passed and Henry was silent she felt pain, then relief. Stephanie, who lived very much inside the lively world of her fantasies, had more than once attempted to ride upon some scheme or other from fantasy into reality. This time, to her shocked surprise, she had very nearly succeeded; but on the whole she was glad to be back again in the freedom of her own dreamy solitude.

She had felt very grateful to Henry but had she ever really loved him or really believed that he loved her? Henry never understood me, she thought, he was always in such a hurry and making jokes, he was never patient with me, never moving at my speed, never really *with* me at all. Talking to Lucius, even to Gerda, was easier. No, Henry was not Mr. Right. She thought, I must have my own sort of happiness and be my own self, and that's never very easy with another person. She had felt so feeble and tired and miserable at the Hall, she felt so much better in health and spirits now that she was on her own again. She began to feel proud of herself for having survived, for having escaped. After all, things had not turned out too badly. She supposed she would go on looking for a husband, since that was what pretty clothes were for and life was all about, but now that she had financial assets there was no need to be in a hurry about it, no need to feel, as she had felt in the past, that she had to grab just anybody.

Still, I do wish I'd known Sandy, she thought, as I would have done if he hadn't died. I'm sure I would have helped him to find himself. And she thought, if Henry had looked like Sandy I could never have left him. I was meant for Sandy really. Henry was an accident, a mistake. She felt like a widow. She thought, I'll wear black for a while, I think it would suit me, and it'll keep people guessing. And she pictured herself sitting in bars and night clubs, ordering the most expensive drinks, a solitary well-dressed mysterious woman.

Yes, and I'll change the flat and make everything different and modern and bright, and I'll spend some of that money they left behind in the suitcase, that ransom money, they must mean me to have it. She returned to the computer dating form she was attempting to fill in. Did she want her choice to have long hair or short hair? Did she like beards? Did she mind if he was Chinese? How exciting the world was after all and full of various possibilities. No wonder she felt so innocent and free and young. One of the questions they asked her was rather fun to answer: *Put your favourite colours in order of preference.* Of course that would show something important. I think I like red best, she thought. Or do I like blue best? Am I a *blue* sort of person, I wonder?

"Your side looks higher, Bellamy," said Gerda. "Rhoda, just hold on would you, dear?"

"I told you those rings were different sizes," said John Forbes.

"Well, it was straight before," said Gerda.

"Perhaps the floor slopes. Or perhaps you didn't notice before."

"It seems a pity not to get it right now."

"It's very heavy, some of the rings have been pulled out of shape, I'll get some new ones."

"All right, just hook it on anyhow, that's fine."

Bellamy and Rhoda descended from their ladders. Rhoda disappeared to the kitchen. Bellamy folded the ladders and carried them away. The tapestry of Athena and Achilles hung once more in its old place. The bright light from outside showed up all its colours. Perhaps it had shed some of its dust or perhaps Gerda had never looked at it properly before. What she had vaguely thought of as black turned out to be a sort of marvellous indigo blue. I wonder what's happening exactly, she wondered. She had never asked anybody.

"I love this room," said John Forbes. The library had returned to its former state.

"Sandy was very fond of it." Gerda found herself constantly uttering Sandy's name to John Forbes, as if continually testing to see how easy it was now to speak of him and how much the pain had changed. She had talked quite a lot to John about Sandy. "Sandy bought those blue and yellow Italian vases we made the lamps out of." There was a steady calm almost pointless bearing of witness which did her good. She said, following her connecting thought, "I do hope Cato will come home for the holidays."

"So do I, but he's still like a madman."

They walked to the window and stooped out onto the north terrace. It was past midsummer and two big shrub roses growing just below on the grass were crammed with huge muddley pink flowers, their red transparent stems bending in great arches. The sun was hot. Gerda was wearing a sun dress with shoulder-straps. John in shirt-sleeves was sweating.

"Let him come here," said Gerda, "we will heal him."

John laughed. "Sorry, but your faith is touching—as if you felt we could heal anybody."

Yes, she thought, I can never be healed of Sandy being gone, never, but at least I can think of it now and talk about it. She wanted to say this to John Forbes, but checked herself. She felt that they both did this, formulated ideas for each other and then kept silent.

John Forbes, his mind tracking hers, said, "Where's Lucius?"

"Still in bed. He's got quite lazy these days."

"Well, I must get back to the building site." John jumped from the terrace to the grass and looked up at her, standing in the sun just beyond the slanting shadow of the house, his eyes narrowing but showing very blue in the clear light.

Without saying good-bye Gerda smiled and turned back into

the house. There was so much happening now, so much coming and going, there was no need for formality any more.

She went back through the window into the library and looked again at the big Italian vases which Sandy had bought. She remembered how he had brought them back one evening swinging them carelessly one in each hand. She touched the deep luscious glaze. And then she was thinking of Henry. Henry was like a young lover to her now, all his wry cleverness which had seemed so destructive now bent upon pleasing. He always evaded her but always returned with a teasing tactful gentleness as if he were dancing about her. Of course he was no substitute for Sandy. The idea that he might somehow take Sandy's place had been a dream of her first grief when she had had to invent some sort of consolation or die. Now she could more calmly see that no consolation was possible. But she had to pretend to be happy for Henry's sake, because she was grateful to him, because she was going to receive after all, beyond her hopes, the best of him, and the effort brought her in fact some sort of genuine joy. She sat down on the club fender and stretched out her bare brown legs in front of her. She felt happy and sad and let the tears gently overflow her eyes.

"Listen to the cuckoo."

"Don't go on about that bird. Need you shower me with pearly drops?"

"Isn't it refreshing?"

"Drop the pole straight, don't wave it about."

"I am dropping it straight."

"No woman knows how to punt."

"Look out, I'm going to ship the pole."

"God, it's hot."

"I'm going to put my feet in the water."

"Don't capsize us. You know you're quite a good-looking girl really."

376

"You're not sorry you married me?"

"The mistake of my life. First you persuade me not to sell the Hall—"

"I never said a word about not selling the Hall!"

"It was extra-sensory influence. You and my mother put on some force-ten telepathy."

"When has any woman made any man do what he didn't want to?"

"You got married in white at Dimmerstone church like you said in the letter—"

"*You* decided not to sell the Hall."

"I oughtn't to have compromised. You tempted me, like Eve tempting Adam. As soon as you start playing with property you're done for."

"You said it hadn't occurred to you that it didn't have to be all or nothing."

"I think it did have to be all or nothing. I've failed."

"How glossy the water is, it's got a sort of silver skin on it. Henry, I want a pair of black swans."

"You'll want peacocks next."

"Well, I want peacocks."

"I've failed. I was pure in heart once, before I met you."

"You were just a terrorist, not pure in heart."

"Look at all this. Christ."

"Why not enjoy it? You can give it away later."

"We shall be able to see the television aerials of the housing estate from the upper rooms of Queen Anne unless those trees grow bloody fast."

"But you are pleased about the housing estate?"

"I am pleased now that that bloody man Duckling or whatever his name is has gone away to plan Rattenbury New Town."

"I love your being jealous of Giles, I never cared for him at all."

"Well, I'm glad he's gone. I'm the architect now. There's nothing to it. This morning I designed a fountain."

"A tufted duck just swam under the punt and came up on the other side."

"I was staggered at what those Cotmans raised."

"It will be a model village, and Dimmerstone will look enchanting too when we've finished."

"We can run all of phase one on selling pictures."

"Do you think that really was a Guercino you found in the attic?"

"Yes, but don't tell Gerda yet."

"You never told her you left all that money at the flat?"

"No, it would impair my superman image."

"Do you think much about Stephanie now?"

"Yes."

"Oh."

"How can I not? You made such a fuss about her, and keeping me out of your bed until the wedding day just out of spite—"

"It wasn't spite. I felt—you'd had all those girls—I wanted it to be different with us, a quite quite different thing."

"Well it is. We're married and done for."

"It was a lovely little wedding, wasn't it. So small and white. If only Cato had come—"

"You don't think I'm too old for you, do you?"

"Well, you are rather old."

"Look, quick, do you see, a grass snake swimming."

"Darling, don't feel it's wicked to be happy."

"It's not wicked to be happy, but one ought to be happy being destitute, it would be better."

"You don't know anything about being destitute."

"I know. It's above my moral level. That's been my trouble all along, mistaking my moral level. That idea of selling everything and clearing out, that was far above me, I couldn't possibly have done it in a proper way. Perhaps someone else could have done it. But with me it was just—yes of course you are right—an act of violence. But that doesn't mean we aren't sunk in corruption."

"Oh, to the neck!"

"And when society's rotten to the core one shouldn't build more beautiful houses even for ordinary guys."

"I've never understood that argument. You don't want to smash the past. Why shouldn't all the good old things gradually reach out to everybody?"

"Because there aren't enough."

"So better wreck it all?"

"Our beautiful housing estate is a snare and delusion."

"Tell that to the people who are going to live there! A house is about the most real of all material things."

"It's a delusion. It's a game. Toys. Fountains."

"Why not make some people happier? Daddy says if the rents can be kept down—"

"I'm running this show, not your father."

"And then we could build on the other side of Dimmerstone church, and on the Oak Meadow. Now that we can get that ironstone compound stuff—"

"You're interested. So am I. That's the trouble."

"All right, we're interested. And isn't this our moral level?"

"That's the trouble."

"Look at that enormous dragon-fly."

"I used to think I was Max. Now I think I'm Leonardo."

"You will write your book on Max, won't you? We will go to Amsterdam and to Leipzig and to Colmar—"

"And to St. Louis."

"And to Santa Cruz."

"You don't mind Russ and Bella coming here in September?"

"You're not in love with Bella, are you?"

"I adore Bella. I love you with every atom of my being. You make me laugh."

"So does she."

"I am addicted to your company. That's what being in love is, plus a few physical stirrings."

"It doesn't sound enough."

"I see into your soul."

"Isn't that dull?"

"Not at all. I see myself there."

"You're a narcissist."

"All the best people were. Leonardo, Shakespeare, Jesus Christ—"

"And you're thinking about Stephanie."

"Everything's happened so quickly. I feel so bloody sorry for poor Steph. I did love her in a way, but it was under the sign of doom."

"What sign are we under?"

"The sign of happiness."

"Is *that* enough?"

"It's a start. Life will teach us the rest. It's just as important to have good starting points as to have good goals. When I suddenly saw I could choose happiness everything became crystal clear. I'd never seen that before ever in my life. I'd always thought I had to choose misery."

"You know, I think Gerda suddenly chose happiness too, when she decided to see Stephanie off."

"If your theory is right. Poor Steph."

"Being sorry for her is a kind of contempt. I think she's done rather well."

"It is true that I was never really interested in her."

"What a monster you are. But you are interested in me?"

"Women will make conversations so personal. When I thought of marrying Stephanie it seemed like doing the unthinkable, something one could only do blindfold and in terror. And I thought marrying anybody would be like that."

"But it wasn't?"

"No. Marrying you was calm and lucid."

"You were trembling."

"The gross effects of passion. You're sure you don't hate sex?"

"Sure!"

"Some girls do."

"I just wanted to wait."

"Perhaps virginity was your magic. Stephanie felt it. She was frightened of you."

"It's all yours now."

"How *can* you love me? You must be making a mistake. How valuable you are. How lucky I am. I say, darling, I thought perhaps I wouldn't tell you but—"

"You must tell me everything."

"Yes, I know I must, it's a neurotic urge. But—it's a bit weird —you know, that ring, the Marshalson Rose—"

"Yes."

"I would have loved to give it to you."

"But it's lost, and I love the ring I've got."

380

"I saw Rhoda wearing it."

"Rhoda—wearing the Marshalson Rose?"

"Yes, at our wedding. It was the most extraordinary thing. You know how Rhoda usually wears gloves, one's got sort of used to seeing her in gloves. Well, when we were coming out of the church, actually coming down the aisle, I saw Rhoda, she was at the end of row, and her hand was sort of hanging as if— as if she wanted to show it—and there was the ring—there was no mistaking it."

"How extraordinary. But you said nothing?"

"To her? Of course not. I didn't tell anybody."

"Why didn't you tell me earlier?"

"I felt so sort of odd about it, I felt I ought to keep it secret. I've always felt a bit odd about Rhoda—"

"Not in love with her?"

"No, of course not—I felt she was eerie. And then, her having stolen that ring and sort of actually showing it, flaunting it, at that moment when you and I were getting married—I felt as if it might be an evil omen. There, I've told you and now you must comfort me. That's what a wife is for. You tell her awful things and she tells you they're not really awful at all and you cheer up."

"I don't think it's awful. What makes you think she stole it?"

"Well, she must have done, what else?"

"Henry, there's something I must tell you."

"Oh God. You're secretly married to Duckling. I shall shoot myself."

"No, listen. There's something that happened years and years ago and I promised I'd never tell anyone, only now I feel somehow that I'm released from the promise—"

"Colette, you're killing me, quick."

"It's about Sandy."

"Oh Colette, Christ in heaven, not—"

"No, no, stop interrupting. It was ages ago when I was about eight. I was wandering about in the garden just here—I think I was looking for you and Cato, you know how I used to follow you about. And I don't know why, I decided I'd climb up to the folly. And I climbed up and—"

"And?"

"I found Sandy there making love to Rhoda."

"Oh—how strange—how—oh God—how touching and—awful and—oh God—"

"Sandy was a bit upset. I don't know what Rhoda thought. She just stared at me with those strange eyes."

"Ibis-eyed. What did Sandy say?"

"He offered me half a crown to keep mum."

"And now you've told."

"I kept the half-crown. I got Daddy to drill a hole in it. I didn't tell him why. I used to wear it round my neck. I've still got it."

"So you loved Sandy too."

"No, I loved you. But Sandy was—sort of grand."

"Yes, he was, wasn't he—sort of grand."

"So you see. Perhaps Rhoda has a right to the Marshalson Rose after all. I'm sure Sandy gave it to her."

"As a consolation prize. You know I felt so sorry for Stephanie because, as I thought, Sandy had been too bloody snobbish to marry her."

"So you felt you had to. I hope you won't feel this about Rhoda?"

"No. Rhoda always scared me stiff. That tiny head, those huge eyes. Now I'm even more scared."

"You mustn't be. She showed you the ring on purpose."

"As a threat, as a warning. To show us she ought to have walked down that aisle with Sandy."

"No, I'm sure she never expected Sandy to marry her. She just wanted to show us that she was sort of one of the family."

"One of the family! I remember now, Sandy could always understand what Rhoda said. I never could."

"And she wanted you to know where the ring was."

"Well, she can keep it."

"You won't tell Gerda?"

"Of course not."

"Do you want me to throw away that half-crown? I'll throw it in the lake. Oh God, I do love you."

"No, angel, darling, keep it. You know I feel—oh so much better about Sandy these days."

"I'm glad. Gerda knows that."

"I hope so. I was a devil when I came home."

"You'll never be a devil to me, will you? I should die."

"Bring your feet on board, I want to kiss them. They taste of lake water. Your lips taste of lake water too. You are a changeling out of the lake. Oh God, I do love you."

"I feel so happy—except that—except that—"

"I know. Cato. And what happened."

"Death is so terrible. *That* death was so terrible."

"I'm glad you talked to me about it."

"Death is awful, awful, it's a private dark place, it separates one more than anything else."

"You must try to forget it. It's not our business, it's not for us to worry about death now, we don't want that lesson, not yet. Happiness is our sign."

"I hope Cato never finds out that it was all for nothing. Oh that poor poor boy, and I could have managed him—"

"Stop it, Colette, I think you rather overdo your confidence in your virginity. The world is rid of a crook."

"Cato wouldn't see it like that. He must be in hell."

"God will look after Cato. God will bring Cato back to us. You know when I saw him in that old black cassock I thought I'd found a spiritual leader."

"He's broken now."

"God will mend him."

"You don't believe in God."

"People like Cato invent God. He exists for them. We can't do it. We lesser folk just sponge on the God that holy men invent. Ah well—"

"You're thinking that if you hadn't married me you might have been a holy man yourself."

"Me? No. I have no identity. I have to be invented too. You'll have to keep me in being by your will."

"I'll do that. Isn't that love?"

I suppose I have made a mistake, thought Henry. I ought to have sold the place and gone away. I ought not to have married. Then perhaps I could have been a holy person after my fashion, diminishing in that little white wooden house in America in the middle of nowhere, diminishing and diminishing into a sort of inoffensive beetle. I was born to be nothing and to have nothing. Of course I know that this house is an illusion, but now I'm stuck with it. And I've let myself be conned into love and happiness and I shall have to play the role of the happy husband and the loving son and one day I suppose God help me the responsible father for ever and ever now. It's so bloody easy to make women happy. And there I shall be manufacturing happiness and tied up to this bloody beautiful house for the rest of my days and I shall never be able to make up my mind to sell it. For a while I shall get rid of things, send the most valuable pictures to the salerooms, but after a while I shall begin to buy things, I shall begin to embellish the place again. I shall become a connoisseur and I shall have good wine in the cellar. I've been caught by property after all and by a young wife. As a spiritual being I'm done for. The pity that I felt for Stephanie was probably the only spiritual experience that I ever had. And he looked up at the house, reclining on its green fold of hill, the southern-facing façade glowing tawny-golden in the sun. Yes, I'm done for, thought Henry. Now I shall never live simply and bereft as I ought to live. I have chosen a mediocre destiny. I shall never finish my book on Max, I shall become like Sandy, which I suppose was what my mother wanted. Perhaps her will has done it all, or Colette's will, or the will of my bloody ancestors. I have failed, but I don't care. I shall be happy. I never expected it, I never wanted it or sought for it, but it's happened. Apparently I am doomed to be a happy man, and I shall do my damnedest to make it last.

"Darling, do leave that scar alone."

"Henry, listen to the cuckoo."

"Bugger that bird."

"Henry—"

"I must go and see the borough engineer."

"Henry—"

"Well, get on with it."

"I think I'm pregnant."

"Oh no! Oh God!"

"Would you like the walnut cake?"

"No thanks, just the anchovy toast."

Bird-headed Rhoda set the tray down on the quilt in front of Lucius and departed.

Lucius felt a little light-headed, giddy. He thought, something odd has just happened. Then he thought what it was. He had understood what Rhoda said. How strange, after all these years. Had he just gradually come to it by listening to her talk? Or was she now speaking more distinctly? Or what? Whatever it was, he had certainly understood her today. And he had understood her yesterday too, he had had a conversation with her about crumpets.

Lucius lay there in bed touching these ideas vaguely, not really thinking. He felt so formidably tired. Still, he felt best at tea-time. The mornings were hell. Hot Indian tea and anchovy toast do concentrate the mind. Thank God there are still some enjoyments left.

The afternoon sun was shining into his room revealing the dust on top of his chest of drawers where his things lay in a muddle. A brush which his mother had given him when he went to college. A comb full of strands of silver hair. Two ties, still knotted. Money. Cuff-links. Dust. He had never had a woman to tidy up for him.

His mouth was hurting, his back was hurting, there was a sort of hollow in the centre of him where a drum was beating solemnly as if for the denouement of some rite. His breath came fast. They had all forgotten him. No one noticed now that he stayed all the time in his room, no one asked him to come down to watch the television any more. Rhoda fed him as one might feed an old pet in a cage. No, all this was unjust and wrong. They did come to see him, they did suggest that it was such a nice day he ought to go out for a walk. They were kind to him. Only he was invisible to them because they were happy. Colette, her face glowing with a dewy light, her eyes vague with joy, was the very presence of youth, the perfect presence of that which sometimes seemed to Lucius as he lay there to be the most precious thing of all, better than virtue or wisdom or art, simply youth and beauty, the healthy human animal, mature and utterly unspoilt, the body, the mind pure and clean in the only way after all in which such merits are ever really acquired, not by dirty old men in caves, but simply by unsullied unpuzzled nature.

Henry was happy too in his secretive way, never admitting it, his dark eyes glowing like stars, his curly hair electric with force. He and Colette ran about a lot and shouted like children. Lucius could hear the regular thud as they leapt the steps from the front door. Gerda was more dignified, trying to conceal her satisfaction at the success of her schemes. When John Forbes came to the house, which was every day now, she either did not mention it to Lucius, or she described his visit as a surprise. She always gave a harmless reason for his coming, that is a reason other than his desire to see her. She looked much younger and had bought a lot of new clothes. Suddenly with a man in the house she was back again in the land of her youth, in the land proper to her own being. She too glowed. Lucius lay in bed or sat in his dressing-gown at his table and listened to Henry's maniac laughter and to the deep authoritative boom of John Forbes's voice.

So I am not a man in the house he thought. No. Henry was not a man either, but then Henry was an elf and would survive elvishly. I used to imagine that I was Tiresias, thought Lucius, but the mantic power was never given. I could have won Gerda, after Burke died, even after Sandy died, if I had been an ordinary man with ordinary selfish appetites and will. I did want her and love her, I do want her and love her, but she can see that I'm a ghost and she rightly prefers flesh and blood. It isn't goodness, this lack of grasp, I used to think that it was. I am simply one of those who have not and from whom will be taken away even that which they have.

I imagined that solitude would instruct me, but when have I ever had real solitude? What an easy life I have had, he thought, and how fast it has fled away. I still feel that I am young and beautiful, that I haven't aged really. Age is something far far away in the future. People have always protected me and looked after me and I have felt it right that they should. I haven't ever suffered and struggled the way ordinary people do. I could not have done it and I can't think how they do it! I always knew I was special. I was always waiting for something for which I had to sit, as it were, in a comfortable anteroom. Perhaps I was waiting for Gerda. Only now at last I know, perhaps I have only just found out, last week or yesterday, that she is lost to me. There was an intimacy, and a kind of nervous loving, only it lacked the coarseness of real life. Now she will despise me and pity me and I shall gradually become a burden to her. Can I ever make friends with Henry? No.

Of course, he thought, I wasn't just waiting for Gerda. I was waiting for that great work of art which was always there hidden behind the veil, my own great work of genius. And now it's too late. All these feeble verses with which I've been covering the paper are just a substitute for the long hard struggle of real art, for the serious effort which I shall never make now. Only I've got to go on believing in them, I've got to go on deceiving myself into writing, if I stop writing I shall die. It's funny, he thought, I did imagine that I could change my life, that I could go back to the literary pubs and sit there writing poetry on beer-stained tables and being a mystery to the young. Could I have done that? Perhaps it would have been better after all if Henry had stripped me and turned me out into the world like a starving dog.

How terribly tired I feel, thought Lucius, even though I have been lying in bed all day. The sun is shining. I must get up. Perhaps I'll put some music on, though it makes me feel so terribly sad now. I wish I wanted a drink, but I don't. I must pretend that there has been a day, that there has been some activity, before the night comes. And then oh God let the sleeping pills work. A hell of sleeplessness now threatened every dark: a hell which he attempted to forget by day and which he could not picture. It was as if by night he became another person. Sleepless he wept sometimes with incoherent grief like a doomed child.

Up we get, he thought, pushing his messy tray, with slopped

tea and toast crusts, away across the counterpane. Why was it now so bloody hard to get out of bed? He must be anaemic or something. He ought to visit the doctor, only nobody had thought to suggest it.

He sat up and manoeuvred his legs over the edge of the bed. His protruding legs were thin and white, covered with a mass of large blue veins. He looked down at his bare knobbly feet, then held his head hard. Intense giddiness had come upon him like a gust of violent wind. The ceiling became black and descended. He reached his hand out for the bed-post which was moving rapidly past him. A frightful pain filled the void where the great drum had been beating.

*

A while later Lucius became conscious that he was now lying on the floor. After a good deal of thought he managed, by some kind of mental rather than physical effort, to sit up, leaning against the chair beside his table. His right hand functioned all right, but his left was without power. So was his left leg, his left shoulder. His left eye. Lucius experimented with his face. He knew it was different. A pain in the back of his neck was forcing his head forward. He sat quietly for some time breathing gently and considering himself. After a while he felt as if he were asking for something, requiring something, asking somebody for something. What was it that he so much wanted now, perhaps the only thing? Something like justice, only certainly not that. Not love. All the words seemed to have left their things and to be flying about free in his mind. If he could only find the right word. What was it? Courage, he thought, Yes, courage.

Very slowly he reached up to the table and pulled his pad of paper and his pen off onto the floor, onto the dusty familiar carpet. He had never sat on the floor like this before. He looked at the carpet: how worn it was, how threadbare and old. It had been a good carpet once. He carefully took up his pen, balancing it awkwardly between his fingers. Was this the way fingers held a pen? He wanted to see if he could still write. The pad was steady against the leg of the table. In a strange scrawling hand he slowly wrote:

So many dawns I was blind to.
Now the illumination of night
Comes to me too late, O great teacher.

John Forbes was in bed with Dame Patricia Raven.

"What I just can't understand," said John, "is why he wrote those awful crawling letters. Imagine writing to your sister and asking her to give herself up to a gang of thugs."

"Only there wasn't a gang."

"He didn't know that, he still doesn't know it."

"He thought you'd prevent her from coming."

"He should have known her better. She would have run through a fire to get to Cato once he'd summoned her like that. She's the heroic one."

"The young knight, you said."

"Yes. Oh God, I can't get over it. Any sort of ordinary manliness, the most ordinary sort of decency and courage, should have stopped Cato from writing those letters, should simply have stopped him in his tracks."

"I suppose it didn't seem too bad to write to Henry about the ransom. After all it was only money and Henry has plenty. Then when he started writing the letters it was easier to go on. And he was hungry and confused—"

"I wouldn't have started."

"One could be very frightened in such a situation, threatened with a knife—"

"By a puny boy."

"A violent person has psychological power. He can frighten the non-violent just by his will. This is a very dreadful fact."

"He can frighten sheep. I would have been so bloody angry. I'd have gone berserk. I can't forgive Cato for taking it lying down, for not being aggressive. All right you'll say it's better not to be aggressive—"

"I wasn't going to say that. But it may be more prudent. I hope no one kidnaps you. You would get yourself murdered."

"It might be better to be dead than living with some memories."

"Oh, come—"

"And the crazy awful thing about the whole business is that if he'd acted bravely and fought the boy the whole hoax would have collapsed at once. The boy must have been amazed, he probably started it half as a joke! And then suddenly there were thousands of pounds and a girl offering herself—I must say I blame Henry too."

"I think everyone acted fairly reasonably. It was a very obscure situation and evil confuses people. Joe might have killed Cato if Cato had fought."

"Cato was led like a lamb to the slaughter. If only he'd punched the boy's face at the beginning he wouldn't have had to smash his skull at the end. There's a sort of feebleness in the modern young. With some of them it's vicious idleness and something for nothing, with others it's just an inability to resist evil."

"Gentleness perhaps. Cato is non-violent. Colette is far more violent than he is."

"Yes, at least she fought."

"Anyway it's done now and Cato's got to live with it and anything we can do to help him to recover—"

"Oh he'll be all right. He'll go back to God. That bloody religion is so debilitating. Pat, darling, what have I done to deserve such children? Cato a Roman Catholic and Colette married to Henry Marshalson!"

"She seems very happy."

"She could have had that clever young architect, Giles Gosling, he was mad about her."

"I thought you were so pleased with Henry's building plans."

"They're my building plans. Henry and Colette are just playing at it."

"Well, I think Henry's a poppet."

"Pat—!"

"I'm getting up."

"I bore you."

"Not exactly, but you understand so little."

390

Patricia rolled out, stood up. She had been a flaming red-head when she was young. Now her abundant hair had faded to a still radiant speckled sandy ginger. Her skin was very pale and her eyes too were a pale blue. She had an air of innocence which could change imperceptibly into an air of fearful candid intelligence as she gazed with those lucid pale eyes. She frightened people. Her clear face was marked only by a faint puckered tiredness upon the brow. Now, dressed in a light brown Indian robe, she smoked a cigar. John Forbes watched her.

"John, I must tell you something."

"What?"

"I'm going to have someone here to share the flat."

"No! Not a man?"

"No, no, a girl."

"Oh hell. But what about me? I've got to be able to come here."

"Things will be so different."

"Oh no, Pat, don't be obscene. I must be able to come. Who is this girl anyway?"

"Miriam Shippel."

"God, not the girl who writes those books?"

"Yes."

"But, Pat, you can't, you must keep times for me—"

"I'm going to retire and work in the Labour Party. Miriam is going to be a candidate. We're going into politics. I'm tired of just fuming and writing letters to the *Times*."

"Pat, you aren't serious—I mean, you're not—ending this?"

"Well, it'll have to end, John, when Miriam's here. Don't take on. You know how I've always felt, how it's always been."

"You've hated it."

"You know I haven't! But I've done it out of love and friendship—"

"I like 'love and friendship'!"

"I've done it to please you, since there wasn't any reason not to. Now there'll be a reason. Sorry."

"Pat, you know I've got to have someone—"

"Of course you have, dear."

"You think I'm coarse."

"Yes."

"Why have you put up with me for so long?"

"Oh well, I just happen to love you. And because of Ruth. I loved Ruth awfully."

"Yes—I know—"

"Why don't you take up with Gerda?"

"Hell, no, I'd have to marry her! You aren't jealous of Gerda by any chance? No, no such luck."

"Well, why not marry Gerda? It seems to me rather a good idea."

"No, no, out of the question. I say, Pat, is it marriage you want? I mean if it is I'd marry you—"

Patricia's laughter echoed through the flat.

"I'm done for," said John. "This is the first time in years that I've seen you really happy."

"You aren't taking any books?" said Cato.

"No."

It was nine o'clock in the evening and Cato was in Brendan's sitting-room. The contents of the drawers and bookshelves lay about on the floor. The little flat was being dismembered. Brendan was going to India.

"I got it all out of that young policeman in the end."

"So you said."

"Sorry, am I drunk?"

"No, no, have some more."

"Colette didn't want me to know. If only I'd done anything, shouted, struggled, anything. God, he might have *laughed*. It's as if—I didn't give him a chance."

"You can't know. Colette told the police that Joe was harmless, but he slashed her deliberately and in a horrible way. And it needn't even have been true that he had no accomplices, that it was only him."

"Oh it was true—the police were convinced when they

searched the place. My father thinks I'm a sort of sick coward. He can't understand how a man could behave as I behaved. I can't understand it now either."

"Don't try to in that way."

"Maybe I was right to choose a non-violent role, if only I'd stuck to it—I keep going over and over it all in my mind."

"At least you can see you oughtn't to do that."

"He respected me once. When I destroyed that respect there was nothing to save him—"

"Did you see his mother again?"

"No. Father Thomas is dealing with her. She didn't want to see me any more. I don't blame her. She's got away from that bloody man anyway. He respected me and loved me and I somehow brought God to him—if only—"

"I hope you don't inflict this on Colette."

"No, only on you. Colette doesn't know I know. I don't think Colette will ever forgive me for involving her in that horror. She despises me. So does my father, so does Henry."

"Colette loves you and her greatest need is to feel that she can help you. You must meet that need, even by pretence until the pretence becomes real. They all need you."

"I can't meet anybody's need, better to keep clear. Who am I, anyway? Perhaps now I shall start jumping on my pupils. A queer in a cord coat he called me."

"Well, accept it. There's nothing wrong with being queer. Only I don't think you should jump on pupils, a teacher has so much power."

"I've lost my self-esteem and I didn't ever know how much it mattered. It's a great defence against temptation. Now it's gone I feel every sin can tempt me, you name it, I'll do it. Once that spiritual decor is stripped away there's nothing but a demon left."

"I know you feel that."

"Oh not even that—I feel I'm nobody, nothing."

"You were always that, my dear, it's what we all are."

"What will become of me?"

"You might become an Anglican priest later on, I'm sure they'd have you."

"Cocoa after wine?"

"Cocoa might do you good. You were always a bit of a drunk, you know."

"Drunk with Christ, yes."

"The priesthood is a marriage. People often start by falling in love, and they go on for years without realizing that that love must change into some other love which is so unlike it that it can hardly be recognized as love at all. Sometimes the first *élan* carries a man right through to the end. Well, that's one way."

"And you? Did you 'fall in love'?"

"Oh well. I had the advantage of growing up with a saint."

"Who was that?"

"My mother. She was the sort of saint that no one ever notices or sees, she was almost invisible."

"And that somehow defused the drama?"

"I never conceived of not being a priest. For you, there was a *coup de foudre*."

"I wish I believed that Joe was in purgatory."

"If you believed it you would not know what you were believing. I wish you would pray for him. I wish you would go on praying. Prayer is the most essential of all human activities, it should be like breathing. You must still feel it yourself, the need to pray, like the need to breathe."

"I feel it. But what does breathing prove? You know, when I was there in the dark in that place I realized at last and quite certainly that there was no God. I had imagined that I had thought this before, but I hadn't. It's as if I experienced the non-existence of God as something absolutely positive. Now, don't look like that. You keep trying to pull every experience, every testimony back inside the being of God. It won't do! I know all that, after all I've been years in the game."

"You say you've been years in the game. It seems to me you don't know what the game is."

"All right, you tell me."

"I've told you. You fell in love. That's a start, but it's only a start. Falling in love is egoism, it's being obsessed by images and being consoled by them, images of the beloved, images of oneself. It's the greatest pain and the greatest paradox of all that personal love has to break at some point, the ego has to

394

break, something absolutely natural and seemingly good, seemingly perhaps the only good, has to be given up. After that there's darkness and silence and space. And God is there. Remember St. John of the Cross. Where the images end you fall into the abyss, but it is the abyss of faith. When you have nothing left you have nothing left but hope."

"*El abismo de la fe.* Brendan, I've heard all this so often. I've even *said* it so often!"

"Try at least to use it now in relation to yourself. You keep going over and over what happened and picturing it and imagining it otherwise. You mustn't. Repentance isn't a bit like obsessive guilt. Think how often you've said that, in one form or another, in the confessional."

"I can't say it to myself."

"Your guilt is vanity, it's to do with that self-esteem you were talking about, which you haven't really lost at all, it's only wounded. Repent, and let these things pass from you."

"Without Christ I can't. Without the bloody machinery I can't. I thought you might be able to do it for me, but even you can't. I feel damned. I loved that boy and I led him astray and I killed him."

"We live by redemptive death. Anyone can stand in for Christ."

"You're crazy."

"Death is what instructs us most of all, and then only when it is present. When it is absent it is totally forgotten. Those who can live with death can live in the truth, only this is almost unendurable. It is not the drama of death that teaches—when you are there facing it there is no drama. That's why it's so hard to write tragedy. Death is the great destroyer of all images and all stories, and human beings will do anything rather than envisage it. Their last resource is to rely on suffering, to try to cheat death by suffering instead. And suffering we know breeds images, it breeds the most beautiful images of all."

Cato put down his glass. He looked up at Brendan who while he talked had been moving, sorting books, and now stood beside the empty shelves trailing his fingers to and fro in the dust.

Cato said, "Christ cheated death by suffering instead."

Brendan looked at Cato for a moment, then was silent, leaning back against the shelves and gazing dreamily ahead of him.

Cato said, "Oh *no*—"

Brendan smiled and flashed his blue eyes and sat down, knocking over a tall pile of books with his foot. Then he actually laughed.

"But you believe in the Resurrection and the Life," said Cato. "If I really did now I'd be laughing too. I'm not sure that I ever did believe. You do, which is why what you've just said must be, for you, a kind of nonsense, a magic spell, made up, oh I know, for my benefit, like things one says in the confessional, only of course much more sophisticated. After all you believe in a personal God—"

Brendan was silent.

"Well, you do, don't you?"

After a moment Brendan said, "That's another picture. We deal in the idea of persons, we have to. But God is unimaginable and incomprehensible and nameless. *Dysphrastos* and *thaumastos*. Oh all this is the old 'game,' I know. But one lives with the game and things change. You've never really lived with it, you've been a provisional priest right from the start. You've been doing the thing on your own terms. Now when at last you might cease to be provisional—"

"And fall into the abyss."

"You talk of giving up."

"I don't just talk of it, I am giving up."

"Are you? Time will show. I don't mean about your being laicized. You can't escape from God just by going through a few formalities."

"But Brendan, do you believe in God or not? I mean, I'm not accusing you of being a fake, you're real, and because of you something else is real—but this doesn't add up to God, I mean even you can't invent Him! *Do* you believe in God?"

"It's impossible to answer a question truly unless you know what the question means to the questioner."

"Oh do stop being subtle. If you don't know whether God is a person what happens to your Christology?"

"I let Christ look after my Christology."

"You should have been a lawyer. I remember Father Bell saying that you were the best theologian we had."

"That was years ago, my dear."

"Have you given it up then? Have you given up thinking, you who were so good at it?"

Brendan pushed the books around on the floor with a slippered foot. "One can get so far but no further."

"What about people in the past? After all, we've all been thinking about it for a long time."

"What can we really know about people in the past? We understand so little of minds we only meet in books. Our whole range of understanding and vision is tiny."

"The New Testament?"

"That's unusual. It's unusualness is one of the few clear things."

"Your friend Plato?"

"Human affairs are not serious, but they have to be taken seriously. We are puppets in the hands of God."

"He said that?"

"We can only see Plato through the haze of his ingenious invention, European philosophy."

"And all that brilliant thinking that went to make the doctrine of the Trinity?"

"Brilliant, I agree. Oh we must think, at least some people must. But thinking, in that way, is simply a matter of keeping oneself from slipping back into all sorts of illusions, it's a way of keeping near the truth, even when, especially when, the truth cannot be formulated."

"Maybe I'm more like my father than I used to realize. He thinks religion is pure mumbo-jumbo. I'm beginning to think that most of it is."

"Oh yes, of course. But, Cato, never mind about reason and intelligence. Just hold onto Christ, the Christ that the Church cannot take away from you."

"Now you sound like a Fundamentalist preacher. But Brendan, is that why you're going to India, to stop thinking?"

"No, not like that."

"Like what then?"

"It was time for a change."

"Too comfy here?"

"No, no, one can do Christ's work anywhere. No—many things—"

"Tell me one."

"I was getting too addicted to speculation. I sometimes felt that if I could hang on just a little longer I would receive some perfect illumination about everything."

"Why don't you hang on?"

"Because I know that if it did come it would be an illusion— one of the most, oh, splendid. The original *felix culpa* is thought itself."

"That sounds to me like despair."

"The point is, one will never get to the end of it, never get to the bottom of it, never, never, never. And that never, never, never is what you must take for your hope and your shield and your most glorious promise. Everything that we concoct about God is an illusion."

"But God is not an illusion?"

"Whosoever he be of you who forsaketh not all that he hath, he cannot be my disciple."

"I don't believe you've given up theology at all. Theology is magic. Beware."

"I know."

"I must go and catch my train to Leeds, it leaves at midnight. When shall I see you again?"

Brendan got up and turned on another lamp. "I'm going into retreat next week and I'm leaving England immediately after that."

"So I won't see you before you go?"

"No."

"Shall I come and see you in Calcutta, if I can raise the money from somewhere?"

"Well, better not."

There was silence for a moment. Cato put on his coat. "So you're giving me up too?"

"I'm giving you up too."

They faced each other.

"I've always kept you as a last resource," said Cato.

"I know. But you mustn't have this sort of last resource.

More conversations like this won't help you. What after all would they be about?"

"Oh hell—" said Cato.

"I'm going, as it happens, the way things fall out, and I probably won't be back, at any rate not for many years. All sorts of things will happen to you—"

"Will you write to me?"

"I doubt it."

"Will you pray for me?"

"Every day."

Cato stood in silence, not looking at his friend.

"It's raining," said Brendan.

"Yes."

"How will you get to Kings Cross?"

"Taxi. I'll be O.K."

"Have you anything to read in the train?"

"I'll get a paper."

"By the way, did you see that Lucius Lamb has died? His obituary was in today's *Times*."

"Really? Poor old chap."

"Did you ever read any of his poems?"

"No. I'm told they were awful."

"Some of the early ones were rather good, at least I thought so when I was a boy. I remember one that impressed me very much. It was called *The Great Teacher*."

"What was it about?"

"I can't recall—I can just sort of conjure up the atmosphere."

"I must go, Brendan."

"Do promise me you'll go to Pennwood soon, at least you must go for Christmas."

"It won't be plain living and high thinking at Pennwood, it'll be Christmas carols and Yule logs and domestic happiness up at the Hall."

"Go and complete their happiness."

"Colette's pregnant."

"I'm so glad."

"Well—"

"Oh, and I wanted you to have this."

Brendan fiddled in a cupboard and brought out a dark green

velvet-covered box. He opened it. The ivory Spanish crucifix was nestling inside.

"Oh Brendan—aren't you taking it?"

"No, I wanted you to have it. I'll take yours, the one you left behind on the bed that night when you ran out on me. It's a good exchange."

"Oh—thank you—it's so beautiful."

"Good-bye then. God bless you."

It was raining hard outside. Cato set off, watching out for taxis. The crucifix, in its case, heavy and awkward inside his mackintosh pocket, banged irregularly against his thigh at each step.